GUILTY
WIVES

Also by James Patterson

A list of more titles by James Patterson is printed at
the back of this book

GUILTY WIVES

JAMES PATTERSON
AND DAVID ELLIS

Century · London

Published by Century, 2012

2 4 6 8 10 9 7 5 3 1

First published in Great Britain in 2012 by
Century
Random House, 20 Vauxhall Bridge Road,
London SW1V 2SA

www.randomhouse.co.uk

Addresses for companies within The Random House Group Limited
can be found at: www.randomhouse.co.uk/offices.htm

The Random House Group Limited Reg. No. 954009

A CIP catalogue record for this book
is available from the British Library

Hardback ISBN 9781846057892
Trade paperback ISBN 9781846057908

The Random House Group Limited supports The Forest Stewardship Council
(FSC®), the leading international forest certification organisation. Our books
carrying the FSC label are printed on FSC® certified paper. FSC is the only forest
certification scheme endorsed by the leading environmental organisations,
including Greenpeace. Our paper procurement policy can be found at:
www.randomhouse.co.uk/environment

Printed and bound in Great Britain by Clays Ltd, St Ives Plc

To Judy Ellis —D.E.

PROLOGUE

JULY 2011

ONE

THEY TELL ME I will die here. This place I do not know, this dark, dank, rancid dungeon, where nobody wishes me well and most speak languages I don't understand—this is the place I will call home for the rest of my life. That's what they tell me. It's getting harder to disbelieve them.

There are people in here who want me dead, some for retribution but most to establish their own notoriety. It would be a sure path to celebrity to kill me or one of my friends, known collectively as the Monte Carlo Mistresses. That was the moniker that stuck in the international media. More imaginative than the earlier ones—the Gang of Four, the Bern Beauties, the Desperate Housewives. Less chilling, to me at least, than the one that ran on the front page of *Le Monde* the day after the verdict: *Mamans Coupables*.

Guilty Moms.

So I wait. For a miracle. For newly discovered evidence. A confession from the real killer. A sympathetic ear to my appeal. Or simply for the morning when I wake up and discover this was all a dream. The last three hundred and ninety-eight mornings, I've opened my eyes and prayed that I was back in Bern, or, better yet, back in

Georgetown, preparing to teach American literature to hungover underclassmen.

And I watch. I turn every corner widely and slowly. I sleep sitting up. I try to avoid any routine that would make my movements predictable, that would make me vulnerable. If they're going to get to me in here, they're going to have to earn it.

It started out as a day like any other. I walked down the narrow corridor of G wing. When I approached the block letters on the door's glass window—INFIRMERIE—I stopped and made sure my toes lined up with the peeling red tape on the floor that served as a marker, a stop sign before entering.

"*Bonjour,*" I said to the guard at the station on the other side of the hydraulic door, a woman named Cecile. No last names. None of the prison staff was allowed to reveal anything more to the prisoners than their first names, and those were probably fake, too. The point was anonymity outside these walls: because of it, the inmates, once released, wouldn't be able to hunt down the prison guards who hadn't treated them so nicely.

"Hi, Abbie." Always responding to me in her best English, which wasn't bad. Better than my French. After a loud, echoing buzz, the door released with a hiss.

The prison infirmary was the length and width of an American gymnasium, but it had a lower ceiling, about eight feet high. It was mostly one open space filled with about two dozen beds. On one side was a long cage—the "reception" area—where inmates waited their turn to be treated. On another side, also closed off and secured, was a room containing medical supplies and pharmaceuticals. Beyond this room was a high-security area that could hold five patients, reserved for those who had communicable diseases, those in intensive care, and those who posed security risks.

I liked the infirmary because of the strong lighting, which lent some vibrancy to my otherwise dreary confinement. I liked helping people, too; it reminded me that I was still human, that I still had a purpose. And I liked it because I didn't have to watch my back in here.

I disliked everything else about it. The smell, for one—a putrid cocktail of body odor and urine and powerful disinfectant that always seized me when I first walked in. And let's face it, nobody who comes to the infirmary is having a good day.

I try to have good days. I try very hard.

It was busy when I walked in, the beds at full capacity, the one doctor, two nurses, and four inmates who served as nurse's assistants scurrying from one patient to the next, putting figurative Band-Aids on gaping wounds. There had been a flu going around, and at JRF, when one person got the flu, the whole cell block got it. They tried to segregate the sick ones but it was like rearranging chairs in a closet. There just wasn't room. JRF—L'Institution de Justice et Réforme pour les Femmes—operated at more than 150 percent capacity. Cells designed for four held seven, the extra three people sleeping on mattresses on the floor. A prison intended for twelve hundred was housing almost two thousand. They were packing us in shoulder to shoulder and telling us to cover our mouths when we coughed.

I saw Winnie at the far end, wrapping a bandage on an Arab woman's foot. Winnie, like me, was a nurse's assistant. The warden ordered that we not communicate, so we were assigned to different cell blocks and different shifts in the infirmary.

I felt a catch in my throat, as I did every time I saw her now. Winnie has been my closest friend since my husband and I moved to Bern, Switzerland, for his job at the American Embassy. We lived next door to each other for five years, mourning the late working hours of our diplomat husbands and sharing each other's secrets.

Well, not *all* our secrets, it turned out. But I've forgiven her.

"Hey." She whispered in her lovely British accent. Her fingers touched mine. "I heard what happened. You okay?"

"Living the dream," I said. "You?"

She wasn't in the mood for humor. Winnie was a stunning beauty—tall and shapely with large radiant eyes, chiseled cheekbones, and silky, ink-color hair—which made it all the harder to see the wear around those eyes, the stoop in her posture, the subtle deterioration of her spirit. It had been just over a year since the murders, and three months since the conviction. She was starting to break down, to give in. They talked in here about the moment when that happened, when you lost all hope. *La Reddition,* they called it. Surrender. I hadn't experienced it yet. I hoped I never would.

"Movie night," she whispered. "I'll save you a seat. Love you."

"Love you, too. Get some rest." Our fingertips released. Her shift was over.

About ninety minutes later, I heard the commotion as the hydraulic door buzzed open. I had my back turned to the entrance. I was helping a nurse dress a laceration on an inmate's rib cage when one of the nurses shouted, *"Urgence!"*

Emergency. We had a lot of those. We had a suicide a week in JRF. Violence and sanitation-related illnesses had been on the upswing with the worsening overcrowding. It was impossible to work a six-hour shift without hearing *urgence* called at least once.

Still, I turned, as guards and a nurse wheeled in an inmate on a gurney.

"Oh, God, no." I dropped the gauze pads I was holding. I started running before the realization had fully formed in my head. The shock of black hair hanging below the gurney. The look on the face of one of the nurses, who had turned back from the commotion to look at me, to see if it had registered with me who the new patient was. Everyone knew the four of us as a group, after all.

"Winnie," I whispered.

TWO

"NO. PLEASE, NO."

I sharply parted the people around me, bouncing off them like a pinball, rushing to Winnie. Two guards saw me coming and moved forward to restrain me as the doctor and two nurses hovered over Winnie, working feverishly.

"Let me see her. Let me . . . *permettez-moi* . . ."

All I could see, between the two guards containing me, was the back of a nurse and the lifeless body of my best friend. The doctor was speaking quickly—too quickly for me to understand—and one of the nurses rushed to retrieve some medicine from the drug cabinet.

"What happened?" I called out to no avail, using the wrong language again in my panic.

I tried again to get around the guards. I just wanted to see her. I wanted *her* to see *me*. But one of the guards threw a forearm into my chest and my feet went out from under me. I fell hard to the floor. My head slammed on the tile. The guards dropped down, using gravity to their advantage, pinning me where I lay.

"Please. *S'il vous plaît*," I managed. "Winnie . . ."

Then, between the two guards restraining me, craning my neck as far off the floor as I could, I saw the doctor, a middle-aged man with long gray hair, straighten up, relax his posture, and shake his head at the nurse. He wrapped his stethoscope around his neck and turned toward the nurse who was retrieving the meds. "Marian," he called. *"Il n'est pas nécessaire."*

"No!" I wailed.

He looked up at the clock on the wall. *"Le temps de mort...ah, il est quatorze heures quarante."*

Time of death, 2:40 p.m.

"You...you...killed her," I said, the last words I heard anyone say before everything went black.

THREE

DARKNESS, EVEN THOUGH the room was well lit. Cold, even though the room was so humid that my shirt stuck to my chest and sweat dotted my forehead. The blood I tasted in my mouth, the searing pain in my ribs, the bruises on my wrists from the handcuffs that now chained me to the wall—those were real. Somewhere, as I swooned in and out of consciousness, I'd put up a fight. Bits and pieces flashed at me. Kicking and punching. I think I bit someone's arm. But it didn't matter. None of it mattered anymore.

I saw it now, what Winnie saw. *La Reddition.* Surrender. Don't fight it, and it will be easier. *La Reddition* was extending her hand to me, but I hadn't shaken it yet.

Time had passed. Best guess, about ten hours since my best friend had died.

The cell door opened. Boulez, the warden at JRF. Dark hair greased back. Immaculate three-piece suit, tie perfectly knotted. He looked like the politician he was. In America, Boulez would be a city councilman planning a run for Congress. In France, he was a prison warden waiting for his chance to move up in the Ministry of Justice.

"I will not waste our time with pleasantries," he said, which seemed appropriate, given that his employees had just murdered my best friend and beaten and shackled me.

I looked around my cell, roughly the size of my walk-in closet back in the States, before we moved. Mildew on the walls and ceiling. Dark spots on the concrete floor, like oil stains in a garage—except these were the product of human, not vehicular, malfunction.

This was Le Mitard, the prison within a prison. Solitary confinement, to Americans.

Boulez didn't enjoy being here. He didn't like to get his manicured hands dirty. He had a purpose for visiting me, and he was about to get to the point.

"Tell me what drug you used," he said. "It will be a simple matter of inventorying the contents of our drug cabinet to see what is missing. Easier for us if you just confess." His English, though heavily accented, was flawless. Most of the educated French spoke fluent English.

I coughed. Blood spattered onto my brown pants.

"I will not ask a second time," he said.

"Good. So I won't have to keep ignoring you."

He blinked his eyes in concentration. His mind took a moment to track what I'd said. Then he grimaced. "Or was it suicide?" he asked. "Each of you had access to the drugs. Either she killed herself or you poisoned her. Which was it, Abbie?"

His delight in saying these words to me was evident. We both knew that neither of those alternatives was true. But he was making it clear that one of them would be the official story.

"Winnie would never kill herself," I said. "Don't you *ever* say that she did."

"Ah." He raised his chin. "So, murder."

He was trying to get a rise out of me. This guy should stay a prison warden forever. There was no better outlet for sadism.

"You would naturally blame her for your predicament," he said.

I coughed again. Same result. I wiped my chin on my shoulder, not having my hands available to me.

"I'm not going to forget what happened today," I said. "Someone's going to pay for this."

"I have a better idea." Boulez walked toward me, confidently enough given my restraints. He stood a few feet away, just outside the reach of my legs should I kick out at him.

"Confess to the double murder," he said. "And what happened to your friend Winnie will be considered a suicide."

Sure. None of the four of us had confessed at trial. Boulez wanted to be the hero who secured my confession, a piece of red meat he could toss to the carnivorous international media—and to the French voters, when the time came.

"And if I don't?" I asked.

"Well, you've already committed two murders. A third? We cannot imprison you beyond your natural life, now, can we? But there are other ways to punish, Abbie." He walked back toward the cell door. "I'll give you forty-five days to think about it."

"I think you mean thirty, Boulez." A French law had been passed recently, limiting time in Le Mitard to thirty-day stretches. But everyone at JRF knew there were ways around that restriction.

"Did I say forty-five? Ah, well." The corners of his mouth curled up. He rapped on the door with his knuckles. It popped open with a buzz.

"Boulez," I said. "You won't win. One day I'm going to walk out of this place."

His eyes narrowed. Then his smile broadened. "Madame, you are the most famous criminal in the history of France. You'll never walk out of here."

With that, Boulez disappeared. The lighting, controlled from outside the cell, went out, plunging me into darkness. For thirty days. Or maybe forty-five.

Or maybe for the rest of my life.

All because of two nights in Monte Carlo.

BOOK ONE

THIRTEEN MONTHS EARLIER: JUNE 2010

CHAPTER 1

JUST OVER THIRTY minutes after leaving Bern's airport, the jet touched down on the tarmac in Nice so smoothly it felt like we'd landed in butter. Or maybe it was the Champagne, already numbing my senses, coloring everything wonderful. Wonderful is what I had been promised. Wonderful is what all of us, for different reasons, needed. We needed to bathe ourselves in luxury. We needed a four-day dream.

"I am officially on vacation!" I announced to the group, taking the last swallow of my Champagne.

"It's about bloody time, love!" Winnie reached across the aisle and grabbed my arm.

Serena, seated across from me in the small cabin, raised her empty glass and tossed her long blond hair. "*Bonjour,* Monte Carlo. And that, my friends, is the limit of my French."

"Don't forget *Chardonnay* and *Merlot,*" I added.

"Touché," she said.

"See, your vocabulary's getting better by the second."

I looked around at my friends. How did I get so lucky? Serena Schofield, the Amazon blonde—a former U.S. Olympic skier who placed fifth in the downhill at Lillehammer. Bryah Gordon, born in Johannesburg under the oppression of apartheid, the youngest of our clan at thirty-one and the smartest by far, our resident encyclopedia on topics large and trivial, a beauty in her own right with flawless coffee-colored skin and kinky African hair cropped at her chin. And Winnie Brookes, of course, the exotic Brit, the Diva, we called her, as breathtaking as any runway model working today, who, most of the time, seemed utterly oblivious to her beauty.

Then there was me. Abbie Elliot. What these interesting and gorgeous women were doing with me was anyone's guess. For all the complaints I had about leaving the States and moving to Switzerland, all I had to do was look around at these women to find a silver lining.

"I think for the rest of this trip, I'm going to speak with a British accent." I turned to Winnie. "Bloody good show, love," I tried, doing my best Monty Python imitation.

"And I'm going to be an American," she replied. "Hey, how ya doin'? You got any countries we can invade?"

We got off the private jet—thank you, Serena—bathed in the rays of a welcoming, lowering sun. An SUV drove us to the area of the Côte d'Azur Airport marked PRIVATE AVIATION, where our bags were waiting for us inside.

"Do we have a car?" Winnie asked.

"A car? Cars are so pedestrian, *dahling*," said Serena in her best Zsa Zsa voice, with a wink at all of us. None of us was poor by any stretch of the imagination, but Serena lapped us several times over. To know her, you'd have no idea how rich she was. She was as sweet and down-to-earth as anyone I knew. But this weekend would be different. She had money, and she clearly planned on spending it.

We followed Serena through a door that led out to a large landing pad—and a large, sleek, silver-and-gray helicopter.

"Serena, really!" said Bryah, with maybe a hint of nervousness. Bryah didn't get out much. Her husband, Colton, was what you might call controlling if you were being polite. If you weren't being polite, you might call him something else. The long and short of it was, Bryah had never been on a girls' weekend like this.

"Why drive when we can fly?" Serena ran over to the helicopter and climbed in. I couldn't believe it—but then again, I could. Money was no object, and Serena wanted us to live a fantasy for four days.

"You couldn't find anything bigger?" I asked.

Once we were belted in, the helicopter lifted quickly, causing a minor rebellion in my stomach. But soon we were soaring over Monaco, and nothing else mattered but the sloping hills of the French Riviera, the blue expanse of the Mediterranean, dotted with yachts and sailboats heading back to port for the evening, and the pink-green sky, against which the sun was beginning its descent toward the horizon.

"Did you know that Monaco is the second smallest country in the world?" Bryah asked.

"Fascinating," said Winnie. She and I made eye contact, suppressing smiles.

"Bryah, honey," I said, patting her leg, "we're going to have fun. Don't be nervous."

A mere seven minutes later, we were landing on a helipad by the beach. We unstrapped our restraints and waited for the pilot to open the door.

"Wait," said Serena. She reached into her bag and removed three overstuffed envelopes, handing one to each of us. I opened mine and found a thick wad of euros.

"What is this?" Winnie asked.

"That's fifty thousand euros each," she said. "Gamble with it. Shop. Do whatever you want. Just promise me you'll spend it."

"Can I buy a car?" I asked. "A small island?"

"How about a movie star?" Winnie asked. "Think I can rent Brad Pitt for the weekend?"

"*Brad Pitt?* Too old, Win," I said. "One of those younger boys. Zac Efron, maybe."

"You want an athlete," Serena suggested. "David Beckham. Rafa Nadal."

"Rafa, maybe," Win agreed.

We looked over at Bryah, who had remained silent. She considered the money, looked at Serena, and allowed a wry smile to play on her face. "You could get into a spot of trouble with this bit of money," she said.

We all looked at each other, giddy and slightly intoxicated, relaxed and eager, and broke into laughter. Outside the window of the helicopter was Monte Carlo, the playground of the rich and famous. We were all stifled in our own way, mothers and wives living in our adoptive Swiss city, and these four days would be our chance to escape. To live someone else's life.

"Bryah," I said, "I think that's the idea."

CHAPTER 2

IT WAS ONLY minutes before we were at the entrance of the Hôtel Métropole. It was near dusk and it looked like the light had been turned down on a dimmer switch. The air was warm and thick. Porters in gray jackets and hats took our bags and cheerily greeted us, first in German—mistaking the heritage of the blond Serena—and then in English.

The hotel was fabulous. We walked through an ivy-covered granite archway that made me feel as though someone should be trumpeting our arrival. The patterned stone path was lined with candles in ornate glass holders, potted Japanese plants, and tall, manicured pine trees that probably had a fancy name but looked like anorexic specimens to me. The hotel loomed before us, basking in the low light. The next thing I knew, I had a Champagne glass in my hand and the bubbles were tickling my nose as I drank and walked. Someone from the hotel was explaining about a recent remodeling, someone named Jacques Garcia, and I nodded importantly and said, "I love his work," even though I had no freakin' idea who he was. Winnie was sashaying in front of the pack, singing something and waving her arms, probably attracting the attention of all the male porters in her tight green sundress.

"So exciting!" Serena hugged me close and we clinked glasses.

The large, airy lobby smelled and looked like money, from the checkered tile floor to the skylight to the elaborate lamps hanging from the ceiling—picture candelabra covered with tents—to the guests, the men in tuxedos and many-thousand-dollar suits, the women in evening gowns and pearls.

"I could learn to like this," I said.

"Schofield," said Serena to the man at reception.

The man hit a few keys and said, "Simon?"

"Simon?" The three of us said it in unison to Serena. Simon was her husband. Think: rich and dull. Nice enough, I guess, though I never saw the connection between those two.

Regardless, the point was that we were escaping this weekend. Four days, just for us—meaning no husbands. That meant something different to each of us, I thought, but something nonetheless.

"Buzz kill," Winnie sang.

Serena laughed. "His assistant booked it for us. Force of habit, putting Simon's name down."

"I can't wait to see this room," said Bryah.

"Forget the room." Serena clapped her hands together. "We're going to the casino. I feel lucky!"

"Forget the room?" Again, the three of us, almost in unison. We overruled her. We wanted to see this suite we'd heard so much about.

"Wow," I said, as though it were a two-syllable word. The presidential suite, a double penthouse. They called it the Carré d'Or. It sounded like a perfume. It looked like a palace. Fresh roses everywhere. Complimentary Champagne and macaroons. Expensive artwork. A view of half of Monte Carlo. As I may have mentioned, I could learn to like this.

I didn't come from money and I didn't have any to speak of, by which I mean that Jeffrey and I were perfectly comfortable—but we had no summer villas, no private jets. And no complaints, either, by the way. Still, it differentiated me from the others. Winnie had grown up with money in London. Bryah and Serena had married into it.

They'd probably seen penthouses like this one before, though the way they scattered like cockroaches to explore it, maybe this was above even their typical expense level.

It was the most opulent thing I'd ever seen. The lounge area, probably suitable for a helicopter landing, was all dark parquet with rich gold and maroon accents. The floor-to-ceiling windows revealed the Mediterranean and a terrace that called out to me. First, I took a peek into a bathroom—marble and sandstone, a delicious ivory-colored tub, a shower big enough for a small family—"Yes, that will do," I decided.

Then I looked into one of the bedrooms, the front one, twice the size of mine in Bern, the walls decorated in flowers and light shades of green and opening to reveal a dressing area and table on one side. I directed the bellman to drop my and Winnie's bags here; we'd be sharing this front bedroom, while Serena and Bryah would share the back one.

Then to the terrace. Winnie was already out there, cutting quite a figure as she looked out over the Monte Carlo Casino, the Mediterranean, and the pink sky beyond. The breeze carried her dark hair off her back.

"This terrace, alone, is bigger than my first apartment in Georgetown," I said. "Twice the size."

"I know, mate. It's just lovely." Winnie turned and opened her arms, as though she were showcasing herself. "Hello, Monte Carlo!" she said.

Serena popped her head into the room. "Get dressed, ladies," she said. "We're going gambling."

CHAPTER 3

LE GRAND CASINO'S exterior displayed the triumphant, ornate architecture of royalty, a palace of gold. We passed a number of sleek foreign cars parked at the entrance and showed our passports at the door. (Citizens of Monaco, Bryah informed us, were forbidden from gambling in the casino.)

The atrium was adorned in gold; it had marble columns and sculptures in glass enclosures, and the double-height ceiling was open to the second floor. It felt like we were at the opera, not a casino. (The person who designed this casino, Bryah explained, also designed the Paris Opéra. We had to get some liquor in her fast.)

We paid our way into a private gambling room that had frescoed ceilings, lavish molding, and sculptures and paintings everywhere. The attire was jacket and tie for the men, gowns and cocktail dresses for the ladies. All of us except Bryah were wearing black cocktail dresses—Serena's and Winnie's were strapless. Bryah, on the other hand, opted for something gold and more conservative.

Bryah always covered up more than the rest of us. I thought I knew why.

Anyway. We were among Monte Carlo's elite, the world's elite—

movie stars and athletes and speculators and Fortune 500 CEOs, wagering staggering sums of money, most for the pure sport of it.

"Roulette," said Serena. "You can't come to Monte Carlo and not play European roulette."

This was something I knew. I didn't gamble much, but when I did, it was always roulette.

The European roulette wheel had thirty-seven individual pockets, numbered zero through 36. Half the numbers were red and half were black. The bettor simply had to guess in which space the bouncing ball would stop. You placed your bets on a board. You could bet on individual numbers; on a block of two or four numbers; on the first twelve, second twelve, or third twelve; on numbers 1 through 18 or 19 through 36; on an odd number or even; on a black number or red. The payout varied with the degree of risk. Winning on an individual number obviously had the biggest payout, thirty-five to one, whereas betting that a number would be red, for example, was only a two-to-one payout because you had a fifty-fifty chance.

Serena took a seat and put down fifty thousand euros, which drew the attention of the other three players and a small crowd behind them. Each of the players—an Indian in a tuxedo, a heavyset Italian with a beard and ponytail, and a young woman who appeared to be American—looked at Serena, trying to place her. A movie star? An heiress?

"She's an international drug smuggler," I told the woman with the Italian, a bleached blonde with a long, curvy body.

The croupier—the dealer—gave Serena fifty yellow chips, each chip representing a thousand euros. Serena placed five of them on the number 5, her finish in the downhill in the Winter Olympics.

A straight bet. A bad bet. Terrible odds. The Indian bet reds. The Italian took 1 through 18. The American placed a corner bet, centering her chip at the intersection of squares 31, 32, 34, and 35.

The croupier spun the roulette wheel clockwise and said, "No more bets." He dropped the ball into the wheel in the opposite direction of the spin. The ball bounced against the tide as the wheel spun, finally landing in the pocket for 19.

"Nineteen, red," said the croupier. The Indian doubled his money. Everyone else lost. Serena lost five thousand euros—roughly six thousand American dollars. That was a trimester of boarding school in New England for one of my kids.

"Place an outside bet," I said to her. "Bet a column, or odds or evens or a color."

"Bor-ing." Serena put another five chips on 5.

"You have less than a three percent chance of winning," said Bryah.

"Oh, let her play. Best of British, Serena!" Winnie said.

"No more bets," said the croupier.

Our drinks arrived. Cosmopolitans for each of us. To me, the vodka tasted better than the Champagne. The bubbly goes to my brain too quickly.

"Eleven, black." Good news for everyone but Serena.

"You can't keep putting five thousand down on a single number," I said.

"You're right." Serena winked at me. She put ten chips down on the 5.

"No more bets."

Serena raised her glass to me in a toast.

"Twenty-two, black."

Serena put another five down on 5.

"No more bets." The ball tripped and danced around, ultimately settling in the pocket numbered 6.

"Six, black."

"I'm getting closer," said Serena. I'm sure that was great consolation after having lost twenty-five thousand euros in the space of ten minutes.

The Italian put two chips down on square 5 as well and smiled at her, his eyebrows dancing. But then he put five chips on reds to cover his stupid inside bet.

"No more bets." The croupier did his thing and the small ball did its little jig.

"Thirty-four, red."

A crowd had begun to gather behind our table. The blond American, throwing money away on thirty-seven-to-one odds, dropping five thousand euros a pop on the number 5.

Soon, Serena had depleted her fifty thousand euros and laid out another fifty for the croupier. People behind us mumbled. I doubt it was flattering talk.

This was classic Serena, always seeking a competition, always sizing herself up against others, never shrinking from a dare. This, I knew, was what she wanted from this weekend, something wild and risky.

I stood behind her. Winnie was talking with a tall man who looked Spanish. Bryah was on her next Cosmo and lightening up, now cheering Serena on instead of explaining the crappy odds to her.

"Sticking with five, then," I said, my hand on her shoulder. It was her money. Who was I to tell her what to do?

"Sticking with five." Serena reached back and patted my hand.

It didn't get any better for her.

"Seventeen, black."

"Twenty-four, black."

"Seven, red."

People began to applaud with each bet Serena placed. I didn't know if it was encouragement or ridicule, but she had drawn quite a crowd.

"You think I'm crazy." Serena looked back at me.

I bent down and kissed her cheek. "I think you're wonderful."

"Love you, sweetie." She was down to her last ten chips, her last ten thousand euros. She put five down on 5.

"Fourteen, red."

The crowd reacted with audible disappointment. I'd been wrong. They admired her spirit, if not her strategy. They were doing the same thing we were doing on this trip, living vicariously through others, watching this woman take wild risks.

Down to her last five chips. "Do I change?" she asked me.

"Do you believe in it?"

She paused. "I believe in us."

I leaned down to her. "Then bet on us. The four of us."

"Madame?" the croupier asked.

Serena looked at me and smiled. She bet her last five chips.

On the number 4.

Another audible reaction behind me. What was she doing? Why change now?

The roulette wheel spun. "No more bets." The ball danced one last time for us.

The crowd went up in a roar.

"Four, black," said the croupier.

CHAPTER 4

MY HEAD WAS throbbing the next morning and I needed to melt for a while. The best beach and pool are the private ones at the Monte Carlo Beach Hotel, which is actually just over the border in France—something I knew without Bryah telling me. Bryah wasn't her normal encyclopedic self this morning, having probably even less familiarity with a night of drinking than I. We had some thoughts of shopping, seeing the royal palace, Princess Grace's grave—but first we all just wanted to chill.

We were all suffering but enjoying it at the same time. By the time we dragged ourselves to the beach club, it was almost eleven. The sun was high and brutally hot. The air was clear and dry and the sky was cloudless. The Mediterranean was an endless deep blue. The good life.

The pool at the Métropole was great, but this one was the place to be. That's what we were told, anyway, and it turned out to be true. The place was at full capacity, making it hard for us to scramble together four chairs. There were plenty of swimmers in the humongous pool, but the sides were lined with people sitting and getting their legs wet. It was like a singles bar.

"A bit knackered, are we, girls? Then nothing like a dip." Winnie slipped off her cover-up, revealing her black bikini. Two dozen men injured their necks in the process of getting a look at her. Serena, though not Winnie's equal in beauty, was even taller and still had an athlete's lithe body. Her bikini was gold. It seemed like we were under a spotlight.

Bryah kept her cover-up on—"It's not like I need a tan," she joked—consistent with her routine. We'd never talked about it. After the sprained arm, the dislocated shoulder, the broken fingers, the bruises on her forearm or thigh or back—somewhere in there it stopped being a coincidence, ceased being clumsiness. It wasn't a regular thing, which meant that her husband, Colton, wasn't a serial abuser. He was just a small, spiteful brute. And it was never Bryah's face. Always a part of her body she could cover up. Which meant Colton was cautious. That, for some reason, made me despise him all the more.

I'd wanted to say something to Bryah so many times, but the three of us made a decision not to: she knew we loved her, that we'd do anything for her. If she wanted to talk, she would.

"Well?" Winnie looked back at us. She fingered the clasp on her bikini top. "When in Monte Carlo?"

Most of the people at the pool were topless. I would not be one of them; a red bikini underneath my cover-up was as racy as I got.

"When in Monte Carlo," said Serena. She was still intoxicated by her performance at the casino last night. It wasn't about the money per se; it was about her competitive nature. She'd turned her last bet of five thousand euros into a payout of 175,000 euros, putting her up 75,000 for the night. That's over 100,000 U.S. dollars, if you're keeping score.

Serena went first, removing her top. Winnie quickly followed. They covered themselves in suntan lotion, with extra for their headlights, and sauntered over to the pool to dip their toes in.

"I hate them," I told Bryah. A waiter appeared out of nowhere. I ordered bottles of water, Champagne cocktails, and fruit plates for each of us.

Bryah settled in, donning fashionable shades and stretching her limbs in ecstasy. She really seemed to be unwinding. Serena and Winnie were making out okay, too. About a dozen men surrounded them within seconds of their approach to the pool. They were the flirtatious ones in our crew.

Sometimes it was more than flirtation. Serena hadn't been faithful to Simon. The marriage had grown loveless, and sexless, years ago. Simon was good to her, by which I mean he provided for her, but that wasn't really Serena's style. Serena craved excitement, adrenaline, and there were only so many times she could jump out of an airplane or race a Formula One car around a track. She wanted passion in her love life. So, on two different occasions over the last five years, she'd found it with another man. And she'd been remorseful both times. She even suspected that Simon knew. My theory: She *wanted* Simon to know. She wanted him to fight for her. She wanted him to want her.

Now, it seemed, all she had was Katie Mei, the child she had adopted from China after two near-term miscarriages had ended her appetite for pregnancy. Katie was everything to her.

And Winnie? She was married to James Bond. Christien had been with British intelligence for years before taking a desk job with the British Embassy in Bern. Christien was handsome and mysterious. Just Winnie's type. They were two drop-dead-gorgeous people with two drop-dead-gorgeous children. But something was off with them. It was hard to pinpoint it. And Winnie wasn't one to complain. It was just the way she talked about Christien, the absence of enthusiasm. Winnie doted on her kids and threw herself into her charity work, raising money and advocating on behalf of autistic children, honoring her autistic brother, Winston. (That's right, Winston and Winnie. Her parents had a sense of humor. Having these two kids, they always said, was a Win-Win situation.)

"If you're a woman anywhere at this pool right now, you hate Win and Serena," Bryah said with a chuckle. She was probably right. Almost every head was turned in their direction, and, look, this wasn't exactly a pool full of homely people. Most of the women here were more done-up than the women at the casino, and at least half of them had improved a body part or two with surgery.

Drinks arrived, and I started on the Champagne. Why not? I was on vacation. I didn't miss Jeffrey, I had to admit. I missed my kids, but I would have missed them in Bern, too. Richie and Elena were in boarding school in Connecticut, the same school Jeffrey attended as a child. I'd objected but lost the argument. I usually did, which was hard for me to admit. It was one thing for the kids to be in Connecticut when we were at Georgetown—Lakeville was about six hours by car, ninety minutes by plane—but quite another when we were in Switzerland. But I couldn't ask Jeffrey to turn down this position at the U.S. Embassy, and I couldn't ask my kids to pick up and leave the only school they knew, a school where they were happy.

"Enough," I said to myself. "I'm on vacation." I finished my Champagne and decided to drink Winnie's, too. One of her poolside suitors had already bought her one.

"Let's jump in," said Bryah. "Want to?"

I looked at her and smiled. What was I waiting for? And why? Jeffrey? He was probably with his girlfriend at this moment.

"That sounds perfect," I said.

CHAPTER 5

NOT EVERYONE AT the Monte Carlo Beach Hotel was having a wonderful time. Four men stood on a private balcony, sharing binoculars, observing the activity by the pool with something less than warm feelings.

"You see what I mean?" Colton looked at the other husbands. "Not just catching a tan, are they?"

"At least Bryah still has her bloody top on, Colt." Christien couldn't say the same thing for his Winnie.

"This is why you called?" Simon asked. "This is why we had to fly down here?"

Colton turned to Simon. "Look at them, man. Your Serena, as much as anyone—but all of them. It's like they aren't married women!"

"Oh, Colt—"

"And you should have seen them last night at the casino. A gaggle of wild *stukkies*, they were. Waltzing in, attracting attention. Not shying away from it, I can tell you."

"Colton's right. We should do something," Jeffrey said in agreement. "This is unacceptable." Tall and lean with carefully coiffed hair, he now looked more like the top U.S. diplomat he was than the Georgetown international relations professor he'd once been, back when he'd first met Abbie.

"There you go, *brah*." Colton's normally pale skin was purple with rage. To the others, he didn't fit with Bryah. A forty-eight-year-old, pudgy, temperamental white man with an exotic young black wife. A cerebral young lady with an angry man who fancied a bulldozer over a handshake.

"And what," asked Simon, "are you planning to do?"

"Not let them get away with it, that's what." Colton lifted his beige shirt, revealing a handgun stuffed in his pants.

"Bloody *hell,* Colt." Christien, with the baritone voice, the detached manner. He took one step back.

Jeffrey stepped back, too, but didn't speak.

"You've lost your mind!" said Simon. Prematurely gray but still physically fit at forty-four. Too focused, he would admit, on adding to a portfolio that already could keep generations in comfort. The adopted girl, Katie Mei, had been good for him, grounding him a bit more.

"This whole thing was a waste of time." Simon looked at his watch. "My jet's leaving in one hour. I need to be back in Zurich tonight. Will you all be joining me?"

Christien didn't answer, keeping a cool stare on Colton's weapon.

"Will you be joining me?" Simon asked again.

Jeffrey, the stuffy diplomat, raised the binoculars again. Abbie was in the pool, laughing at something a young man said to her. The man was younger, more muscular—more exciting than Jeffrey. He lowered the binoculars and looked alternately at Colton and Simon.

"I want to hear what Colton has in mind," he said.

CHAPTER 6

AFTER THE POOL, we returned to the hotel. Winnie and I, sharing the front bedroom, chatted like schoolgirls about the cute boys at the pool while we put on makeup and plucked eyebrows and drank Champagne from long-stemmed glasses. Winnie went through a box of tissues as her allergies momentarily flared up. I was doing fine except that I had some water in my ear from the pool that numerous Q-tips failed to remedy. Life's rough, right?

Then dinner in our hotel at Yoshi, Joël Robuchon's Japanese restaurant. Quaint in terms of size—seating only forty—but not in design, which was luxurious Japanese modern with muted colors and stone. At the far end, the room swept open to a second story, from which hung a pearly eight-foot spiral chandelier. Beyond the far wall of glass was an ornate Japanese garden.

Serena and Winnie sat on the burnt-orange silk banquettes along the wall. Bryah and I took the comfy yellow chairs across from them. The table was set with black plastic mats, black-and-clear water glasses, and glass plates. A soft light burned in a green glass in the center of the table. Before we could say *banzai* we were drinking the house's Bruno Paillard Champagne.

We were, quite simply, having a blast. We were sun-drenched and intoxicated and giddy. Over salmon sashimi and our first flask of sake, we decided to forgo our usual topics of conversation—global warming, nuclear proliferation, emerging markets in Latin America—in favor of describing the looks on our husbands' faces during sex. In a nutshell: Simon looked like a chipmunk holding his breath. Colton, a seal giving birth. Christien gnashed his teeth as though he were about to pass a bowling ball. My Jeffrey was always a quiet one, closing his eyes intensely as though he were trying to remember the lyrics to a song.

"When was the last time, for any of you?" Bryah asked. She actually won; she and Colton were intimate last week. For Winnie, it was weeks. For me, months. For Serena, years.

"Wait," I said. "Do you mean, when was the last time Jeffrey had sex? Or the last time he had sex with me?"

The joke fell flat. Even I had surprised myself with the comment. Winnie knew about Jeffrey's affair, and I'd alluded to it previously with the others but never so explicitly.

"I don't think Simon cheats," said Serena. I was alarmed at how matter-of-factly she put it. She poured from a new flask of sake, which had been recommended by the sommelier. "He's only attracted to things he can buy or sell."

"Honestly, I don't know about Christien," Winnie chimed in. "I don't think he cheats, but I never know anything about him. Y'know, last week he had a bit of the lurgy? I only found out when I heard him puking in the loo. And then I took his temperature and it was bloody through the roof. Not five minutes before that, I'd asked him if he was feeling up for a jog and he said, 'Could be,' with that straight face of his. Then he's keeled over on his arse spilling his guts. He's just got one speed, that one: man of mystery. Sometimes I want to remind him that he stopped playing Double-O Seven eight years ago."

The edamame—salted, boiled soybeans in the pod—were fresh and firm and the octopus salad and boiled potatoes were seasoned to perfection. We shared orders of prawns tempura and vegetable fritters and grilled black cod wrapped in a banana leaf. A broth soup with tofu topped it off until dessert. I preferred the lime snow eggs but everyone else liked the lychee sorbet best. Ah, well, we celebrate our diversity.

More sake, and we were perilously close to being drunk—or perilously close to being so drunk we no longer realized it.

"Colton is just so insanely insecure," said Bryah. "Whatever else—and I know what you all think of him—it all comes down to that. Insecurity."

"I'd like to box his ears right, I would," said Winnie, the alcohol loosening her discretion.

"No, I mean—oh, this is yummy." Bryah had her first taste of the new sake.

"By all means, keep drinking, Bryah," said Serena with her patented wink. Bryah was the most petite—probably a hundred pounds soaking wet—and I was a lot closer to her than to our tall, leggy friends across the table. Bryah and I were matching them sip for sip, regardless.

"But here's an example. We were at dinner a few weeks ago and Colton's talking to the waiter. The waiter's a grad student in psychology. He said he was doing a thesis on the relationship between psychotherapy and Christianity. Colton makes a comment that Jung is the founder of psychotherapy. The waiter didn't say anything, but later on, Colton realizes he meant Freud. It bothers him so much that he looked stupid to the waiter that he finds out the waiter's schedule and makes us go back there for dinner again, just so he can strike up another conversation with the waiter and correct himself."

"That would qualify as insecure," Serena said in agreement.

"So here's a question." Bryah was coming out of her shell more and more as the weekend traveled on. "Raise your hand if you're still in love with your husband. Honest, now."

I looked at each of the ladies. Eight hands among us, all resting on the table.

I raised my hand.

"Abbie, really?" said Serena.

"No, I have another question," I said. "Why are we spending our time on our getaway weekend talking about our husbands?"

"As of now, we aren't," said Winnie. "Promise?"

Our hands all met in the center of the table. Screw the husbands. We had each other. And the night, as they say, was still young.

CHAPTER 7

HE WATCHED THEM from the other side of the street, across from the Hôtel Métropole and the restaurant, Yoshi. Laughing and stumbling and hugging, the four lovely ladies. The four gorgeous troublemakers.

They'd spent the entire afternoon at that pool, then had gone back to the room to shower and prepare. Cocktails on the terrace, no doubt, then dinner at Yoshi at nine. A busy day for them. A day that, from the look of things, was far from over.

He stamped out his cigarette, his first in more than ten years. Excusable under the circumstances, he thought. Being nervous was natural, even for someone who prided himself on his focus during storms.

He did feel nervous, yes, but in a positive way. He felt invigorated. He felt dangerous and volatile and he liked the feeling of empowerment. Light on his feet and ready for action. And always comforted by this fact: the decision would not be his. It would be her decision. No—*their* decision, the four of them.

He was merely reacting. Eradicating a wrong. Avenging an injustice. This wouldn't be his fault.

Also comforted by this fact: he could always pull the plug. Abort. Right now he was only thinking, preparing. He could always change his mind.

But his pulse was popping. He felt anger in the clench of his jaw, saw it in the white of his knuckles. He wasn't going to change his mind. This was unacceptable. He could be a lot of things. He'd been called a lot of things.

"But never a fool," he said.

CHAPTER 8

"ACTING YOUR AGE is overrated!" I shouted—forgetting that I was a mother of two and a forty-one-year-old wife who'd been married seventeen years. Not that anyone else heard me. The music's bass line pulsated like a collective heartbeat throughout the dance floor, where about two hundred of us were gyrating and throwing ourselves around and screaming for no apparent reason, other than that it was fun. Overhead scanner lights swiveled about desperately, cutting through the darkness. Fluorescent-tube lights adorned the walls, sometimes emitting a strobe effect, which made us all look like we were moving in slow motion as we danced around at top speed and the DJ above us orchestrated the entire thing.

It was sticky-hot and we were wall-to-wall people and I kept thinking, Who concert, Who concert, but it would have dated me if I'd said anything to the vast majority of the dancers, whose average age was probably late twenties. The place was huge, the dance floor the principal focus, but there were still plenty of people crammed into the bar and seating areas, where they would have the privilege of dropping almost thirty euros for a bottle of water or a Diet Coke. Mix in some liquor and you needed a second mortgage.

Well, I would, anyway. These were the jet-setters, the sheikhs and celebrities and assorted robber barons—and their adult children, vibrant and aimless in their ignorant youth. I missed ignorant youth. But I was living it again tonight.

Someone grabbed my arm. Winnie. "I'm going to the bar!" she yelled. She had to repeat it twice over the pulsating *thump, thump* of the music—or maybe that was my heart beating.

"If you need to sell an organ to buy a drink, make it a kidney," I said. "You have two of them."

"All right, then," she said, which roughly translated to: "I can't hear a word you're saying."

I thought of following her but this was too much fun. I danced back-to-back with Serena and we almost stuck to each other from the sweat. I looked up to the open-air ceiling, through the exposed pipes to the freckles of stars overhead.

Nice night, I thought. This must be someone else's life.

Three songs later, I'd burned off all the calories from Yoshi. Even Serena, the Olympian, was in need of a break. We couldn't find Bryah.

We danced back to our seats, a semicircle of red leather within which were nestled tiny cocktail tables topped by candles. Winnie was seated next to a well-heeled man in an expensive suit with a full head of hair and a manicured beard, easy enough on the eyes but attractive more for his carriage, his evident ease with himself. He had his arm over the back of the leather and, thus, over Winnie.

"Who're the hotties?" Serena said to me in what passed in this place as a whisper, meaning she was practically screaming in my ear.

Another man, wearing a dark suit and white shirt with an open collar, was chatting with Bryah while he nursed a glass of clear liquid that could have been anything. He was younger and stockier than the guy with Winnie, an athlete, maybe.

"Hey!" Bryah grabbed my hand and pulled me to her. "This is Luc," she said. "These are my friends Abbie and Serena."

"*Enchanté,*" he said in a deep voice, giving each of us the European double-kiss greeting.

"He's a race-car driver," Bryah said. "He raced the Grand Prix here."

"Really," said Serena, her interest piqued.

My eyes stole around the two of them to another man in a cream silk shirt and black slacks talking to another woman. His eyes met mine and he managed a seamless departure from his conversation. The next thing I knew, he was extending his hand to me. He was dark and swarthy, a few days' growth of beard on his face, thick dark hair messed in a haphazard style.

It took just that long for my brain to connect the dots, to recognize the face from the dozens of movies I'd seen.

"Damon Kodiak," we said simultaneously.

"*Enchanté,*" he said, then the kiss to each cheek. His cologne was something outdoorsy.

I felt something warm course through me, and it wasn't the bass line of the music. Yeah, I thought. *Enchanté.*

"You're stunning," he said to me. "If I may."

It was like a dream. The darkness punctuated by the fluorescent colors. The thousand-dollar bottle of Cristal on the table. The alcohol numbing one part of me and awakening another. The attention of an A-list Hollywood actor with a barrel chest and a deep voice and piercing blue eyes focused, for the moment, on me.

"You may," I said. You definitely may.

CHAPTER 9

I DIDN'T KNOW if time was standing still or accelerating. It became irrelevant. Two bottles of Champagne became four. The dizzying lights began to seem natural. The throbbing, percussive music became my pulse.

The darkness cast Damon's face in shadow, but somehow I could see him clearly. The powerful, scruffy jaw, the warm eyes, the messy hair. At some point, his hand had become planted on my knee. At some point, that had felt natural, too.

"I love this song!" Winnie shouted. Something in French, a woman's husky, sultry voice over pounding electronic music. The four of us had become eight. Winnie with the wealthy Frenchman, a man named Devo. Serena with the Grand Prix driver, Luc. Bryah was with a well-dressed musician from Morocco named François.

Make that nine of us. An American, whom Damon seemed to know, a heavyset man in a silk shirt, assorted jewelry on his fingers, and a goofy hat. He was pretty goofy himself, but it seemed like he was springing for the booze and nobody was complaining.

"Do you want to dance?" Damon asked me. The way those signature eyebrows arched, I could see that he didn't.

"I'm fine where I am," I said. We'd formed our own little cocoon at the table.

"Are you?" That strong hand, moving slightly on my leg.

I leaned into him. "Can I be honest?"

"Of course."

"I didn't like *Four's a Charm*. I liked *Three*. And I thought *Five* was funny, too. But *Four*? Four guys break out of prison and steal all the evil warden's money? C'mon."

Damon nodded. "They wanted that one. I didn't want to do it but they did."

"They?"

"The money men," he said. "The financiers. I had a ten-movie contract with them and they usually let me decide, but—once in a while..."

"Once in a while they make you do one that stinks."

He smiled widely, as if genuinely amused. "I have to tell you, Abbie, most women wouldn't admit to me that they hated one of my movies."

"I'm not most women."

"No." He sipped from his Champagne. "No, you're not."

A group of women half my age stood a distance from us in slinky, sparkling outfits, noticing the famous actor making my acquaintance. One of them called out to him. He turned and gave them a warm smile, sending them into hysteria, before turning back.

"Admirers," I said. "Does that get old?"

He considered that. "Only when I'm trying to focus on something else. Or some*one* else."

Bryah broke into hysterical laughter, something François the musician said. Winnie was stroking the trimmed beard of her Frenchman, Devo, as if she thought it was funny. She'd grown very comfortable with him, and he with her. Serena was leaning in so close to the hunky race-car driver that they were on the verge of kissing.

So was I, I suddenly realized, as I turned back to Damon. "What project are you working on now?" I asked.

His eyebrows arched. "Right now, I'm working on you. How am I doing so far?"

He smelled so good. I was getting lost in those eyes. *Dreamy* was a word I used as a child, and I could see why. A fantasy. Someone else's life, right?

"Tell me something nobody else knows about you," I said. It felt exciting to ask. It felt intimate. It felt right.

He thought about that a moment. "I guess there is one thing," he said, his eyes sparkling. "Whenever one of my movies comes out. I've never told anybody."

"Tell me," I said.

He brought his lips to my ear. The whiskers from his two days' growth brushed against my cheek. He whispered to me, sharing something nobody else knew. Or so he claimed. But I believed him. I believed everything about him right now.

"I think that's cute," I said, when he was finished.

"Cute," he repeated. "Cute."

"No, I mean—it shows how much acting means to you."

"A window into my soul? Something like that?"

"Something like that," I said.

"Let me tell you something else." He leaned in again. I felt a chill run up my spine. "I want to touch you, Abbie," he said. "I want to put my hands on you. Tonight. Just one night."

"Where?" I said without thinking. I was done thinking. I was finished with rational calculation. I was ready to surrender. "Tell me where you want to touch me."

He never moved from my face. But he answered in a whisper, his lips tickling my ear. He told me where.

CHAPTER 10

SOMEONE HAD THE idea of returning to the casino. It might have been the chubby American, but whoever it was, the idea gathered steam, and soon we were piling into someone's limousine. Damon sat across from me and didn't take his eyes off me. It was like I was the only person in the limo. His eyes met mine, then they slowly lowered, then went back up, covering every inch of my body, up and down, before joining my stare again.

Someone made a joke and I laughed harder than I could remember ever laughing before. And I didn't even know what the joke was. But everything was heightened: every comment was funnier, every sip of Champagne tastier, every moment more delicious than the last.

"You have been to the Grand Casino, yes?" It was the wealthy Frenchman Devo. I was pretty sure he was wearing a toupee, which made me howl with laughter.

"Serena's a star there," said Bryah, leaning against the Moroccan musician.

I looked over at Serena. She was busy nuzzling noses with the race-car driver Luc.

Then we were suddenly there, and out of the limo and making a grand display of our entrance. Damon walked up and took my hand and a jolt of electricity shot through my body. We weren't three feet inside the ornate atrium and people were all over him, the big movie star. Everything was moving fast and spinning and then we were in a private room, different from the last one but with the same elaborate frescoes and lavish surroundings and the roulette wheel was spinning and everyone was cheering. At one point I was sitting down with money in front of me, too, and I was betting it all on number 4, as Serena had.

I was aching for him. I wanted to run my hands through his hair and over his chest and feel his hand slide up my leg, but he wasn't there. Bryah was back at the table: I didn't know she'd been gone, and she was giggling uncontrollably, something about how the toilet seat washed itself after you were done. That made me laugh, too. Anything and everything made me laugh. And the Champagne kept flowing.

"You are a very beautiful woman," said Devo the Frenchman, sitting next to me. Winnie threw a playful elbow into him and I thought of his toupee and I started giggling again. I never giggled but now I couldn't stop. Serena threw her arm around me and pulled me close and laughed along with me and I turned to kiss her on the cheek but she turned, too, at the same time, and we ended up kissing on the lips. That made Devo say, "Yes, *yes*," in that cartoonish French accent and both of us howled with laughter and then kissed each other again.

I lost track of myself, time, everything. Expensive cologne and sweet Champagne and beautiful scenery and roulette wheels spinning and laughter and my best friends in the world and Damon, where was Damon—

And then some of us were in the limousine again and heading somewhere, I didn't know where.

CHAPTER 11

A DOCK. THE COOL, fresh, salty air of the Mediterranean. The four of us were walking down a dock. Heels clanking on steel. Bryah's arm was joined in mine. She was singing a song from her native South Africa—"Oh, take me back to the old Transvaal, there where my Sarie lives"—and I lifted my face up to the stars, thinking again about my friends: how did I get so lucky?

I spilled Champagne all over my dress and threw the glass in the water and found the whole thing funny. I said, "I love you, Bry," and she kept singing her song and Winnie and Serena were climbing aboard this enormous yacht and then the fat American was opening his arm like a host, welcoming us inside.

Inside, Serena had her arms around the neck of the Grand Prix racer Luc. Winnie was stroking the beard of Devo the French Tycoon again and whispering something to him. "Drinks!" Devo announced and I laughed. I laughed at everything the man did now. But the hair thing aside, he had a commanding, confident presence and he had Winnie's attention and there was something familiar about him, but I couldn't place it and couldn't imagine we'd ever met.

Racer Luc was showing Serena a large handgun and I did a double take and it should have bothered me, I was thinking, but it didn't and Winnie said, "I want to shoot it," and Luc said, "No, no," and Devo said, "It's okay, let her," and Luc looked at Devo and said, *"Vraiment?"* and Devo said, "Yes, yes," like he was annoyed and I didn't know why Devo was suddenly the boss of Luc, why a race-car driver would take direction from a toupeed tycoon and I couldn't imagine where they were going to shoot a gun unless we were going to start shooting each other and I started laughing and then Devo said, "You are afraid she'll kill a fish?" and that made me laugh even harder. I had passed being drunk three stop signs back.

We went through two doors and then up some stairs and we were outside. It felt great out here with the breeze and the harbor was dark but the shadowy water beneath us looked beautiful and endless.

And then I jumped when the gun went off.

CHAPTER 12

"I LOVE IT!" Winnie said. I, on the other hand, didn't love it so much and felt a little bit sick. Luc said, "Here, now," and removed the gun from Winnie's hand and placed it inside his jacket and the fat American—yes, he was fat and I was too drunk to feel generous toward him—the fat American was up on the deck with us and he was holding a camcorder at his shoulder. Bryah preened for the camera and then so did Serena and then they were hugging and laughing and the fat American was encouraging them. I was still staring out at the Mediterranean and I felt wobbly and then somebody said something that made us go back inside but I still felt unsteady.

Inside. An expansive room, bigger than my living room, with plush gold furniture and a bar, as if we needed anything else to drink. The fat American whose name I forgot was still using the video camera and Devo the Tycoon said, "*Now,* drinks!"

I took a glass of something, whatever it was, and drank a toast to group something. The liquid was harsh and I spit it out and I said, "Wait, what? Group *what?*" And Devo said it again, "Group *sex,*" and I burst into laughter and Devo said, "Ah, *l'Américaine* laughs." He was right, I was laughing and then Bryah started laughing, too.

Devo opened his hand to indicate Winnie and Serena and said, "Are your friends not beautiful?" I said, "My friends are gorgeous," but I was still laughing and Bryah thought this was funny, too, except that she also seemed to be considering it, and Serena didn't appear to hear what Devo had said or maybe she did and didn't care; she was consumed with Luc the Driver, and I was drunk—as I may have mentioned. Everyone started moving toward another room, and I looked inside and I saw a bed and an elaborate light hanging over it and soft carpeting and then all of them were inside, Winnie and Serena and Bryah, who said, "When in Monte Carlo," and then I felt it, I felt something snap.

Snap.

I stumbled backward in my heels but stayed on my feet. My head was spinning and my stomach was in revolt and I suddenly felt the weight and volume of what I had consumed over the last fifteen or sixteen hours.

"No," I said, taking another step back.

"No?" Devo said to me.

"No." I took a deep breath, my legs shaky beneath me.

"*Quel dommage.*" Devo nodded respectfully and closed the bedroom door behind him.

CHAPTER 13

I WASN'T SURE what to do. I paused momentarily, wondering if I should knock on the door or something, but I heard Bryah's muffled laugh and then Serena's, too, and I knew Winnie could handle herself so I walked out of the room adjoining the bedroom to place some distance between us. I really wasn't in the mood for sound effects.

"Damon," I said. Where had I lost him? The casino, I guess.

I walked into the next room of the gigantic yacht, the main room, where we started. I heard a noise on the dock outside the boat. It must have been the fat American. He hadn't joined the fun in the bedroom. I hoped he wasn't still carrying around that stupid camcorder.

My head was beginning to roar from the booze, laser shots of pain against the inside of my skull. There was a refrigerator in the corner of the room and I fished around for a bottle of water.

"Damon," I said again.

The boat moved a bit, and I could tell that someone was coming aboard.

"I believe that's my cue."

That voice, like a song. I turned and straightened up and there he was, at the opposite end of the room. My heart started pounding.

Headache—what headache? It all came back in a rush, the intoxication, the giddiness, the loss of inhibition. I realized it then: it wasn't the booze that had turned me upside down tonight.

"Have we met, monsieur?" I asked.

Damon took a step toward me. His eyebrows pitched, a hint of a playful smile. "Sorry I'm late."

I took a step forward. We were inching toward each other. Every switch inside me had been flipped on. My legs didn't feel shaky anymore.

"But you're here now," I said.

A scene in a movie, I thought. Ironic given my dance partner, a man with his own star on Hollywood Boulevard.

Damon reached for his shirt, started to unbutton it.

"No," I said.

He didn't move. "No." He didn't say it as a question, but I knew it was.

"No," I repeated. I walked toward him. Damon Kodiak, international film star, stood silent, watching me.

I reached him. I placed my hand where his was, at his collar.

"Let me do it," I said.

CHAPTER 14

ONE BUTTON AT a time. Slipping it out of its buttonhole. Slow, measured, careful. As though each one were a tiny gem that required concentrated precision. His breathing quickened; his powerful chest expanded, contracted.

There. All done.

My hands began above his waist, over his rocky abdominals, slowly gliding upward into a thicket of curly dark hair. Then his chest. Feeling the curve of his muscle, then his nipples. His heartbeat ricocheting into the palm of my hand.

"You'll let me know when it's my turn," he said.

I put a finger to his lips. I ran my hand down his unshaven face, then his neck. His shoulder. He spread his arms, allowing the shirt to fall to the floor.

I took my time with his belt, a rich leather. Sliding the long end out of the belt loop. Pulling it back and slipping the prong out of the hole. Once undone, two quick tugs around his waist and it was on the floor, too.

His breathing continued to accelerate.

Now the pants. He was visibly excited. My eyes met his briefly and

I smiled. Mischievously. I worked the button and the zipper. Then I looked up at him, our eyes locked now. I watched him struggle to restrain himself as I pulled and yanked until his pants had dropped.

"Abbie—"

"Don't say my name." I shook my head slowly. I was someone else. Someone else with her hand inside his cotton boxers. Someone else touching, caressing, stroking. Not too quickly. Not too slowly.

"Okay," I said. "It's your turn."

CHAPTER 15

HE WAS BEHIND me, unzipping my dress slowly, sliding his hands inside, running them along my ribs. The dress dropped to the floor. His hand over my throat, my shoulders, my breasts. His other hand gripped my hair forcefully, a gasp escaping my mouth at his sense of entitlement, his ownership of me.

He pulled my head back, his tongue grazing my neck, his breath hot in my ear, his free hand brushing my stomach, then sliding inside my panties.

A noise from my throat, something guttural and foreign, as his fingers explored me, then slowly, expertly glided inside me. I was weightless. I was his.

"Show me," he commanded in a whisper.

My hand joined his now, directing him. A kernel of sensation, unfamiliar and primitive, began to build and he felt it in the urgency of my hand on top of his, in the quickening of my breath, in the vibration of my pulse, and then an exhilarating rush and I cried out in a voice I didn't recognize, someone else's voice, and my entire body spasmed and collapsed against him.

And then there was nothing else. We were animals gripping and pawing and pulling. Then he was on top of me, his muscular arms spread on either side of me, palms flat on the carpet. He slid inside me easily and I called out, I don't know what I said, *Right now you have me, you own me,* and we found a rhythm, writhing and moaning, and his jaw was clenched and I pulled his hair and *This isn't who I am but maybe, maybe it's what I am becoming* and I wrapped my legs around him and my heels dug into his back and I felt it again but this time I recognized it and I let it wash over me and *I want him inside of me forever and I want this, I want whatever this is, I have never known this but I don't ever want to lose it, whatever this—whatever this—what—*

I cried out and then his back arched and he thrust one last time and let out a wail, his eyes shut, his body shuddering.

We were motionless, panting, for a time. Sweat from his forehead dripped onto my neck. My hair was plastered to my forehead and cheeks. He eased himself out of me and I sat up. He pulled me to my feet and we stared at each other, each of us spent but still curious. He'd found a bottle of water from the fridge and took a drink, then gave me some. I took his warm hand and led him into the next room, a bedroom. I knew he needed time to recharge his batteries, but I thought I might be able to help him. So I did, pushing him against the wall, dropping to my knees. I helped him. Slowly at first, playfully, then more urgently and then his fingers were lacing through my hair and he started responding, and I smiled and I helped him some more and then he was standing at attention. He was ready.

Or at least he thought he was. I climbed him, attacked him, kissing his mouth hard and gripping the thick hair on his chest. He slapped a hand on each of my buttocks and lifted me into the air, my legs wrapped around his waist. We were greedy and selfish and grunting and moaning and I begged him to go faster and I laughed, for some reason I laughed, incomprehensible laughter, and I felt tears in my eyes, and I didn't know what had taken me so long to find this, I didn't know where this—this, whatever it was—had been hiding inside me.

I am lost, I am lost in this, it is happening and I don't know anything, I don't know anything but this, it is all I am, it is all I want.

I was free and open and vulnerable and angry and relentless and then I was dreaming, and in my dreams I didn't recognize myself and I didn't recognize my lover and I knew something had happened, just like that—

Pop-pop-pop-pop

—and everything was different.

Everything would be different, forever now.

When I opened my eyes, the sun was on my face.

CHAPTER 16

BY THE TIME the sun had come up, he was long out of Monte Carlo, driving north on the A8 toward Lyon. Traffic was sparse. It was a Saturday at dawn. Who in their right mind would be driving now?

He chuckled, betraying his nervous energy. Was *he* in his right mind? Arguably not, after what he'd just done. But maybe his mind was right for the first time. Maybe *this* was right, and everything that had come before was wrong.

He stretched his limbs as he drove. He was full of electricity but he knew it was induced by the adrenaline; he knew it was temporary; and he knew he would crash hard when it was over. He hadn't slept, after all, and he still had more than two hours to drive.

He pulled off the highway near Rousset, a village near Aix-en-Provence, one of the most picturesque parts of France, but the scenery wasn't on his mind this morning. He needed to urinate, he needed caffeine, and he needed something in his stomach. Nothing more. In a perfect world, he wouldn't stop at all; he would remain alone and anonymous in the automobile, driving straight to Lyon. Nobody to see his face. Nobody to remember him later, to recount to the authorities: *Yes, now that I'm thinking of it, he did seem rather nervous. Like he was hiding something.*

He'd even filled up the tank late yesterday so he wouldn't need to stop on this trip for fuel. But he hadn't brought along anything to eat or drink in the car—truly an unforgivable oversight; how had he missed that?—plus he wanted to use a decent bathroom, not one of those freestanding toilet facilities along the French highways that suffered, to put it delicately, from inadequate plumbing. In any event, it was decided: he would stop. He found a gas station and killed the engine.

He had no disguise. He had ditched it hours ago, after everything had happened. His reasoning: if he were pulled over by the French police for some reason—either for what had happened in Monte Carlo or for something as innocuous as a moving violation—he wouldn't want to have to explain why he was traveling incognito. How does an innocent man explain a disguise?

That was the dilemma, of course: he could remain disguised and assume that risk, or he could go au naturel and take a different chance—that he would be caught on some security camera, leading to the obvious question of what he was doing two hours outside of Monte Carlo at dawn.

He zipped up his light windbreaker, pulled his baseball cap down low, and adjusted his sunglasses. He checked himself in the car's mirror. Not good. He looked like someone trying to conceal his identity. But again with the dilemma—wouldn't that be preferable to smiling for the camera?

Yes, and so he got out of the car and walked without incident to the front door of the gas station's shop. He reached for the door handle and looked through the glass door and saw the security camera and wondered just for a moment if he had taken leave of his senses and should just live with hunger pains and drowsiness, and he could always take a piss on the side of the road—

In his distraction with the camera he missed the door handle and his momentum carried him into the door itself, where the brim of his baseball cap collided with the glass, pushing the cap back off his face and nearly off his head altogether. This bit of embarrassing clumsiness caught the attention of the girl behind the counter inside, who, from the looks of it, had been reading something but now turned in his direction.

What to do? Cut your losses and make a run for it? Stroll inside as if nothing had happened?

He wasn't good at this. He'd been remarkably adept in Monte Carlo, if he did say so himself. The pre-event planning had been careful and he'd carried it out with icy precision. Why was he so pitiful with the getaway?

He fixed his hat atop his head once more, adjusted his shades, and walked in. He tried to whistle, which he didn't do very well but which signaled calm. He nodded to the girl behind the counter, a young petite woman with a button nose and inquisitive eyes.

"Hall-o," she said in stilted English. Damn her. He hadn't opened his mouth, and already he was exposed as a foreigner. So much for blending in.

He didn't answer, fearing his voice might betray his nerves. His lips formed into some kind of conciliatory expression and he pretended to be fascinated by the assorted soft drinks and bottles of water lined up in the refrigerated case on the back wall. In the reflection of the case's glass he could see her watching him. But why? What about him was arousing her suspicion? What *else* could she tell simply by watching him? Something obvious he had missed? Was he tracking in *blood,* for the love of God? Surely not, but the problem was, he couldn't very well inventory himself right there in front of her. Why had he come here? Why was he risking everything just so he could piss in a clean urinal and fill his stomach with empty calories? How breathtakingly stupid could he be?

It flashed through his mind: he could kill her with his bare hands and then steal the security tape. But where would that tape be located? He could get that information from the girl, he could make her tell him before he killed her—

Without further thought, he walked across the store to the bathroom. He was headed to a urinal but suddenly found himself opting for a stall. His hands went flat against side walls and he balanced himself, as his heartbeat ricocheted against his chest and his legs buckled.

What had he missed? What mistake had he made? Why had he done it? In the end, why was it worth all the risk involved?

Then he exhaled and raised his chin. Remember, he told himself. Remember the anger. The betrayal. The wound to your pride. Let it motivate you now, just as it did last night, before you carried it out. Stay focused. Stay mad.

He took a breath, finished his business in the bathroom, and assessed himself in the mirror. He felt better. Screw up now, and everything you've done is for naught.

He strode confidently out of the bathroom and brought three power bars, a bottle of Evian, and a large cup of store-made coffee up to the register. The girl had returned to her paperback novel, which she laid facedown, revealing a crumbling spine and the words *La comédie des menteurs*.

Menteurs. Liars. He smiled at the girl but didn't speak. He paid in cash and left. Once he was safely inside his car, he felt very much like laughing.

CHAPTER 17

I GAVE MY ARMS a long stretch and smiled at the ceiling. I was lying naked on a bed in a small bedroom. The pillows and comforter were all over the floor. A chair lay overturned.

I got up, feeling the full effects of last night. Every muscle was sore, every movement painful. My head was pounding.

And I felt great.

I found a cotton robe in an adjoining bathroom and threw it on. I walked into the large main room, where everything had started last night with Damon. No sign of him. I sighed. He was a man of his word. "Just one night," he'd said.

Just one night, but everything was different. The dose of fantasy had really been a dose of reality. I couldn't go back to Jeffrey. Whatever I'd tasted last night, not love but *something*—I had to have that something. I wouldn't become Serena, dabbling in occasional affairs to keep life interesting. I wouldn't be Winnie, living with a mysterious, distant man she no longer knew.

Richie and Elena. It would be hard. But it wasn't like they lived with us much, anyway. I'd move back to the States. I'd move somewhere close to their boarding school in Connecticut. Hey, I'd ask them if they even wanted to *stay* in boarding school. Jeffrey hadn't given them much choice. But screw him. Let him stay in Switzerland and fuck the ambassador to his heart's content. I wasn't living a charade anymore. Not for another day. I was done.

No—I was just beginning. I hadn't been playing someone else this weekend. I'd *become* someone else.

Winnie stumbled into the main room. She looked like someone else, too, but not in a good way. Her hair was flat and her eyes dull and bloodshot. She had on a large T-shirt and her legs were bare.

"Top of the morning," I said. "Was it fun?"

"They're gone," she said, retrieving a bottle of water from the refrigerator.

"Devo, Luc, and François?"

She nodded and sunk into a chair.

"And that disappoints you?" I asked. "You expected a whirlwind romance from those characters?"

She started to answer but then we both heard it, the commotion outside. Something chaotic, people shouting, the noise of urgent footsteps rattling on the dock.

And then I remembered something, something tickling me from the recesses of my memory last night. *A noise, a pop—*

"Wonder what the ruckus is," Winnie said.

—a burst, muted and distant, several in succession—

"The bloody hell?" she said.

—a gunshot? Had I heard gunshots?

And then the unmistakable sound of the yacht's door swinging open, the pounding of footsteps entering the yacht, men's voices shouting something in French. Winnie and I jumped to our feet.

Just as three commandos, in full combat gear, rushed into the cabin and trained assault weapons on us.

CHAPTER 18

THREE OF THEM initially, then three more spilling in behind them, dressed in blue, combat helmets with face shields, dark masks covering everything from their necks to their noses, bullet-proof vests, weapons galore on their belts, thick gloves, and heavy combat boots.

"*Allongez-vous face contre terre! Face contre terre!* Down!" Their assault weapons swept across the room. One of them motioned to the floor, lest we misunderstand, while others fanned out throughout the yacht.

"*Face contre terre!*" One of the soldiers moved toward me and I crouched down. He pushed me flat to the floor and I lay still. Winnie had done the same thing.

Shouting, from other parts of the yacht. Bursting through a door—the bedroom door. Serena's inquisitive voice. More shouting. I caught Winnie's eye. She was staring forward intently, perfectly still and perfectly terrified.

Chaos all around us. Serena and Bryah, pushed into the room at gunpoint and forced to the floor beside us, Serena in a T-shirt and panties, Bryah stark naked.

"What's going on?" Serena shouted. The soldier behind her put a foot on her back.

"Silence!" he ordered.

I said, "Just do what they say—"

"Silence!"

That soldier stood sentry over us, training his gun on our backs, while the others stormed the various rooms of the yacht.

"Qui est-ce qui est dans le yacht? Comment?"

Comment? How many? I thought he was asking how many people were on the yacht. I didn't know, other than the four of us. Devo, Luc, François, and Damon were gone. The fat American?

"Quatre ou cinq," I answered. Four or five.

The soldiers called out to each other, announcing each room clear, I assumed, but I really didn't know. I didn't know much of anything. I was in a foreign country where an armed militia was overtaking our yacht. What in the world had happened?

The fat American, in a T-shirt and boxers, his hair standing on end, was pushed into the main cabin and forced to the carpet as well. The soldiers gathered and seemed satisfied that they'd rounded us all up. They went to each of us and grabbed our hands and fastened them behind our backs, some kind of a hard rubber restraint. Handcuffs, but not like the police used. At least not in America. But this wasn't America.

I was lifted off my feet and pushed forward. Each of us was forced up the stairs and onto the dock. Outside, the air was clammy and the sun was low in the east. What would ordinarily be a sleepy dawn was a frenetic scramble of people and vehicles.

It was as if France had declared war on tiny Monaco. Gray helicopters hovered low overhead. A couple of planes that looked like fighter jets circled the sky. Official-looking cars swamped the harbor. The same military group, wearing combat gear and brandishing assault weapons, was pulling people out of all the other yachts moored in the harbor. The entire dock was lined with people lying flat on their stomachs in handcuffs.

We soon joined them—and this time, we didn't require an order.

We fell to our knees and then lay face down. Soldiers moved us with their feet until they had arranged us on the diagonal, clearing a lane on the dock for foot traffic.

"What in the world is going on?" I said, my head turned toward Winnie, each of us lying prone on the cold, dingy dock.

"Oh, God," Winnie said. "Oh, God, no."

"What?" I asked.

"Silence!" one of them barked at me.

Winnie closed her eyes, and the chaos escalated around us. She complied with the wishes of the French soldier, not speaking but simply mouthing the words.

Oh, no.

CHAPTER 19

TEN, TWENTY MINUTES passed. I was lying flat, my head turned toward Winnie and beyond her, to the harbor. A French soldier stood only a few feet away. Soldiers and people in civilian clothes ran back and forth. I heard several splashes, telling me that people were diving into the water. Some of the soldiers entered our yacht again. Troopers were boarding yachts with dogs, German shepherds, who wore large blue vests that covered their torsos.

What had happened?

"Talk to me, Winnie," I said, but a boot came down between our faces.

"*Une arme!*" The shout came from someone standing at the door of our yacht.

"*Qui est le propriétaire du yacht? Celui-ci?*" shouted a man whose boots were inches from my face. "*Qui est le—*"

"I am," the fat American said. "It's my yacht."

"*Levez-vous!*" A soldier grabbed me by the wrist restraints and lifted me to my feet. "*Allez-vous! Allez, allez!*" All of us, the four of us ladies and the fat American, started marching toward the harbor.

"What's going on?" Serena said in a hushed tone.

"Don't worry, sweetie, this is some kind of mistake," I called back with no conviction whatsoever.

Commandos had raided every boat. The parking lot was swarming with officials, mostly in plain clothes, not in uniform. An area around one particular car, a black convertible, was cordoned off with barricades.

Soldiers were lifting everyone to their feet and lining them up single file on the dock. But we were getting the royal treatment. We were marching ahead of them, all by ourselves.

We were being singled out.

CHAPTER 20

THE DIN IN the parking lot had reached near-deafening levels—everyone was shouting over each other and barking orders, sirens were blaring, helicopters were hovering. The four of us were each placed into a separate unmarked black SUV. Slowly, the vehicles started to move in a caravan. A helicopter flew overhead, trailing us. Soldiers jogged alongside the procession, holding their machine guns in ready position. A series of large vans passed us going the other way on a narrow road, heading back toward the dock, presumably to transport the occupants of the other yachts. Why, I had no idea.

"I'm an American citizen and I have rights," I said to the driver and the soldier seated next to him in the front seat. "I demand to know what's going on."

They didn't respond. They didn't even look back at me.

We pulled into the same airport in Nice where we landed only two short days ago, the Aéroport Nice Côte d'Azur. But this time it was lined with military vehicles and armed soldiers. I was led into a small plane, where I was placed in a seat and my handcuffs were fastened to something else, locking me into the chair. Then a blindfold was placed over my eyes.

"Is that really necessary? For God's sake, I'm handcuffed and—"

"*Silence!*" someone yelled in my face.

I heard others board the plane. My friends. I heard sobbing. I thought it was Winnie but I couldn't be sure. I couldn't even be sure that the sobs weren't my own.

I couldn't be sure of anything right now.

We sat in stunned silence. I could hear the rapid breathing of my friends, all of us bound and blindfolded and clueless.

Then some more men jumped onto the plane and said something that I missed. The plane soon moved down the runway. And then it lifted in the air. Less than forty-eight hours after arriving in Monte Carlo, brimming with anticipation, we were leaving in handcuffs and blindfolds, with absolutely no idea where we were going or what was happening.

"Ladies, you have rights," I called out. "Demand a lawyer. Demand someone from the emb—"

A blow to my chest, a flat palm whisking the wind from me. My head slammed against the wall. I was woozy for a moment but I had to think, to focus. But focus on *what?* Nothing made sense.

It seemed like we were in the air for about an hour and a half. That was three times the time it took to fly from Bern to Nice two days ago. But Bern felt very far away right now.

Paris, I assumed. After our landing, we were released from our seats and marched down a flight of stairs. I was wearing nothing more than a robe, nothing underneath and nothing on my feet.

A mistake, I told myself. A misunderstanding.

I walked in blindfolded darkness, a strong hand clutching my arm, into another car. The car was blaring a siren, which echoed similar sirens from the other cars in our caravan. I thought of so many things—Richie and Elena, even Jeffrey, what in the world could have possibly happened—and lost track of time. The only thing I noticed was that the car never stopped, hardly even slowed, during the entire trip.

Then we stopped. A door opened, a blast of warm air, and I was being handled again, forced out of the car, stubbing my bare toes on asphalt. A soldier on each side of me kept me from falling. They were carrying me as much as I was walking.

From asphalt to tile, the inside of a building. From tile to an elevator. We climbed three stories, by my count. Nothing but darkness through the blindfold. My wrists were abraded and one of my shoulders was cramping from my hands being held behind my back for so long.

Then more tile, then a room, a very cold room. I was put into a chair, my cuffed hands placed behind the back of it, and locked down.

I smelled aftershave, body odor, sweat. I sensed the presence of others in the room. One or two, I thought, but I wasn't sure. A door opened and closed several times. People entered and exited. They whispered and they conferred. Someone lit a cigarette. I thought the French had banned indoor smoking, but I wasn't entirely sure I was even *in* France and I doubted I would score any points raising an objection, in any event.

My head was pounding and my heart was racing. The silence was worse than the chaos on the dock.

And then the blindfold was ripped off my face.

CHAPTER 21

I BLINKED INTO the glare of a brightly lit room. The walls were shiny white and bare, and there were blinding fluorescent lights overhead. The ceiling had a pitch to it, sufficient to allow the can lights on the angled surfaces to shoot directly into my eyes. A modern version of the spotlight shining in the face. What with the frigid temperature in here, it felt like sunshine in the middle of winter.

Two men stood across from me. One of them was young and wiry with a ruddy complexion and a square jaw and hair cropped in military fashion. The other was probably fifty; he wore a suit and a civilian hairstyle.

"*Comment vous appelez-vous?*" asked the older man. French. Did that mean I was in France? It made the most sense.

"*Je m'appelle* Abbie Elliot," I said, struggling for a calm, firm demeanor. "*Je suis une citoyenne américaine. Je veux*—I'm an American citizen," I said in English, flustered, "and I want to speak with a lawyer or someone from the embassy."

"Who do you work for?" The younger one, the square jaw, was talking now. He seemed like the one who would play the heavy hand. And he seemed to relish it.

"Work for? I don't work for anyone," I said.

Square Jaw approached my chair and bent down, as if to get a better look at me. "You are lying," he said. His English was as good as his older colleague's, but his accent was thicker. "How many of you are there?" He wasn't letting me break eye contact, moving his face to keep my eyes focused on him. "Hmm? How many?"

"You've made a big mistake," I said. "The only group I'm a part of is a group of ladies on vacation. Whatever happ—"

"Tell me!" he hissed, gripping the back of my hair, his hot breath on my face. "*Comment?* How many?"

"I'm in Monte Carlo with three friends," I said, trying to project some measure of confidence, but it wasn't easy. Cold sweat was running down my armpits and along my ribs. My hands were shackled behind me, locking me to the chair, rendering me immobile. "Serena Schofield, Winnie Brookes, and Bryah Gordon."

"Who do you work for?" he asked me again. "Le Groupe Islamique Armé?"

Islamique? "I'm not Islamic," I said. "I'm the daughter of a Methodist—"

"ETA?" he went on. "Mujahideen-e Khalq? FLNC? Al-Qaeda?"

Al-Qaeda?

I drew back, in the limited space I had before my head touched the high back of the wooden chair to which I was tied. I looked alternately at Square Jaw and the older guy, as though I were waiting for a punch line. Or for someone to pop out from behind a curtain and tell me this whole thing was a prank, like on *Candid Camera* or the MTV version of it my son watches.

But there were no curtains, nor were the facial expressions of my inquisitors anything but deadly serious.

I laughed, but no one joined me.

"You think I'm a *terrorist?*" I asked.

CHAPTER 22

MY INITIAL REACTION, of all things, was relief. I'd had some time to think about this on my travels from Monte Carlo to wherever I was currently, and I'd decided that the most likely explanation for what had happened on the harbor was drugs. A raid—the French equivalent of the DEA searching boats for illegal narcotics, which they would probably find in abundance on those vessels. Given that the occupants of our yacht were singled out, I figured that meant they had found some drugs on our yacht. And I figured that could be a problem for us, even though the drugs weren't ours, simply because we'd been staying there.

But *terrorism?* That meant these guys were way off base.

I spent the next half hour fending them off as they lobbed names of terrorist groups at me, even names of specific terrorist leaders, reading me for a reaction, waiting for something in my eyes or my body language to tell them they'd hit their mark. I'd protested initially, to the point of shouting: I wasn't a terrorist; I was a housewife and mother on vacation; I was about the least threatening person on the face of this earth. We were talking past each other, missing each other completely. My interrogators were probing for an exact spot on the map while I was telling them they had the wrong planet.

When that line of questioning ran aground, they started in on what would happen next. "What else is planned?" they asked me, again throwing out details, presumably the most visible terrorist targets in France. L'Assemblée Nationale? Notre Dame? Roissy? L'Arc de Triomphe?

It was almost comical—a relief, as I said. Before this weekend, my idea of adventure was to order a wool sweater online, sight unseen. Now I was being asked whether I was going to bomb the Eiffel Tower or assassinate the prime minister.

I say it was *almost* comical because there was one thing missing from this comedy show: comedy. These men were not just serious. They were scared. Something had happened, an event of some kind that had shaken them to the core and made them determined not to let something else transpire on their watch. They were trying for an even-handed approach, peppering me with questions in a staccato, back-and-forth style without expressing much emotion, keeping their voices level and trying to substitute intensity for what, it seemed to me, was their rawest emotion—fear.

That, more than the setting or their questions, unnerved me. Something very bad had happened.

"This is a misunderstanding, guys," I said in English, not knowing the French equivalent. "Whatever it is that happened, I have no idea—"

"That is a lie," said Square Jaw, whose name, I had learned, was Durand. "Do not tell us you have no idea." He was still on his feet, stooped at the waist and looking at me face-to-face.

"I really don't."

"You insult us with these lies." The older guy was named Rouen, the good cop, I suppose, to his younger and tougher partner. But neither of these men was revealing very much to me at all.

"I'm not saying another word until you tell me what's going on," I told them.

Durand slowly moved his eyes off me. *"Montrez-lui les photos,"* he said to his partner, the elder statesman Rouen.

The photos, Durand had said. A crime scene? What had happened? Damon, I thought, with a shot of dread. Had something happened to Damon? The murder of an international movie star could probably elicit the response I witnessed, at least fifty cops or soldiers, or whatever they were, swarming the harbor.

My head started pounding. On a good day, following the intake of as much alcohol as I had last night, I would be barely able to move. But I'd been knocked around on the dock and on the plane and I was in desperate need of a painkiller. And I had a pretty good feeling that what was coming next wasn't going to make me feel any better.

Not Damon, I prayed.

The two men moved a long table so that it was positioned in front of me. The older guy, Rouen, placed a large glossy photo on the table before me.

"Oh, God." It was a close-up shot of a man sitting in a car, wounds to his chest and neck. No matter how garish and surreal the sight of his dead body was, I had no trouble identifying him.

"Devo," I said.

CHAPTER 23

"DEVO," DURAND SCOFFED, looking at his partner, Rouen. "Yes, *Devo,* as you say."

Rouen dropped another photo on the table, a different man, sitting dead in the same car, similar wounds, including a bullet to the forehead.

I turned my head away. It was Luc, the race-car driver.

Devo and Luc had been murdered.

I lurched forward and vomited into my lap.

"Perhaps now we can...dispense with your games? You will tell us what happened?"

I looked up at Durand, catching my breath. "Surely...you don't think *I* had anything to do with that? You don't think we...*killed* them?"

Durand dropped both palms on the table and leaned into me. "We know you did," he answered. "It is just a matter of how long it will take you to admit it."

No. No. This was wrong. This couldn't be. *Don't talk, Abbie. Get a lawyer. Don't be an idiot. This is* murder *we're talking about.*

"My husband works for the American Embassy in Switzerland," I said. "I want to speak with him. I want a lawyer and I want someone from the—"

His hand flew up so quickly I didn't have time to react. A blow to the head, to the soft part of my skull near my temple and hairline. Not enough to send me to the hospital, or even to exhibit a bruise later. But enough to send a message.

"You are not in Switzerland and you are not in the United States," Durand said, his anger rising. "No phone calls. No husbands. No lawyers. Not until you confess this to us."

"I'm not saying another word," I managed.

"Then you are saying something with your silence." This time it was Rouen. "In this country, when you do not talk to us, it appears you are hiding something. This is not America," he reminded me for the second time.

Durand said, "You must understand, this is for your benefit. If you are able to show—what is it, *remords*—if you show you are sorry, yes?"

"Remorse," said Rouen. "It is your only chance. You will spend your lifetime in prison if you do not—"

"I didn't kill anybody," I said. "I don't know anything about it."

Stop, Abbie.

"That is . . . not helpful." Durand looked disappointed. "And your friends? You can say the same of them?"

"My friends would never kill anybody."

Durand held the photos of Devo and Luc up to my face. "They were on your yacht, yes?"

"Yes, we were all on the same yacht—"

"And by this you mean you and your friends."

"Yes. Correct. And Devo and Luc."

"And Monsieur Ogletree? *Le propriétaire?*"

Ogletree? The fat American. The owner of the yacht. "Yes," I said.

I'd left out one person: Damon. But I didn't see where he figured in. Surely this whole thing could be resolved without my having to talk about *that*. It wouldn't really come to that, would it? I wouldn't have to choose between admitting to infidelity and being charged with *murder.*

Would I?

"And when you declare your innocence, you do the same for your friends? You can…make excuses for your friends at all times? Account—account for them? At all times?"

I couldn't, of course. Nor could they account for me, not once the bedroom door closed with Serena, Winnie, Bryah, Devo, and Luc on one side and me on the other.

Shut up, Abbie. What are you doing? Even innocent people can get in trouble during interrogations. Shut the hell up.

And hope your friends are doing the same.

"She does not respond," Durand said to Rouen.

"She is protecting her friends, perhaps," he answered back.

"I want a lawyer," I said.

"We give her an opportunity to explain her facts and she does not," said Durand. "So, instead we ask her friends."

He turned back to me, one last comment, almost as a whisper, his nose inches from mine. "Your friends will be as loyal to you as you are to them? Only a fool would believe this."

The two of them walked out of the room, leaving me sitting amid the bleached white walls and blinding lights. Leaving me in a cotton robe stained with vomit, my head woozy and throbbing. Leaving me to my imagination and fears.

Leaving me alone, more alone than I'd ever felt.

CHAPTER 24

DURAND DID A slow walk around the room, circling the single chair positioned in the center. "So it was you, Serena, and Winnie," he said, struggling with the names. *SEHR-ee-na. WEE-nee.*

Bryah's eyes dropped to the floor, in part out of shame, in part because of the blinding lights in her face. "Yes," she said quietly.

"Not Abbie. She did not...accompany you in the bedroom?"

Bryah thought for a moment. She was staring into her lap, into the center of a gray smock that most closely resembled surgical scrubs, which soldiers had thrown over her on the dock in Monte Carlo after pulling her naked from her bed. It did little to protect her from the cool temperatures in the room.

"Abbie slept somewhere else."

"You do not make excuse for her?"

"I don't...what?"

"You cannot account for her," said Rouen.

"I—no. I don't know what Abbie did," Bryah admitted. "But she isn't capable of killing someone."

"Ah." Durand bent down and spoke into Bryah's ear. "She will not say the same of you. They will blame you. All these white women of . . . privilege will blame the black *Islamique,* yes?"

"I'm not Islamic, you idiot. Just because I'm black you think—"

"Enough," he hissed. "You will be taking a risk, allowing them to give their story first. The first story will be the one that is . . . believed."

Bryah closed her eyes. "I didn't kill anybody and neither did they."

"But you say you were . . . *endormi.* Asleep. Now you tell me you know for certain they are innocent. You are telling me lies. These are lies."

"Tell us who it was," said Rouen, leaning against the wall. "The killer will spend a lifetime in prison. The ones who help us? Not so long."

"Are your friends so brave as you?" It was Durand, again, in her ear. "Can you be sure?"

Serena coughed as she tried to concentrate on the question. She was ill already from last night's events. After being roused from sleep at gunpoint and then seeing the photo of Luc dead, it took all her will not to vomit. She'd collapsed into hysterical sobbing upon seeing that photo and took almost half an hour to recover.

"Abbie wouldn't hurt anyone," she said.

"That is not my question," said Durand. "Shall I ask it again?"

Serena struggled against her restraints. She had a pinched nerve in her shoulder that flared up every so often, and now—when she was in the unnatural position of having her hands restrained behind her back and cuffed to a small wooden chair—was one of those times.

"After we went into the bedroom, I didn't see her again. I can only assume she went to sleep."

"But you cannot say."

She shook her head. "I don't know where she was," she said.

They'd decided to interview Winnie last. She'd been the most emotional, the most unglued of the four women during the trip from the harbor to headquarters. Let her stew in it, whatever it was—sadness, terror—so she would be ready to burst when it was her turn.

Winnie's head had fallen. Her eyes were puffy and bloodshot from her sobbing.

Durand approached her, squatted down so he was face-to-face with her. But she wasn't looking at him. She hadn't acknowledged their entrance at all.

"He's dead, isn't he?" she whispered.

CHAPTER 25

THE DOOR OPENED. Durand and Rouen again. I didn't know how much time had passed. Best guess was three hours. Maybe four. I was dehydrated and nauseated and completely off-kilter. I was, I assumed, exactly as they wanted me.

It was all about control, after all. Manipulation. They held all the cards, Durand and Rouen, and I held none. None except my complete innocence, if that counted as a card. I hoped that it still did.

"I need to use the washroom and I need some water," I said.

Durand shook his head dismissively, as if my request weren't even in the vicinity of reasonableness. "Not until you . . . explain to us."

That wasn't going to happen. I'd spent the last few hours steeling myself. Don't say a word, I thought. Wait for a lawyer, no matter how long it takes. What in the world was I doing talking to these people? They didn't have any proof. They couldn't possibly.

Keep telling yourself that, I thought.

"I want a lawyer," I said yet again.

"You do not have that right," said Rouen.

"Do the French still have to prove people guilty? Or did you dispense with that, too? Will I even get a trial?"

Durand held up a large plastic bag and walked over to me. Inside was my black purse.

"This is yours?" he asked.

I stifled my initial instinct to respond. I'd just spent the last few hours promising myself I would remain silent.

Durand looked at Rouen. "A simple question, I would think."

"It's my purse," I said.

Durand, wearing a smug expression, returned to the door, where he made an exchange with someone in the hallway and returned with a second bag.

It held a handgun. Not the one Luc had last night; this gun was smaller. He displayed the weapon to me with pride, watching my reaction. I didn't know *how* to react.

"Okay, so? It's a gun."

"It's *your* gun," he said.

"It's not my gun. I don't own a gun. I've never seen that before."

"Why do you lie to us? Admit it. Admit this is your gun."

"Go to hell," I said. It felt good, empowering.

He held it still closer, only inches from my face, shaking it for emphasis.

I turned my head. "I have nothing else to say."

"Nothing else. Nothing else. I am...so sorry to hear that. I hoped you could explain to me something."

I looked at him. "Yeah? What do you want explained to you?"

He leaned into me, a gleam in his eye. "This gun that you say is not yours? If you would please explain to me why we found it in your purse."

CHAPTER 26

THE AMERICAN EMBASSY in Paris was a beautiful stone building located near the bend of the Seine just west of the Place de la Concorde, an enormous public square—actually an octagon—each of the eight corners featuring a statue representing a different French city. Where the guillotine once served its bloody function during the French Revolution's public executions now stood the majestic Obelisk of Luxor, flanked by fountains on each side, glowing in the city's darkness this evening.

This was the heart of Paris, overlooking the gardens of the Champs-Élysées; steps from the high-end shopping district and the Musée de l'Orangerie and, of course, the Louvre; across the Seine from the Palais Bourbon and the Assemblée Nationale.

The embassy grounds were protected by gates and by United States Marines. Visitors' identification was checked twice before admittance. At the secured entry, visitors were required to check and turn off their cell phones. They passed through metal detectors and, given today's events, were subjected to a physical search and an armed marine escort as well.

Now they stood, two American expatriates, Jeffrey Elliot and Simon Schofield, in the office of the attaché from the United States Department of Justice, Daniel Ingersoll, an assistant U.S. attorney from Washington, D.C., serving a two-year stint in Paris.

"Terrorists," Simon scoffed. *"Terrorists?"*

Ingersoll, an approachable man with a youthful face and sandy hair, had been here all of four months, and this monumental international incident was being dropped in his lap. It had sounded interesting at the time, this job—a fresh start after the divorce; a chance for his teenager, Molly, to attend a couple years of high school in Paris; and interesting work free of the stress of federal courtrooms. Yeah, right, he thought to himself. This case was going to dominate the rest of his time in Paris.

"They've begun the investigation as a terrorism investigation," he said to Simon. "It doesn't mean it ends that way."

"And this means what again?" Jeffrey demanded.

"Walk Jeff through it, Dan." It was the voice of the United States ambassador to France, Tristan Souter, over a speakerphone, as he traveled back from Australia.

"Sure." Ingersoll sighed. He looked at the two husbands, who were wearing expressions he'd seen many times as a federal prosecutor—not so much on the defendants but on their families: desperation, anxiety about their lack of control over events, and overpowering worry, which bent their shoulders and distorted their mouths.

"The French can detain anyone as long as there's a plausible reason to believe that a crime was committed," he explained. "If it's an act of terrorism under investigation, they can effectively hold a detainee for what is really ninety-six hours. Four days. Technically, three, but it's always extended by the prosecutor. It could be extended to five or even six days. But four is customary."

"And during this time?" Simon asked. "What protections does my wife have?"

Ingersoll did a slow nod, trying to be deferential to the panicked husbands. "Very few, Mr. Schofield. They can deny her any outside communications. They can deny her a lawyer. For terrorism, they don't even have to videotape the interrogations. She will see a lawyer at the end of the third day—after seventy-two hours—but only for thirty minutes, and the lawyer will not have seen any of the evidence. And some of us here believe—well, we don't know but we *suspect* they record these attorney-client visits. So we always advise our citizens not to reveal anything."

Simon flew out of his chair, pacing the room in small circles. "You're telling me they can interrogate Serena for four days straight and no one will watch them? No one can represent her? She can't talk to anyone?"

"Unfortunately, yes," said Ambassador Souter over the speakerphone.

Simon waved his arms. "They're considered terrorists all because of who this man was? I mean, how were they supposed to even *know*?"

Ingersoll didn't have an answer for that one. He knew virtually nothing of the facts of the case. Still, a terrified husband could be forgiven for asking unreasonable questions. All that Ingersoll knew for certain at this point was that the French were stiff-arming him, playing things close to the vest for the time being.

Jeffrey checked his watch. "And it's only been about twelve, thirteen hours since they were detained?"

"About thirteen hours, we think." Ingersoll cleared his throat. "All we know is that at approximately seven hundred hours this morning, the GIGN raided the harbor in Monte Carlo."

"The GIGN?" Simon asked.

"I'm sorry, the Groupe d'Intervention de la Gendarmerie Nationale. It's an elite counterterrorism group. A military unit. Like our Delta Force." Ingersoll sighed. "They took virtually everyone in the harbor into custody, but most have been released. Your wives, and their other two friends, are obviously their focus."

"And you haven't seen them?" Simon asked. "Aren't they supposed to let you see them?"

Ingersoll grimaced. "Typically, someone from the embassy is allowed to visit an American citizen on a daily basis during the *garde à vue*—the detention period." He shrugged his shoulders in apology.

"But not today. This is no ordinary crime, sir. It's not even an ordinary act of terrorism."

Jeffrey ran a hand over his face. "Where are they? The Palace of Justice?"

"We don't know, Jeff," said the ambassador over the speakerphone.

"You don't *know?*"

Ingersoll said, "The GIGN could have taken them to their headquarters in Satory, out west. But we think they're being held by the Central Directorate of Interior Intelligence. DCRI. French intelligence. We think they're in DCRI headquarters in Levallois-Perret. A suburb of Paris."

"This is absolutely—this is outrageous," said Simon, who was all but bouncing off the walls. His face was ghost-white. "What—what's happening right now? What do you think they're doing? Are they eating? Can they sleep? Are they—"

"The French are building a case," said Ingersoll. "They're questioning the women and gathering evidence and incorporating new information into the interrogations. This case will receive the highest priority, so the evidence is coming in fast. Evidence that takes months to process will take hours."

"They've got our wives all to themselves for four days, interrogating them hour after hour and doing God knows what to them," said Jeffrey. "And we know nothing? They haven't told you a single thing? Not one scrap of information?"

Ingersoll paused, nervously scratching his head, debating. "I've exhausted my contacts. I've not been given any details. The lid is being shut extremely tight on this one."

That wasn't altogether true. He'd largely been kept in the dark, but he had a few sources of his own, some relationships he'd built up within the Paris police force. He hadn't been told anything concrete, but he'd been given one piece of information, probably better described as opinion than fact.

He was told that the evidence against the four women was very, very strong.

CHAPTER 27

I WAS LOST in a sea of white light. I couldn't very well sleep, even had I wanted to, given the brightness of the room and the cool temperatures, which had given me a permanent chill. Or maybe the slight tremble in my body was because of my jangled nerves, a simmering fear that shot up to a full-scale boil whenever I let my imagination get the better of me.

Time had passed, but I didn't know how much. There was no clock in this time warp of a room, nor were there windows or any sense of the world beyond these walls. The typical indicators of time—the movement of the sun, meals, human interaction—all were denied me. I had only my internal barometers, hunger and drowsiness, neither of which were reliable in my current state.

I didn't know if it was day one or day two now, if it was midnight or noon. My best estimate was that I'd been in this wooden chair for approximately eighteen hours, but I wouldn't have bet a nickel on that guess.

Nor was I having a great day from a physical perspective. A rather consistent pain shot from my buttocks up my spine to my neck. My arms had grown numb. My neck was sore from the rolling, side-to-side motion of my head along the back of the chair.

Make the suspect uncomfortable, off balance. I got it. Their tactics were predictable, even primitive. But they were working, regardless.

They had fingerprinted me, swabbed the inside of my mouth, drawn my blood, and run tests on my hands and forearms. Otherwise, I had been left alone. More alone than I'd wanted, in fact. I'd called out regularly in the beginning—requesting water, the bathroom, a moment to stretch my limbs—and soon realized that I would settle for an angry confrontation. Some interaction. More information. Anything. I was left alone with this puzzle, of which I had only two pieces: Devo and Luc had been killed, and the murder weapon had been found in my purse.

Or so they'd said. I didn't know what to think. Either they were lying to me or someone had put a gun in my purse. Either way, this was a mistake. It *had* to be.

"Hello!" I called out, recognizing the incongruity of my actions: refusing to talk but wanting someone to visit; recognizing that I should have a lawyer present but wanting to talk to Durand and Rouen anyway, wanting to know what other information they had, why they thought I was a suspect, what the other ladies had told them.

It was a ploy, this silent treatment. They had shown me a damning piece of evidence and then left me alone for about twelve hours, enough time to let my imagination interact with my fear and concoct all sorts of heart-stopping, worst-case scenarios. A traditional tactic, maybe, but traditional for a reason—it was effective.

The door opened. Durand and Rouen again. The brute and the stately elder.

"I need…water," I said. "And a bath—"

"You would like a meal and a bathroom and a phone call," said Durand. He unscrewed the top of his water bottle and took a long swallow. Then he screwed the top back on. Taunting me. "Like your friends have had," he said.

"What…about my friends?" My voice cracked as I spoke. My mouth was so dry that my tongue was sticking to the roof.

"Bathed and fed," he answered. "Now they are sleeping on beds.

Because they told us. Madame Elliot, you have little time. We know what happened. We do not know why. *Mais* soon, we will have no need for a statement from you."

"Tell me...what they said."

"Your friend Winnie? Winnie says that it was you. You fired the weapon and it was your idea."

"It was my idea to kill Devo and Luc? That's ridiculous. She wouldn't say that."

Durand shrugged his shoulders.

"And why would it be *me*? I wasn't with Devo or Luc. I was probably the only one who wasn't, frankly."

Stop, Abbie. This is what they want. They want us to turn on each other.

"Then perhaps," Rouen offered, "this is why they are all saying it was you. Because you were separated from them last night."

"They can blame you," Durand added, "without blaming themselves."

Rouen said, "If it is of consolation to you, your friends Serena and Bryah were...*réticent*. Reluctant? Yes, reluctant—they were reluctant to say it was you."

"You, who have no alibi." Durand.

"You, whose purse contained the gun." Rouen.

"Now is the time, Abbie." Durand moved in close.

I shook my head. No. No. This couldn't be. This couldn't be right. My friends wouldn't have done that. This couldn't be happening.

I took a breath and made a decision. Once the words came out, they couldn't be put back in.

"Damon Kodiak," I said. "Damon is my alibi."

CHAPTER 28

EVERYONE WAS DIFFERENT during the *garde à vue*. Some were indignant. Others, scared silly. Some would ramble incessantly while others wouldn't open their mouths. Some wanted desperately to please the authorities while others spat in their faces.

This one, this suspect, had been different from the other three women from the start. More visibly upset. More remorseful, less combative. Almost despondent.

"You were in love," said Durand.

"No." Winnie shook her head slowly. "I don't know. Maybe. I cared for him...yes...I cared for him...maybe I loved him..."

"You hoped he would obtain...divorce."

"No. That wasn't..." She sighed. "That wasn't...possible...for a...lot of reasons."

"It would be understandable that you would be...upset," Rouen chimed in. "This man you cannot have? This life you cannot have?"

Winnie didn't answer. Her head continued to rock back and forth, as if it were no longer a denial but merely her attempt to stay conscious.

"And you still deny touching this gun we found?" asked Durand.

Winnie moaned. "Why do you keep asking me the *same questions?*"

"Because you have not given me the truth."

"I have! For God's sake, I have! Twenty...times now."

"Why would Serena do such a thing as kill him?"

"She wouldn't."

"And Bryah? And Abbie? What reason?"

"No reason. They wouldn't hurt a—"

"Then it is you, Winnie. There is no other possibility. We know that you pulled *la détente*. The trigger. We know it was you."

"Tell us why you killed him, Winnie," said Rouen.

She didn't answer. Her head fell back against the chair.

"You wanted money," said Durand. "If you could not have him, you wanted him to pay."

"You think...I killed him...for the money...what money? He wouldn't pay me...he wouldn't pay me money. Why would he...pay me money?"

"To be quiet about your affair," said Rouen.

"No...that's...ridiculous. Please...I need some...I need water and a bath—"

"Soon, Winnie. Soon," said Durand. "Tell us about the money."

"I don't need...money. None of us...does. Well, Abbie...Abbie doesn't have money...but she...she wouldn't...please...just some...water?"

"When you show remorse, Winnie."

"Show remorse, Winnie," Rouen urged. "Say that you are sorry."

"Sorry?...I'm sorry...he's dead....I would give anything...to bring him...back...but I didn't...I didn't do anything..."

The two interrogators looked at each other and made a decision—they could work with that statement. Winnie would get a bottle of water and her bathroom break. They had, for the moment, what they needed.

CHAPTER 29

"YOU WERE IN LOVE."

"No. I don't know. Maybe. I cared for him...yes...I cared for him...maybe I loved him..."

"It would be understandable that you would be...upset. This man you cannot have? This life you cannot have?"

"Tell us why you killed him, Winnie."

"I killed him...for the money...he wouldn't pay me...he wouldn't pay me money...I'm sorry..."

Durand turned off the small, handheld voice recorder. After he had secretly recorded Winnie's statement, he had spent an hour reviewing the recording and making editing decisions, then a technician had spent another hour cutting and splicing Winnie's words so that only the damning ones remained, making it sound like a seamlessly flowing conversation.

Bryah shook her woozy head. "No...no...it...can't be...Winnie wouldn't...she couldn't..."

"She has already confessed. You can no longer help her. Your only question is whether you help yourself." Durand was freshly showered and refreshed from sleep. Rouen was wearing the same suit but

94

with a different white shirt underneath. Each of them was holding a bottle of water.

To Bryah, handcuffed to a rickety wooden chair, it had been one long day-and-night-and-day of blinding lights and white walls. As much as she'd tried to track the time, she could do no better than a very rough estimate. Thirty-six hours was her guess. They'd fed her a cheese sandwich and a small bottle of water and they'd let her sleep on the floor for some time—how long, she had no idea, but probably just long enough to make her desperately want more.

Her head bobbed. She began to cry. It was Winnie's voice on the recording, no doubt.

"She already confessed to shooting them," said Durand. "You can deny all knowledge and join her in prison for life. Or," he added, "you can tell us what we already know. You will have a... very short sentence."

Bryah shook her head, as if she were shaking away cobwebs.

"She already confessed to shooting them over the money," said Durand. "Say it. 'She shot them over the money.'"

"No—"

"Say it. 'She shot them over the money.'" Durand nudged her shoulder. "And then we can permit you a bath and get you something to eat and drink. You want... sandwich? Croissant? *Café?*"

With dark, tired eyes, Bryah looked up at Durand. "I... can't. No..."

"Why this nonsense?" Durand flailed his arms. "We already know! You simply say what we already know! You do this and you leave prison in two years. You do *not* do this? Then you are a liar and you are equally to blame. You never see your *famille* again. You spend thirty years in *la prison*. Maybe a lifetime."

"Madame Gordon," said Rouen. "*Écoute-moi bien.* Winnie has admitted she killed him over the money. This is a benefit to her. It means for her that this was not *une action terroriste*. Not an... act of terrorism. You see? For *le terrorisme,* we have stronger laws, yes? Harsher punishments. Lifetime in prison. But what your friend has confessed? This is not terrorism. The penalty is... much lower.

Yes? So you must help her now. You must...support what she says."

Durand pressed a hand to his chest. "We? We do not know that what Winnie says is true. She wants us to believe this so she receives the lesser sentence. If you want to help her, you say only what she has already said *herself*. You help her avoid a *terrorisme* charge and you help yourself by...cooperating."

Bryah tried to control her sobbing. She'd heard about France's terrorism laws, the lengthy detentions, the harsher penalties, the outcry from human rights groups. She wasn't a lawyer and she didn't know the details, but what they were saying rang true. And—

And it *was* Winnie's voice on that tape.

"She shot them over the money," said Rouen. "She shot them over the money."

Bryah's head dropped.

"She shot them...over the money," she said.

CHAPTER 30

THE DOOR OPENED. I'd drifted off, by which I mean my mind had wandered, my vision had become cloudy and unfocused. Some might define that as sleep. I couldn't define anything now. I'd barely slept the night of the partying and the yacht and Damon—and since then I hadn't had more than a few winks. I thought I'd drifted off when they put me on the floor for a few hours last night—or was it noon? The morning?—but otherwise I had fallen into a semiconscious haze.

Don't say anything, I tried to tell myself. Your brain isn't working.

They showed me papers. I stared at them for a time, my head wobbly. *Procès-verbal d'audition de la personne gardée à vue,* they said. Some kind of a witness statement.

"Your final...opportunity," said Durand. "You can see that the others have complied. Your friend Winnie has confessed."

I closed my eyes, or maybe they were already closed.

Winnie...no.

"The others have confirmed—yes?"

"Corroborated," said Rouen.

No...impossible...a bad dream...someone else's nightmare...

Durand pushed my chin up from my chest, so I was facing him. "Winnie says you gave her the gun. You assisted her."

No... not the gun... not my gun...

"No," I managed. "Never... touched a... gun." My tongue was heavy; my words were coming with great effort.

Durand shook the papers, the witness statements, in my face for emphasis. "You see here. All of them say it. It was *le chantage*. Blackmail, Abbie."

"Black... blackmail... who...?"

"Still? *Still* you insist you know nothing?"

"Why would we black... blackmail Devo?"

"*Devo,*" Durand scoffed. "Do not call him that again."

"What should I... call him?"

Rouen approached me, holding up an official photo of a balding man in a suit, his posture proud and confident, giving a speech with the flag of France behind him.

It took me only a moment, my mental inebriation notwithstanding. Put a beard and a toupee on the man in that photo...

"Oh, no," I whispered.

Devo the Tycoon was Henri Devereux.

I was being accused of murdering the president of France.

CHAPTER 31

THE CELL DOOR OPENED. Dan Ingersoll looked in before entering. The woman was sitting on the floor in the corner, her elbows on her knees. Her hair was shoulder length, greasy, and flat against her head. Her face was pale and drawn. Her eyes were heavily bloodshot and vacant. Her gaze slowly made its way up to him.

"Abbie Elliot?" he asked.

She wet her lips and raised her chin. "Who are you?"

"My name is Dan Ingersoll. I'm with the U.S. Embassy."

"Congratulations." Her head fell back against the wall. The cell was all concrete. It was cold and clean.

He wasn't sure where to start. He'd never done this before.

"Have you been treated okay?"

She rolled her neck. It was probably a dumb question. Four days in French custody, being interrogated mercilessly. "They forgot the mint on my pillow," she said.

"I'm serious."

"Oh. You're serious." Her eyes tracked up to the ceiling. "But not so serious to come visit me even once during four days of this?"

"They denied me access," he said. "This isn't like Ameri—"

"Oh, I swear, if another person reminds me that I'm not in America, there's going to be a third murder to prosecute."

He could hardly blame her. She didn't look like the type who had a history of spending time with angry cops and investigators. This must have been a nightmare.

"How are the others?" she asked. "Have you talked to them?"

"Only Serena Schofield," said Ingersoll. "You two are the Americans."

"How's Serena doing?"

Ingersoll thought about his answer. He prided himself on his bluntness. An FBI agent once told him that he didn't talk like a lawyer. He took it as a compliment. "It's a difficult situation," he said.

"I didn't ask you if it's a difficult situation. I actually figured out that much all by myself. I asked you how Serena is doing."

He deserved that, he thought. "She's distraught," he said. "Terrified."

She nodded slowly. The sleep deprivation was evident. She appeared to be numb at this point, suffering from sensory overload. Four days of fear and anxiety and manipulation was too much for anyone. He wondered if Abbie had confessed. Most would under these circumstances.

"I didn't kill anybody," she said.

He didn't answer. It wasn't relevant—not for his purposes. She was an American citizen, and he needed to make sure she was given her rights. He wasn't there to exonerate her.

"And I sure as hell didn't know that guy was the president of France. How was I supposed to know that?"

It was the same thing Simon Schofield had said in his office a few days ago. *How were they supposed to know who he was?* Ingersoll didn't have an answer then and he didn't have one now.

"Have you talked to my husband?" she asked.

"Of course. He'll be here soon."

"And what about my kids?"

"I understand that they're on their way to France," he said.

Abbie's dry, dead eyes filled at the topic of her children.

She didn't look like a killer, he thought, even knowing how silly that thought was. He'd seen all kinds as a prosecutor. Some of the quietest, tamest people were some of the most vicious criminals. You just never knew.

"This is everywhere, isn't it? I mean, our identities? We're all over the news?"

Ingersoll nodded. "Your names are known, I'm afraid."

Abbie tilted her head in the direction of the door. "What are they telling you? About the evidence?"

He shook his head. "I don't know much about that."

She stared at him for a long time. "Mr. Ingersoll, be the first person in here who *doesn't* bullshit me."

It seemed out of character, the cussing. For some reason that he couldn't pin down, he had a feeling that Abbie Elliot was a very good mother.

He would see her on almost a daily basis now, assuming they incarcerated her somewhere close. He'd watch out for her and Serena. They were American citizens. He owed it to them. It wasn't his job to save their hides, but he'd look out for them as best he could. His chest swelled at the thought.

"Okay, no bullshit," he said. "This thing is quickly spinning out of control. It's a lynch-mob mentality. A very popular president is dead, and right or wrong, everyone seems to think that four beautiful, privileged foreigners did it. The people of France want blood. They want to bring back the death penalty just for you. The U.S. government wants to duck down and hide, because two of the suspects are American. My advice would be to get the best lawyer you can find."

He took a breath. Abbie's face disappeared into her knees.

"But Ms. Elliot, no bullshit, if there's any way I can help you, I'll do it."

She nodded her head, her face still buried between her knees. Her way of showing appreciation for his candor. She probably felt incredibly alone right now.

As Ingersoll exited, he could hear her weeping softly.

He wiped sweat from his face, as if Abbie Elliot's anxiety had trans-ferred itself to him. This was perhaps the biggest case the French had ever prosecuted, he realized.

There was no way they were going to let these women walk free.

BOOK TWO

NINE MONTHS LATER:
MARCH 2011

CHAPTER 32

LE PROCÈS COMMENCE, blared the front page of *Le Monde* this morning. "The Trial Begins," requiring no further elaboration; anyone in France who didn't know what that meant was either comatose or a newborn. The *International Herald Tribune,* in its typically sedate way, informed the public that it was "Day 1 in Devereux Assassination Trial." *USA Today* announced, "Trial of Monte Carlo Four Opens." All this I knew courtesy of one of the guards at the jail in southern Paris where I spent the last two nights before my trial. They'd moved me from the prison where I was staying so that my route to the courthouse would be unknown. The French were taking the death threats seriously.

I traveled in a blue vehicle with sirens on top, a cross between a minivan and an SUV, the word GENDARMERIE stenciled in white on the side. I sat in the back along a bench, where I was restrained at the wrists and ankles and shackled to the bench itself. Across from me sat two armed gendarmes. Our area in the vehicle's rear was sealed off from the driver's cabin by a plastic shield, which had a slit that opened only for communication. There was some light back here, courtesy of the tinted, bulletproof windows.

From what I understood, there were four separate vehicles for the four of us—each of which was taking a different route—and there were decoy vehicles as well. Whatever else the French wanted to do to us, they didn't want us gunned down by some grief-stricken protester. They'd had enough high-profile security lapses for one decade. The heads of the entities primarily responsible for the safety of the French president, the Groupe de Sécurité de la Présidence de la République and the RAID unit—Recherche Assistance Intervention Dissuasion—had resigned following President Devereux's death. Apparently it was no excuse that the president hadn't wanted his security detail, other than Luc Cousineau, to accompany him to Monte Carlo; they weren't supposed to take no for an answer when it came to presidential security, and after his death, heads had to roll.

The trial was at the Palais de Justice, which houses the Parisian police force and the courts, including the country's supreme court, the Cour de Cassation. The Palais is located on the Île de la Cité, an island on the Seine that is home to the Cathédrale Notre Dame de Paris as well. Next to the Palais is the Sainte-Chapelle, a chapel where Jeffrey and I, years ago, had spent an afternoon listening to a six-piece orchestra play Vivaldi's *Four Seasons* as daylight streamed through the stained-glass windows.

The roads bordering the Palais de Justice were barricaded. A few news trucks had been let in but otherwise the only vehicles allowed passage were the decoys and the ones carrying the defendants. Spectators were lined up along the streets, many of them holding signs. Some of the signs were in French, some in English. Some supported us—FREE THE MONTE CARLO MISTRESSES—but most did not: JUSTICE POUR HENRI; DEATH TO THE KILLERS! The collective commotion of the crowd, which I heard through the thick windows of the vehicle, left me with the sensation of putting my ear up to the door of a rock concert.

On the Boulevard du Palais, our vehicle passed through the magnificent wrought-iron gates into the courtyard of the Palais itself. I bent my head down to peer up through the window at the main building, where the supreme court was located—the long set of stone steps, the four majestic columns, and the words that I couldn't make out but I knew were there, carved into the structure: LIBERTÉ, ÉGALITÉ, FRATERNITÉ.

In the courtyard, which was still open to public view, the vehicle went through an arched passageway that led into a loading area. I was taken out of the vehicle and walked through a series of empty hallways, the gendarmerie at my front and back.

I'd made this trip often over the last nine months, but the security was much tighter this time—the barricades, the decoy cars. The threats had escalated in the last few weeks. The Palais de Justice had been emptied one day last week after a bomb threat, and since then the Sainte-Chapelle had been closed to tourists and the Palais limited either to people having business with the court or members of the public willing to undergo the screening, which rivaled that of an Israeli airport.

Or so I'd been told. I'd been cut off from the outside world. I hadn't spoken with, much less seen, my three friends for months, except during court hearings. I'd had only Jeffrey and my kids as visitors. I got most of my information from my attorney or the prison guards. The guard at the Paris jail for the last two nights was a chatty character named Solly, who was eager to touch any part of the biggest criminal case in modern French history. Solly had made the comment that I was the most famous *criminel féminin* since Marie Antoinette, which I think he intended as a compliment, but I don't recall it turning out so well for her.

We reached the door of the holding area. One of the gendarmes used a key. I turned to the one holding my arm, a man named Guy, whom I had come to know and who liked to practice his English with me.

"Wish me luck," I said.

I moved into the holding area and a door closed behind me. I heard Guy's response through the door.

"*Elles n'ont pas besoin de chance,*" he said to one of his colleagues. "*Elles ont besoin d'un miracle.*"

He didn't think I could hear him. No matter. He wasn't saying anything I hadn't heard a hundred times already. And I couldn't bring myself to disagree.

They don't need luck, he'd said. They need a miracle.

CHAPTER 33

THE HOLDING CELL was a nondescript anteroom where the accused awaited the start of trial, handcuffed and guarded. I was the first to arrive, for no particular reason. I didn't know where the others had been kept the last few days. I didn't know much about my friends at all lately.

We'd barely spoken in nine months, the four of us. The investigating judge assigned to our case had ordered our provisional detention while the murder of the president and his bodyguard remained "under examination," as the French put it. A special judge hearing questions of custody—*le juge des libertés et la détention*—had upheld the decision to keep us in custody pending the close of the investigation. All of that meant that we weren't going anywhere until trial.

For some of this time, the four of us were detained in separate facilities. The stated reason was our personal security, as we had become rather notorious, to put it mildly, but I always figured they wanted to keep us separated so we wouldn't communicate with each other.

Winnie was the next one in. She looked terrible, primarily because she looked so different. Her silky, flowing mane of hair had been replaced with a close crop that hung lifelessly at her shoulders. Her eyes were sunken. Overall there was a withered quality about her: she had lost at least ten pounds that she couldn't afford to lose, and her normally confident, almost regal carriage had been replaced by a defeated, wincing expression and slumped shoulders. It was, to me, as heartbreaking as anything that had happened over the last nine months.

I smiled at her, and she at me. A moment of warmth on a day that was going to be very, very cold.

Bryah was next, and then Serena, each looking about as bad as Winnie. All of us had been run through the wringer, our lives turned upside down, our dirty laundry aired for the world to see, our families humiliated, and our futures looking very, very grim indeed. We were scared and frustrated and bewildered and exhausted. And the trial hadn't even started yet.

But we had each other, together in the same room. We didn't speak because we all knew by now that it was prohibited; we'd been to enough court hearings together to know the drill. But the looks on each of our faces told me that we were still a foursome; we still loved each other.

No small chore, that. They'd done everything in their power to turn us against each other from the first day we were detained. *Serena says it was all your idea. Winnie kept a lot of secrets from you. Whoever confesses first gets the most lenient sentence. Your friends won't be your friends for very long.* The French intelligence officer Durand, and the Paris cop Rouen, had worn out the groove on those lines for four days straight.

Once the *garde à vue* had ended, the case was assigned to an investigating judge, whose role was theoretically an impartial one, seeking to discover the "truth" without favor to either the prosecution or the accused. But that judge was no different from Durand and Rouen, urging us to implicate ourselves and each other from the outset. The only "truth" I could glean from his investigation was that he wanted to confirm our guilt and get his name in the paper as often as possible.

The prosecutor, a strident, ambitious woman named Maryse Bal-lamont, had offered to reduce the charges if we would sign written statements implicating the others. Even my own lawyer had impressed upon me over and over again that I should not try to "shield" my friends, that we were on a sinking ship and it was every woman for herself.

"Keep your chins up, mates," I said to my friends. One of the gendarmes clucked his tongue at me and put a hand on my shoulder. But really, what were they going to do to me—keep me in prison *beyond* my natural lifetime?

Don't think like that, Abbie. I had to keep alive some small semblance of hope, some kernel of possibility that there would be a break, that everyone would figure out they had the wrong suspects and we'd walk out of here free women.

"*Temps de commencer,*" said one of the gendarmes, wearing his courtroom-best powder-blue shirt and navy-blue cargo pants. He was carrying a baton and firearm on his belt. The four of us stood. I winked at Bryah, who looked as if she were about to wilt. Serena blinked back tears. Winnie lowered her head and took a deep breath.

And then we began the march to the courtroom. Our trial was about to begin.

CHAPTER 34

SALLE NUMÉRO TROIS—courtroom number three—broke into a collective hiss as we entered the courtroom from the side door.

"Meurtrières!" someone shouted.

"Assassins!"

"Monstres!"

I kept my chin up, trying to maintain a sense of dignity, taking my seat in the cage of bulletproof glass and staring forward as if nothing were happening around me. The sky-blue shirts of the gendarmes were everywhere, and they had apparently decided to let the spectators get a little venom out of their systems before enforcing the rule of silence in the courtroom.

Try as I might to remain resolute, it was impossible to ignore the spectacle; it was like trying to meditate in the midst of a tornado. One man got to his feet and charged toward us, not getting very far before being subdued by the gendarmerie. An object—a shoe—slammed against the glass cage only a few feet from where I was sitting, having been thrown from the balcony.

I was seated at the end of the cage farthest from the spectators, and from this vantage point I could see the expressions of each of my friends. Bryah shrunk back, looking positively terrified. Serena watched with horror, tears falling down her cheeks. Winnie kept her head down and her eyes squeezed shut.

I bit my lip and recalled the stern warnings of my lawyer: don't show emotion. Don't get mad. French judges don't like outbursts from the defendants. It took all my will not to react as I watched the crowd rise up against us.

I'm innocent! I wanted to scream. *How could you possibly think we're killers?*

Surely something would happen, I told myself throughout the investigation. Surely some piece of evidence would appear, some lead would crystallize—surely they'd realize they have the wrong people!

More gendarmes entered the courtroom. Several surrounded our glass cage and soon there was at least one gendarme standing at each row of spectators. Their batons were drawn but their firearms remained holstered.

It became a mob mentality, a feeding frenzy, all decorum discarded as the gendarmes called out for silence and people shouted their opinions and gestured in our direction. Some were supportive, including a couple who looked like American students, shouting something about saving France's ass during World War II. People were yelling at us and at each other, the small minority who supported our cause trying to shout over the majority without success. The reporters filling most of the front two rows and seated in the folding chairs in the back were trying to take this all in and scribble some notes.

Our husbands, all four of them—Jeffrey, Simon, Christien, and Colton—turned from their perch in the front row and watched the brewing rugby scrum, with Simon shielding his four-year-old adopted daughter, Katie Mei, and Christien placing a protective arm across his two children. After a time Simon got into the fray, not moving from his seat but yelling back at the protesters. He was hardly a threatening presence, but he was pointing his finger menacingly and working himself up in his frustration and concern.

Then the wheels came off: from one of the middle rows, a guy in a leather jacket and spiky hair, who I assumed to be British, pushed someone, knocking him into a gendarme. A number of gendarmes rushed to separate and restrain the two people, and at some point, not surprisingly, someone overreacted to someone else's overreaction and before long the scuffle involved a number of spectators and police.

"Allons, allons!" The gendarmes inside our cage lifted us to our feet and hurried us out of the courtroom. The door closed behind us. We were ushered into the holding area and placed in handcuffs again.

Each of my friends looked shell-shocked. We were accustomed to being the subject of strong opinions. We'd all read the various accounts of our case in the international media, stories from every continent, the most ridiculous rumors and speculation, even Facebook and Internet sites devoted to us. But this was different. This was our first encounter, up close and personal, with the reaction of ordinary French citizens.

Even though we'd read the papers and heard the stories—the overwhelming consensus of the French people was that we were guilty, guilty, guilty—it was still shocking to see it firsthand. They wanted our blood.

"We're screwed," said Serena. "We are so screwed."

CHAPTER 35

UPON OUR SECOND entrance into the courtroom, the mood was decidedly reserved. There were more uniformed gendarmes than members of the public. Some of the original onlookers were no longer there, replaced with others who had been waiting in line to come in—a line that, from what I'd been told, wound through the hallways of the Palais de Justice and out onto the street.

The courtroom was fairly modern, and distinctly non-American. The back half of the courtroom was for the spectators, half a dozen benches of blond wood and some chairs placed along the back for additional seating. Over the spectators on the ground level was a balcony holding several additional rows of seating.

We were on the left side of the courtroom, enclosed in bulletproof glass that had one rectangular slit that allowed us to communicate with our attorneys, who sat in front of our cage. On the side opposite us was the prosecutor, Maryse Ballamont, seated behind a long pine table much like the one in front of the defense attorneys. At a right angle to us, seated in front of the spectators, was the *partie civile*—the civil party—in this case the former first lady of France,

Geneviève Devereux, a stunning and fashionable redhead who once held the crown of Miss France.

The judges hadn't yet appeared, but all the lawyers were dressed in black robes and thin white scarves that hung straight down from the center of their collars like glorified bibs. All that was missing were the old-fashioned wigs.

I turned and looked at my husband, Jeffrey, in the front row among the spectators. The families of the accused had the right to attend the trial, and all four of the husbands were there. Winnie's two gorgeous children sat next to Christien, and Simon held his and Serena's daughter, Katie Mei, on his lap. Bryah's son wasn't there and neither were my kids, at my insistence. This entire ordeal had been devastating enough for Richie and Elena—it was unbearable for me to even think about it—and they didn't need to see this trial firsthand.

Jeffrey slowly nodded his head in my direction and gave me a warm smile. It was weird, to say the least, between us now. Neither of us was sure how to handle it. Like the rest of the world, he knew of my fling with Damon Kodiak, but he hadn't so much as acknowledged it—I'd like to think because of the dire circumstances I faced, but probably also because his own infidelity had spanned some two years, not one night, so he could hardly throw stones from his glass house.

Regardless, Jeffrey had been decent to me over these last months. I knew this had been hard for him, too, both professionally and personally. He'd been accustomed to my caring for the home and children, when they were around, and now with our kids transferring to a school in Bern while my case was pending, Jeffrey was trying to run a household for them while managing to keep afloat at work. And that was just the day-to-day part; the emotional aspect was doubly difficult. It was Jeffrey who saw the effects of this case on our children; he was the one who held their hands as they cried themselves to sleep; he had suffered some embarrassment of his own. The list of casualties from our weekend in Monte Carlo seemed to have no end.

A high-pitched bell sounded. From the long table in the front of the courtroom, the *huissier*—the bailiff—stood and announced, *"Le Cour."*

I stole one more glance at my husband, then the entire courtroom got to its feet as the judges entered.

CHAPTER 36

IN A TYPICAL French murder trial, the case would be heard by three judges and nine laypersons. But this wasn't a typical murder trial. The murder of the French president was being treated as a terrorist act, something with which our lawyers took issue. So they brought our case all the way up to the Cour de Cassation, France's supreme court—which decided that trying us as terrorists sounded like a perfectly good idea.

That meant that our case would be heard not by a combination of judges and ordinary citizens but rather by a panel composed exclusively of judges. I didn't know if that was good or bad. My lawyer, always trying to buoy my spirits, never directly said that our chances were diminished because of the all-judge panel. But the fact that he fought the decision all the way to the nation's highest court told me that it wasn't the preferred outcome for us.

The long table where the judges sat was raised about two steps higher than the rest of the courtroom, but it wasn't like the judge's bench in an American courtroom. It was just one long table, with ordinary gooffsenecked desk lamps in front of each seat. I was used to the courtrooms I saw on American television; this looked more like a city council meeting.

From behind the wood-paneled wall, a door opened, and the judges entered the courtroom. Like the lawyers, they were wearing black robes and thin white scarves. The presiding judge—who was the only one wearing a red robe—sat in the center, and everyone in the courtroom took their seats after he did.

The four of us put on headphones, old-fashioned, clunky models with thick cushions on the ears. The presiding judge—*le président juge*—began to speak in French to the courtroom, but what we heard through the headphones was a woman's voice, translating his words to English. It added just another odd element to the completely bizarre package of horrors that was the last nine months of my life.

The lawyers formally announced themselves—the lawyers representing the four defendants as well as the lawyer for the president's widow, the civil party. The *président juge* then asked if there were any applications regarding "publicity," which I didn't understand initially but then I remembered: trials are open to the public in France unless there is a determination that allowing them to be open would constitute a danger. After what had happened thirty minutes ago, a decent case could be made that the trial should be closed. But none of the lawyers so requested, and it wasn't likely that the judge would have granted the request, anyway. To the French citizenry, this was the most important trial in memory. It needed to take place in the open. Besides, by now there were enough gendarmes in the courtroom to invade a small country.

"The clerk will read the transfer judgment," said the woman in her calm, soothing voice in my ear, translating the words of the *président juge*. This had been explained to me as the French equivalent of an indictment. After the investigating judge determines that there is a basis to charge the accused with a crime, a panel of judges hears the matter and makes the ultimate determination about whether the case should be transferred to the trial court—the Cour d'Assises. My lawyer told me that this written transfer order was typically a rather dry exposition of the evidence, but in this instance, maybe because of the high profile of this case, the panel of judges used very forceful language in describing the case against us.

I'd had the judges' order read to me several times previously, but it was no less painful hearing it again, especially through the maddeningly moderate tone of the female translator. And it was more than painful—utterly mind-blowing, worthy of Kafka, the words delivered so gently but landing with such a damning impact. The gunpowder residue. The fingerprints. The DNA. The incriminating admissions. The misleading and deceptive statements (for which I was singled out several times). The eyewitnesses. The immoral behavior. The blackmail.

When the reading was completed, I thought to myself, This isn't the greatest way to start a trial. *Here's everything bad we think about you... now let's get started!*

I let out a sigh and looked up at the ceiling of the courtroom, at the narrow skylight that provided the only natural light in the windowless room.

A miracle, I thought. God, please give me a miracle.

"Before we begin, I would like to say a few words," said the presiding judge.

CHAPTER 37

MONSIEUR LE PRÉSIDENT JUGE, Alfred Reynold, was a man in his late fifties with a weathered face and flowing white hair. He placed a piece of paper before him and folded his hands, which were mostly obscured by the sleeves of his red robe.

"On the day of nineteen June, 2010, this nation was attacked," he began, via the female translator in our ears. "No bomb was detonated. No building collapsed. No city burned. But we were attacked no less.

"It was a day that will never be forgotten. Each of us will recall forever where we sat or stood when we learned of the death of the president of the French. Each of us will recall forever the sadness, the anger, and the fear. And the resolve that justice be served on those responsible for President Devereux's death.

"On that day, we did not belong to the Union for a Popular Movement or the Socialist Party or the National Front. We were not conservative or liberal or green. We were not white or black or brown. On that day we were only French. Together we suffered. Together we mourned. Together we moved on, changed forever but resolved to honor the legacy of President Devereux.

"And together we will find justice for the president and his bodyguard, Luc Cousineau. Together we will carry out these legal proceedings with careful deliberation, firm resolve, and heavy hearts, but never forgetting that the ultimate end is justice. Because to do any less would be to disrespect the legacy of fairness and compassion that marked the public service of President Devereux."

The courtroom was utterly silent as the judge completed his statement. Henri Devereux had been something of a rock star in this country, a flashy soccer player in the eighties who dated movie stars and heiresses, later ascending quickly through the ranks of public service. In 1995, he married Geneviève Rousseau, Miss France 1993 and fifteen years his junior, in a spectacular countryside wedding in the Loire Valley at a home owned by the family of his mentor, François Mitterrand. That same year he lost his race for the presidency but won in his second effort in 2002. He was reelected in 2007 in a landslide. With his gorgeous wife at his side and three young children, he was flamboyant and charismatic and controversial. I'd recalled various accounts of affairs and sexual exploits, but this wasn't exactly unexpected in a French president, and there had been no indication that the citizenry's affection for the man had dimmed whatsoever.

We were accused of killing, by all accounts, the most popular president in the history of France. And now here was the presiding judicial officer at my trial, promising the country that there would be justice for his murder.

It couldn't get much worse than that, could it?

Famous last words.

"The court will now hear from Major Rouen," said the judge.

CHAPTER 38

THE PRESIDING JUDGE had before him the dossier, the voluminous file that constituted the totality of the evidence gathered by the investigating judge from witness interviews, expert and forensic reports, and the like. This was, on paper, their case against us. In theory, they could skip witnesses altogether and just read through the file, let the lawyers make arguments, and announce a verdict.

The dossier was divided into four parts. Two of the parts were largely technical—official documents explaining the gathering, retention, and transfer of evidence between the police and prosecutor and court, as well as the legal decision relating to our pretrial detention. A third part was devoted to the four defendants' *personnalités*, or character, if you prefer. Everything from birth certificates to interviews with friends and families.

The presiding judge, however, turned to the final section of the dossier, entitled *"Pièces de fond"*—On the Facts. This section contained more than two hundred documents, including witness interviews, forensic reports, photographs, and summaries of the evidence and investigation.

"Good morning, Major," said the presiding judge.

"Good morning, Mr. President." Major Rouen stood in the center of the courtroom, at a podium fitted with a microphone. In one corner of the room, the courtroom deputy—the *greffier*—angled a camera on a tripod so that it captured both the presiding judge and the major. This was not a media camera—they were barred under French law from courtrooms—but a camera ordered by the presiding judge to keep an audio and visual record of this trial, which would be held, with the official transcript, under seal.

"Major, do you have any personal or familial connection with the accused?"

"I do not," said Rouen.

"Then please tell us what you can about the matter under examination."

André Rouen, an eighteen-year veteran with the Paris police department, seemed like a good witness, at least judging by his appearance. He was on the tall side and fit, with sandy hair rimmed with gray at the temples, an unassuming middle-aged man who normally would blend into the background.

Major Rouen did not take an oath. In French courtrooms, cops were not sworn in because it was already their duty to testify truthfully. Rather, he proceeded directly into his narrative, including the account of his initial receipt of the phone call from the Monte Carlo police—"a call I shall never forget," he said—and his flight down to the harbor.

"We coordinated our response with the RAID unit and Brigade General Favier of the GIGN," he said. GIGN and RAID handled the paramilitary aspects of the operation, securing the dock and the surrounding area while Major Rouen and the National Police conducted its investigation.

Major Rouen took the presiding judge through several of the photographs contained in the dossier, discussing the positioning of the bodies of President Devereux and his bodyguard, Luc Cousineau, and the search of the Bentley convertible where they were found.

The presiding judge, leafing through the massive dossier stacked in front of him, detailed the procedures undertaken by French intelligence and the police in recovering and analyzing forensic evidence during the investigation. He then asked Rouen to summarize the ultimate findings.

"We recovered various samples of DNA from the vehicle that were tested for a match," he said. "This included hair follicles, mucus, blood, and cerumen."

It included a lot more than that, but he was focusing on the relevant parts.

"We obtained a match for hair follicles on the dashboard belonging to the accused, Winnie Brookes," said Rouen. "We obtained a match for hair follicles on the passenger seat and floorboard belonging to the accused, Serena Schofield. And we obtained a match for hair follicles on the dashboard and on the rear seat on the driver's side belonging to the accused, Abbie Elliot."

The courtroom broke into a collective stir, visibly and audibly evident even through my headphones. Technically, the investigation of the *juge d'instruction* was confidential. There had been leaks, bits of information and rumor coming in weekly drips, but none of it had been confirmed until now.

"A small sample of mucus was located on the interior of the driver's side door that matched the DNA of the accused, Winnie Brookes," said Rouen. "A blood smear on the front passenger seat was confirmed as the blood of the accused, Serena Schofield.

"And a sample of cerumen, a glandular substance commonly known as earwax," he said, "was located near the gear shift between the two bodies. The sample was a DNA match for the accused, Abbie Elliot."

"Please remind the court, Major," said the presiding judge. "During questioning of these accused, you inquired as to whether any of them had been inside or around that vehicle?"

"Yes, Mr. President. We made that inquiry of each of the accused."

"And how did they respond?"

Major Rouen turned his head ever so slightly in our direction, though from his position he couldn't see us.

"Each of the accused denied ever being inside that vehicle," he said.

CHAPTER 39

THE SPECTATORS' COLLECTIVE reaction began to rise in volume, and the presiding judge called for order.

"And after being confronted with this evidence," the presiding judge asked Rouen, "did the accused continue to deny having been in that Bentley vehicle?"

"They did," said Rouen. "Each of them continued to deny it."

My lawyer had prevailed on me to admit being in the automobile. He'd tried to shape my story so that I maintained my innocence but admitted to that one fact. "Why fight it?" he'd said to me over and over. "If you deny something so obvious, you lose your credibility and you lose any goodwill you have with the court."

Serena shook her head, her jaw clenched and her eyes cast upward to the ceiling. She was a fighter, a competitor, but in this case she was flailing at shadows. My attorney was right: we had no credible explanation for this DNA evidence.

The presiding judge gestured in the direction of the glass case that was positioned to the right of Major Rouen, where the physical evidence was held. The courtroom deputy removed the murder weapon

125

from the case and handed it to Rouen. It was a subcompact handgun with a black grip, a Beretta Px4 Storm.

"The weapon was recovered aboard the *Misty Blue* yacht owned by Mr. Ogletree," Rouen explained.

"Please explain where, within the yacht, the weapon was found."

"Mr. President, the weapon was recovered within this black purse."

The presiding judge referenced another exhibit. The *greffier* removed my black purse from the glass evidence case and handed it to Rouen.

"The purse belonged to the accused, Abbie Elliot."

"Did the accused Ms. Elliot admit *this* much at least?"

Someone in the gallery snickered at the judge's sarcasm.

"She did, Mr. President. She admitted that the purse was hers."

"And the weapon?"

"She denied the weapon belonged to her."

"Did the accused Ms. Elliot offer an explanation as to why the weapon was in her purse?"

"No, Mr. President. She did not."

Rouen continued to recount, consistent with the dossier, how the weapon was processed and analyzed for fingerprints, and how the four of us were fingerprinted.

"Please tell us the results of the fingerprint analysis."

Major Rouen cleared his throat. If he was doing it for added drama, he needn't have bothered; the courtroom was hanging on his every word.

"A fingerprint matched to the right index finger of the accused, Serena Schofield, was found on the barrel of the weapon," said Rouen. "A fingerprint matching the left thumb of the accused, Abbie Elliot, was found on the grip."

"And the third one, Major?"

"A fingerprint on the trigger of the weapon was a match for the right middle finger of the accused, Winnie Brookes," the major said.

The presiding judge nodded solemnly, taking in this information with a sense of gravity. He already knew this information, of course, and there had been rumors in the media for weeks, but this was the first time it was publicly acknowledged: fingerprints belonging to Serena, Winnie, and me were found on the murder weapon.

Winnie, sitting next to me, stared forward into the bulletproof glass, numb from the whole ordeal, unable to muster any emotion, even upon hearing the most damning evidence against her. Serena was tearing up again, surprising me by her emotional vulnerability—she was in many ways the toughest of us all.

I wasn't having a great time myself. Now, in addition to the DNA evidence placing me inside the vehicle where the dead bodies were found, it was revealed that the murder weapon had my fingerprints on it and was found in my purse.

And then there was Bryah, passive, staring forlornly up at the ceiling, listening to the evidence.

Evidence that, thus far, had miraculously avoided implicating her in any way.

CHAPTER 40

MY LAWYER, JULES LAURENT, stood and adjusted his microphone. Jules was tall and trim and clean-shaven, conveying a neat overall appearance save for his head of wild black curls that danced as he moved about. Jules was a good man. He'd spent hours listening patiently as I rambled incessantly about my innocence and my crazy theories about what had happened. And he'd taken some grief from some of his law partners for agreeing to defend me, though he was receiving a handsome sum for doing so—courtesy of Simon Schofield, who was bankrolling all the lawyers.

"Major Rouen," Jules began, standing just in front of our enclosed cell. "You recovered DNA evidence relating to Winnie Brookes, Serena Schofield, and my client, Abbie Elliot, in the automobile where the bodies were discovered."

"Yes," said the major, turning to face my lawyer.

"Saliva, hair follicles, blood, and a tiny bit of earwax."

"Yes."

"But no fingerprints?" asked Jules.

Major Rouen took a moment. "No fingerprints in the vehicle. But recall that we found their fingerprints on the murder weapon."

"Exactly," Jules agreed. "All three of these women were careless enough to leave their fingerprints on a gun that would have been perfectly easy to wipe off. *Perfectly* easy. And yet, when they were in and around the car, they were exquisitely *careful,* so much so that not a single fingerprint was found among them. Odd, yes?"

Major Rouen inclined his head. "Presumably they didn't expect the gun to be found. But the bodies—they knew those would be discovered."

Pretty good answer. Rouen had given this plenty of thought, no doubt.

"Still," Jules persisted. "Your position is that these women managed to leave all sorts of DNA throughout the automobile, and yet not a single fingerprint."

"I would imagine they were unaware of leaving behind this evidence," said Rouen.

Jules nodded. "But does this not leave room for the possibility that the DNA evidence was transferred from another site—not by these women but by someone else? That in fact these women were never in that car, as they have claimed, and instead someone else transferred that evidence into the car?"

"I don't consider that likely," Rouen answered. "I would suggest that these women shot the president and his bodyguard while the men were in the car, and that they checked on the men to be sure they were dead. They would not necessarily have touched the inside of the car or even climbed inside."

"Really." Jules delivered the word as an incredulous statement, not a question. "Well, take my client, Abbie Elliot. You found Abbie's hair on the driver's-side rear seat and on the dashboard. And her ear secretion on the gearshift between the president and Mr. Cousineau. How do you suggest Abbie managed to get her head between the two men, such that some of her earwax could have fallen onto the gearshift? And she was in both the front and back seat at different times, each time with her hair falling out? But not a single fingerprint?"

Major Rouen allowed a brief smile. "Mr. Laurent, we cannot reconstruct every movement. Nor should we assume that, simply because we did not recover a fingerprint inside the vehicle, that this somehow means that the women were not inside the vehicle. Sometimes you don't leave a fingerprint."

"But tell me, Major: can you eliminate the possibility that the DNA evidence was planted there by someone else?"

Rouen opened his hands, as if his patience were being tested. "Eliminate it? No."

Jules nodded, having gained a concession.

"And perhaps I might be more skeptical," Rouen added, "if two of the accused hadn't confessed."

I heard some laughter from the gallery before the female voice in my headset had finished translating Rouen's answer. I had to admit, it was a nice zinger.

"We'll get to that," said Jules. "But Major, as you said, your theory is that President Devereux and Mr. Cousineau were shot while in the car, correct?"

"That is correct, Mr. Laurent. We believe they were already in the car."

Jules informed the presiding judge that he would be referencing a photograph from the dossier. He produced a blowup of the photograph, which showed President Devereux and Luc Cousineau dead in the Bentley convertible. Luc was seated in an erect position, head back against the headrest. President Devereux, in the passenger seat, had fallen to his left side.

Jules placed the blowup on an easel. "Major Rouen, from the angle of the wounds, you concluded that President Devereux was shot while he was falling to his left, just as he was found. In other words, he didn't fall to the side *after* being shot; he was already in that position when shot."

"That was our conclusion, yes."

"And likewise, Mr. Cousineau here, seated upright. You concluded that this was his position when he was shot. He wasn't moved afterward."

"Yes."

"Now, I suppose you might say that the president was attempting to duck from the shots."

"I would, yes."

"But is it possible, as well, that the president was reaching for Mr. Cousineau? Trying to help his friend?"

"Possibly."

"Mr. Cousineau, on the other hand…" Jules pointed to Luc, who was seated completely erect in the driver's seat. "He appears to have made no movement whatsoever in the direction of his president—the man he was sworn to give his own life to protect."

"Mr. Laurent," said the presiding judge. "The deceased, Mr. Cousineau, is not on trial here for his bravery or professionalism. And you are not making a point that is helpful to your case, I must tell you."

Jules nodded respectfully to the judge. "Mr. President, with all respect, that is not my point."

Jules gestured toward the blowup photo. "My point is simply that it appears that the bodyguard, Mr. Cousineau, was shot before the president was. And I am wondering why."

CHAPTER 41

DENIS GISCARD WAS the second in command in the presidential security force, the Groupe de Sécurité de la Présidence de la République. Giscard reminded me of his former boss, Luc Cousineau. He was built like a pro wrestler and had the intense eyes of a bodyguard, the rigid posture of a military man.

"I have served four years in the GSPR," he told the presiding judge.

"Lieutenant Giscard, are you acquainted with the accused, Winnie Brookes?"

"Sir, that is correct." Giscard spoke in crisp sentences with a respectful, military tone. "Sir, I first met Ms. Brookes in July 2009."

"What was the occasion?"

"Sir, I was providing security detail for President Devereux at the G8 summit in L'Aquila, Italy. There was an evening cocktail reception and the president made the acquaintance of Ms. Brookes."

Winnie sat motionless, seemingly holding her breath, as one of President Devereux's bodyguards recounted Winnie's yearlong affair with the president.

"Sir, I would estimate that it was approximately monthly. There were times when the president would see the lady every week. Other times, several weeks would pass."

"Did you come to witness the interaction between the two?"

"Sir, that is correct. As a bodyguard staying very close to the president, you cannot avoid observing some things. Sir, it was my impression that Ms. Brookes treated the relationship differently than did the president."

The red-robed presiding judge waved a hand. "Please elaborate."

"Sir, the lady, in my opinion, pursued the president. She initiated many of the contacts. She was...aggressive. I did hear her speak once of marriage." The former bodyguard paused. "I heard her say that she wished to leave her husband and wished the president to leave his wife."

The spectators responded audibly and the presiding judge demanded decorum. In my peripheral vision I could see the figure of Winnie's husband, Christien, immobile in the first row of spectators as he listened to this very public account of his wife's infidelity. Presumably he'd had no idea of what Winnie had been doing. Certainly I hadn't, and I was her best friend. In hindsight, the signs were there. Some of her weekend trips to visit "friends from the university" or some unnamed relative in another country, or spontaneous overnight trips to tend to a "sick auntie" were really her rendezvous with the president. I even recall noting a change in her, a certain glow about her, a spark in her eyes. I once said, "Maybe you should visit your sick auntie more often, Win," which caused her to burst into laughter. But still, I never allowed my brain to travel to that place; it never once occurred to me she was having an affair.

"When did the accused Brookes make this statement about leaving her husband?"

"Sir, I recall it was early March 2010. The president was campaigning for the regional elections in Alsace. Ms. Brookes accompanied him during some of his travels."

After our arrest and the revelation that Winnie had been carrying on an affair with President Devereux, the press had gone into overdrive trying to obtain photographs of Winnie with the president.

They found one. It was taken in February of 2010 in Kigali, Rwanda, when President Devereux became the first French head of state in more than a quarter century to visit that country. It had been notable because the president had expressed regret over France's role in the 1994 Rwandan genocide. Now, however, it was far more notable for the photograph taken of President Devereux at the genocide memorial, which included in the background a beautiful woman in a royal-blue dress who, at the time, had probably blended in as part of the delegation. The number of times that this still photograph had appeared in print and television since our arrest probably rivaled the number of times that the video of Monica Lewinsky, at a rally for President Clinton, had run on TV.

"And how did the president respond to the accused Brookes when she said she wanted him to leave his wife?"

"Sir, the president indicated that he would not leave his wife. 'Not an option,' he said."

"And did the accused Brookes respond?"

The lieutenant took a breath. "Sir, she indicated that the present situation was not acceptable. 'Not enough,' she said."

"Lieutenant, did this conversation cause you concern?"

"Sir, that is correct. One of my principal responsibilities is threat assessment. I considered her a threat for violence. And for blackmail," he added.

"And did you convey this concern to the president?"

"Sir, I did. The president indicated that he understood."

The presiding judge flipped to another portion of the dossier. He mentioned the new document he was referencing and waited a moment as the lawyers turned to the appropriate page.

"Lieutenant, the trip to Monte Carlo in June of 2010," said the presiding judge. "You did not accompany the president."

"Sir, that is correct. Captain Cousineau was the only member of the detail to accompany him."

"That was a breach of protocol."

"Most definitely, sir. And rare, but not unheard-of."

"What was your understanding of the reason?"

"Discretion, sir. The president was going to visit Ms. Brookes while she was on vacation. That was not the norm. The norm would be either a visit from Ms. Brookes in Paris or, otherwise, she would accompany him on an official trip. She would simply travel with the delegation. Monte Carlo was different. President Devereux wished to conceal his identity. Leaving behind his security detail was part of that."

"Did you approve?"

"Sir, I did not. I conveyed as much to Captain Cousineau. In fact, I conveyed my concern to President Devereux directly."

"What did the president say in response?"

Lieutenant Giscard turned his head to the left ninety degrees, so instead of seeing the back of his head, I could see his profile. But he wasn't doing it for me. He was doing it for Winnie. It was as close as he could come to turning and looking at her.

"Sir, the president indicated that he was going to end the relationship with Ms. Brookes in Monte Carlo. He told me that this was going to be their last trip."

CHAPTER 42

BELOW THE PALAIS de Justice were jail cells that held inmates while they were standing trial. The cells for the women were remarkably pristine, thanks to an order of nuns in Paris who washed the linens daily and scrubbed the floors and walls. I'd never spent the night here—security concerns compelled the government to keep moving the four of us around—but sometimes they placed us here temporarily prior to a court appearance. During the trial, before we were shipped off for the night to some undisclosed location, they sometimes allowed us to use this location for brief visits with our families.

Jeffrey had left court a few minutes early to pick up our kids, Richie and Elena. Because of his diplomatic status, the U.S. government had provided housing for Jeffrey in Paris ever since I was arrested. At least it gave him a permanent place to stay as he bounced back and forth between Switzerland and Paris over these last several months.

My kids had largely stayed in Bern at their new school, coming for visits on the weekends. Today was a school day, but it was also day one of the trial, and although I refused to let them be in the courtroom, I could understand their wanting to be in Paris today, their wanting to see me. Had I any energy to object and insist on their attendance at school, I would have done so, but the truth was that the rule book, at this point, had been thrown out the window. None of us, parents or children, had any clue how to handle what was happening.

"Don't just say you don't like it," I said to Richie, seated next to me on the bed in the cell, which was just a long plank with a thin mattress on top.

"Why do I have to like it?"

"You don't, sweetie." I stroked his hair. "But tell me why."

"I don't like Holden. He's stuck-up. He doesn't like anything. Everyone's a phony to him. He just makes fun of everything, like he's too good for everybody. I mean, seriously, Mom, why does everyone think that book is such a classic?"

Richie was fifteen now. His face was maturing, his jaw squaring like Jeffrey's, his cheekbones gaining prominence, and—God help me—his chin showing the first signs of facial hair. He had my eyes, but that was all he inherited from me.

"There is a bit of Holden in every boy growing up," I said, placing the palm of my hand against his cheek. "Holden is scared, honey. He's scared so he's pushing everyone away, and he tells himself he's pushing them away because they're superficial and phony. And sometimes they are, but really he's justifying his fear. He just doesn't realize it."

"Maybe," Richie conceded. "Or maybe the book just sucks."

Elena, age twelve, was sitting on the other side of me, her hand clutching mine and her head resting against my shoulder. She took after me more than Richie did, with her petite body, tiny nose, and large brown eyes—even the cowlick parting the right side of her hair. Her prepubescent body was developing now, her hormones beginning to flare up—major changes, without her mother there for her.

I was an emotional powder keg in the presence of my kids. This was the only time I had with them and I had to maximize it. I was on the verge of tears and wanted to do nothing more than kiss them and hold them and squeeze my eyes shut and wish all this away. But I had to be their mother. I couldn't imagine how extraordinarily difficult this must be for them—all I could do was guess. I saw them, at most, twice a week for limited visits, during which everyone was trying to keep up a brave front. I was left with little more than what I could force out of Jeffrey, and I could only assume that Jeff was sugar-coating matters to spare me greater pain. *They're doing fine. It's hard but their spirits are up.*

I was losing them. I was slowly losing all of them. And here we were, debating the merits of *The Catcher in the Rye* while inside each of us was devastated and absolutely petrified.

"How's your Chinese teacher?" I asked Richie. It had been his favorite class in boarding school in Connecticut. We hadn't told him to study any particular language; he'd been drawn on his own to Chinese, which we thought was a savvy move for the twenty-first century—especially if the boy is interested in a diplomatic career, Jeffrey had noted more than once.

Richie seemed momentarily at a loss for words.

"He's not taking Chinese," said Elena.

"He's—you're not taking Chinese at your new school, Rich? Why not?"

Richie shrugged. "Just taking a trimester off, I guess."

"I don't understand." I looked over at Jeffrey, standing in the corner of the cell, but he was no help. "You love Chinese. Are you taking a different language instead?"

"Mom, who cares?"

"He's learning French," Elena said. "So am I."

"*French?* Why are you—?" When it came to me, when I got it, it was like a blow to the chest. I gathered my arms around each of my kids and pulled them close. We didn't move for a long time, save for the slight quiver of Elena's body as she began to cry. It was all I could do to keep my composure, and then the dam broke.

"Don't you ever give up hope," I whispered through my own sobs. "Not ever." But clearly, everyone was bracing for the worst, even my children, who were preparing themselves for the possibility of spending a lot of time in France over the coming decades, visiting their mother in prison.

CHAPTER 43

DAY TWO OF the trial. The four of us entered the Palais de Justice the same way, traveling in separate vehicles from different locations. I'd spent the night at a local jail on the southwest side of Paris, which I would remember for its stench of body odor and for the two prostitutes, Lorissa and Florence, who were placed in the empty jail cell next to me and who spent the night singing off-key renditions of old Madonna songs.

The next witness was Richard Ogletree, the fat American from that fateful night in Monte Carlo. Nine months later, he was still fat. His hair was still greasy, too. But he was dressed in more subdued attire, a blue sport coat and white dress shirt open at the collar, and his mood was decidedly less spirited. When he passed us on the way to the podium, where he would address the court, I noticed that his hairline was wet from perspiration. He nodded in the direction of Maryse Ballamont, the prosecutor, whose return nod was almost imperceptible.

Because Ogletree's primary language was English, all the principals concerned with his testimony—the judges, lawyers, and Ogletree himself—donned headsets like the ones the four of us in the defense cage were wearing. It lent a stilted quality to the proceedings, with a pause after every statement.

"I'm primarily an investor, Your Honor," said Ogletree. "I have also coproduced some movies."

"Mr. Ogletree, please refer to me as Mr. President or the presiding judge. This isn't the United States."

The fat American raised his hand. "Sorry, Mr. President."

"Very well. Mr. Ogletree, please tell us what you can about the matter under examination."

"We were filming a movie in Paris, and we were on break for the weekend," he said. "I wanted to go to my yacht in Monte Carlo." His voice slightly trembling from nerves, Ogletree provided a brief summary of the events of that night in Monte Carlo—the trip to the nightclub, the casino, and then returning to his yacht, the *Misty Blue*. "Finally I went to bed," he said. "I left all my guests, who were still enjoying themselves, and went to my quarters to sleep. That was the last I knew before the next morning, when the French officials boarded my yacht and arrested all of us."

After the questioning was completed, the prosecutor, Maryse Ballamont, stood to ask some follow-up questions. She was a tall, thin woman with very attractive features, taken by themselves—shiny jet-black hair, prominent cheekbones, expressive green eyes—but her overall look was severe and humorless, though I will admit to being biased against the woman who was trying to put me in prison for life.

All business in her black robe, holding the headset up to her right ear, she cut right to the chase. "Mr. Ogletree, in your testimony you refer to President Devereux. That night, did you know that the man who called himself Devo was the president of the French Republic?"

Ogletree nodded eagerly—too eagerly. "Yes, Madam Prosecutor. He introduced himself to me at the club. He explained his hairpiece—the toupee—and his beard as a disguise so he could enjoy himself that night without being swarmed by people. To the public at large that night, he didn't want to advertise who he was. But in the small group? We all knew."

"I will convey to you, sir, that this is a matter of contention," said Ballamont. "So let me focus on the four women who stand accused. In your presence, did you hear them refer to the man who called himself Devo as the French president?"

"Yes. All of them did. I recall that someone would call him *Monsieur le President* and he would quickly say 'Devo,' to remind them to keep things quiet. He—for example, I remember he was talking about the American presidential election and how he'd known Hillary Clinton for years because she'd been the first lady and he'd met Senator Obama a few times—things the president of France would talk about."

I shut my eyes. He wasn't just lying; he was creating entire conversations out of whole cloth. How could this be happening?

"Abbie Elliot?" Ogletree said in response to a question. "Yes, I recall her specifically saying to me, at the nightclub, what a unique experience it was, having drinks with the president of France."

"And are you certain of this?" the prosecutor asked. "Ms. Elliot in particular. You are certain she knew this man was the president of France?"

"I am absolutely certain, Ms. Ballamont. Because it is the last thing I remember about that night."

Maryse Ballamont nodded. This felt like a well-rehearsed script playing out before us. "The last thing that night," she repeated back to him. "You testified that you had been using your camcorder to record what was taking place on the yacht."

"Yes, that's correct. Before I went to bed, Ms. Elliot asked for the camcorder."

The prosecutor paused a beat. "Tell the court why Ms. Elliot said she wanted the camcorder." Then she pressed the headset to her right ear to hear the answer translated into French.

The fat American, who had been turned to his right to face the prosecutor, turned his attention back to the court.

"She said she wanted to make a sex tape starring Henri Devereux," he said.

CHAPTER 44

"I'VE GOT SOME bad news, Mom." Richie entered the jail cell beneath the Palais de Justice for our nightly visit before I was transferred to some undisclosed location. He held up his iPhone. "MonteCarloMistresses.com," he explained. "Of the four of you, you were voted only the third hottest."

My heart did a brief flutter, the adrenaline shot at the mention of bad news, before I settled into a smile. "How did *you* vote?" I asked.

Richie kissed my cheek. "Winnie won. She was your problem. You split the Caucasian-brunette vote. Bryah took second and Serena finished last. The Amazon-blonde thing must not be in these days."

I laughed, only because my son was trying to cheer me up and I wanted him to know that he had. But I wasn't thrilled that he was checking out websites like that one. I had hoped to insulate him and Elena as much as possible from what was happening. That, I suppose, was a pointless exercise at this stage. By various accounts, there were as many as five websites and six Facebook pages devoted exclusively to the four of us, the deadly-but-lovely assassins of the

French president. At least two books were being written. Last week, on CNN International, I watched Larry King interview a former college roommate of mine who said I always had a rebellious streak but it was hard to imagine that I would kill someone. Score one for me, I guess.

Elena, looking like the young schoolgirl she was in a white sweater and pleated skirt, was reading from her iPhone as well. A frown covered her face and she didn't respond when I asked her what she was reading. These kids, with their electronic toys. The Internet was all well and good, but I didn't need to access it 24-7.

"Let me see." I took her iPhone to read it. It was a blog from a *New York Times* reporter named Joseph Morro, who was covering the trial. I knew Morro because he'd repeatedly tried to interview me. "Mr. Ogletree's testimony was devastating, in particular to the American, Abbie Elliot," he wrote. "With his testimony that she wanted to 'make a sex tape starring Henri Devereux,' he showed her to be a schemer with a motive, as well as a liar."

Wonderful. Great. But it was hardly the first time I'd read something to that effect, and anyway, I didn't want to poison what little time I had with my kids with this negativity. I put her iPhone down on the bench in the cell and extended my arms. "Enough of the high-tech gadgetry," I said. "Your mom wants a hug."

We came together and held each other for a long time. I took in the warmth of her body, the smell of her shampoo, the indescribable feel of a child's embrace. These were the truest moments, and therefore the cruelest. I felt Elena's tears on my own cheek. How quickly we could roller-coaster from levity to despair.

"This is so unfair, Mom," Elena managed with a shaky voice.

It wasn't fair, not even close to fair, for these wonderful kids. I could only imagine what it was like for them at school, as they watched television, as they read media accounts such as the Morro blog, as they lay in their beds at night, visited by their darkest fears. But I couldn't speak without losing all composure, and I couldn't do that, I wouldn't do that to them right now. They needed my strength more than I needed theirs.

"We'll figure this out," I whispered, the most I could muster. I didn't know if it gave them any comfort.

And I didn't know if it was true. But the truth was out there somewhere. Some piece of evidence had to materialize, right? Sooner or later the dam *had* to break, didn't it?

CHAPTER 45

"COLONEL BERNARD DURAND of the Central Directorate of Interior Intelligence," said the next witness. Durand was Major Rouen's partner—Square Jaw. He had been the intimidator, a role that came naturally to him. Even dressed in his courtroom best, he looked like a thug. He had a rough complexion that suggested a childhood illness or hard living or both, narrow eyes that emitted a cold glare, a military crew cut, and a thick neck. I knew firsthand that he was not a guy you wanted on the opposite side of a confrontation.

"The women had grown desperate," said Durand. "Winnie Brookes was facing the end of her affair with the president and an obviously unhappy marriage. Abbie Elliot, her closest friend and neighbor, was also in an unhappy marriage, as she admitted, and as her husband admitted during the investigation. And, like Ms. Brookes, Ms. Elliot lacked independent wealth. For both Ms. Brookes and Ms. Elliot, leaving their husbands would lead to financial hardship. Thus the need for blackmail money.

"Serena Schofield acknowledged an unhappy marriage as well. And though she is wealthy, she and her husband, Simon, have a prenuptial agreement that would limit her to one million dollars in the event of a divorce. One million American dollars would be significant to most of us, but not to someone who is married to a man worth more than six hundred million dollars, like Simon Schofield."

The presiding judge, for the record, referenced all the pages in the dossier that chronicled the interviews with each of us and our husbands. In the years I'd known her, Serena had never mentioned that she'd signed a prenup with Simon.

"The blackmail attempt obviously did not work," Durand continued. "Winnie Brookes confronted the president with the video recording as he and Captain Cousineau were leaving. She shot the men in the Bentley convertible. Presumably, she did so because the president did not respond to the blackmail attempt to her satisfaction."

"There are no living witnesses to the shooting," said the presiding judge.

"That's correct, other than Ms. Brookes, who has denied these facts."

"Yes, yes." The presiding judge's eyes crept toward the defense cage. "Colonel, you can say with certainty that it was Winnie Brookes who shot the deceased?"

"Yes, we can, Mr. President. First, we can say so because of the statements signed by Bryah Gordon and Serena Schofield. They each swore that Winnie Brookes confessed to the murders when she returned to the yacht."

"These are statements that Ms. Gordon and Ms. Schofield have since disavowed?"

Durand seemed amused. "Once they retained attorneys, Mr. President. Yes, at that point, they decided that they no longer wished to stand by those statements. But I can assure you that they were very clear with me at the time they signed them."

The judge waved a hand, as if there were no need to elaborate, as if he fully agreed with Durand's take on the matter. "In any event, Colonel, even if we disregarded the signed, sworn statements, you have other proof that Ms. Brookes shot the men?"

"Yes, Mr. President. We tested each of the women for the presence of gunshot residue when they were taken into custody."

"And?"

"Ms. Brookes's right forearm tested positive for the presence of gunshot residue." Durand nodded. "Mr. President, there is no doubt that Winnie Brookes is the one who fired the weapon that night."

CHAPTER 46

PICTURE FOUR WOMEN on vacation, strolling into the lobby of a gorgeous hotel in their sundresses, holding glasses of Champagne and full of anticipation for a four-day weekend in Monte Carlo. At the reception desk, the well-groomed hotel clerk says something to the tall blond woman and the other three women react, making faces and raising mock complaints to the blonde.

This was a scene everyone in the courtroom was watching on a large projection screen, courtesy of a digital surveillance tape from the Hôtel Métropole made on the day we arrived. I remembered the moment captured there; the receptionist had mentioned Simon's name because he'd booked the suite for Serena, and we'd all recoiled at the mention of Simon, one of our husbands, on a trip that was supposed to be about everything *but* our husbands. Well, we'd certainly managed to make it about something else, hadn't we?

"This was twenty hundred and forty hours," said Colonel Durand, gesturing to the screen. "This was the moment on seventeen June when the four accused arrived at the hotel."

He meant 8:40 p.m., near dusk, which jibed with my memory. Durand pointed to a stack of small black boxes that were contained in the glass evidence case. "Mr. President, we reviewed surveillance tapes for the entire week surrounding the morning of nineteen June, the day that the bodies of President Devereux and Captain Cousineau were discovered. As you can see, we were able to clearly see whenever hotel staff created a new key card for guests to enter their rooms."

"And tell us what your review showed," said the presiding judge.

"We identified every single person on the surveillance tapes who received a key card during that one-week time period. We were then able to interview guests at the hotel from that time period as well, to match names to those faces."

"And what did your investigation yield?"

"Mr. President," said Durand, "from the moment the four accused arrived at the Hôtel Métropole until the discovery of the bodies, nobody but these four women received key cards to their suite, the Carré d'Or."

"Is it possible, Colonel, that one of the four women misplaced her key card and someone else picked it up and used it?"

"No, Mr. President. Each of the accused, when arrested, was in possession of her key card."

"Very good, Colonel. And did you conduct any further investigation?"

"Yes, Mr. President." Durand drank from his water glass. "We considered other claims the women argued during the investigation: that someone might have bribed hotel staff for a key card, so he wouldn't have to walk up to the front desk and be caught on camera; or that one of the hotel staff broke in."

The presiding judge turned to a page in the dossier and referenced it for the record. "Proceed, Colonel."

"Mr. President, as the dossier indicates, the Hôtel Métropole interviewed each member of its staff in my presence. We focused most particularly on staff members who entered that suite during the time period for turndown service or cleaning. But every single staff member was thoroughly investigated. Each one submitted to a lie-detector test. And everyone passed the test. We are confident that no staff member, either intentionally or accidentally, permitted anyone other than those four women to enter their suite, and that those employees who did enter the suite committed no wrongdoing whatsoever."

"So let us be clear." The presiding judge closed the dossier and paused a moment. "During the investigation, the accused claimed that physical evidence found at the scene of the murders was planted."

"Yes, sir."

"That hair follicles found in the car must have been taken from their hairbrushes in their hotel suite and placed at the scene of the crime."

"Yes, sir."

"That mucus belonging to Ms. Brookes was taken from a used tissue found in the hotel suite. That Ms. Elliot's cerumen—ear-wax—came from a cotton swab in the hotel room. That the blood droplet belonging to Ms. Schofield was taken from the hotel suite. You are aware of these claims."

"Yes, sir."

"And to those claims you would say?"

Durand nodded triumphantly. "Mr. President, I can say with ut-most certainty that nobody received a key card to the Carré d'Or suite other than those four women. And no staff member from the hotel allowed anyone else into that suite during that time period.

"Mr. President," he concluded, "there is no way anyone else en-tered that room to steal evidence and plant it at the murder scene. The defense's claims are more than just absurd. They are impossible."

CHAPTER 47

I SPENT THE NIGHT in a local jail on the south end of Paris. As always, I was assigned my own cell for security reasons, which meant I had the overflowing toilet and cockroaches all to myself. They didn't have a mattress, but they scrounged up some blankets and laid them along the bench for me to sleep on.

The cops at the jail were passing around a French magazine called *Bruit* that, on its laminated cover, claimed to contain exclusive sexy photos of Winnie Brookes, who had briefly aspired to modeling back in her early twenties. Some British photographer realized that he had shot these pics of Winnie years ago and, not wanting to miss out on the ravenous frenzy for anything related to the Monte Carlo Mistresses, had sold them to the highest bidder. Winnie hadn't posed nude, but she got as close as she possibly could—mostly bra-and-panties shots, including a few with another scantily clad female model, which were immediately identified by the Neanderthal cops as their favorites.

"Thanks, I'm good on photos of my friends in their undies for now," I said to whomever was approaching my cell door. I was lying flat on my poor excuse for a bed, staring up at the ceiling, and not very interested in seeing another picture of Winnie.

"I don't have any photos of your friends in undies. But I'd be willing to take some."

I lifted my head enough to make out a man in a leather jacket and jeans, with an unshaven face and long red hair pulled back in a ponytail.

"I've seen you in court," I said.

"Joe Morro," he said. *"New York Times."*

I put my head back down. "The blog. The guy who used to call me all the time."

"Right."

"The guy who trashed me in last night's edition. 'A schemer and a liar,' I think you said. My daughter read that."

"Maybe we can help each other."

"How's that? You going to break me out of here? Confess to the murders? Those things would help me out."

He laughed. "Give me exclusive access to you. Talk to me, on and off the record. And I'll be a resource for you."

I rolled my head over toward him. "How did you get in here?"

He laughed. "I know, I know. Security's tight. One of these cops is my friend. I wrote an article about his sister once. But don't worry, they gave me a full-body search before they let me pass. I'm no threat to you."

"Last I heard, the pen is mightier than the sword."

He liked that. "How do you prove a frame-up?" he asked. "That central intelligence guy Durand—he says nobody else had a key card to the hotel suite. So how does anyone get your hair and mucus and all that stuff? Plus who even knew President Devereux was going to be in Monte Carlo? He was traveling incognito. An advance plan or frame-up is a tough sell, Abbie."

"So now you're going to tell me how much my case sucks?" I moaned. "Joe, I'm tired and I need sleep. If I can think of something I need, you'll be the first to know."

"I think you're innocent," he said.

That line, I had to admit, got my attention. I wasn't hearing a lot of that these days. I looked at him again. "Don't say something like that unless you mean it."

"I mean it. I think Winnie did it, personally. She was on a pretty self-destructive path, don't you think? I think the rest of you are getting screwed. She shot him and then came back onto the yacht and dumped the whole thing on the rest of you guys."

"That's not true," I said.

"Okay, maybe not that exactly. But I'd bet my journalism degree that Winnie Brookes is the killer. And I'd also bet my degree that you aren't sure whether I'm right or wrong."

I didn't answer. He was trying to goad me. It was working.

"I can help you," he repeated. "I can be very resourceful when I need to be."

"So you claim," I said.

"I found you here, didn't I? At your undisclosed location?"

He dropped his business card inside my cell.

"Call me," he said.

CHAPTER 48

THE COURTROOM WENT still at the call of his name, like a classroom suddenly going quiet upon the teacher's entry. Heads turned back to see him. He walked with the smooth confidence of someone who was accustomed to such attention. He was dressed in a beautiful black suit with a thin black tie and expensive Italian loafers.

He was a fish out of water, walking through a criminal courtroom instead of down the red carpet at the Oscars. But he was an actor, after all; he could play a part and he played this one well, maintaining the appropriate sobriety for the occasion.

On just about every level, the experience of watching Damon Kodiak testify in court was about as surreal as it got. Even under the perilous circumstances in which I found myself, I couldn't deny having a physical reaction to him. He had drawn something out of me that I'd never known existed. The memory of that time was somewhat tempered, admittedly, by being arrested hours later, dragged from the yacht, and put on trial for my life, accused of a crime I didn't commit. But that was the thing: it was more than just some memory. It was an indelible mark he'd carved inside me.

And then, of course, there was Jeffrey, sitting only a few dozen feet away from me right now. Who would have thought that I'd find my-self in the same room with my husband and my one-night stand, and that our affair would be the *least* of my problems?

Damon answered the preliminary questions easily enough. He tes-tified to being in Monte Carlo on the night in question, during a break from a movie he was filming. He freely admitted to meeting me and the others at the nightclub and to taking a particular interest in me.

"I enjoyed talking to Abbie very much," he said. "Did I find her attractive? Sure. I suppose you could say we flirted as well."

Yeah, you could probably say that.

"Mr. Kodiak," asked the presiding judge. "Were you aware that the man who referred to himself as Devo was, in fact, the president of France?"

"No, I was not," Damon answered. "Though I joined the group late, and I confess to having enjoyed a few cocktails by that point in the evening. It's possible that the others knew who he was. But I did not."

No matter how Damon qualified it, this testimony was very helpful to the defense, especially after Richard Ogletree said that we all knew "Devo" was President Devereux. Damon was the first person to cor-roborate our position.

"I recall the Grand Casino, yes, Your Honor," he said. Apparently he didn't get the memo from Ogletree about calling the judge Mr. President. Then again, the presiding judge wasn't rushing to correct the international movie star.

"I recall arriving at the casino with Abbie and her other friends after the nightclub. That much, of course, I remember. And I remem-ber having a good time at the casino, as I always do." Damon seemed to think that this comment merited some favorable reaction, which the spectators gave him.

"As best as I can remember," he said, "I didn't spend any time with Abbie, personally, at the casino. We sort of lost each other."

That was true. I'd lost Damon at the casino. And the surveillance cameras at the Grand Casino backed this up.

"Mr. Kodiak," said the presiding judge, "when did you next see the defendant, Ms. Elliot?"

"When did I next see Abbie?" Damon scratched the back of his head, then turned and looked in my direction briefly, though we didn't make eye contact.

"Yes, Mr. Kodiak. After you became separated at the casino, when was the next time you saw the accused, Abbie Elliot?"

He opened his hand, gesturing toward me, before he gave his answer.

"Today," he said. "When I walked into the courtroom."

"You are aware that Ms. Elliot has used you as an alibi. That she has claimed that the two of you had a romantic encounter on the yacht, which could account for her whereabouts during the time of the murder. You know all this."

"I do, Your Honor. I do." He paused. His eyes rose to the ceiling, as if he were pondering the most delicate, diplomatic way to put it.

"She...was a very nice woman," he said. "A very aggressive woman. I think it's safe to say, from my perspective, that she was interested in sleeping with me."

"But that did not happen?"

"It didn't happen." Damon glanced at the judges with a look that said it all: *What would a superstar like* me *be doing with a woman like* her?

Anyone who wasn't looking at the dashing and charming Damon Kodiak was looking at me. I could only stare straight ahead and try to keep my composure. *What did they threaten you with, Damon?* I wondered.

"Your Honor," said Damon, "I'm afraid what Abbie Elliot told you is either an alibi she invented, or a fantasy in her mind."

CHAPTER 49

"GOOD MORNING, MR. KODIAK." Jules Laurent cleared his throat and glanced at a notepad on his desk.

"Mr. Laurent." Because Jules was speaking in English, Damon removed his headphones.

"You testified you were never on the yacht, the *Misty Blue,* on the night or early morning in question."

"That's correct."

"You're aware that one of your fingerprints was located on the doorknob of a bedroom door on that yacht."

"I am, yes," said Damon. "And as I told the investigators, I've been on Dick Ogletree's yacht many times. Just not that night."

"The bedroom door I reference—you are aware that this is the very bedroom that my client says was the location of your...intimate relations?"

"I wasn't," he said. "I am now."

"A coincidence?"

"Apparently so."

"So I will assume...you also are not aware that Abbie, my client, identified this particular bedroom to the authorities *before* she knew that your fingerprint was on the doorknob of that bedroom?"

Damon, of course, didn't know that. Jules referenced the various pages of the dossier, establishing the date of my statement to the police and the later report of the fingerprint results.

"So of the five bedrooms on this yacht, Abbie just happened to pick the one where a fingerprint of yours would later be found? She just got lucky in her guess?" Jules asked, wagging a pencil in his hand.

Damon bowed his head ever so slightly. "Mr. Laurent, I doubt she would consider herself lucky at this moment."

A murmur of laughter rippled through the courtroom. Jules acknowledged the moment.

"A poor question," he said. "A better one: Mr. Kodiak, knowing that you are alive and well, and perfectly able to... rebut what she said... knowing all of this, yes?... can you think of a reason why Abbie would make up this story about you? Knowing that you would immediately deny it and... expose her as a liar?"

Damon, who had been wearing the trace of a smug smile, lost a bit of color.

"This woman," Jules went on, waving an arm with a flourish, "whom the prosecution claims to be a criminal mastermind—she would have to be quite... oh, stupid, yes? To make up such a silly alibi?"

The prosecutor rose, presumably to object, but the presiding judge was already admonishing Jules to avoid speeches at this point. Jules bowed slightly to the presiding judge and moved on.

"The murders occurred on nineteen June, Mr. Kodiak. Yet you were not questioned until twenty-four June. Five days later. Do you recall this, as I do?"

Damon's eyes danced a bit before he nodded. "I think that's right."

"They came to you," he said. "Not you to them?"

"That's also correct."

"You hadn't heard this news of President Devereux's death before twenty-four June?"

"Of course I had. I believe I heard about it when everyone else did."

"And you knew it had taken place in Monte Carlo."

"Yes," Damon said, the answer coming more slowly, as he grew more wary of his adversary.

"And the news of the arrests." Jules gestured to the four of us in the defense cage. "These four women. Their names and faces were splashed everywhere. Almost immediately. Were you not immediately aware that they had been arrested?"

Damon coughed. Stalling for time, I thought. "Mr. Laurent, the sequence of events is not something I remember particularly well. At some point, yes, I heard their names. And yes, to answer your next question—yes, I recognized them as the women I'd met at the nightclub."

"But you did not initiate contact with the French authorities, did you, sir?"

"I did not. I didn't think the fact that I had met them at the nightclub made any difference. What could I tell the French authorities? These women were fun to party with?"

More laughter in the courtroom, but subdued this time. This wasn't the time for levity.

Jules was moving in on Damon, and everyone sensed it.

CHAPTER 50

"MR. KODIAK, THE dossier indicates that the authorities first tried to reach you on twenty-one June." Jules referenced the dossier for the record. "Is that date . . . consistent with your memory?"

Damon scratched at his cheek. "I couldn't be specific."

"Do you have a reason to doubt the accuracy of the police record in the dossier?"

Damon shook his head. "No. I do know that I was filming some water scenes in the Mediterranean and it would have been difficult to speak with them."

Jules dropped his hand and stared at Damon for a long, pregnant moment. "It would have been difficult to take a boat or helicopter to shore and speak with authorities about the murder of the French president?"

"No, I suppose it wouldn't have, if they'd asked, but they didn't," Damon snapped, the first break in his cool demeanor. "We were spending entire days out there on the water and if they had told me it was an urgent matter, I would have—of course I would have come ashore." He took a breath and calmed down. "They said it could wait."

Jules nodded aimlessly. He was probably thinking to himself that he'd pushed this too far. What Damon was saying sounded somewhat reasonable.

"It wouldn't be the case," Jules said, "that you were trying to...get your story straight?"

"No, it most certainly wouldn't, Mr. Laurent." Damon pointed a finger at Jules. "After the nightclub and the casino, I left and went to my friend's place in Cannes. I stayed there until the morning and got up and took a helicopter to our film site on the Mediterranean. What story is there to get straight?"

"Your friend's place in Cannes. That friend is...Oliver Kurtz?"

"Yes." Damon nodded emphatically. "Ollie told the authorities the same thing."

"Ollie is a personal assistant, is he not? He was...renting a house in Cannes?"

"That's right."

"So you call him a friend. But he is your employee, yes?"

Damon sighed. "He is both an employee and a friend."

"I see." Jules smiled to the spectators. "And he'd like to remain both of those things, yes? Especially your employee. He would like to please his boss, correct?"

"He wouldn't lie for me, if that's what you're saying, Mr. Laurent."

"Of course not." Jules pondered a moment. Finally, he flipped a page in his notepad. Moving on to another topic. "The name of this film you were shooting was?"

"*Overboard.*"

"Ah. *Overboard.* And the film company was Mirastar, I believe?"

"Mirastar Entertainment, yes."

"You had a...ten-movie contract with Mirastar."

"Yes."

"And *Overboard* was your last of the ten."

"Correct."

"It was with Mirastar that you made these 'Charm' movies, yes? *Three's a Charm, Four's a Charm, Five's a Charm.*"

"Yes."

"And also...let me see." Jules checked his notes. *"Renegade, Beat of an Eye, Last Man Standing?"*

"Yes."

"Action movies, yes?"

Damon inclined his head. "I suppose you could call them that, yes."

"Mr. Laurent," the presiding judge chimed in. "Is this necessary?"

"I will...get to my point, Mr. President. Many thanks."

Jules focused again on Damon. "Mr. Kodiak, you were...in negotiations for another contract at the time of the murders?"

He nodded. "Yes, sir."

"You are forty-seven, Mr. Kodiak?"

"Thank you for reminding me, Mr. Laurent." More chuckles from the gallery. I didn't know he was that old. He was sure holding up well. I would swear to *that* under oath.

"I mean no disrespect, sir. But is it fair to say that...that a man of your age will find it more difficult to...star in action movies?"

"I don't know about that."

"Well, then could we agree that your more recent movies have been less popular at the box office?" Jules picked up a piece of paper. "Or should I read you some figures?"

"The answer to your first question is yes," Damon said with some ice.

"All right, then. You were in the midst of negotiations with Mirastar. And others as well, yes?"

"Yes."

"And would I be correct in saying that the money that was being offered was...less than the money in your previous contract?"

Damon was no longer deriving any enjoyment from this conversation. "You would be correct."

Jules waited a moment. He wanted to be sure he had everyone's attention. He certainly had Damon's.

"And in the midst of this negotiation, Mr. Kodiak, did you think it would help your negotiating position, or hurt it, if the moviegoing public knew that you'd been on a yacht with the president of France at or near the time he was murdered?"

"I must object." Maryse Ballamont shot to her feet.

"I wasn't on that yacht," said Damon. "I wasn't!"

"Of course you weren't." Jules was done. He thanked the witness and took his seat. I caught Damon's eye as he looked about the court-room. He held my stare for a split second before he shook his head and looked away.

CHAPTER 51

ANOTHER CRAPPY JAIL cell, another restless night of sleep. Despite what I thought was an effective cross-examination by Jules, the online media coverage was brutal after Damon's testimony. Joseph Morro's *New York Times* blog said that "Ms. Elliot's alibi, which had always felt like quite a stretch, was obliterated today by Mr. Kodiak, who seemed almost amused at the idea." (This from the reporter who told me the night before that he thought I was innocent.) The Paris paper *Le Monde* said that my alibi sounded like "the fantasies of a frustrated, deranged housewife." A daily online poll in *Le Monde* now had 82 percent of respondents believing we were guilty. A similar poll in *USA Today,* which I had hoped would be a bit more favorable, had 71 percent believing us guilty.

The next morning, following a "shower" that consisted of running water through my hair at a sink and scrubbing my armpits with hand soap, it was time for court. I was once more put into the back compartment of the oversized gendarmerie vehicle, the restraints placed again on my wrists and ankles. The gendarmerie assigned to my security treated me, as always, with some reverence given my celebrity, but even they had grown chillier toward me as the evidence had come in, blow by blow. At least we didn't have to obey the stoplights, so our cavalcade of three vehicles—one in front and one behind—made good time on the narrow Paris streets.

I heard them as soon as we crossed over the Seine, the hostile chants of the protesters waiting to greet us. *"La mort aux meurtrières!"* they cried. Death to the murderers. I peered through the window at the swollen throngs lining the streets, straining against the police barricades, shaking their fists in the air and holding signs that did not exactly speak well of the four of us on trial.

"Anyone ever hear of the presumption of innocence?" I mumbled.

Before the words were out of my mouth, everything began to unravel.

The sounds came in quick succession, two thumps against the side of the rear cabin, where we sat. Someone had thrown something at the car. Then the unmistakable crash of glass shattering on the hood of the vehicle, and then the explosion. Through the slit in the plastic between us and the front cabin I saw a cascade of orange-red flame snake across the windshield.

Our vehicle veered sharply to the right and abruptly stopped. I was pitched forward on the left-side bench, thrown as far as the momentum of the sudden stop had carried me against my wrist and ankle restraints. The guards fell into each other and started shouting to one another and to the front cabin.

One of the guards pushed me back up to a seated position, where I sat, helpless, as the guards frantically readied their weapons. One of them was on his radio, urgently trying to get direction from his superiors. Through the narrow back window I saw several fireballs on the street topped with thick black smoke. I saw people spilling over the barricades. I saw French troops in riot gear, late in reacting, advancing on the crowd with shields up, batons raised, and in some cases rifles poised at the shoulder.

But there weren't enough of them, and they hadn't been prepared for this. Protesters scattered like cockroaches in all directions.

Some of them ran directly toward our vehicle.

"Nous devons sortir d'ici!" one of the guards shouted.

He was right. We were sitting ducks. Our vehicle was on fire and the protesters were headed for us.

We had to get out of here.

CHAPTER 52

THE CARGO DOOR of the vehicle burst open and armed gendarmes jumped in. My restraints were removed and I was carried out of the vehicle by guards on either side of me. In the open air, the smell of burning gasoline filled my nostrils and the chaotic shouts of the turbulent crowd drowned out the thumping of my pulse.

Through the blur of activity, people dashing madly about and shouting and colliding violently with riot police, it was clear that I was being steered toward the rear vehicle in the convoy, which thus far was intact. But between the vehicle and us were a half dozen men, wild-eyed in their rage, who now had me in their sights. The riot police, trying to intercept them, fired on them. Two of the protesters took shots to the chest and fell backward. One of them ran from the riot troopers and hurled an object at me, a brick that hit one of the guards to my left. He fell to his knee and I went down with him, as he was holding my arm. On the ground, I picked up the brick because I figured I should have a weapon of my own. The guard pulled me to my feet and we tried to navigate forward.

Another man, shouting wildly, tackled the riot police head-on, lunging at their shields and receiving swats from their batons for his trouble. The noise had grown deafening, the movements of the people a dizzying collage of desperation and rage...

But then there was the man who stayed just outside the immediate fray, who, for a split second, seemed not to move at all, despite the turmoil around him. That was the man who, by his stony pose, drew my attention. That was the man who lifted his shirt and revealed a gun.

He widened his stance and drew the weapon from his waistband. I was unable to speak but my arm was working fine. By the time he was raising the gun, I had thrown the brick at him. It grazed his shoulder, startling him more than anything, but it was enough to throw off his aim. The gun went off in the air while he regained his balance. Then one of the gendarmes fired and hit him. Blood splattered from his midsection and he dropped to the ground. Riot troopers converged on him, separating him from the gun, flipping him over, and cuffing him.

The bloodshed seemed to scatter the remainder of the protesters from the immediate area and I ran, with the two guards, to the rear vehicle in the convoy. They pushed me into the backseat, did a quick U-turn, and floored it.

I looked back through the rear window. Flames on the street, one vehicle on fire, several protesters lying prone, others still battling the riot police.

"You are...safe," said the guard next to me, panting, as we sped away.

"Safe?" For now, maybe. But I was beginning to wonder if I was even going to make it through this trial alive.

CHAPTER 53

I DIDN'T KNOW where I was, which somehow seemed fitting under the circumstances. This gave new meaning to the term "undisclosed location"; it wasn't even disclosed to me.

I knew this much: I was at a French military compound, and I was in some kind of stockade made of twisted wire that, I was told, would cut me if I tried to grab it.

I was alive and relatively intact. Given the attempt on my life, my physical injuries were comparatively minor—abrasions on my knee when I fell and more serious cuts to my wrists, which I suffered when our vehicle had jerked to the right and thrown me off my seat, straining me against the handcuffs. Some military doctor had dressed the wounds on my wrists with gauze and tape.

"You okay, Ms. Elliot?" It was Dan Ingersoll, the Department of Justice attaché to the U.S. Embassy. He was dressed in a nice blue suit—courtroom attire, as he'd attended every day of the trial. He addressed me formally, which is pretty much the way he'd related to me over these many months while I awaited trial. He'd visited me several times each week, making sure I was being kept secure and fed and not being stripped of all those nice human rights that diplomats look

out for. That was his job, to make sure I was being afforded basic dig-
nities while I awaited trial. And he'd limited his conversations with
me to those topics.

Still, his formality aside, Dan seemed to genuinely care about my
predicament. On the rare occasion when I lodged a complaint, he followed up on it for me. If I had a question, he got the answer. If I just
needed to vent, he was an attentive listener.

His eyes moved to my bandaged wrists. I knew what he was thinking. "From the handcuffs," I explained. "I'm not suicidal."

"Ah." He nodded.

"Where am I?" I asked.

"An air force base in Creil," said Dan. "About thirty miles north of
Paris. No more random jail cells. They're keeping you guys on a military base from now on. You'll be flown to and from court in a military
helicopter."

I didn't know if that meant my accommodations would be better
or worse. I suspected the latter.

"Who tried to kill me, Dan?"

He shrugged his shoulders. "They don't know too much about
him. He was twenty-two. Dropped out of Sorbonne University. He
was a political supporter of Devereux. Apparently he had some psy-
chological problems."

"You're using the past tense," I said.

"He was killed." Ingersoll sighed. "Three dead, in all. Thirty-some
wounded. I think they arrested like sixty people or something."

"I saw at least three people get shot," I said.

He shook his head. "The riot squad used rubber bullets. Non-
lethal. Only the guards escorting you had weapons with real bullets. They killed the guy who tried to shoot you. Another guy died
from a baton blow. A third guy, an older man, died from cardiac
arrest."

I shuddered. Three dead, more than thirty wounded. I closed my
eyes and dropped my head. The list of casualties from our fun little
weekend continued to grow.

"Oh, and the New York Yankees called," Dan added. "They saw the video of you hurling that brick and they want to sign you to a minor-league contract."

I tried to manage a smile. I appreciated his attempt at levity.

"It was your basic Molotov cocktail," Dan explained when I asked him what had caused the fires. "Fill a bottle with petrol, tie a rag around the stopper, soak it with alcohol, light the rag, and toss the bottle. Homemade incendiary devices. They've worked for centuries."

"They worked today."

He smiled for some reason, then grew serious. "We've been in touch with the interior ministry about the safety of you and Ms. Schofield. And they're on the same page with us, Ms. Elliot. What happened today was a black eye for them. They look out of control when something like this happens. And governments don't like to look out of control. Especially new ones formed after their last president was assassinated." He drew a breath. "Your safety will be guaranteed," he assured me.

Something told me he enjoyed that paternalistic role. I was willing to bet he had a daughter.

"During the trial, you mean," I said. "My safety will be guaranteed during the trial. But not afterward."

Dan didn't debate me. What could he say? Look what these people did while I was surrounded by armed escorts. Imagine what would happen when I was alone in a prison cell, or out in the prison yard.

Don't think that way, I told myself. Once trial resumed next week, we had our defense. We had several weeks' worth of evidence. We would testify. Our experts would testify about evidence being planted and hotel key cards duplicated. Our husbands would testify that, whatever our faults, we weren't murderers.

We hadn't begun to fight. We still had our defense. There was still a chance.

"Don't give up hope," I always told my children. I had to keep reminding myself to follow that same advice.

CHAPTER 54

I AM DROWNING in a sea of boiling water, my flesh tearing from the bone. I try to cry out; nothing escapes from my mouth but a desperate whisper. When my head goes back underwater I see the wavy images of my children, Richie and Elena, above me. They are calling to me, offering a hand to me, but I don't want to reach out for them; I'm afraid that the water will scald them. *Go away now,* I silently plead with them. *Go away before you get burned—*

I popped up in bed, sucking in deep breaths of air. A man was standing at the door of my cell, raking a metal key across the wired bars.

Still pulling myself out of the dream, out of that water, I blinked through bleary eyes.

The man opened the cell and approached me. He was dressed all in black. I could hardly make him out at all.

"Get up," he said.

I got out of bed and he led me by the arm out of the cell. Another man, also in black, was waiting out there and followed behind us. I struggled to keep up with the man pulling me forward. I was hardly awake and my socks had no traction on the slippery floor. We walked down two flights of stairs. Then he led me into what appeared to be another cell. It was pitch-black, but I sensed it wasn't empty. I could hear labored breathing and noticed a smell I couldn't quite make out. The smell of fear—

The lights went on. Bryah, Serena, and Winnie were each sitting in a different corner of an unfurnished cell, each wearing a gray gown like the one I was provided. We glanced at each other, squinting with bewilderment. They looked like I assumed I did—bloodshot eyes, hair all over the place, roused from the depths of sleep.

A few minutes passed in silence. None of us spoke. None of us understood. Then we all turned as we heard the echo of footsteps on the concrete floor.

Colonel Durand—Square Jaw—entered the room. He stopped in the middle and looked around at the four of us. He studied each of us with something close to amusement. Then he began to stroll about the room casually, nodding his head and cupping his chin with his hand.

"Winnie Brookes killed the president. This is...beyond debate, of course. The rest of you? You knew of the scheme to blackmail, but that is all. You did not intend any murder. You played a role in concealing it, but this was...afterward. As for Winnie, it was not her intention to commit murder. She...snapped? Snapped. There was no plan. No...premeditation. A blackmail scheme that...went bad."

Durand stopped and looked around at each of us.

"Is that a question or a statement?" I asked.

"A statement," he answered. "A statement that each of you will make when court resumes on Monday. And then the trial will end. Monday, the trial ends."

Monday? "No," I said. "We have weeks' worth of testimony ahead."

Durand shot me a confident look and ambled over to Bryah. "What I have described is quite like the statement that you signed, Ms. Gordon."

"You tricked me," Bryah spat.

He wagged a finger at her. "No more of that. You cooperated previously and you will cooperate once again. You will state what I have just described."

"In exchange for what?" she asked.

"Ten years," he answered. "The prosecutor will recommend ten years of prison. And the court will accept that recommendation."

"How could you possibly know that?" I called out.

Durand ignored me and walked to the corner where Serena sat. "Ms. Schofield. I say the same to you. You also previously signed this statement. You will also receive ten years." He opened his hands. "Ten years is a gift. Your children will still be young when you are released."

Serena and Bryah were still, but their faces had grown intense.

"Ms. Brookes." Durand turned to Winnie. "The evidence against you is…quite overwhelming. You are facing a certain life sentence. You are quite fortunate that France does not have the death penalty." He rolled his hand. "But now you will receive forty years because of the absence of intent. A long time, yes, but preferable to life. You will still have good years left."

Winnie was speechless. It wasn't a terrific offer but Durand had struck a chord with her. The evidence against her was very strong. In her wildest dreams, she hadn't expected to receive an offer of any kind from the prosecution.

"And Ms. Elliot," he said, turning to me.

I took a breath.

"You did not cooperate, but neither did you shoot the men or plan a murder. For your lack of cooperation, you will receive a sentence of twenty years."

I shook my head. "You couldn't possibly have the authority—"

"You'll really just give me ten years?" Bryah cut in.

"I'll really just give you ten years," said Durand, still staring at me. "And Ms. Elliot, you think I do not have the *authority?* I am Central Intelligence. I *am* the authority." He looked at his watch. "It is two hundred hours. You have until sunrise to make a decision. Then the offer will expire."

He gestured to the two goons, who followed him out the cell door.

"Oh, and one more thing," he said, peering at us through the bars of the cell. "This is what you call a package deal, yes? Either all of you accept, or none of you accepts."

He slid the cell door shut with a metallic *clang* and disappeared.

CHAPTER 55

WE ALL SAT for a moment in shock. Could this be? Was this some cruel, sadistic hoax? No, I thought. The French government wanted this trial over now, before there could be any more bomb threats or riots or assassination attempts. "What happened today was a black eye for them," Dan Ingersoll had said. Of course. They wanted a quick confession, the passing of a sentence, and closure.

"I'll take the deal," Serena announced.

"Oh, you'll take it, will you?" Winnie sprang to her feet. "What happened to 'They tricked me into signing that statement'? You'll just throw me under the bus, then?"

Serena popped up as well. "I'm not the one who made us go to that nightclub. I'm not the one who was secretly meeting her boyfriend. And I'm not the one who forgot to mention that her boyfriend was the damn president of France!"

"As if that would have mattered. You had your eyes—and hands—all over Luc the moment you saw him. Don't make this *my* fault."

"No?" Serena moved closer. "And how do we really know that while we were sleeping, you *didn't* go out and kill them, Winnie?

How do we *really* know that? I mean, it sounds like your president boyfriend was about to dump you!"

"You think—you actually think that *I* could have—" Winnie gasped and placed a hand on her chest.

"Guys," I said. "Come on. Don't do this. This is what they want."

I was sure of that last point. Durand knew as well as anyone that we'd been separated from each other since our arrest. We'd each harbored some resentments and this was our first opportunity to vent them. Durand was forcing an all-or-nothing plea bargain. He was making Serena and Bryah an offer so inviting that they couldn't possibly turn it down, thus forcing the hands of Winnie and me.

"I'm accepting it, too," said Bryah, standing next to Serena. "Craig's only four. I have to think of him. Winnie, the cold fact of the matter is that whether you did it or not, they have you dead to rights. You're right lucky to get forty years, you are."

"Well, isn't *this* just lovely?" Winnie stepped forward, her hands in fists. "And Bryah, I couldn't help but notice that all the blood and DNA and fingerprint evidence—you seem to have been left out of it completely."

"Everyone stop," I said.

"What is *that* supposed to mean?" Bryah cried.

"Oh, I'm just saying how very convenient that is for you, love. The rest of us look guilty but not you—"

"Convenient?" Bryah stepped forward and slapped Winnie hard across the face. "*Convenient?* You think *any* of this has been con—"

Winnie lunged at Bryah, punching her shoulder and grabbing her hair. They locked in a struggle, an awkward dance, slamming against the wall before I managed to slice an arm between the two of them and separate them.

"Stop now!" I demanded, holding each of them at arm's length. "This isn't going to solve anything."

"She has to face facts, Abbie," said Bryah, panting. "If she doesn't accept the deal, none of us gets it."

"This is your fault, Winnie." Serena poked the air. "You got us mixed up with these people and now our lives are ruined!"

Winnie started to respond but halted. She looked back and forth at Serena and Bryah, two of her closest friends, and then collapsed to the floor. She began to sob uncontrollably, wailing like a wounded animal, pounding the floor with her fist, her body convulsing as if she were being shot full of electricity.

Serena looked at me. "You have to convince her, Abbie. You're the only one she's ever listened to."

Winnie went on like that for what felt like an hour. Her wails finally turned to dull moans, and then she curled into a fetal position and grew still. She stared forward at nothing. I didn't need to convince her of anything.

"I can't...do this anymore," she said, her voice flat and scratchy, void of any life at all. "I'll take the deal."

I dropped my head. Look at us. Winnie was deteriorating before our eyes. So was our four-way friendship. We were scared beyond comprehension and trying to find a way, any way, out of this mess. There were no good options—only shitty ones and less shitty ones.

Twenty years, I thought. Objectively, a decent offer. My lawyer would be thrilled.

A life. Some kind of life, when I got out. If I got out alive.

"So we're all agreed?" Serena asked.

"A package deal," Durand had said.

Three down, me to go.

Hope, I always preached to Richie and Elena. Something to look forward to. A light at the end of the tunnel, even if it's a twenty-year tunnel. A chance to watch my kids blossom as adults. A chance to spoil grandchildren.

I took a deep breath. My head fell back against the wall. I looked upward. Maybe I was searching for a sign.

A sign that I was about to make the biggest mistake of my life.

"I'm sorry," I said. "I can't agree to this deal."

CHAPTER 56

I WAS ALONE now in every sense of the word, after three hours with my friends, who had tried everything in their power to talk me out of my position. They'd begged me. They'd tried guilt. They'd threatened me. They'd even offered me money.

When Durand had arrived at dawn, Serena and Bryah pleaded with him to let them accept the deal without me, to sever me from the "package." But he was steadfast. The point was to end the trial, and without me confessing, it wouldn't end.

No deal, he said, unless I agreed to it.

"You can't do this to us!" Serena cried to me, as the guards pulled her out of the room.

"Please, Abbie. *Please* reconsider!" Bryah pleaded as they dragged her away.

I was left alone in the room while the others returned to their cells. I buried my head in my hands and let time pass. At some point, sweeping exhaustion overtook the stress and I lay down on the concrete floor. I think I drifted off a couple of times for a few minutes, but mostly it was a long, timeless stare at the wall, pondering how my life had come to this and what lay ahead.

I raised my head at the echo of footsteps on the concrete floor. My stomach was calling to me, so it must have been somewhere approaching noon, but I really had no idea.

My husband walked through the cell door. A guard closed it shut behind him and walked away.

"Rough night," Jeffrey said.

I nodded. I got to my feet with some effort, pain shooting along my spine up to my neck.

"Abbie, this guy Durand? He said you have one more chance to say yes."

I wiped at my eyes and shook out the cobwebs. "I can't," I said.

"What does that mean, you can't? Of course you can."

I looked away from him.

"Think of your friends—"

"Don't do that," I snapped. "Don't make me responsible for them. It wasn't my idea to make it a stupid package deal."

"Then think of our family, Abbie."

I looked at him. How could he say such a thing to me? What did he think I was doing? How could he not realize that my family was the *only* thing I was considering? Even at the height of my pain, after discovering his infidelity, I'd never felt a chasm between us as wide as the one I felt now. It was as if Jeffrey Elliot didn't know me at all.

"Jeff, how can I ever look Richie and Elena in the eye again if I admit to something I didn't do? How can I teach them to live their lives with integrity and courage if I abandon my principles the moment the going gets rough?"

He stepped toward me. "You tell them you did it so you could get out of prison someday. So you could spend time, later in life, with your children and with *their* children. I mean, really, Abbie." He placed his hands together, as if in prayer, as if beseeching me. "Are the kids better off with a principled mother who spends the rest of her life in a shitty French prison?"

I brought a hand to my face and tried to keep my composure. "They'll know that their mother had the courage to stand up for the truth. Doesn't that count for anything?"

"Abbie—"

"And what about figuring out what the hell really happened, Jeffrey? Why aren't you and Jules spending every waking moment trying to turn over every possible stone to figure out who really committed this crime? Has that thought ever crossed your mind?"

Jeffrey took a breath. "That's not fair, Abbie. You know we've done everything we can."

"Nearly nine months," I said. "Nine months, and not a *single* clue as to who framed us? How is that even possible?"

"That's not the point. Not anymore."

I grabbed my hair and held my breath. This was sensory overload. Too much. Finally, I gathered myself and gave it one last thought. "I'm sorry," I said. "But I can't."

"Oh, my God." Jeffrey opened his hands. "You're really going to turn this down."

"Jeffrey," I said.

He put a hand against the wall to steady himself, shaking his head furiously.

"Jeffrey," I repeated. "I need you to be with me. I can't do this alone. Everybody—" My throat choked closed. I tried again, in a hoarse whisper. "Everybody else is against me. I need you on my side. *Please.*"

"No." He shook his head emphatically. "I can't support this. I won't. You're screwing over your kids, your friends, and me." He raised his hands in surrender. "And why? Out of principle? Because of the truth?"

I drew a breath and took a hard look at the man I've called my husband. I had the distinct sense, at that moment, that I wouldn't be calling him that much longer.

"That's exactly why," I said.

Red-faced and flustered, Jeffrey moved his face within an inch of mine.

"You realize, Abbie, this is all on you now. Like it or not. Whatever happens to Winnie and Bryah and Serena. Whatever happens to our family. It's all because of this decision you're making. It's all on you and you alone. Are you prepared to roll the dice on all of that?"

I wasn't prepared for much of anything that was happening to me. And I wasn't rolling any dice. I was just doing my best to keep my nose above water.

I'd lost so much. My privacy, my reputation, my life as I knew it. There was only one thing I still owned—my integrity. I couldn't let them take that away, too.

Jeffrey was right. Fair or not, I was making this decision alone. And that, I now realized with a sensation so palpable it stole my breath away, was how I was going to get through this entire ordeal.

Alone.

CHAPTER 57

FROM OVERHEAD IN a helicopter, the west end of the Île de la Cité, the tail of the dolphin-shaped island, looked like occupied territory. The bridges on that end—the Pont Neuf, Pont Saint-Michel, and Pont au Change—were closed, blocked by armored vehicles. Civilians were not permitted in the quarantined zone. French commandos patrolled the streets. To the east, the army had closed all streets within a block of the Palais de Justice except one, the Quai de la Corse, where a checkpoint was set up; all unauthorized vehicles were turned away.

The effects of the rioting were visible from the air: streetlamps had been pulled down; portions of the roads still bore the torch marks from Molotov cocktails; collateral damage to some of the nearby restaurants and cafés and shops was evident from boarded-up windows or plastic sheets. Authorities had estimated the damage to the Île would reach the millions of euros.

"All because of us," I mumbled, as the helicopter swooped into its descent.

The French had considered moving the entire trial to a military installation but ultimately decided against it, presumably because it would be symbolic of defeat. Still, the four of us defendants were now spending our evenings under military detention. French troops would occupy the perimeter of the Palais de Justice. The only members of the public who could enter the quarantined zone were the media, and only after showing their credentials and being escorted through the checkpoint in armored vehicles.

The helicopter landed, under heavy guard, in the courtyard of the palace complex only steps away from the building that housed France's highest court. It was a full-scale military exercise just to get me out of the copter, involving soldiers in formation, shouting to each other and forming a protective cover around me as I was whisked into the courtroom building.

We shared one moment together in the anteroom, the four of us. Serena and Bryah looked at me with tears in their eyes. This was their last chance.

"You can't do this to us," Serena said. "Please don't."

And then the guards beckoned us and we filed into the courtroom.

Today, I would testify.

CHAPTER 58

INSIDE THE COURTROOM, the presiding judge's face was crimson with anger as the session came to order. This was the first time the court had convened since the riot and the judge wanted to say his piece. "This is a court of law," he said. "And in this court of law, justice will not be deterred. It will not be delayed. It will not be denied."

He looked in my direction as he spoke, as if the riot had been my fault—as if it had been some elaborate scheme on my part to get a day off from trial.

"We will conduct this trial with deliberation but with dispatch," he went on. "We will waste not another day on distractions. The people of this great republic want justice and they want it with all deliberate speed. They will have it."

The court gave a presumptive nod and then turned in my direction.

"Ms. Elliot," he said. "You wish to testify at this time?"

I rose and approached the microphone in the cage. "I do, Mr. President."

"It remains your intention to contest these charges?"

That was a strange question to ask. He was referring to my refusal to go along with Durand's plea offer.

"Yes, Mr. President."

"I am disappointed to hear that."

Disappointed? "Mr. President, I didn't do anything wrong and I—"

"We have already heard this from you, have we not?" The presiding judge, needing both hands to do so, held up the dossier and then dropped it with a loud *thud.* "You testified in full to the investigating judge, did you not?"

"I did."

"And you stand by what you said?"

"Every word."

"Every word." The presiding judge looked at the other judges on the panel.

"Mr. President, the court has heard other evidence that was previously detailed in the dossier. I would respectfully ask for the same—"

"The court does not require a lecture on its procedures, Ms. Elliot."

I took a breath. "May I pro—"

"The court has reviewed your statements to the investigating judge at great length. The members of this court do not have any questions for you. If you have anything to supplement what you have previously said, the court will hear that testimony. But your general claims of innocence are well known to this court."

I wasn't sure what to say.

"Do you have anything to add to your previous statements, Ms. Elliot?"

"Mr. President, I—I guess I'm not sure how to proceed."

"Proceed by answering my question. Do you have any new information?"

I let out a breath and tried to calm myself as the heat came to my face.

"Mr. President—"

"Are you able to substantiate your claim that you were framed by another individual? Are you able to tell us who could have possibly possessed all the information and resources necessary to frame you?"

"I—no, I can't give you a *name*."

"Then we are left with your general denials. Which we will review again during our deliberations." The presiding judge took a moment to look among his colleagues, to confirm their unanimity. "There is no need for any further testimony from you at this stage."

"I don't get to testify?" I cried. "Are you kidding me?"

Jules jumped up. "Mr. President, if I may have a brief moment with my client."

The presiding judge stared at me, then at Jules, for a long count. "If you must. One minute. We will not recess."

Jules leaned against the glass cage, speaking through the mouth holes. I put my hand over the microphone and leaned forward, too.

"Abbie," he said in a harsh whisper, "you must accept the deal. We can see if it's not too late to change our minds."

"No," I said.

"They must be getting pressure to end this trial. They're going to blame you for dragging this out."

"No," I said.

"Abbie, listen to me. It's over. You can see it in their faces. I'm sorry but it's over—"

"No!" I shook my head violently. I removed my hand from the microphone and turned to the court. "This isn't fair! I have the right to testify as much as anyone. I didn't commit any crime and I don't care how much you threaten me or pressure me—I won't admit to something I didn't do. You can't do this! *You can't do this!*"

The presiding judge said something to the bailiff and the sound to my microphone was cut off. It didn't stop me from continuing to yell at the judges. Gendarmes approached me and ordered me to my seat. When I refused, they each took one of my arms and forced me down.

I ripped off my headphones as I sat seething, my pulse racing so wildly that my vision was spotty. But I could see enough: Jeffrey, in the front row, with a hand covering his face in horror. Serena, Bryah, and Winnie, all with tears streaming down their faces, their fates now sealed. The presiding judge, admonishing me furiously. I couldn't make out what he was saying but it didn't matter.

Because I knew. Everything was unraveling, any last chance at hope. We probably never really had a chance. Maybe my pride, my stubbornness, my blind hope had prevented me from seeing it earlier. It no longer mattered. Regret was irrelevant. Hope was a continent away.

It was over.

CHAPTER 59

"LISTEN," I SAID.

I placed my hand gently against my daughter's wet cheek. Her shoulders were bobbing, her chest heaving. Eye contact was difficult for her, but she recognized the moment as much as I and struggled to contain her emotions.

I rested my other hand on Richie's trembling shoulder. He was quiet but his grimaced, tearful expression made him almost unrecognizable.

"Listen," I repeated, trying to keep myself stable. "I want you to understand that I had to stand up for the truth. I had to do it. I couldn't let them make me say something that wasn't true. Your integrity, your dignity, your honor — they aren't for sale. Not ever. Not to anyone. Do you understand?"

Each of my children nodded, emotion choking their throats.

I took a deep breath. "You know what I care about the most? I care about the two of you making the most of your future. You have so much going for you and you're going to be wonderful at whatever you do. Whatever you do. I don't care if you become nuclear scientists or schoolteachers or garbage collectors. Just promise me you'll love what you do and that you'll do it with all your heart.

"You're going to accomplish amazing things. You're going to make lifelong friends. You're going to fall in love and, I hope, have children that fill your heart with love like you—like you fill mine," I concluded with a whisper.

I brought them closer and we collapsed into each other. Still, after all this time, it was utterly incomprehensible to me that this was happening, that events had spiraled so wildly out of my control.

I closed my eyes and listened to them breathe. I pretended that this moment wouldn't end, that if I never let go of them, this moment would never end.

CHAPTER 60

I WAS LED into the anteroom, where I joined the three others. They'd had similar partings with their families, as indicated by their red, swollen eyes and lifeless expressions. They didn't even have enough energy to hate me, at least not for the moment.

The trial was over. It had lasted just longer than three weeks. Our forensic experts and investigators had been given their opportunity to testify. The judges tolerated their testimony but didn't appear to be listening much at all. They just had to be able to say they gave them their chance to speak.

The court deliberated for two days in closed session. I can't imagine what took them so long. My guess was that the sentencing, not the verdicts, had tied them up.

In the courtroom, the three other husbands were there with their children. Jeffrey had taken Richie and Elena and left the Palais de Justice; they were on their way to Orly Airport for a flight back to Switzerland. That was my request. I didn't want any of them to see me like this.

The presiding judge adjusted his microphone and cleared his throat.

"Today, we close one chapter and begin another. What will remain in history as among our republic's most trying challenges, suffering the loss of a beloved president, has in some ways brought out the worst we have to offer. But ultimately, upheld by our republic's resilient spirit, we will look back and see that this challenge has summoned the *best* we have to offer. We have proceeded with conviction but with compassion. We have proceeded with courage but with caution. And it is with the utmost certainty that this court believes, unanimously, that we have discovered the truth.

"The accused will stand.

"Winnie Brookes, it is the finding of this court that you are guilty as charged in the transfer judgment. You will serve a term of natural life in prison.

"Bryah Gordon, it is the finding of this court that you are guilty as charged in the transfer judgment. You will serve a term of thirty years in prison.

"Serena Schofield, it is the finding of this court that you are guilty as charged in the transfer judgment. You will serve a term of thirty years in prison.

"And Abbie Elliot, it is the finding of this court that you are guilty as charged in the transfer judgment. You will serve a term of natural life in prison.

"The prisoners will be remanded to the custody of the Minister of Justice and Liberty. With all deliberate dispatch, the prisoners will be transferred to the Women's Institute for Justice and Reform.

"The members of this honorable court, having reached a final judgment by unanimous vote, have determined that this matter is concluded. The court stands adjourned."

Everyone reacts differently. There's no manual for it. Most of the spectators cheered upon the judge's final words. Maryse Ballamont shook hands with her assistants. Winnie didn't move. Serena's legs nearly buckled. Bryah was the only one who actually wept.

Me, my reservoir of tears had dried up. I had exhausted every emotion of which I was capable. So, like any observer, I watched as the other women were led out and allowed one final embrace, albeit handcuffed, with their husbands and children. Reporters spilled in, now that the court had adjourned, and from a safe distance—one that was determined by the gendarmerie—they snapped photos of Bryah and Serena and Winnie with their grief-stricken families.

My family was gone. Gone for now, and gone forever. And still I couldn't summon the energy to scream or cry. Instead, I just let my head fall back as far as it would go. I looked up to the ceiling, to beyond this courtroom.

And I burst into laughter.

BOOK THREE

APRIL 2011

CHAPTER 61

IT WAS A whir of gray outside as the bus sped along the A20 on its way toward Limoges. Gray, because the cold, dry winter had been unkind to the landscape of central France. Gray, because the concept of color had essentially disappeared for me.

The bus had a police escort, squad cars at our flanks and front and back. The *thwoop-thwoop* of the helicopter overhead competed with the sound of the bus's engine as it coughed and struggled its way southward at high speed.

There were thirty-four of us, spread out over twenty rows and split by a single aisle down the middle. Almost three dozen of France's newest prisoners or transferees. The worst of the worst. Killers and terrorists and sex offenders and drug dealers. An even mix of black and brown and white faces, hard-looking women with bitter eyes, their postures rigid, brimming with violence.

We were shackled at our wrists and ankles. Each row on the bus was bracketed by a steel cage that prevented prisoners from contacting those in the seats in front or behind them or across the aisle. We were caged chickens being taken to slaughter. And it smelled even worse. The odor from the lack of showers and fear-induced perspiration was almost suffocating.

"Maman! Papa!" a woman two rows in front of me, across the aisle, called out. *"Où sont mes parents?"* Her head rolled back and forth as she moaned, pining for her parents.

In the front of the bus, Winnie stared aimlessly out the window, her washed-out expression and slumped shoulders neatly summarizing her condition. Her wrists and forearms were so bony that it was hard to imagine how the handcuffs could have restrained her. Her hair was flat and unwashed. She looked like someone had awakened her from several days' slumber and thrown her on this bus.

I looked back over my shoulder. Near the rear of the bus, Serena sat silently, her expression hardened, as if she were willingly numbing herself. The Olympic athlete inside her was rising to the surface; she was preparing for the mental and physical task of incarceration. She had heard the same things I had about this prison.

Bryah and I were in the same row, across the aisle from one another. She looked like a child enduring a nightmare. Her eyes were wide with dread as she scanned the bus's occupants, a sampling of the population at the maximum-security prison where we'd soon be housed. She looked far younger than her thirty-two years. She was pretty and petite and as passive as they came. A guppy tossed into a pool of barracudas.

She looked at me and said, "I can't do this. Not for thirty years." I could hardly hear her over the engine and the helicopter. But I didn't need to hear the words. I could see it in her eyes, in her trembling lips. She was coming unglued.

"You don't have to get through thirty years," I told her. "You just have to get through today."

"Maman! Papa!" the woman cried out. *"Où sont mes parents?"*

"Écoutez," hissed the woman in the seat behind Bryah. "Hey, girl."

I would have ignored her. Avoiding provocation in French jails had become instinctive for me, natural as blinking my eyes. But Bryah turned back to the woman.

The woman was heavyset and unkempt, with thick jowls, beady

eyes, and eyebrows that looked like they'd been painted on. Her accent was heavy but her English was decent. "The woman who...asks for her parents?" she said. "She *killed* her parents. She...set them on fire."

"Oh, my God." Bryah put her manacled hands over her face.

"Do you want to know...who *I* killed?" she asked.

"No, she doesn't," I called out. "Leave her alone."

"I killed my...cell mate...at Rennes...for...*ronflemont*...for snoring."

Bryah burst into violent sobs, her shoulders trembling.

"Do you...snore, girl?" the woman asked, putting her forehead against the steel enclosure separating her from Bryah.

"Shut up!" I said.

"She was black, like you," the woman said to Bryah. "I like black girls."

"Don't listen to her," I called to Bryah.

"Do you want to be my...cell mate, black girl?"

Bryah curled into a ball, her body still trembling. "I can't do this!" she cried. "I want to go home! Abbie, I want to go *home!*"

"Honey, hang in there! It's going to be okay!" I shouted, gripping the steel cage. I wanted to sound calm and reassuring but it probably came out more like a desperate plea. Because it was. This was not a good time for Bryah to come apart at the seams. If she entered the prison like this, she'd be a walking invitation to anyone looking for an easy mark, to any shark sniffing for blood in the water.

With that, Bryah lurched forward and vomited on the floor. That flipped everyone's switch on the bus. They cheered and shouted and heckled Bryah, the weakling, the loser in the Darwinian struggle inside this bus.

The fat woman behind Bryah didn't let up. If anything, Bryah's vulnerability seemed to encourage her. She banged the steel cage separating her from Bryah as though it were a drum. "*Une jolie fille comme vous serez très populaire dans ici,*" she taunted.

A pretty girl like you will be very popular in here.

"Shut up! *Taisez-vous!*" I yelled at the woman, banging on my own steel cage. I was only adding to the commotion, which had reached near-deafening levels.

"Vous pouvez fendre votre gorge avec ces menottes," she said to Bryah.

You can slit your throat with these handcuffs.

My blood went cold. She was explaining how Bryah could save herself the burden of prison and end her life right here on this bus.

"Vous avez tué le président!" the fat woman shouted for the whole bus to hear. *"Quelqu'un va vous tuer."*

You killed the president. Someone will kill you.

"Shut up!" I cried. "Bryah—Bryah! Look at me. Bryah—"

"Fendez-vous votre gorge!" the fat woman yelled. It became a chant on the bus. "Slit your throat! Slit your throat!" It was like a game for these animals. Who would be the first to break one of the newcomers?

Bryah, at this point, had her face between her knees, her shackled hands over her head. Trying desperately to hide, to drown out everything else. I don't think she even heard my words of encouragement over the thunderous heckling and whistles and jeers.

She would need help in prison. We all would. Because what the fat woman had said was true.

Prisoners or not, most of these women were still French citizens. We killed their president. Somebody, at some point in this jungle we were about to enter, would try to do the same to us.

CHAPTER 62

THE BUS FINALLY left the A20, slowly navigated the round-about—a traffic circle from which numerous roads branched off—and took a local road. As we neared our destination, the guards, safely ensconced behind a secure door at the front of the bus, insisted on quiet.

Bryah hadn't spoken for some time. An unceasing tremor vibrated throughout her body. Otherwise, her glassy eyes just gazed forward.

The bus rolled up to a set of large, ornate gates, built in a bygone era. From a small booth raised ten feet off the ground, like a tollbooth on stilts, a prison guard nodded at the driver and punched a button that opened the gates. I watched them close behind us as we entered the facility. I was now in prison.

The bus passed an open area that you'd call a prison yard, if a yard consisted solely of asphalt. It was like a sidewalk the size of half a football field. About a hundred women, most huddling in groups, most smoking cigarettes. Some were kicking around a soccer ball. Others strolled the perimeter, next to the twenty-foot fences.

The prison was mostly brick, five stories high, the top four of which housed the inmates. It was divided into four blocks—A through D—one of which we approached as the bus came to a stop. They were already greeting us, waving pieces of cloth through the barred windows or dumping garbage to the ground.

The four guards on the bus rose. Two got out. The other two unlocked the cage separating them from us and ordered us to our feet, row by row. We got out without incident. The air outside was cool and dry. There was an aroma of food. Chicken soup, I thought.

Outside, as we marched single file toward the main building, the jeers from the prisoners through their cell windows drowned out pretty much everything else. Much of it I couldn't make out, either because it was French spoken too quickly, French lingo I hadn't picked up yet, or another language altogether. But I did catch a few words, like *assassins* and *le président* and *Monte Carlo*. We were clearly the star attraction of the incoming prisoners.

We walked through a small courtyard toward a nondescript building that could have been any government office. As I was in the middle of the pack, I waited outside while the first people entered the building. Guards walked alongside us, sizing us up, intimidating us. They were all women, though some of them were more masculine than many men I knew. They were dressed in navy-blue uniforms and tall black boots, and carried batons and cans of pepper spray at their waists. I looked up at the barred windows, where the prisoners continued their taunting and garbage throwing. The guards seemed oblivious to it. They probably liked it. Whatever put the newbies in their place, from the outset.

Up ahead, the same woman started wailing again—"*Où sont mes parents?*"—and her legs buckled. None of the prisoners moved. But the guards quickly took note. One of them had her baton raised before she reached the prisoner. "*Où sont mes parents?*" the prisoner cried before the guard slammed a blow across her back. She fell to the asphalt and kept up her desperate sobbing. Two of the guards kicked her repeatedly, each blow a sickening *thud* against her torso, followed by a pained grunt. They didn't stop, even after the prisoner was quiet, motionless. They were going to kill her—

"Stop!" I shouted.

"This is... interest to you?"

I jumped at the words; a guard had snuck up from behind, suddenly only inches from me, harsh nicotine breath on my face.

"What—what?"

"This is interest to you?" She had a wide face, with a thin scar along her right eye, and a crooked nose.

"That woman—she isn't—"

I felt a searing pain in my ribs from the end of the baton. I tried to keep my wind and my balance but failed at both. I doubled over to the ground, breathless. The prisoners, from their cell windows, roared with approval.

The guard yelled something at me but I couldn't hear her over the shouting. I looked up at her and she swung the baton, as though it were a golf club, into my ribs again. I couldn't breathe and tried to blink away the black spots forming before my eyes. I braced myself against the asphalt and pushed myself up. The baton slammed down on my back and I collapsed again, chin first, to the hard surface.

She was yelling again, instructing me, but I couldn't understand her and, it was now clear, I wasn't going to win no matter what I did. When I stayed down, she hit me. When I pushed myself up, she hit me. When I looked at her, she hit me.

She was playing to the crowd, to the prisoners peering out their cell windows and egging her on with their cheers. She batted me around as a kitten would a mouse, striking me repeatedly on my back, my arms, my legs, my ribs.

I stared at her boots, thick and black and scuffed at the toe, taking the abuse until finally another guard came over and got me to my feet.

"Ne me regardez pas!" the first one shouted, only inches from my face. This time I caught it. Don't look at her. That much I had figured out.

The guard stood so close to me, her nose was touching my cheek. *"Vous êtes en France et vous parlez français,"* she said.

"Je... comprends," I managed through halting, pained breaths. Don't eyeball the guards, and speak French when you're in a French prison.

Lessons I wouldn't forget. And if I did, they'd be quick to remind me.

CHAPTER 63

ONCE INSIDE THE building, I lined up my shoes at a red marker, gave my name to someone behind a window, and was directed into a room. I moved gingerly. My ribs were so sore it hurt to breathe. My lower back was seizing up. But I made it. The room had white walls and a desk. A guard stood with a clipboard and motioned me in.

I gasped when I saw a woman lying prone in the corner. It was the woman asking about her parents, the one they'd beaten until she stopped asking.

"Elliot," said the guard. *"Parlez-vous français?"*

"That woman needs medical attention," I said. *"Elle a besoin d'un docteur."*

"Ah, English." The guard didn't even look up from her clipboard. "You have . . . wedding ring?"

"This woman needs to see a doctor!" I repeated.

"She is okay. You have—"

"No, I don't have a wedding ring." You're allowed to bring your ring into prison, but I figured it wouldn't last long in here, and I wanted Elena to have it one day when she got married.

The woman in the corner stirred. Her head lifted and turned. Blood trickled from her mouth. Her right eye was swollen shut.

"Help this woman!" I demanded, raising my arm and pointing at her—and wincing as I did so, the pain rocketing through my ribs.

"Watch?" the guard continued. "Yes, you have watch. Watch is okay."

The woman in the corner managed to look in my direction. *"Où sont mes parents?"* she mumbled.

"Take off...clothing," the guard said.

"No." I took a step back. "That woman is mentally ill and she's been seriously injured. I'm not taking off my clothes until you help her."

The guard, for the first time, looked up at me. "The clothes," she repeated.

I stood my ground and shook my head.

The woman reached into her pocket and removed a whistle. She gave it two quick blows. Almost instantly three more guards burst into the room.

"Elle ne se déshabillera pas," the guard said to the new reinforcements.

They hardly broke stride as they moved toward me.

"No!" I cried, but they were on me before I could even raise my hands. Their batons were still at their waists. They were using their hands. I tried to push them away, to squirm out of their grip, but it didn't seem like a good idea to start throwing punches or kicking or scratching them, so I never stood a chance. They forced me to the floor and pinned down my arms. One of them tugged at my shirt with both hands until she managed to make a tear in the cotton at the top. Then she ripped my shirt right down the center. The same guard ripped my bra off from the front before tugging on my pants until they came off. It took her a few tries at my panties before she ripped them apart, too, leaving me naked.

When it was over, the guards stood up and moved away from me. I was naked. My clothes were in shreds. And the door to the room was open, so every prisoner who'd been behind me in line was watching everything that happened.

"Là," said the guard with the clipboard. "Now the clothes are off. Stand up."

I got to my feet with considerable pain.

"Raise the arms," she ordered me. After I did so, she continued with her demands, part of the ritual search. "Open the hands. Lift the feet."

Then she snapped on rubber gloves. "Open the mouth." With no enthusiasm whatsoever, the guard inserted a tongue depressor in my mouth, probing underneath my tongue and along each cheek. I just about gagged a couple of times.

Then she ran her fingers through my hair. Finding no contraband in my hair or mouth, or under my arms or feet, she had one place left to look.

"Turn and...bend...bend over," she said.

I took a breath, turned around, and reached for my toes, stark naked as I was. She shone a small flashlight into my anus.

The prisoner in the corner was lying motionless again, her head back down on the floor.

"Cough," the guard said.

I manufactured a cough. A couple of the guards whispered and laughed. They made me stay in that contorted, vulnerable position, my privates exposed to the guards and the prisoners, for what must have been ten minutes. Unless there was something incredibly interesting about the inside of my anus (and in forty-two years, nobody had ever said so), or unless one of the guards was an aspiring proctologist, it seemed the guards were simply making a point.

They were humiliating me, violating my privacy, and making sure everyone understood they could do it with impunity.

CHAPTER 64

I WAS GIVEN a yellow smock and thin green cotton pants that made me look like a color-blind hospital patient. Next I met with a prison administrator, whom I had to assure that I was not pregnant and not suffering from HIV, hepatitis, or tuberculosis. I requested the infirmary as my work assignment and set up a commissary account.

Then six of us followed a guard through three consecutive doors of webbed steel, spaced a good twenty feet apart. A buzzer sounded and the first door popped open. The guard walked through, followed by the six prisoners assigned to cell block D, and then the door closed. The second door buzzed open, we walked through, and it closed. Then the first door opened again and the rear guard in our group walked into the first containment area. No more than one door was ever open at the same time. It prevented anyone from getting a head of steam, from acting aggressively. And the guard at the rear was never in the same containment area as the guard at the front with the prisoners, so if by some chance there was trouble, the guard at the rear was free to take action, or at least call for help. All this had been explained to me before I got here.

The six of us prisoners marched single file, holding our bed linens out in front of us. On top of each stack of linens sat a large clear bag of toiletries. When we finally walked through the third door, we entered an open space and my heart started hammering.

This was cell block D.

On either side, going up four stories, were cells with wooden doors. Guards patrolled narrow aisles lined with high green railings. A series of metal walkways connected the two sides to each other; stairways allowed access from one story to another. A guard tower, large enough to hold two guards, rose from the open middle of the cell block. The whole place was dimly lit, and the last time I smelled this odor, I was with my kids in the ape house at the National Zoo.

The catcalls began in force, the hazing as the prisoners smelled fresh blood entering the system. They came to their doors and yelled through the small openings covered with metal wiring. Even if I had possessed the vocabulary to understand them, I wouldn't have been able to, as their shouts blurred together in one taunting cacophony.

I steeled myself and moved one foot in front of the other. We climbed stairs. Two of the prisoners were taken, by one of the two guards, to cells on the second floor. Then we climbed another set of metal stairs and repeated the procedure. Finally, I was taken to a cell on the fourth floor.

Maybe this was the penthouse suite. Maybe they wanted me on the top floor so I could have a better view of the countryside. But I wasn't crossing my fingers.

The number 413 was stenciled in faded black on the wooden door. I heard chatter on the other side. Through the small hatch, I caught sight of only a couple of prisoners. The guard unhooked the latch.

She opened the door, introducing me to my new home.

"Oh, my God," I mumbled.

CHAPTER 65

AS THE CELL door opened, the odor that wafted to my nostrils, even over that of stale cigarette smoke, was mold. Decay.

I thought again of my daughter, as the cell was approximately the size of her bedroom in our town house in Bern. There were metal bunk beds to the right and left. A table protruding from the wall, a shelf above that, holding some cans of food and a loaf of bread and some books. A small freestanding closet in one corner, a dingy toilet and basin in the other.

There were six women in here. Two on the top bunk, left side, their legs dangling over the edge. Two on the bottom bunk, opposite side. One sitting on a stool. The sixth sitting on the toilet.

Six plus me, last I checked, equaled seven. I looked again at the sleeping arrangements. Four beds, seven women. I wasn't a math major, but I had trouble finding an equation in which this arrangement turned out well for me.

The mild chatter I heard outside the door had cut off when I entered. Six pairs of eyes appraised me in silence as the guard led me inside by the arm and closed the door behind me. All the prisoners were white. Five thin—not fashionably thin but malnourished—and one heavy. Five dark-haired and one blond.

The dead bolt latched closed again. I considered a smile but it didn't make any sense. I made a point of looking around for a place to unload my bed linens and blanket and toiletries. I moved toward the bottom bunk, left side.

One of the women on top, who had a butch haircut, dark eyes, and chiseled arms peeking out of a shirt whose sleeves had been cut off, clucked her tongue and shook her head.

"*Où?*" I asked.

Nobody wanted to tell me where I could throw my stuff. It seemed as though everybody else in the room was following the lead of the butch haircut.

"*L'Américaine,*" said one of them on the bottom. "*Elle est celle qui riait.*"

The one who laughed. She was referring to the photo they had snapped of me after the verdict, which had appeared on the front page of *Le Monde* the following day. Under the headline MAMANS COUPABLES—Guilty Moms—were a photo of Bryah and Serena hugging their children and one of me, seated in the defense cage, my head reared back as I burst into laughter. A still photograph, void of context—the ice queen who gunned down our beloved leader and thought the whole thing was hilarious.

"*Papier.*" The woman on the toilet, her pants at her ankles, was curling her fingers at me. "Paper? *Papier toilette!*"

"Oh." She wanted toilet paper. I had a roll in my toiletries bag. I managed to get it out while balancing the linens and tossed it to her.

One of the women sitting on the bottom right bunk bed, with sickly pale skin and sunken eyes, popped up and approached me. I steeled myself but couldn't think fast enough. She reached for my toiletries and produced the toothpaste. She held it up and said something in French I couldn't catch and returned to her bed, celebrating.

I wasn't going to sit there all day with all that stuff in my arms, so I placed it carefully in the corner. The floor was concrete. It was scuffed and dirty and cracked. The same was true of the walls, thick with mildew and badly splintered at the intersection with the floor. T-shirts and pieces of paper were stuffed in the crevices.

"We knew...we were getting one of you," said the woman next to the butch haircut, the blond one of the bunch. English! At least one of them could communicate with me. Butch didn't seem happy that the blonde was speaking to me, apparently without consent, but the blonde returned the elbow when Butch threw her one.

"You are the one...who laughs," she said. "We were...hope—hoping?...for you."

"Why?" I asked.

"You are..." She leveled her hand horizontally in the air. "More short?"

"Shorter than the others." Easier to fit into this thimble of a room.

"Vous allez pouvoir dormir sur le plancher," said the leader, the butch haircut.

She was telling me I would be using the floor for my bed. The concrete floor was decorated with numerous stains. While I pondered the origin of these stains, a gigantic gray rat with a long black tail, which looked more like a small dog than a rodent, scurried out from under one of the bunk beds and into one of the crevices at the base of the wall. I jumped back, evoking laughter from my cell mates.

Even the sympathetic blond woman couldn't contain her amusement.

"That's Iggy," she said.

Great. The rat had a name.

"Elle s'habitue à eux," said the heavyset woman.

I'd get used to the rats, she was saying. She was probably right. And that was the worst part of all.

This would now be normal. This was now the only life I would ever know.

CHAPTER 66

MY CELL MATES regarded me as part celebrity and part pariah. They barely acknowledged my presence, which I thought might be some kind of ritual for a newbie. Only the blond woman was willing to speak with me. I suspected she was the only one who spoke English.

Her name was Linette. She was a car thief. She had been convicted of a third offense more than three years ago and was serving a five-year sentence. She had soft blue eyes and a youthful face, though her skin was blemished and her nose crooked.

I sat on the bottom bunk with her, after she threw the two extra mattresses off and gave me a seat. She opened a large plastic box that had a long number on it and offered me biscuits from a can. I ate a few. They were dry and stale but it was food. I hadn't eaten dinner. Or lunch. My stomach was howling at me.

"Do not tell them I gave you food," said Linette.

"Why not?"

She didn't speak for a while. She seemed to be struggling with what she could say to me.

"Do not tell them," she said.

Linette was the only person who had treated me like a human being here, so I decided not to push it.

She checked out my fashionable wardrobe, the smock and thin pants. "Those clothes are for . . . *les pauvres*."

The poor, she meant. The indigent prisoners who couldn't afford their own clothes. I didn't qualify as poor. Stubborn and naive. But not poor.

"Ah, you . . . argued? With the guards? You should not do that."

"Dix minutes pour les lumières!" The guard's voice, calling for lights out in ten minutes, crackled through the intercom speaker by the door of the cell. I looked at my watch. It was ten minutes to eight.

I considered the sleeping arrangements again. Seven of us. Four beds. Two extra mattresses for the floor. I assumed I was the odd person out.

Linette got up and pulled her blanket off her bed on the top bunk. She laid the blanket out in the small space on the floor that hadn't been taken up by the two extra mattresses. She then put my bedsheet over the blanket. I would use my own blanket, apparently, to cover myself.

"Do not . . . argue with the guards," she repeated.

"Tomorrow's another day."

With that, the lights went out. Everything was dark.

"I am not . . . speaking of tomorrow," Linette whispered. "I am speaking of tonight."

CHAPTER 67

I DON'T KNOW what time it happened. Maybe two in the morning, maybe three. I hadn't slept, fighting off the mounting fear and revulsion as I heard the scurrying of rodents in the dark near me, as I swatted away buzzing flies, as I slapped something that bit my leg.

It happened quickly. A loud rapping at the door. The lock unlatching. Two guards entering, yelling "Elliot!" and lifting me off my feet.

They walked me down the stairs, back through the doors where I had entered cell block D, and then we turned right down another long corridor, and then finally went down two more flights of stairs, narrower and winding. The air grew warmer with each step I descended, until it became downright steamy. It was dark and my sleep-deprived eyes weren't working so well to begin with. My body, especially my ribs and legs and back, was sore from the beating I'd taken earlier.

A series of pipes hung down from a low ceiling. Hot water dripped on me as I was led into a dimly lit basement room. Finally, the guard behind me told me to stop. She took my right hand and slapped a handcuff on it. Then she raised my arms and drew the other end of the cuffs around the top of a thick overhead pipe running the length

214

of the room. Then she cuffed my left hand. The pipe was about six or seven feet off the floor—high enough to force me to stand on the balls of my feet, my arms stretched to their limit over my head. My wrist touched the hot pipe and I recoiled.

The guard left me to the hissing steam, to the hot drips on my neck and face and in my hair. Time slowly ground forward. My calves were burning and my back, already suffering from the beatings, was soon in agony. Every time my calves relaxed a bit, I had to choose between burning my wrists or cutting them on the handcuffs, which bore into my flesh when the force of gravity on my arms took over.

I gritted my teeth and refused to speak, to make any noise at all. That's what they wanted. They wanted to hear my pain.

After what felt like a century, my calves on fire, my back and neck and shoulders locking up fiercely, I heard footsteps approaching, the hard knock of boots on concrete, the occasional splash from the accumulated pools of warm water on the floor.

The guard who came into my view was the one who had beaten me in the courtyard. I made a point of avoiding eye contact, but in the dim lighting the scar near her eye seemed more prominent, almost fluorescent.

"*Je m'appelle Sabine,*" she said, introducing herself. Just Sabine. I'd heard the guards didn't give out their last names, a security measure. "*Je suis le chef. Vous me comprenez?*"

She was the leader, she was saying. The one I had to answer to.

"*Dis-le,*" Sabine said. Say it.

I didn't answer. She could call herself whatever she wanted, but that didn't mean I had to acknowledge it.

"*Vous ferez tout ce que je dis,*" she said. You will do whatever I say.

I didn't answer.

"*Dis-le,*" she insisted, but before I could speak, the butt of her baton stabbed my stomach, whisking the wind from me. I doubled forward, though of course I was physically unable to do so. The pipe scorched both wrists and I struggled to get back into position. I couldn't stand much longer. My legs were on the verge of collapse.

"*Dis-le,*" she said again. "You do...whatever I say."

It was a time before I could recover my breath. She gave me that time. She wanted to hear me acknowledge her power over me. That was the point. Finally, I got a good breath and cleared my throat. I thought of Linette's advice not to argue with the guards.

So I didn't argue with Sabine. I just spat in her face.

She showed her disapproval with her baton, swinging the club into my left ribs three times in succession. It was all I could take. My legs gave out and my head fell backward. I was dangling from the thick pipe by my wrists, bloody now from the cuts made by the handcuffs and gravity. Sabine said something and another guard, with some effort, unlocked one cuff—dangling me sideways—then the other, and I fell hard on my shoulder to the damp concrete.

"Quelqu'un at-il de vous donner la nourriture?" Sabine said to me.

I shook my head. "Nobody . . . gave me . . . food," I managed.

"Vous voulez une nourriture?" she asked.

"Oui," I said. I wanted food.

"Et une douche?"

"Oui." A shower, too.

Sabine called out to somebody, something about food and a shower, and I heard more footsteps. I raised my head and considered the possibility of lifting myself to a sitting position. My arms were useless and every inch of my body was in excruciating pain. No matter. Before I could even get up on my elbows, I was forced down by a gush of liquid, dousing my hair and my shirt.

It wasn't water. After a moment, I recognized the smell.

Soup. It was the chicken soup I smelled this morning.

"No!" I cried, as guards lifted me from either side, the handcuffs slapping over one bloody wrist, around the thick pipe, and then around the other. "No!"

"Bonne nuit, Elliot," Sabine said to me. Good night.

My muscles were completely useless. I dangled from the pipe, the flies and mosquitoes and other assorted insects instantly recognizing the scent of my bloody wrists and the soup broth soaking my clothes and hair. My protests echoed throughout the enclosure.

I am Abbie Elliot, and I am in hell.

CHAPTER 68

THERE WAS NO WAY for me to know how long I was there. I couldn't process information—such as how much time had passed—and the basement was shut off from any daylight there might have been. My head was ringing from having been furiously shaken from side to side, my best defense against the insects that swarmed around me. At least I kept them off my face. My body was another story. My muscles were paralyzed, my arms entirely numb, and the insects feasted on my limbs and torso without impediment. I was like a human piñata, immobile and helpless, hanging from the thick steam pipe by my arms.

I was awake when they came for me. I might have been awake the whole time. I wasn't sure. A waking nightmare, at some point, becomes indistinguishable from a sleeping one.

They had to carry me back to my cell, where my mates were eating breakfast on the tin plates we were provided. There is no mess hall in a French prison; they bring the food cart around from cell to cell and dish out the food and you eat it right there in your cell.

Everyone recoiled when they got a glimpse—or, more accurately, a whiff—of me.

"Permettez-lui de prendre une douche!" Josette, she of the butch haircut, complained to the guards. She was telling them to let me take a shower, but it was more out of self-interest than kindness. I wouldn't want me in here looking and smelling like this, either.

I wasn't welcome on anyone's bed so I just lay on the floor. My arms were limp noodles. I thought there might be nerve damage. My wrists bore bloody rings where the handcuffs, aided by my body weight, had torn severe gashes. The rest of my body was so terribly sore that I couldn't find a comfortable position. My skin was red and swollen, having been ravaged with bites of various kinds. I itched in every conceivable part of my body but I just tried to put it out of my mind, because I couldn't scratch anything with arms and hands that didn't function.

Without a word, following a consenting nod from Josette, two of the women came over to me. One was Linette, who had thus far been the only one to address me and seemed to be the only one who spoke English. The other, I knew from what Linette had shared with me last night, was Lexie, the diminutive one who had stolen my toothpaste. Lexie had set fire to a bookstore in the Latin Quarter of Paris and had five years left on a seven-year sentence. Apparently, Lexie hadn't left cell 413 for the last eighteen months, couldn't speak comprehensible French, and by all accounts was certifiably insane.

Lexie didn't speak to me, but she bunched up my blanket and sheets and managed to make a comfortable cushion for me to lean against. She smiled at me and I almost burst into tears at the small gesture. Linette offered me apple juice and poured it into my mouth as though I were an infant.

"Tienes hambre?" asked a woman on the bottom bunk. Her name was Penelope—a dark-complected young woman, originally from Seville, Spain, who had killed her boyfriend three years ago in their apartment in Lyon. As Linette had explained it, Penelope claimed that her boyfriend was abusing her but apparently got nowhere with that defense. She was serving twenty-two years.

She was speaking Spanish, which I knew far better than French, having double-majored in it in college. She was asking me if I was hungry. Same thing Sabine asked me last night, and it turned out to be a trick question. Besides, I didn't think I could hold anything down beyond a little juice.

Josette jumped down from the top bunk and washed her tin plate in the water basin. When she was done, she walked over to me, which in this place took all of six or seven steps. Josette's expression and tense posture were as severe as her butch hairstyle; everything about her was angry. Four years ago, according to Linette, she had killed a woman in a bar fight. If I had the story right, she had beaten the victim with a beer bottle and when the bottle shattered, she took a jagged piece and slit the woman's throat. That's what you got, apparently, for flirting with Josette's girlfriend.

Mental note: if Josette has a girlfriend in here, don't flirt with her.

She eyed me now. It felt like some kind of a test. I'd taken a few sips of apple juice and was resting in relative comfort—the operative word being *relative*—and now the unofficial leader of the cell was sizing me up.

"*Comment aimez-vous la prison jusqu'ici?*" she asked me. How do you like prison so far?

It was a taunt, delivered with cold eyes and a flat tone. The others retreated. When Josette spoke, everyone else went quiet.

"*La soupe de poulet est délicieuse,*" I answered.

The chicken soup is delicious.

Josette blinked twice, thought a moment, then turned to Linette. For a moment, I figured this could go either way.

Then Josette burst into laughter. The rest of them, the tension now broken, followed suit. Everyone had a good chuckle. Even I managed to crack a smile. Josette's eyes made their way back to mine. She nodded at me with grudging approval.

I had earned something with her. It was a start.

CHAPTER 69

THE GUARDS CAME for me after breakfast. I didn't know why. They marched me to the showers, which were otherwise empty. They ordered me to strip, and my darkest fears quickly surfaced.

But sexual assault wasn't on the agenda this morning. I disrobed and got two whole minutes under the weak spray with soap they tossed me. I dried off with a towel the size of a bath mat and put on a new, clean set of prison garb. I was eager to scrub the soup broth off my body—as best I could with arms that were just regaining function.

They marched me down one of the prison hallways, apart from the four cell blocks, through lots of security—hydraulic gates and doors requiring key cards. I saw a metal sign that said LE GARDIEN and I finally realized I was going to visit the warden of the prison.

Inside, the office was spacious and orderly, the walls filled with photos that displayed the warden's ego to the hilt, awards and citations and diplomas and photos of the warden with various dignitaries—including one with the fallen president, Henri Devereux.

His name was Boulez. He looked like a man of power. Dark hair slicked back. Expensive clothes, a vest over his crisply starched shirt and yellow satin tie—a three-piece suit with the jacket off. His man-icured hand clutched a gold timepiece as he looked me over. It took me five seconds to dislike him.

"Welcome," he said to me, as if they'd thrown a Hawaiian lei over my neck when I got off the bus. I thought it best not to respond.

"Ah, it is always difficult at first." He waved a hand. "Most learn to adjust to this life. Some do not. It is all a choice, Ms. Elliot."

He hadn't offered me a seat, which I suppose was his attempt to establish superiority. Under the circumstances, he didn't have to try very hard.

Boulez weighed the timepiece in his hand. "You have the choice to be cooperative. Your time can be...difficult if you do not."

"Like last night? Would that be an example of difficult?"

He winked at me. This asshole actually winked at me.

"Your friends? They cooperated last night. They slept comfortably in their cells."

I reverted to silence, unsure of what I might blurt out. I'd devel-oped a defiance, a defense mechanism during my ten-month stay in the French penal system. It was how I was wired. Call it stubborn-ness. Call it pride. I wasn't going to make it easy for these people to break me. *Thank-you-sir-may-I-have-another* wasn't in my vocabulary.

"Your attitude, Ms. Elliot...did not lead to good results. Not for you. Not for your friends. I am correct? I am told your friends have *you* to thank for their harsh sentences."

I didn't need to be reminded of that. It was on my mind constantly. "They have your government to thank," I said.

Serve and volley. He wasn't going to debate me. He didn't need to.

"Choices," he said again. "You have a...unique opportunity, no? Another chance to...correct?...correct your mistake."

The appeal, he meant. In France, every convict gets a second trial with new jurors or, in my case, judges. But nobody was holding out hope. My lawyer, Jules, had explained that the court would likely rely almost entirely on the investigating judge's report and not call live witnesses. They wouldn't want to reopen the nation's wounds.

No chance, Jules had bluntly assessed. No chance of winning.

But Boulez was talking about the sentence. If I confessed, he was saying, perhaps the court might lighten my sentence.

"A written confession," said Boulez. "That is your choice."

"I'm innocent."

He found that amusing and made sure I knew it. Then he grew serious.

"Confess," he said, "and your conditions here will be . . . better."

They could stick my head in a toilet and it would be better than last night.

"Safe," he elaborated. "You will be protected. And a personal recommendation from me to the court for a less harsh sentence. You understand, this is a difficult thing for me personally." Boulez got up and lifted the photo of himself standing next to President Devereux off the wall. He stared at it with reverence. "I considered Henri Devereux a personal friend."

"But did he consider you one?"

Boulez looked at me as if I'd slapped him. "What is this you say?"

I pointed at the photograph. "It looks like this was some fancy event where everybody in the room wanted their picture taken with the president. He probably posed for a hundred photos that night. See how his shoulders are turned away from you? And his eyes are looking past you? It looks to me like he'd never met you before, and he wouldn't care if he never saw you again."

Nice one, Abbie. Way to make friends. But I'd hit my limit with this prick.

Boulez's face colored. He didn't want to give me the satisfaction of a reaction, but he gave me one regardless. His jaw clenched and his eyes bored into me. It was obvious to both of us that I had hit the nail on the head.

"Okay, suit yourself," I said. "You guys were best friends."

Boulez took a moment to reboot, to regain the upper hand in the room. He sat back down and formed a tent with his hands. A wry smile appeared on his lips. He nodded to the guards flanking me.

"Ms. Elliot needs some time to consider my offer," he said as the guards escorted me out. "Make sure she has all the time she needs."

CHAPTER 70

THE BLOOD IN my mouth was warm and bitter. Beads of sweat streamed down my face, into my eyes and mouth and ears, dripping off my chin. My thighs and lower back were in searing pain. I tried to keep my breathing even by exhaling in quick bursts. More than anything, I was trying not to pass out.

My back was against the wall and my thighs were at right angles to it, parallel to the floor. It was exactly like sitting in a chair, but minus the chair. I was steeling myself against the wall, trying not to let myself slide down to the floor.

The guard monitoring me was named Lucy. She was, by all accounts, the only guard nastier than the head guard, Sabine. To my horror, she actually looked like me, if you added an inch of height, twenty pounds of muscle, and a creepy smile. My cell mates called her my *belle-soeur laide*—my ugly stepsister.

"*Voulez-vous cesser?*" she asked me as she lit a cigarette.

Did I want to stop? She knew I did. I'd been in this position for almost a half hour. My legs were trembling. My face was twisted in agony. But I wasn't going to give Lucy the satisfaction of an answer, because sure as sunrise, she would respond with a cruel direction to remain in this position for another half hour.

It had been six nights like this, each of them with Lucy. At first she went back to the steam pipe, handcuffing me over my head. One night, she just made me stand all night, twelve hours straight, with my arms out, something they called *l'épouvantail,* or the scarecrow. My ankles were so swollen I couldn't walk the next day. Another night, she let me fall asleep on a hard floor but woke me up every thirty minutes by splashing water in my face.

I started to slip down the wall. My thighs felt like they'd been set on fire.

Lucy patted the baton against her leg, watching me.

I collapsed, my butt landing hard on the concrete floor. I stretched out my legs. I panted and moaned and spit blood.

"I did not tell you...you could stop," she said, holding the baton against her side.

I braced myself for what was coming next. So far, they hadn't hit me in the face; they'd limited the abuse to the torso, back, and legs.

"Get...up," said Lucy. She knew I wouldn't. She knew I couldn't.

"Just give me a minute," I pleaded. "Just one—"

The spray hit me on the left cheek, just below my eye. But pepper spray, I had come to learn the hard way, didn't need to make direct contact with the eye to cause serious disability and pain.

Within seconds my face felt like it was on fire. My eyes shut involuntarily. I gasped for air and broke out into convulsive coughing. I was on my hands and knees, fighting for whatever air I could take in, my face ravaged with fiery heat.

I panted and gagged and shrieked. It would be a half hour or forty-five minutes before the effects would completely wear off. At which time Lucy would demand that I reassume my position on the wall. Or she'd pull out the OC spray once more.

"*Ce va être une longue nuit,*" my ugly stepsister called out to me.

She was right. It was going to be another long night.

CHAPTER 71

LINETTE MOREAU TOOK Giorgio's hand in hers and stroked it. Most of the time during these two-hour visits, which took place every other Sunday in an airy room filled with other prison visitors, they just gazed into each other's eyes and held hands and touched foreheads from across the table separating them. This day, they'd killed the first hour on gossip: Linette's best friend, Sophie, had broken up with her boyfriend; Linette's mother was trying to quit smoking for the twentieth time; Giorgio's rock band, Noise Pollution, was this close to getting a gig at the Élysée Montmartre, a big break if they could pull it off.

Oh, how she loved this boy. Two years her junior, which made him twenty-eight, a tall Italian with soulful eyes and a smile that leveled her. And he was clean now. They both were. It was the cocaine that had made them do stupid things like steal cars and boost stereos and pick pockets. That chapter of their lives was closed. Giorgio had two legitimate jobs—a courier for a law firm and a bartender at Baxo—while he pursued his dream of making music at night and on the weekends, always carrying that ratty notebook where he penned his lyrics or toting around his prized Les Paul, strumming chords and humming to himself.

She loved him so furiously it made her eyes water, her throat constrict. Just two hundred and six days now until they could be together forever. They would be married on a hillside overlooking a vineyard in Bordeaux.

"So?" he said to her in French. Giorgio was learning English with audio recordings, but he had nowhere near Linette's knowledge of the language. Occasionally they tried to speak in English, but he always defaulted to French. "Tell me about her."

Linette shrugged and responded in French. "If I chose one word? Tough."

"Choose more than one word, Linny. Come on. Everyone is so excited that you're sharing a cell with one of them."

Linette frowned. "She's a sweet girl. And she's tough. The rumor is that the guards are trying to get her to confess to her crime. Sabine assigned Lucy to her."

"Lucy? Ugh."

"Right. The worst of the worst. Every night, they drag her out of the cell and work her over. They gave her the 'bath' the first night. Since then, it's probably their usual bullshit—stress positions and depriving her of sleep. But Abbie hasn't confessed. She just takes their punishment. She doesn't even complain to us."

Linette looked about the room, which held two rows of long tables, filled to maximum capacity with husbands and boyfriends and parents and children, all desperately trying to make the most of the short time they had with the prisoners, trying to fit weeks' and months' and years' worth of love into one hundred and twenty minutes every other weekend. There was not one person among them, prisoner or visitor, who wouldn't leave this room bruised, full of despair and longing and heartache.

"I'm worried about her," Linette said.

"That's why I love you, baby." Giorgio touched her face for a moment. Anything beyond that would catch the attention of the guards. *Contact minimale* was the rule, except for children under the age of twelve, who could sit with, or on the laps of, the female prisoners. "Don't worry," he said. "Time will pass. It will get better."

"Time will pass," she agreed. "But it will get worse. Right now, they can't really hurt her badly, because of the media. The reporters constantly want to visit. Sooner or later, the warden will have to let them in. They can't have anyone photographing Abbie with a broken nose or a black eye. But once the reporters move on to the next scandal? Abbie will have no protection from Lucy and Sabine."

"They'll get what they want," said Giorgio, having served a stint in prison himself.

"Either she'll confess or they'll kill her. One of their famous suicides, maybe."

The next table over, a young child was wailing as he sat on his mother's lap. She was trying in vain to soothe him, but he was inconsolable.

Linette shook her head and sighed. "Sooner or later, they're going to win," she said. "They always do."

CHAPTER 72

SEVEN THIRTY. I counted the minutes. Seven forty. Ten till. The guards called out the ten-minute warning before lights out.

The others settled in for sleep, or to light up their hash and blow the smoke out the window. It was quite a rogues' gallery in cell 413. We had a car thief (Linette) and two killers (Josette and Penelope). We had a deranged arsonist (Lexie). Then there was Camille, in for selling cocaine, though by all indications—stringy hair, pale face, trembling hands, and constant smoking—she was more of a user than a seller. Camille was in rehab but it wasn't going so well. She mumbled to herself and chewed her fingernails down to bloody nubs. Her forearms looked like they'd been attacked by cats.

Finally, there was Mona, a large, nasty woman from a town in northern France called Rouen whose crime, as far as Linette understood it, was dating a Saudi man who was accused of terrorist activities within France. They called her charge criminal association, or something to that effect, and she'd been at JRF for almost three years without having been put on trial.

Other than Linette, they didn't talk to me much. Josette, the unofficial leader, had made it clear to me that my problems could not become my cell mates' problems. They might help me inside the cell, but outside these narrow walls, I was on my own.

Today hadn't been a bad day. I did a shift in the infirmary, where I worked as a nurse's assistant, and helped them save an attempted suicide. Played gin rummy with some of the women in the day area. Dinner included a pork chop that was actually edible. My cell mate Camille, the cocaine addict, showed me photos of her little boy, Gregory, and I helped her make a collage she taped to the wall. In my world, this was an up day.

But it could be a bad night. I never knew. They didn't come for me every night anymore. Maybe Lucy didn't like working the overnight shift every day. Or maybe she and Sabine figured it was more effective to mind-fuck me, that the anticipation would be worse than the actual torture. They'd be right. I didn't sleep well, waiting for them, listening to every footstep I heard outside the cell, wondering if it was one of them coming for me, if it was going to be the steam pipe or the "scarecrow" or the "seat." Batons or pepper spray. Sleep deprivation or screaming in my face all night.

When they didn't come, I would do it all to myself anyway, in my dreams, my nightmares, except that those were worse. There was blood and violent rape and they tore at my flesh and my children were there, watching and calling out to me and sobbing.

Lucy and Sabine were with me even when they were physically absent. And they knew what they were doing. Even when they gave me a night off, they walked by the cell, they hovered at the door a moment, they rattled the latch. They made me wonder. They made me sweat. Sweating wasn't hard when it was more than ninety degrees outside and about a hundred within this cramped cell.

I'd been there six weeks. I don't know precisely when it happened. But I was starting to change. I was curling inward. I saw deprivation and fear and despondency all around me, but I found it harder and harder to worry about anyone besides myself. I started to lose everything that made me human.

Yesterday, I watched Penelope the Spaniard, whose tooth had become infected and had turned black, scream into the intercom for a dentist for the fifth day running, and all I could think was that her problems paled in comparison to mine. I watched Mona, the overweight one, who is in prison basically for having a boyfriend from Saudi Arabia, as she coughed incessantly for the third day in a row, and my only concern was that I didn't want to catch whatever she had. (Of course, I would. We all caught each other's maladies.)

I was no longer Abbie anymore. I was D-11-0215—*onze deux cent quinze*. The number tells anyone that in the year 2011, I was the 215th person admitted to JRF, and that I was assigned to cell block D. The red border around my ID told everyone that I was considered an "extremely high escape risk."

Josette and Mona lit up their hash a few minutes ago, trading the cigarette back and forth and blowing the smoke out our barred window. They knew that the guards, if they came for me, wouldn't come for a few hours yet. And even if they did, they wouldn't object to the hash. They're probably the ones who sold it to them. If they didn't, then they turned a blind eye during visitation while it got passed from visitor to inmate. And they didn't turn a blind eye for free.

Nothing was free in this shithole. Possession isn't nine-tenths of the law at JRF; it's ten-tenths. Prisoners guard whatever item they possess, from a cigarette to a comb to a book to half a cup of apple juice, with uncompromising propriety. You want something, you give something. It's an old-fashioned barter system. The currency could be anything. The most common forms are cigarettes and sex. Or something you want from the commissary—toiletries, a radio, clothes, stationery. Sometimes it's a favor. Mona, for example, not being the most ambitious or tidy gal, let Penelope get high with her last night if she agreed to make Mona's bed for a week (we can't leave our cell unless our beds are made, which isn't a problem for me, as I don't *have* a bed).

Lights out. Josette and Mona kept smoking, the orange tip of the cigarette glowing in the darkness. Penelope read a fashion magazine with her night-light. Lexie, the crazy arsonist, hummed to music on her headphones.

An hour passed. Two. Three. With my own night-light, I read

and reread letters from Richie and Elena. They were glad to be back in Connecticut, I could tell. Back with their friends. The ink was smeared from my tears, which fell in healthy quantities off my cheeks. This was when I cried. When the lights were out or when everyone was asleep. When nobody could see me.

Near midnight I heard footsteps. I watched the small sliver of light under our cell door, waiting for the shadow to cover it. It happened soon enough. The shuffle of boots on concrete, coming to a stop at my door. The latch unlocking. My heartbeat fluttered. I held my breath. One part of me mentally prepared for another night. Another part begged them to go away, to make the monsters go away, to leave me alone.

Leave me alone. Please leave me alone! Just one night of peace!

I hadn't waved the white flag yet. But they were winning.

CHAPTER 73

I TOOK A seat in the large room in F wing and looked around. Prisoners were spilling in and looking for seats, sometimes in groups with friends.

It was movie night. The prison got a different film every month and showed it on various nights to accommodate the two thousand inmates. I signed up for this one because it was an American movie—*Sex and the City 2*—so it would be easier for me to follow. But truthfully, any time I spent out of my cell was like a reprieve.

And I was hoping that I might see one of my friends. I hadn't laid eyes on Winnie, Serena, or Bryah since we arrived at the prison. Each of us had been placed in a different cell block. The warden had a built-in excuse—we were still subject to our appeal, so we weren't supposed to communicate. But the truth was, he wanted to keep the heat on us, especially me. If only I would confess—

There. There she was. Winnie. I stood up and saw her before she saw me.

My heart swelled. I hardly recognized her. She looked haggard, depleted. An unhealthy kind of skinny, with sunken eyes.

When she saw me, she lit up. Before we reached each other, we were both crying. Everything that had happened so far, the terror and pain and despair, came pouring out. We held each other until a guard divided us with a soft rebuke. When we separated, I noted how many people were observing us. I sometimes forgot we were celebrities in here.

We took seats in a middle row, creating a distance between us and the guards, who mostly sat in the back. We had our arms around each other. We stroked each other's hair. We touched heads. The room went dark and the screen lit up with the movie, but neither of us was watching it.

"It's just bloody awful in here, isn't it?" she whispered.

I moaned. "Let's not go there. Have you talked to the others?"

"I saw Bryah once. She's in with the Muslims, y'know."

I'd heard. They separated the races in here. As best they could, at least. Most of the prisoners in here were white. The blacks and Muslims, together, formed about a quarter of the prison population, so they were put together.

"I saw her at the library," Winnie added. "She's learning Arabic."

We both laughed. That was *so* Bryah. God, it felt good to laugh.

"What about Serena?" I asked.

Winnie shrugged. "I saw her once. She's doing pretty well, actually. Nobody messes with her. I guess being so strong and athletic helps. She's in cell block A and has only one other person in her cell, an elderly woman."

"Wow." That must be nice. Luck of the draw, I guess. Or maybe Serena had proven herself early on, with her fists. Either way—good for her.

"Bryah told me...she said they're being awful to you. They're trying to get you to confess?"

It figured that Bryah would have a grapevine in here. Once an information junkie, always an information junkie. "I'm a big girl," I said. "Have you seen Christien? The kids?"

We'd been here ten weeks now, so with visitation privileges limited to every other week, she could have seen Christien four or five times by now.

Winnie was quiet a moment. "It's... hard. It's the best part and the hardest part. Right?" Then she looked at me. She knew, presumably, of the rift between Jeffrey and me. "Have you seen your family?"

I shook my head no. "I don't know if I can stand the thought of the kids coming here, seeing this. And Jeffrey... he's coming next week, I think. We're writing letters."

"Christien said Jeff's going back to the States. Is that true?"

It was. Jeffrey's days at the U.S. Embassy in Switzerland had been numbered since my arrest, even more so once his affair with the ambassador became public knowledge. They weren't so barbaric as to fire him while we were in crisis mode, but now that the trial was over, the writing was on the wall. Jeffrey was going back to Georgetown. On the plus side, he'd be a lot closer to Richie and Elena, who had returned to their boarding school in Connecticut. On the down side...

"He'll be so far away," Winnie whispered.

I leaned into her. "I think that's okay with him, Win. Know what I mean?"

She let out a pained sigh. "Oh, God. I'm so sorry. Abbie, I'm so dreadfully sorry about all of this. All of this is my fault—"

"Shh." But Winnie couldn't be consoled. She broke down, quietly sobbing. I held her and closed my eyes and savored the warmth of my friend. It went on like that for a good thirty minutes. I didn't mind a wet shoulder. It felt so good having Winnie close again.

When it was over, when her body had stopped trembling, Winnie was quiet for a long time. Then she put her mouth up close to my ear.

"I can't do this," she said. "I'm not going to make it in here much longer."

CHAPTER 74

I SAT WAITING in the visitation room, watching the female prisoners interacting with their children and siblings and spouses. It was hard to watch. Hard to watch couples wanting desperately to embrace but being limited by the rule of *contact minimale,* nothing more than a brief kiss upon entry and departure. Hard to watch mothers being pried away from their kids at the end of a session. Hard to listen to the agonizing wails of small children who didn't understand why Mommy couldn't come home with them.

These women had it rough. The vast majority of them were inside because of drugs or because of the man they were with. Most of them lacked a high school education. Many of them were illiterate. Most of them would get out of prison with little hope of making it and would end up addicted again, or they would commit another crime, or both.

My visitor was late, so my eyes dropped back down to the newspaper I was reading. We usually got the French papers a day late, and the American papers two or three days after publication. But it made no difference to us prisoners. The papers were our only consistent source of news, so the information was current as far as we were concerned.

I was reading a *USA Today* from three days ago, an article on a guy I once knew named Damon Kodiak.

Damon had been pushing a film for several years, without any takers in Hollywood. *Der Führer* would be a controversial movie, to say the least. A biopic of Adolf Hitler that explored in depth his childhood, his friendships, his relationship with Eva Braun. A sympathetic portrait of a man whom history regarded with little sympathy.

Hollywood had flatly said no. Kodiak had a concept, but he didn't have money. Still, he didn't stop. Over the last eighteen months he'd managed to scrape together financing—private money—and finally made the film. His first time behind the camera, also starring in the lead role. Written by, directed by, and starring Damon Kodiak. It would be his *Passion of the Christ,* or it would be a colossal flop.

Last weekend, *Der Führer* had opened in the United States with a box-office gross of seventy-two million dollars. It was the biggest opening of Damon Kodiak's career and perhaps signaled his rebirth at age forty-eight. The movie would be opening soon in Europe, where it was projected to set box-office records.

So our lives had taken slightly divergent paths since our night together in Monte Carlo.

"Sorry I'm late." Joseph Morro, the Paris correspondent for *The New York Times,* dropped his satchel on the table and pulled out a notepad. "Thanks for agreeing to the interview."

"I agreed to talk to you," I said.

Morro didn't seem to catch the distinction. He looked down at my newspaper. "Reading about your boyfriend, I see." He didn't try to conceal his sarcasm. He'd made it pretty clear in the daily blog he wrote during the trial that, like most everyone else, he found it utterly implausible that a gal like me would have spent the night on a yacht with Damon.

"I'm innocent," I said to him. "And I intend to prove it at my appeal. I will find the real killer if it's the last thing I do."

He cocked his head. "Great. Now can we start the interview?"

"I didn't agree to an interview. I agreed to talk to you."

"You agreed—" Morro drew back, replaying the words. "You're not going to let me ask you questions?"

"Now you're catching on, Joe. Here's my quote for you: I'm innocent. I intend to prove it at my appeal. I won't rest until I find the real killer." I stood up from the bench. "Have a safe trip back."

"Abbie, c'mon. There's nothing for me to print."

But he'd print it. These guys were starving for news on the Monte Carlo Mistresses. It would be a nice lead-in for a story on the upcoming appeal. It wasn't much, but it was more than any other reporter had from me.

And for my purposes, it was all I needed to do.

CHAPTER 75

IN THE WARDEN'S office, the phone receiver remained in its cradle. The government-issued cell phone rested on the warden's desk as well.

No, this was a call the warden, Boulez, would take on his private cell phone.

"You know why I'm calling, don't you?" the man said to Boulez.

"I believe I do." Boulez had the Internet open on his computer, to the lead story by the *Times* correspondent in Paris, Joseph Morro. The headline alone said it all: ELLIOT: "I WILL NOT REST UNTIL I FIND THE KILLER."

A defiant Abbie Elliot, proclaiming her innocence to *The New York Times* and vowing to prove it at her appeal.

"How did you let that happen?" the man asked.

"I cannot keep reporters away," Boulez whispered into his cell phone. "And I cannot control what she says to them."

"You're the goddamn warden, Boulez. You control *everything*. So control *her*."

Boulez looked at the photos on his ego wall, a shot of him receiving an award for distinguished service from the Minister of Justice and Liberty. He saw his reflection in the glass and looked away.

"We have tried," he said. "She is...exceptionally resistant to persuasion."

"'Exceptionally resistant'?" The man scoffed. "Then be exceptionally persuasive."

"I will...evaluate our methods. Perhaps—"

"Perhaps," the man said, "there is an alternative to a confession. So that we'd never hear from Abbie Elliot again?"

Boulez paused a beat. The thought had crossed his mind, of course. "But now?" he said to the man. "After she just gave this...defiant statement to the press? It would be more than just a coincidence if something happened to her now. And a suicide would be impossible to believe."

The man was quiet a moment. "She probably knows that," he said. "That's probably why she said those things to the reporter. To insulate herself."

"Perhaps so," Boulez conceded. "She is smart."

"Then you'll have to be smarter, Boulez, won't you?"

Boulez exhaled slowly. "There are still two months remaining before her appeal."

"I don't *have* two months, Boulez. Which means you don't, either. Get this done right away. I want that confession yesterday. And if you can't do that, then take care of the problem the other way."

The line went dead. Boulez pinched the bridge of his nose. Abbie hadn't cracked yet, hadn't confessed and dropped her appeal. And he was running out of time.

But surely he could think of something.

CHAPTER 76

"THE SUITE WAS like a square," I said to Linette, as she sat on one of the beds in the infirmary. She had a laceration on her arm. The nurse, Leonore, had treated it and now I was wrapping it with a bandage. "Winnie and I were in the front room. Bryah and Serena stayed in the back room, by the balcony."

"How long would it take?" Linette asked.

I thought for a moment. "Not long to get to Winnie's and my room. That was right by the front door. Pull out some Kleenex that Winnie had used from the trash for her mucus. Grab one of my used Q-tips for the earwax. Pull hair out of our brushes. Find something with our fingerprints. Two, three minutes?" I estimated. "Then do the same in the other bedroom—Bryah and Serena's bedroom. Then plant the evidence at the crime scene."

"But why didn't they get any DNA from Bryah? Serena, yes, but not Bryah?"

I shrugged. We could never figure why there was no evidence planted at the crime scene that implicated Bryah. The three of us, dead to rights; Bryah, nothing.

"Maybe…they only got to the first room," Linette suggested.

"Yours and Winnie's. Maybe they were afraid to stay longer than that."

I shrugged. That made some sense, of course. Whoever it was, not wanting to linger and be caught, might just pop into the first bedroom and then get out. But that logic had one obvious flaw. "That would explain why they had nothing from Bryah," I agreed. "But then how did they have forensic evidence of Serena?"

Linette shook her head. She didn't have an answer. Neither of us did.

The dimensions of the infirmary reminded me of my high school gym, except the ceilings were very low here. It was exceptionally bright—so bright that I had to squint every time I walked in. But I welcomed the contrast from the dreariness.

There were twenty-five beds on one side and a cage on the other side, where the prisoners waited to be seen. On one of the short sides of the rectangle was *la pharmacie,* the room with medical supplies and prescription drugs. On the other short side was the room where Linette and I were right now—a secure area, big enough for five patients, usually reserved for special cases, such as people with contagious maladies or those who posed security risks. If the room was otherwise vacant, as it was now, we used it for overflow.

Up in the corner of the room, a security camera monitored us. This room, with its wall of thick glass separating us from the main room, its privacy blinds, and a door that locked from the inside, could otherwise be pretty private if not for the surveillance camera. A fortress, actually. That thought drifted in and out of my mind.

"Abbie, I need ampicillin." The nurse, Leonore, was in the main room, treating a prisoner with a bladder infection. She spoke passable English and liked to practice it on me. "Can you re—receive it for me?"

"I can *retrieve* it for you," I said with a smile. She laughed at her mistake. She handed me the key to the pharmacy. This was, as a technical matter, strictly forbidden. Only doctors or licensed nurses could enter the room. But as a practical matter, the nurse couldn't afford to spend her time going back and forth to the drug room. The infirmary was notoriously understaffed. We were lucky if even a single nurse showed up on a daily basis; a doctor came, at most, every other day. The waiting line to get treated usually went out the door. So time was precious, and if an assistant could be trusted to run back and forth to *la pharmacie,* so much the better.

That was a big "if," though. Letting a prisoner near drugs was like letting a bank robber into Fort Knox. So Leonore was saying something here by trusting me.

You took what good you could in here. It didn't come often.

After I delivered the ampicillin to Nurse Leonore, waited for her to use it, then returned it to the pharmacy and signed it back in—all under the watchful eye of a security camera—I returned to Linette in the secured room.

She was done now, her bandage wrapped. She wagged a finger at me.

"That's what you have to figure out," she said to me in French, the language in which she felt more comfortable. "You have to figure out why they had evidence of Serena, but not Bryah."

CHAPTER 77

SEVENTEEN HUNDRED HOURS, or five in the evening, was the time for "lockup." With very few exceptions, all prisoners were required to be in their cells from then until morning. For *la compte,* the nightly accounting of inmates before nightfall, we had to stand at attention in the middle of our cells for the guards to see us through the hatch and count us. Usually, somewhere along the way they would miscount and have to start over. Once we were all accounted for, dinner was served.

After we were counted and recounted, we settled in and waited for dinner. I watched with indifference as a rat the size of a Chihuahua poked its head out from under one of the beds and then retreated. He must have heard about dinner, too.

"Lexie," Josette called out. I wasn't sure what Josette had done to become the unofficial leader of our cell, but the leader she was. She was telling Lexie, the deranged arsonist who never left the cell, that she had to find the spot from which the rat had entered the cell and plug the hole. All along the intersection of the floor and the wall, we had stuffed newspaper, pages from magazines, or, if we had nothing else, balled-up underwear or T-shirts in the cracks.

Lexie jumped off the bunk, pulled some newspaper out of the trash, and crawled under the bed. Lexie was afraid of leaving her cell—hell, she was afraid of her own shadow—but the rats and roaches didn't faze her.

"Where's Mona?" I asked. Mona, the only overweight one of our bunch, usually ate her own dinner and then some of ours.

"*La bibliothèque.*" The library, Josette explained. Mona worked there, and tonight a new shipment of books had come in that would require the removal of some old periodicals to make room.

The prisoners with the most privileges—or, if you prefer, the drug dealers—were the "porters" who delivered the food on wheeled carts. They knocked on the door and we held out our tin plates, on which they dropped our meat and vegetable and starch, plus juice or water. Usually a quarter loaf of French bread as well. And then some extra goodies, like a hash cigarette or pills, for those who had made that purchase.

They slipped the hash to Josette tonight, not even trying to conceal it from the rest of us. I retreated to the corner with my plate of mystery meat, green beans, and something brown that could have been sweet potatoes or maybe baked beans. Another gourmet meal *chez* JRF.

At midnight, the door latch popped open. My heartbeat fluttered. It was Lucy. Another night of torture.

We walked in silence, the two of us. Lucy kept a distance behind me. I wasn't handcuffed but she'd frisked me, as always, so she knew I wasn't carrying a weapon.

She was humming to herself. Having a grand time. After descending the stairs, we walked back through several barred doors to the center of the prison—to get from any block or wing to another, you first had to return to the center—and turned toward H wing.

This was different. Usually we went to the basement.

Each wing was secured by a guard at the intersection of the wing and the center. If there was a way out on the other side of the wing, such as H wing's exit into the prison yard, there was a guard at that end, too. Always in a booth with bulletproof glass and a weapons stash.

Lucy removed her pepper spray and handed it to the guard in the booth. Same for her handcuffs. That was also different. I'd never seen her surrender these weapons.

Where were we going?

It was sickly hot in the corridor, the humidity lingering from the scorching temperatures today. And my nerves were twitching. It wasn't like I enjoyed being subjected to the "scarecrow" or the "chair" or the pepper spray—but at least I knew what to expect. Something was different tonight, and I doubted it would be a pleasant surprise.

We stopped at room H-11. When the door opened, I saw a cot and a card table, on top of which was a bottle of vodka and three paper cups.

And Sabine, the head guard, standing in one corner with a grin on her face.

CHAPTER 78

LUCY PUSHED ME into the room. I lunged forward but then stopped and turned so that my back was to neither Lucy nor Sabine. I backpedaled to the wall.

In French, Lucy said, "Take off your clothes."

We were required to submit to a strip search upon any guard's request at any time. I had no legal right to say no. "No," I said.

There was one window, covered with iron bars, that looked out over the courtyard where we first got off the bus, where Sabine first beat the piss out of me. Lucy closed the inside shutter, leaving the three of us in total privacy.

Lucy and Sabine looked at each other, and they seemed to make a decision that Sabine would be first. I wasn't sure what that meant but I had an idea.

Lucy poured herself and Sabine a cup of vodka. She even offered me one but I was too tense to respond. My hands balled into fists.

The two guards saluted each other and downed their shots. Sabine sat on the cot and loosened the belt on her pants.

In French, Lucy said, "You will pleasure us. First, Sabine."

I didn't respond, didn't move, which itself was an answer.

Sabine pulled down her pants and lay flat on the cot, resting her disgusting little head on the pillow. Lucy advanced on me with predatory eyes and her baton drawn. "You will do this," she said.

I shook my head no. Lucy got close to me and swatted the baton in my direction. She wasn't trying for serious contact, but she caught my hand, raised in defense, rapping my knuckles hard. I shuffled away from her, as if we were doing a dance around the room. She was herding me toward the cot, where Sabine had now pulled her underwear down to her ankles and awaited me.

"You will do this," said Lucy in French, "or you will never walk the same again."

She swatted the baton at me once more, this time landing with a crack on my wrist. I was like a trapped mouse, my back against the wall, ready to move in either direction, while Lucy shadowed me.

"No!" I blurted out with rising panic.

"Lucy," Sabine called out. In my peripheral vision, I saw Sabine hike up her underwear and pants. *"Nous devons commencer avec elle."*

We will have to start with her. A shudder coursed through me.

Sabine got off the cot, took her baton, and joined Lucy. Lucy handed her baton to Sabine, so her hands were free.

In an instant, Lucy was on me, grabbing my hair with one hand and tearing at my shirt with the other. She wrestled me to the floor and I tried to scream but sheer terror prevented me from uttering a sound. I moved my legs furiously and tried to push her off me but she was far stronger than I was, and her fury seemed to outweigh my fear.

Her forearm to my face held me down and she yanked off my pants. I tried desperately to find my voice, as if it would do any good to scream in here, as if anyone would listen, and I realized that as brutal as the physical torture had been, it didn't hold a candle to this, to this violation, this utter invasion—

"Hold still!" Lucy grunted into my face. I was now naked from the waist down, as Sabine approached me with her baton in one hand.

Tears blinded my eyes, my pulse exploded through my body, bells and whistles screaming in my brain—*DON'T, PLEASE DON'T*—

And then the alarm bells went off. Real ones, booming sirens throughout the prison. All of us froze. We looked at each other for a beat before panic spread across Lucy's face.

Real alarms. Sirens with a distinctive cadence—three quick beeps, buzz. Three quick beeps, buzz. I'd never heard them before, but they'd been explained to me. They could mean only one thing.

Someone was trying to escape.

CHAPTER 79

I QUICKLY DRESSED and Lucy handcuffed me to the cot. She and Sabine rushed out, bolting the door behind them. I dragged the cot toward the window and used my free hand to open the shutter.

If I hadn't seen it with my own eyes, I wouldn't have believed it. The rooftop lights were all turned on. A searchlight coming from the prison yard provided further illumination, sweeping across the midnight sky as it tried to stay locked on the helicopter hovering over the rooftop.

The copter was blue with white trim. A rope dangled down from the copter and a woman was climbing it, struggling as the rope swayed from side to side and the copter bobbed like a buoy in the ocean. From the copter, gunfire erupted from some kind of rifle toward the courtyard. The guards in the towers on each side of the front gate, to my right, had opened fire on the copter. The woman was struggling to climb the ladder. She was heavyset and her ponytail—wait—

"Mona," I said. My cell mate Mona was escaping. Right—she'd been working late tonight in the library, which was in the back of the prison.

The gunfire abated from the guard tower nearest me. Had someone been shot? I didn't know. Guards in the tower on the other flank were still firing on the helicopter, sparks flying off the copter's body as it bobbed and spun, making it difficult for Mona to climb.

She was halfway up the rope when the helicopter rose. A decision by the pilot. Escaping with Mona dangling from the rope was preferable to being shot out of the sky.

Right decision, but too late. A burst of flame came from the rear of the copter and it began to spin out of control. The copter rose a bit higher and then veered sharply to its left, toward the courtyard, moving almost sideways through the air and losing altitude.

I averted my eyes but not in time. I saw Mona lose her grip on the ladder and fly through the air before plummeting to the courtyard face-first. My eyes moved away just as I saw her head burst open on impact. A moment later, the helicopter crashed down on its nose, not twenty yards from Mona's body, bursting into flames.

I felt the heat on my face, the sting in my eyes. This was happening right in front of me, maybe thirty yards away. The tactical-response guards didn't stop shooting into the helicopter until the fire department showed up, maybe twenty minutes later, spraying the orange flames and dark clouds of smoke until nothing was left but a melted, twisted bird.

I closed the shutter as the smoke drifted toward me, closing my nose to the putrid scent of burned gasoline. It reminded me of the Molotov cocktails, of the attack on the police convoy during the trial. But I had lived to see another day.

Mona Mourcelles would not.

CHAPTER 80

THE SIX OF US STOOD, handcuffed, outside cell 413 while the guards tossed the room. *Une recherche,* they called it—a search. The prison retained the right to inspect our cells at any time for contraband. They went through the mattresses and our books and opened our personal boxes—each of us had a rectangular box where we could hold any personal items, from candy to cigarettes to CDs, whatever we bought from the commissary that would fit in there.

The guards removed a bunch of stuff from the cell. Then they marched us down to the basement and interrogated us. They stripped us naked, hosed us down, and threw out a few questions to us while they beat us with their batons. It wasn't much of an interrogation. It was more an outlet for their anger.

Mona and the two Saudis in the helicopter—friends of her boyfriend—had perished in the failed escape. But more important than all that, a prison guard in the tower had died in a spray of gunfire. The guards had lost one of their own, and someone had to pay. Might as well be Mona's cell mates, even though, as far as I knew, none of us had been aware of Mona's plans.

The six of us lay huddled on the floor, shivering from the cold spray that hit us every few minutes, covering our heads while the guards rained down blows with their batons. Lexie, lying next to me, was positively terrified. This was the first time I'd seen her outside the cell. She'd gone about twenty months, at this point, without leaving it.

"*Qui a su du plan?*" they kept asking. Who knew of her plan? The longer we failed to answer, the angrier the guards became. They had lost control of their rage. They were swinging the batons wildly, striking our feet and ankles, our midsections, even our heads. I'd been on the receiving end of a lot of abuse, but I'd never seen anything this violent, this uncontrolled.

"*Elle ne nous a pas dit!*" Linette protested, sitting up. She didn't tell us, she was saying. Yelling back at the guards didn't seem like a bright idea here, even if Linette was speaking the truth.

One of the guards whom I didn't know moved toward Linette after her outburst. But Lucy intervened, putting a hand on the guard. Lucy wanted to handle this one herself. She smiled broadly at me, then grabbed Linette by the hair and dragged her out of the room.

"Linette!" I started to crawl toward her, passing Lexie, when I heard something from one of the guards and then it hit me, square on the mouth, a blow from the baton.

My head snapped back. My eyes rolled back in my head. And then everything went black.

CHAPTER 81

I WOKE UP vomiting on a stained concrete floor. My jaw ached so badly I thought it might be broken. My face felt puffy. I was so dizzy that I couldn't maintain my balance.

I surveyed my surroundings. The room was about six, maybe seven square meters. A high ceiling from which a lone lightbulb hung. Walls covered with mildew and laden with graffiti. Stains all along the floor.

This was segregation. Solitary confinement, as it's known in the States. Le Mitard, they called it here.

I crawled over to the faucet, which jutted out from the wall like an outdoor spigot, and turned it on. The pressure was weak, the water lukewarm. I held a hand under it and splashed it on my face. Drank a little. It was potable, but bitter with the taste of iron. I spat blood into the drain on the floor.

The intercom, up high on the wall, crackled. *"Mettez votre dos à la porte et les mains par l'ouverture,"* the voice said.

I forced myself to my feet. My knees were dirty and bloody and stiff. The front of my shirt was covered in blood and vomit. I was woozy but I managed to comply with the guard's directive. I stood against the door and placed my hands behind me, through the opening. A pair of handcuffs slid over my wrists.

"*Reculez-vous de la porte.*"

I complied again, standing back from the door, my hands cuffed behind me. A guard entered and grabbed me from behind by my handcuffs, directing me out of the cell.

"What happened to Linette?" I asked. "*Qu'est-il arrivé à Linette?*"

The guard didn't answer. She just marched me back to my cell. My head was ringing and my nausea was replaced with a sense of dread.

The guard opened my cell door. Inside, the place was a disaster from the guards tossing it, searching for contraband. Four of my cell mates sat silently, as if in shock.

Josette, the leader. Penelope, the Spaniard. Camille, the drug addict. Lexie, the deranged arsonist.

Mona, of course, was dead from the aborted escape.

That left Linette as the only one unaccounted for.

"*Où est Linette?*" I asked.

Josette was the only one who would make eye contact with me. Her expression was as hard as ever, but her eyes were brimming with tears.

She shook her head slowly.

It took a moment before it registered, before I absorbed it. "No!" I cried. I collapsed to the floor. "No!" I pounded on the concrete and just screamed, guttural cries, my throat filled with anguish and venom. Another wave of nausea surged through me and I retched several times, dry-heaving bile, the contents of my stomach having long been expelled.

"Not Linette," I pleaded in vain. Not when she was only months away from release, when she was going to marry the love of her life, Giorgio.

After a while I was merely panting like a rabid animal.

"*Ils l'ont tuée,*" I said. They killed her.

Josette looked up at the ceiling. "*C'était un accident,*" she said. "*Elle est tombée et a frappé sa tête.*"

"What?" I raised my head. "She didn't slip and hit her head. This wasn't some *accident*. Lucy killed her! Lucy killed her!" I repeated.

"*Non*." Josette's voice trembled. "*Un accident*."

I stared at Josette, then at the others. They were all nodding along with Josette. I realized I'd been mistaken. My cell mates weren't in shock. They were terrified. Scared to death. Even Josette, the hardest of the bunch, was singing the company line: Linette had fallen and struck her head. Nobody was willing to say that Lucy had beaten our friend to death.

Because if they did, the next "accident" would be theirs.

"We can't let them get away with this!" I said, getting to my feet. I repeated myself, this time in French, but I could see it didn't matter which language I spoke.

"*Nous n'avons pas un choix*," Penelope said.

"Of course we have a choice," I pleaded. "Of *course* we do."

But I was arguing in vain. There was nothing I could say that would talk them out of their fear.

Linette, my dear friend—*our* dear friend, *everyone's* friend in JRF—was dead, murdered by Lucy, and we were going to turn our backs and pretend the whole thing was a slip-and-fall.

"Murderers!" I banged on the buzzer for the intercom, screaming into it. Josette and Penelope rushed from their beds and grabbed me, restrained me. I fought them off initially and kept whacking at the intercom, which never answered me. Finally they tackled me to the ground, where I lay sobbing and hyperventilating until the lights went out at eight o'clock.

CHAPTER 82

"YOU SHOULD SAY something," said my husband, Jeffrey.

Six days had passed since Linette's death. Six days of staring at the walls of my cell, at the bed once occupied by Linette, hardly eating, hardly speaking other than when I went to the infirmary for my job. The prison had conducted its typical "investigation" into Linette's death and come back with the unsurprising "finding" that Linette Giselle Moreau had died when she slipped in her cell and struck her head on the floor. Four of her five cell mates, in their interviews, corroborated this version of events. I was the lone holdout. The official paperwork described me as *peu coopératif*—uncooperative—and "unwilling to give a suitable account of the event."

The guards had been shrewd in their write-up. They estimated the time of death as falling between 7:30 and 8:30 in the morning, which placed the occurrence right near the 8:00 a.m. shift change. This, I had come to learn, was how it worked when fatal "accidents" occurred at JRF. If there were ever an official inquiry by the Ministry of Justice and Liberty, not only would it be difficult to isolate a particular guard as the culprit, but it would be impossible to even identify which *shift* of guards was on duty at the time—the crew that was ending at 8:00 a.m. or the one that was just starting.

"Anything," said Jeffrey. "Tell me what you think."

Across from me, dressed comfortably in a button-down shirt and blue jeans, sat my husband. This was Jeffrey's first time visiting me. It only took him three and a half months. Sometimes he'd tried excuses—the move back to the States, getting settled back into civilian life at Georgetown, spending weekends with the kids, who were still having a really tough time with all this. Take your pick: Jeff could invent a reason not to visit.

Sometimes he didn't even bother with an excuse.

I couldn't totally fault him. We hadn't parted on good terms, after all, and it wasn't like our marriage was in fabulous shape before my arrest.

"Abbie, c'mon," Jeffrey repeated. "Talk to me."

I gave him a cold smile. "You pass on a dozen chances to visit. You wait almost four months before you show your face. Then, within ten minutes of gracing me with an appearance, you tell me you want out of our marriage. And now the burden's on *me* to say something."

"Abbie—"

"How about, 'Fuck you'? Does that work, Jeff?"

A large part of me wasn't surprised. I guess I should have been grateful he didn't just drop the divorce papers in the mail.

"Listen, Abbie," he said, knifing a hand on the table. "We both made some mistakes—"

I laughed out loud. "You have a speech prepared? Are you kidding me?" I leaned into him. "Yes, we both made mistakes. Letting you talk me into dropping my career and moving to Switzerland, for starters, so you could fuck the ambassador while I stayed home waiting like a helpless little housewife—"

"And I believe the entire *world* knows of *your* indiscretion," he hissed back. He read the expression on my face. "Oh, what—your little romp in the hay was different? It doesn't count if it's with a movie star?"

Incredibly, this was the first time we'd ever discussed the topic.

Both of our "indiscretions," as Jeff put it, became part of my trial, part of the overall story, part of the tabloid hysterics the world over. But we avoided talking about it one-on-one.

"You'd already broken us," I replied. "You, with your damn affair. What I did was wrong, and I take responsibility for it. But it wasn't some planned, long-term relationship, sneaking around behind your back and inventing all sorts of excuses. It was an impulse, after I'd drunk more alcohol than—"

"Oh, just spare me that 'spur-of-the-moment' crap, all right?" Jeffrey waved a hand. His face was crimson and his eyes rabid. "Like you didn't go to Monte Carlo looking for it. Like you weren't looking for it earlier that day at that pool. You were carrying on like a little tramp! Giggling and flirting at the pool in your skimpy little bikini—"

One of the guards slapped a hand down on our table. *"Si vous ne restez pas tranquille, votre mari devra partir,"* he said, threatening to end the visit if we didn't quiet down.

"Excusez," Jeffrey said in apology. He took a breath and settled down.

My blood had gone cold. I just stared at Jeffrey, my body still as a statue but my mind racing. I was pretty sure that the color had drained from my face.

Jeffrey let out a long sigh. "I'm sorry for what I did. I've paid a pretty damn high price for it—but I'm sorry all the same. But now it's a—"

I felt myself get up from the table. Suddenly, I couldn't be in the same room with this man. "You can have the divorce," I said, or words to that effect. I don't know what I said. I just wanted to get away from him. I needed to think.

Like you weren't looking for it earlier that day at that pool.

Carrying on like a little tramp. Giggling and flirting at the pool in your skimpy little bikini.

"I really am sorry," Jeffrey said. "But really, Abbie—you can't be surprised."

Surprised? It depended on what he meant.

I wasn't surprised that he was asking for a divorce. I knew that day would come.

But I was very surprised indeed to learn that Jeffrey had been in Monte Carlo on the day that President Henri Devereux was murdered.

CHAPTER 83

I STOOD AT THE door of my cell at twelve forty-five, standard operating procedure when moving about the prison. Stand at your cell fifteen minutes before your assignment—work, library trip, visitation, whatever—and wait for the guard to escort you where you needed to go. My shift at the infirmary started at one o'clock.

My brain was buzzing from what Jeffrey had told me this morning. Not the divorce, of course, but his comments about my behavior at the Monte Carlo Beach Hotel on the afternoon before President Devereux's murder. It was a slip of the tongue, in the heat of the worst kind of argument—one between unhappy spouses, in which the rawest of emotions surface. Jeffrey hadn't even realized he'd said it. He apparently had no idea what he'd just revealed to me.

I thought about it over and over. Yes, the evidence presented at trial established that we had spent some time at that hotel swimming pool. But there weren't any photos of us. Zero. And there wasn't any mention of us flirting with anyone, or of my wearing a bikini. Nobody had said one word about how we conducted ourselves at that pool.

No. Jeffrey would have had to see these things himself, personally.

Jeffrey was in Monte Carlo that day.

I didn't know how to process that information. I didn't know what, exactly, it meant. He never told anybody, that much was clear. In fact, he'd lied about it. But what did it mean? I hadn't, for even one second, considered the possibility that Jeffrey—my *husband*—no, it couldn't be. No.

No?

All I knew for sure was that certain avenues, previously closed to me, were now open. I needed to talk to Winnie.

I was handcuffed and frisked and escorted to G wing. I gave my ID number to the guard stationed there and then walked the corridor unescorted. I passed a door on my right, which led down to the underground parking garage for the prison staff, accessible only by a key card and monitored by a guard at a secure booth. I walked past another door that I had been told was a fire escape. I stopped at the red line before the infirmary, where another guard was stationed in a secure booth, complete with a weapons arsenal, security cameras looking inside the infirmary, the whole thing.

"Hi, Abbie." The guard was named Cecile. I liked her. One of the decent ones who treated us civilly, either out of compassion or because she realized that we were easier to manage when treated with some measure of respect.

After a loud, echoing buzz, the door marked INFIRMERIE released with a hiss.

I squinted into the bright light and fought off the impulse to gag when I inhaled the wretched smell of bodily secretions and powerful disinfectant. It was like not showering for a week but bathing yourself in cologne. Like riding in a cab in New York City.

The beds were filled, as usual. Pack two thousand people into a space reserved for roughly half that many and even the most mundane virus or malady becomes an epidemic. Plus, being sick gave people an excuse to get out of their cells. But it cost them. Unless you were really sick, getting the okay to visit the infirmary was like everything else around here. It wasn't free.

I saw Winnie at the far end, wrapping a bandage on an Arab woman's foot. Her shift was ending. The warden didn't allow us to communicate, so they tried to arrange our shifts so we never worked together. It wasn't a perfect system, but typically we only saw each other, as we did now, in passing.

"Hey." She whispered in her lovely British accent. Her fingers touched mine. "I heard what happened. You okay?"

Everyone had heard about Linette. She was a favorite around here. "Living the dream," I said. "You?"

She wasn't in the mood for humor. "Movie night," she whispered. "I'll save you a seat. Love you."

Movie night. I would tell Winnie tonight. I would tell her what Jeffrey had inadvertently blurted out to me. She could help me figure this out.

"Love you, too. Get some rest." Our fingertips released.

I quickly went about my assignments. This job, the chance to help people, was about the only thing propelling me forward now. I did some bandage wraps. I helped flush some minor wounds. I fetched some drugs from the pharmacy across the room for the nurse. An hour passed. Two o'clock was a shift change for the guards, and out the window I could see various cars driving up the ramp from the underground garage. Pulling up to the large main gate. Swiping their key cards to open it. Waving to the attendant, who was raised ten feet off the ground in a fortified booth. Driving off to freedom, once the gate opened.

Another half hour later, I heard the commotion as the hydraulic door buzzed open. I had my back turned to the entrance. I was helping a nurse dress a laceration wound to an inmate's rib cage when one of the nurses shouted, *"Urgence!"*

Emergency. Not uncommon. We had a suicide a week in JRF. I turned as guards and a nurse wheeled in an inmate on a gurney.

"Oh, God, no." I dropped the gauze pads I was holding. I started running before the realization had fully formed in my head. The shock of black hair hanging below the gurney. The look on the face of one of the nurses, who had turned back from the commotion to look at me, to see if it had registered with me who the new patient was. Everyone knew the four of us as a group, after all.

"Winnie," I whispered.

The guards saw me coming and restrained me. I fought them, tried to break through them, as the doctor worked feverishly on Winnie. I cried out as the guards forced me to the ground, slamming my head against the tile.

This was too much. Overload. Not Winnie, too. Not *Winnie*.

I fought and I screamed and I pleaded. The doctor stopped working on her and called out the time of death and I shouted and kicked and I felt something inside of me die, something that would never return.

CHAPTER 84

OVER THE NEXT ten hours I put it together.

I awoke in Le Mitard, solitary confinement, handcuffed to the metal ring protruding from the wall. Blood in my mouth, burning pain in my ribs, bruises on my wrists.

My first instinct was to scream, but my vocal cords were worn raw. And I'd cried enough already. I'd shed enough tears to fill the Seine. That reservoir was now dry. And another emotion had overtaken my sadness: fear.

I gave myself a window of time, eyes squeezed shut, thinking about my dear friend Winnie, my neighbor for so many years in Switzerland, all the times we'd shared a bottle of wine while our diplomat husbands were off on their travels, how many times I'd wiped the noses of her children. She'd been more like a sister than a friend. She'd made mistakes, yes, but she hadn't deserved what came her way the last year. I would remember her for her generous soul, her animated spirit, while the rest of the world would remember her as a cold, calculating killer.

But then, after a couple of hours, I took a deep breath and

refocused my mind. Because if I was understanding things correctly, my own window of time would be closing soon, too.

It wouldn't do any good to mourn Winnie if I was dead, too.

So I lay in the solitary cell and just thought.

They'd killed Winnie as they had Linette, right around a shift change for the guards. Winnie's time of death was called at 2:40 p.m., but clearly she'd been poisoned earlier than that. No doubt the official investigation would place the time of her poisoning just before, or just after, the 2:00 p.m. shift change. Just as they had with Linette, the guards, once again, would have cover.

Two murders in six days. First my best friend inside this place, the person I saw on a daily basis. Then my best friend, period.

Not a coincidence. Not even subtle. Just the opposite. They were sending me a message. They wanted my confession desperately, more intensely with each passing day, as my appeal quickly approached.

But they couldn't keep killing my friends. Winnie, maybe, as she was the most clearly guilty of all of us and had never really disputed it. Anyone watching our trial remembered her as despondent, defenseless, defeated. The public wouldn't have trouble believing that Winnie had killed herself, which I assumed would be the official story.

But Serena? Bryah? If the Monte Carlo Mistresses kept dropping left and right just before their appeal, even the most cynical of observers would raise an eyebrow.

The cell door buzzed open and, predictably, in walked the chief asshole of the prison, Boulez. Dressed, as always, to the nines, looking more like a greasy politician than anything else.

"I will not waste our time with pleasantries," he informed me.

It didn't matter. He could be pleasant or unpleasant.

"Tell me what drug you used," he said. "It will be a simple matter of inventorying the contents of our drug cabinet to see what is missing. Easier for us if you just confess."

I coughed. Blood spattered onto my brown pants.

"I will not ask a second time," he said.

"Good," I said. "So I won't have to keep ignoring you."

Nothing had changed. I bit my teeth fiercely into my tongue to suppress the rage, to hide it from Boulez. I didn't want to give him the satisfaction.

"Or was it suicide?" Boulez asked. "Each of you had access to the drugs. Either she killed herself or you poisoned her. Which was it, Abbie?"

We went back and forth like that for a few rounds, Boulez taunting me, yours truly ever defiant.

Boulez walked toward me, confidently enough given my restraints. He stood just a few feet away, just outside the reach of my legs should I kick out at him.

"Confess to the double murder," he said. "And what happened to your friend Winnie will be considered a suicide."

He was still trying. Looking for the path of least resistance. A simple, signed confession from me and all his problems were solved. I played along with the banter, but there was no way I was going to confess. Not a chance.

"Boulez," I said. "You won't win. One day I'm going to walk out of this place."

His eyes narrowed. Then his smile broadened. "Madame, you are the most famous criminal in the history of France. You'll never walk out of here."

It was clear to me now. He'd sent all the messages he could possibly send. He couldn't kill another one of my friends.

And he couldn't stop my appeal from starting, less than a month from now.

He was out of alternatives.

They were going to kill me in here.

CHAPTER 85

THE LAST TIME I'd seen Giorgio Ambrezzi was ten days ago, when the prison had a memorial service for his fiancée, Linette. It had been a surreal affair given the circumstances of Linette's death. A hundred inmates had attended. Giorgio had looked broken beyond repair. Surely he suspected that Linette had suffered more than an accidental slip-and-fall in her cell, but his grief, for the moment, had overtaken his anger, and it hadn't been the time or the place for me to raise the subject with him.

Now was the time.

After Winnie died, I spent seven days in solitary, Le Mitard. Boulez had threatened a thirty-day stay—in fact, he'd even mentioned forty-five days, which was beyond the legal limit—but I knew he was bluffing. I knew it was a bluff for one very important reason: they couldn't kill me in solitary confinement. It would be impossible to blame anyone but the guards if I died in Le Mitard. They needed me out.

Now I was out. And I wasn't safe. It was just a matter of time. Days, not weeks.

I'd met Giorgio twice before the memorial service. He always had a gentle expression, an artist's carefree perspective. He'd been in good spirits because he was counting down the days until Linette would come back to him, when they would, once and for all, move on with their lives after their addictions and criminal behavior.

Now his eyes were sunken and lifeless. He was unshaven and pale.

"J'ai entendu les nouvelles de votre ami," he said to me. He'd heard about Winnie. Everyone had. The official story was that Winnie had committed suicide. She had returned to her cell, they said, and self-injected a very high dose of methadone—a drug used to treat addiction. She was found unconscious in her cell. The time of her poisoning was said to have been between 1:00 p.m. and 2:15 p.m.—right around the 2:00 p.m. shift change for the guards.

My favorite guard, Lucy, as it happened, had worked the shift ending at 2:00 p.m.

The official story was that Winnie couldn't bear another trial, revisiting her shame once more. It was a pretty good story, actually. Winnie had been the only one of us who was not pursuing an appeal, so this whole thing fit into a nice, neat package. There was the typical rumor and intrigue following her death, but all in all, nobody had trouble believing the official line.

"Winnie's death wasn't a suicide," I told Giorgio in French. "And Linette's wasn't an accident."

Giorgio stared back at me, his face and body posture intense. He blinked his eyes to indicate his acknowledgment. He'd figured as much. He'd been in prison. He knew enough to know that the prison guards had their run of the place and could make almost any story stick; and he knew enough to know that they were watching us now, and he had to contain his emotions.

"Pourquoi?" he whispered. Why?

I thought he already knew the reason. I pointed at myself. "She's dead because of me," I said in French.

Giorgio's face twisted in agony. Tears fell. I told him I was sorry, over and over again, and I cried as well. He took my hands and squeezed them hard.

"Elle vous aimait," he said. She loved you.

I loved her, too. I loved them both, Linette and Winnie. This was so unfair. So unbelievably unfair.

I cleared my throat and got hold of my emotions. I wasn't doing this only for myself. I was doing this for them, too.

"Giorgio," I whispered. *"J'ai besoin de votre aide."*

I need your help.

"Mais il pourrait être dangereux."

But it could be dangerous.

Giorgio let my words sink in for a moment. He wiped at his eyes and then fixed them directly on me. He answered me in one word. In English.

He said, "Anything."

CHAPTER 86

TODAY, I WOULD begin to fight back.

I tried to sleep a bit to keep my strength up. My dreams were hor-rifying. Ghoulish faces and fanged animals and water filling my nose and mouth and lungs as I cried for help.

In the morning, I tried to eat, limiting myself to bread. Carbohy-drates for energy. I didn't taste it. Didn't enjoy it.

I had a shift at the infirmary at eight. I walked down G wing, past the key-entry door for the staff's underground parking garage, past the fire-escape door, to the guard booth. I gave my ID number to the guard, Cecile, and listened to the buzz of the door. I worked like a ro-bot inside, dressing wounds and mopping floors and looking through the window outside as a shift of guards left the prison, pulling up to the front gate in their cars, waving to the guard in the tower ten feet above, sliding their key cards, waiting for the gate to open, and leav-ing this hellhole for a time. Freedom.

"Abbie," said Leonore, the nurse, in English. "I need...ceftriax-one."

For a while now, I'd been one of the assistants the nurses trusted with drug retrieval. Technically, it wasn't permitted. But practically, these nurses needed all the time they could get with the inmates, and having us retrieve drugs for them saved tons of time.

Still, there were rules. After unlocking the cage door, close it behind you when you're inside, so nobody else can come in. Remove the drug vials from the shelf and write down what you took on a designated sheet. Don't take the syringes out of their wrappers, just bring them wrapped, along with the vials, to the nurse or doctor. Deliver the drugs, and the keys, to the medical professional and only that person.

In the end, you were delegated this task because they trusted you. But it wasn't simply an honor system. One of the four security cameras in the infirmary was located right here in the pharmacy room. Two others were located in the main room of the infirmary. The last one was in the secured room. Lots of eyes watching you.

There was also a nightly inventory of the drugs, and it was your ass if there was anything at all missing, even a bottle of aspirin. And finally, you were frisked upon leaving the infirmary. There was pretty much no way you could sneak drugs or a syringe out of this place. A few, over the years, had tried. All of them had regretted it.

I took the key from the nurse and walked over to the locked cage. Once inside, I found the ceftriaxone that Leonore had requested. Without missing a beat, without any hesitation whatsoever, I also retrieved a second vial of drugs, one that Leonore hadn't mentioned.

I then got a syringe for Leonore to use, and a second one for me to use with the other vial of drugs.

From the standpoint of the guard outside watching the security monitors—if she was watching at all; if she wasn't asleep or socializing or playing solitaire—there was nothing to see. That guard didn't know how many drugs I was there to retrieve. Two vials of drugs instead of one, two syringes instead of one—no reason for her to care.

Had she been so inclined, she might have cared about what happened next. I turned back to exit the pharmacy, which meant I turned my back to the security camera. As I walked, I unwrapped one of the syringes and removed the protective cap as well. Then I stuck the needle into the vial and withdrew the narcotic, filling the syringe. Finally, I recapped the syringe and slipped it into the waistband of my pants. All this was a piece of cake for a mother who had given her son allergy shots for more than a decade.

Maybe, just maybe, someone monitoring the room would wonder what I was doing with my back turned toward the camera, but I doubted it, especially because I never broke stride.

If she had become suspicious, I would find out immediately.

When I stepped out of the pharmacy, I saw nothing amiss. The prison guard seated in the corner was not exactly on high alert; she looked as if she were going to doze off any minute.

Then I heard the buzz of the main door, and the outside guard, Cecile, bursting through it.

CHAPTER 87

I HELD MY BREATH and kept walking toward Leonore as if nothing were wrong, just doing my job. The guard sitting in the corner, an older woman named Nadine, got to her feet as Cecile walked briskly in my direction.

"Here you go," I said to Leonore, who preferred English. My heart was slamming against my chest.

But Cecile walked past me, shouting at two of the inmates near the far corner, near the secured room. Apparently they were having a minor disagreement and had squared off. Cecile had seen it on the security camera. She seemed ticked off that Nadine, inside this room, hadn't noticed.

I let out my breath. I handed Nurse Leonore the ceftriaxone and the capped syringe. She didn't check or even look at my other hand—where I had palmed the other vial. Nor did she ask me to lift up my shirt so she could see whether I had slipped a syringe inside the waistband. Why would she? She was too busy with this inmate's urinary tract infection, and I'd long ago earned her trust. Besides, she knew as well as anyone that there were twenty ways you'd get caught if you tried to sneak drugs out of the infirmary.

The difference here was, I had no intention of sneaking this syringe out of the infirmary.

Leonore unwrapped the syringe cover, uncapped it, filled the syringe, and injected the drug into the patient's thigh. Then she recapped the syringe and handed everything back to me.

I returned to the pharmacy, where I put the two vials of drugs back where I got them and disposed of the used syringe in the sharps container mounted on the wall.

I occupied my time collecting some used towels on the floor, mopping up a mess, all the while hiding a syringe full of narcotics in my waistband.

So far, so good.

A half hour later, Nurse Leonore requested another drug. I repeated the same procedure to the letter. It worked the first time, why not a second?

So now I had two syringes full of drugs for my own use tucked in my pants.

I went into the secured area, where the five individual beds were placed for special cases—people with contagious infections or those who posed security risks. It was behind a locked door, but for the time being nobody was in those beds, so the door was left ajar. My job was to put fresh linens on the beds.

My eyes casually glanced up at the security camera in the corner. The small red light in the bottom corner was glowing, meaning the camera was on. I started with the bed in the far corner, the one farthest from the camera. When I tucked in the sheets under the mattress, I made a point of bending at the knees and shoving my hands far under the mattress. It was probably unnecessary, but that wasn't the point. My purpose was to make it appear that this was my standard way of making a bed, so when the guard watching the security camera saw me do it with the first bed, then the second, then the third and fourth, she wouldn't be surprised—or suspicious—when I did it with the fifth bed, the one closest to the security camera.

Even if the guard were closely monitoring my actions, which I doubted, it would have been highly unlikely that she would have noticed that I was tucking two syringes full of narcotics into a small space under the bed where two reinforcement bars overlapped.

Almost half a year working in the prison hospital taught you a few things.

It might just save my life, too.

I would find out soon enough.

CHAPTER 88

MY LAWYER, JULES LAURENT, sat back in his chair and squinted at me in concentration.

"Are you serious?" he asked.

I had exceeded the number of visitations I was customarily allotted, having received a visit from Giorgio yesterday, but the prison made special exceptions for one's attorney, especially when a court proceeding was scheduled in the near future. I had summoned Jules down here on short notice. Bless his heart, he had dropped everything and taken the train down here this afternoon.

"You can do that, right?" I asked. "They're, like, subpoenas?"

"They are—yes. They are called *commissions rogatoires*. But—are you sure?"

"I'm absolutely sure."

"This...will be difficult," he said, sighing. "The prosecutor will object. I cannot say with...certainty that the *juge d'instruction* will grant this request."

I nodded. "But we'll never know unless we try, right? I mean, if the investigating judge says no way, then he says no way. We're no worse for trying."

"No worse for trying?" Jules shook his head. "Abbie, this could get you killed in here."

"A chance I'm willing to take."

Jules thought for a moment. Really, what did we have to lose? He ultimately came to the same conclusion.

"Okay." He slapped his hands down on the desk. "I'll file the necessary papers."

CHAPTER 89

THE PRISON YARD. Our one hour outside. It was thick and steamy today, the sky overcast. I stood against the chain-link fence so nobody could come up behind me. I watched the other inmates kicking a soccer ball or socializing.

The prison yard. This was where it would happen. I was almost sure of it. Two reasons. One, they could use a prisoner to do their dirty work and keep their grimy fingerprints off the whole thing. They owned plenty of these inmates. There were plenty of inducements they could offer a prisoner to kill me.

And two, the cameras. There were surveillance cameras out here, just as there were everywhere inside, but with one difference: out here, the cameras weren't stationary. They moved at the direction of the monitoring guard inside. So it would be a simple matter of making sure that the camera was turned in another direction when one of the inmates came after me.

I stood, braced, for the entire hour. Not letting any inmate within ten feet of me. Watching the cameras, heightening my awareness whenever the cameras appeared to move off me. I stayed on the perimeter but in the dead middle of the fence, so it would be harder for the cameras to avoid me than if I stood in a corner.

I made it through the hour. The next challenge was the line going back inside. Single file. Easy enough for my killer to slip in line behind me, and then slip something sharp into my back or over my throat.

I found two of my cell mates, Josette and Penelope, and wiggled myself between them. They didn't seem too thrilled but they didn't protest.

Lucy, as always, was watching me in the hallway as I returned from outside. I knew from Linette, who had worked in administration, that Lucy was working double shifts for the next month—the afternoon and evening shifts. Same with Sabine. That would give them maximum freedom to plan whatever they had in store for me.

I avoided Lucy's eye contact as I shuffled back in. I'd had a near miss with her and Sabine when they tried to rape me. But since that night, when Mona perished in the helicopter escape attempt and then Linette was bludgeoned to death, Lucy and Sabine had stayed away from me. They were going to pick their moment, and before that time, it was probably best, from their perspective, to keep their distance.

I made it inside and into the day area—the common area, the bottom floor of cell block D, where inmates played cards or watched the one television or socialized. We had three hours in the day area daily. They could try to kill me here, too, but there were a lot more cameras. This was much safer.

I'd made it another day. But today's work wasn't done.

Now I had a phone call to make.

A call that might save my life.

CHAPTER 90

I SAT IN ONE of four booths at the end of the day area, where we could make our phone calls. Inmates were permitted phone privileges on a daily basis, provided that they had set up an account (mine was billed to Jeffrey) and that the numbers they dialed were preapproved. I had six approved phone numbers I could call. One was for my attorney; two were for Jeffrey, cell and home; and there was one each for the cell phones of my kids, Richie and Elena.

My sixth number was that of Linette's fiancé, Giorgio. I had added him two months ago as a favor to Linette, as she and Giorgio were struggling financially and I'd offered to put him on my account. I'd never called him. Linette had, using my account with my permission.

Well, sometimes good deeds are rewarded.

I dialed my personal code and then Giorgio's cell phone number. He answered on the fourth ring, just as I'd begun to fear that I'd get his voice mail.

"*Allô?*"

"*Giorgio? C'est Abbie.*"

"*Bonjour,*" he said.

"*Comment ça va?*"

"Ah, elle me manque."

Opening pleasantries: how are you, I miss Linette, etc. We had to keep up appearances. The prison reserved the right to record all phone calls, aside from those with your attorney. A lot of us around here thought that they recorded those, too. But my call to Giorgio was surely fair game, so we had to be careful.

"I wrote a song about her," he said in French.

I took a breath. That was the cue.

"Really?" I replied, also in French. "What's the name of the song?"

"'Avec Amour,'" he said. "With Love."

"'Avec Amour.' C'est bon, c'est bon," I said with approval.

Avec Amour. Okay. That was easy to remember.

Now it was my turn. We'd worked this part out in advance. I asked him if he'd had a good day today.

Giorgio responded with a bitter laugh. In French, he laid it out for me. "Linette and I owned a safe with valuables and mementos. I tried to open it today but I couldn't remember the combination. I spent hours trying to remember."

"C'est terrible," I said into the phone, projecting sympathy for anyone who might have been listening. Then, in French, I asked the million-dollar question: Did he finally remember the combination?

"Oui," he answered with a bitter laugh. *"Trois-quatre-deux."*

Three-four-two : 3-4-2.

Reverse it, which was part of our code: 2-4-3.

Avec Amour, 243.

"C'est bon," I replied. We then spent some time discussing the funeral for Linette—the real one, outside these walls. He told me about the plot of land and the weather and the family in attendance. It had been a private funeral, to which only close family members had been invited—a tasteful affair in a cemetery surrounded by gently rolling hills. My eyes glistened with tears but I had to keep focused. We weren't done yet.

"You were going to read a poem at the funeral," I said in French.

"Yes, I did," he responded in French. "I read that song that I wrote."

"'Avec Amour?'" I asked.

"Oui, 'Avec Amour.'"

Avec Amour, 243, *Avec Amour.*

I repeated it silently in my head: *Avec Amour,* 243, *Avec Amour.*

Thank you, Giorgio. We spent another ten minutes on the phone commiserating about Linette and briefly discussing my upcoming appeal. As the conversation petered out, I noted an edge to Giorgio's voice. He knew as well as I that my life was in danger.

He knew as well as I that we might never speak again.

CHAPTER 91

I FELT A WAVE of dread in my stomach as I stood outside the door of my cell with my mates, waiting for our hour outside today.

Today could be the day, I thought. Today could be the day they made their move in the prison yard. Presumably, they'd want to put as much time as possible between Winnie's death and mine, for appearance's sake, but they also had my upcoming appeal on the other side. They were running out of days. And every day it didn't happen made the next day more likely.

We slowly marched down to the day area, out to the administration quarters in the center, and then down the corridor of H wing.

I spotted her standing in the hallway, monitoring the inmates as they trudged forward. Lucy. As always, waiting for me on my way to the prison yard.

I felt a spike of adrenaline. My heart battered my chest as though a prizefighter were using it as a punching bag.

Votre belle-soeur laide, my cell mates called her, though not to her face. My ugly stepsister. I had plenty of reasons to hate Lucy. First, her attempt to make me submit to her sexually, which would have turned very nasty had it not been interrupted by Mona's attempted helicopter escape. More to the point, she murdered Linette, blud-geoned her with a smile on her face, doing it for me, because of me.

We made eye contact. She gave me a smile of smug superiority, of eminent satisfaction.

In response, I winked at her.

Lucy did a double take. She hadn't expected that and she didn't like it.

"Elliot, le mur à l'attention!" she shouted. She was calling me out of the line, telling me to walk to the opposite wall and to stand at at-tention.

I walked to the wall as instructed, stood as straight as a statue, eyes forward, arms down, as Lucy approached me. She stood at my side, looking at my profile. An inch or two taller than me, her mouth lined up neatly against my ear.

In French, she said, "Is there something wrong with your eye?"

"No," I answered.

"You don't wink at me," she said.

I didn't answer. But I smirked. That probably pissed her off even more.

After a moment, she moved still closer to me. Still in French, and in a far quieter voice, she said, "What a shame about Linette. At least she died quickly."

I didn't respond. I kept my eyes forward.

"But Winnie?" she went on, still whispering. "Winnie didn't die quickly. It was long and painful."

I did a slow burn. Lucy. I'd always suspected it. But hearing it, hav-ing it confirmed, filled me with venom. Lucy had poisoned Winnie and watched her die.

In French, she whispered, "Have you ever seen someone struggle to breathe? It can be very difficult to watch. But in Winnie's case, it was fun."

I forced my mouth to stay shut, no matter how much I wanted to respond.

"Nothing to say, Elliot? You're not feeling so funny anymore?"

My eyes moved toward the top corner of the hallway, the security camera, the red glowing light reminding us that they were watching our every move.

"That's all," Lucy said in French. "We're done."

The signal for me to return to the line of prisoners. I turned back toward the long row of inmates.

But Lucy was wrong. That wasn't all. We weren't done.

Instead of getting back into line, I pivoted and lunged at Lucy.

CHAPTER 92

LUCY WAS FAR superior to me in strength and fighting ability, but she hadn't expected me to advance on her like that. She managed to throw up an arm in defense but not before my hand reached the left side of her face, just below the eye. I dug in my nails and clawed downward with all my might, cutting skin, drawing blood, getting a good inch or two of epidermis before she shifted her weight and pushed me back violently.

Lucy shrieked in pain. A siren went off and it was only a couple of beats before several guards were on top of me. It didn't matter. I dropped to the floor and covered my face. I didn't want any bruises to my face. I took a couple of hits with the baton to the midsection, but I didn't care. Lucy got some retribution as well, with her hard boots, kicking my legs and then getting me in the ribs a couple of times before the guards, cognizant of the all-seeing security camera, restrained her. The last thing they needed was a Rodney King video.

"*Chatte!*" Lucy screamed at me, the left side of her face torn and bloody. "*Salope!*" These were not words of flattery.

They turned me over on my stomach and cuffed me. I offered no resistance. I had no need to resist.

"I want to die!" I shouted. "I want to die! I can't take this anymore!"

I kept up like that, screaming almost incoherently, as the corridor filled with prison guards. A small fight can lead to a bigger one, a riot, and the guards had to make sure nobody was getting any ideas.

I was glad for that. I didn't want a riot. I hadn't wanted to overpower Lucy, either.

I just didn't want to go to the prison yard, where some prisoner—whether today or sometime soon—would await me with a shank or a razor. There was no way that the guards, after such a brutal encounter had been caught on camera, could justify dusting me off and sending me outside for an hour of recreation. You lost fresh-air privileges just for mouthing off to a guard. I'd viciously attacked one.

And I have to say, it sure was an added bonus to put that scar on Lucy's face.

CHAPTER 93

BOULEZ SLAMMED HIS fist on his desk in anger. Abbie Elliot should have been dead by now. An attack in the prison yard. But things had obviously changed.

"Where is she now?" he asked, in French, of the two guards standing before him—the head guard, Sabine, and the enforcer, Lucy.

"Solitary, of course," Sabine answered in French.

"No, no, no!" Boulez pounded the desk again. He raised his hands. "How do we get to her in there? Think, Sabine, *think!* How do we get to her in solitary and pretend that it wasn't the guards who did it? Solitary is the safest place in this prison for her!"

Sabine bowed her head.

"And we won't be sending her out to the prison yard any time soon," Boulez added. "Someone who attacks a guard? She wouldn't see fresh air for a month. And we don't *have* a goddamn month! This was supposed to happen *today!*"

Boulez swept a pile of papers off his desk onto the floor. He took a couple of breaths and tried to calm himself. A temper tantrum wouldn't help matters.

He looked at Lucy, who was wearing a large piece of gauze on her face, fastened with long pieces of medical tape. She looked awful, of course, but more than anything she was full of rage. She'd received more than a dozen stitches on her face. Lucy had been, objectively speaking, a moderately attractive woman—albeit hard and nasty—but she wouldn't be attractive any longer. The scar would fade with time, but it would be permanent.

"The infirmary," said Lucy.

Boulez drew a couple more breaths and did some thinking. "The infirmary..."

"She suffered some injuries today," said Sabine.

"She also said she wanted to die," Lucy said, a smile creeping over her damaged face. "More than a hundred people heard her say that today."

Boulez nodded. "So we make it a suicide." He frowned. They'd used that ruse with Winnie Brookes. A second suicide by one of the Monte Carlo Mistresses, within the space of three weeks? It wasn't ideal. But he was running out of options.

Sabine said, "We'll put her in the secured room. We'll make sure there's a bed strap or something in that room. We'll hang her."

Boulez sank into his chair. "You're on until—when?"

"My shift ends at 2:00 a.m.," Lucy answered.

"Mine, too," said Sabine.

"Wait." Boulez snapped his fingers and shot forward. "The security cameras."

The room went quiet for a time. Everyone stewed on that.

"We have paperwork going back months on those lousy cameras," said Sabine.

"They went out last week," Lucy recalled. "Remember?"

"Right. That's right," Sabine agreed.

Boulez groaned. They were right. There was a history with those cameras in the infirmary. Budget cuts had prevented the purchase of new ones, so they had just made temporary repairs to the existing ones. No, it wasn't ideal. But it could sell. Given Abbie's suddenly erratic behavior—her suicidal comments today and her uncharacteristic outburst in H wing—it would pass the smell test.

"Then the cameras have to go out for a while," Boulez said. "We can't have them going out just between 1:45 and 2:00 a.m., though. That would be too coincidental. You understand?"

Both guards nodded.

"All right, then." Boulez slapped his hands down on the table and released a breath. "We keep this between us, as always," said Boulez. He pointed at each of them. "Nobody else is involved. Especially this time. Are we clear? Nobody else."

"I'll assign myself to G station two tonight," said Sabine, referring to the guard booth outside the infirmary. "I'll clear out solitary so that booth stays empty, too. I won't assign anyone to G station three, either," she added, referring to the guard booth at the door leading downstairs to the parking garage. "It will just be me tonight on G wing."

"Fine. You call my private cell when it's over. And ladies?" Boulez called to them as they walked toward the door. "Make damn sure it's over tonight."

CHAPTER 94

SABINE KEPT A close watch on Abbie Elliot for the remainder of the day. From time to time she would peer into Abbie's cell in solitary through the hatch. From what she could tell, and from all other reports she received, Abbie Elliot had done nothing but moan and sob and babble incoherently on the floor of the cell.

After the shift change at 8:00 p.m., Sabine had Abbie transferred. There was simply no way Sabine could stage a suicide in solitary. There was no way to kill yourself in there. The suicides, when they happened, almost always occurred in a regular prison cell or the infirmary. And there was no way Sabine could justify putting a prisoner who had just violently attacked a guard in a standard cell.

Thus the infirmary was the only option. When the guards came for Abbie, she was limp as a wet noodle. It took four guards, each taking a limb, to carry her out. It was as if she'd just had a lobotomy.

From G-2, the guard booth just outside the infirmary, Sabine watched on the security camera as the guards placed Abbie in the secured room. They put her in the first bed on the right, nearest the security camera—standard regulation, always filling the beds from right to left. One of a thousand regulations in this place.

The guards watched Abbie for a moment. She appeared to be borderline catatonic, devoid of any life whatsoever. Then they left, locking the door behind them.

Abbie was all alone inside the secured room, staring up near the ceiling, her aimless gaze somewhere between the clock and the security camera.

Sabine checked her watch. It was 9:42 p.m. She took a breath to settle her nerves. And she waited.

Ten p.m.

Ten fifteen.

As the warden said, they couldn't just shut off the security camera five minutes before attacking Abbie. There had to be a record of problems with it tonight.

Ten thirty.

Ten forty-five.

Eleven p.m.

It was probably about time now. They weren't going to pull this off until a bit before the shift change at 2:00 a.m., so now would be a good time to start with the "camera trouble."

At 11:06 p.m., Sabine shut off the security camera.

CHAPTER 95

LUCY USED A key to open the primary door to the infirmary. None of the loud buzzing of the automated system. The noise might alert Abbie.

Abbie would probably be asleep. She was asleep twenty minutes ago—at 1:00 a.m.—when Lucy had used the key to sneak in, tiptoe toward the secured room, and check on her through the window. There had been no movement from Abbie. Her eyes had appeared to be closed. She was either asleep or she was in the same catatonic state she was in when they'd dragged her from Le Mitard into the infirmary earlier this evening.

Lucy looked up at one of the security cameras in the corner of the main room. The red light was off, of course. The clock on the wall said 1:20 a.m. She would probably not need more than fifteen minutes, maybe twenty, but still there was plenty of cushion built in. She could take all the way until 2:00 a.m. if necessary, then hustle out of the infirmary and head downstairs to her car in the garage. The shift would change but it would probably be some time before a guard would check on the patient in the secured room. When all was said and done, it would be impossible to say for certain that Abbie Elliot had hanged herself before or after the shift change at 2:00 a.m.

Her gun drawn, Lucy tiptoed up to the secured room. She looked through the glass window—glass that was bulletproof and, more important, soundproof. She saw the same thing she saw twenty minutes ago. Abbie was perfectly still. Lying on her back. Sheet and blanket up to her chest. Left arm hanging out over the blanket. Right arm underneath. Eyes appeared to be closed.

Lucy put the key in the lock and turned it slowly, watching Abbie the whole time. She entered the room and raised her gun. She shuffled toward Abbie's bed.

Still no movement.

Lucy kicked at the bed. "Wake up," she said in English.

Abbie didn't move.

Lucy grabbed Abbie's leg through the bedcovers and shook it.

Abbie moaned and her eyes blinked open. She squinted and finally focused on Lucy. She looked at Lucy's gun. But her face didn't register fear. Her face didn't register anything.

Lucy pulled her handcuffs from her belt and tossed them onto the bed. They landed on Abbie's stomach.

"Put...them...on," she demanded in English.

"Kill...kill me," Abbie mumbled.

That's what I'm trying to do. "Put them on," Lucy repeated.

Abbie clearly presented no threat whatsoever, but Lucy wasn't going to take any chances. She was going to handcuff Abbie first, then hang a strap from a hook in the ceiling, then force Abbie onto a chair. But first and foremost, the handcuffs.

"Put them on or I will...shoot." She trained her handgun on Abbie as she moved to the right, going around to the side of the bed to Abbie's left.

It was an empty threat. The last thing she could do was shoot Abbie. How would she explain *that?*

Abbie's eyes wandered. She seemed unable to focus.

Lucy cursed under her breath. She didn't have time for this. She tucked her gun in the back of her pants and gripped Abbie's left wrist. She slapped the handcuff on.

One wrist down, one to go.

"*L'autre*," she said. "Give me...your...hand...your...other hand!"

Lucy held down Abbie's limp left wrist with her own right hand. She reached over Abbie's body, holding out her left hand, palm up, fingers curled and wiggling with impatience.

"Your hand," she said. "Your other—"

Abbie's right hand flew out from under the covers. Before Lucy knew up from down, Abbie stabbed Lucy's extended forearm with a syringe and injected its contents into her bloodstream.

In disbelief, Lucy stared for a moment, just one beat, at the needle sticking out of her forearm, and then she reacted, instinctively reaching with her right hand to remove the syringe.

Instinctive, but a poor choice. And Abbie was way ahead of her, anyway. Abbie's right hand clawed Lucy's left cheek, the damaged one with the enormous bandage. Lucy howled in agony, even as she realized something dark and terrifying:

She had completely lost control of the situation.

She was off balance, stretched over the bed, the needle still sticking out of her arm, her left cheek in scorching pain.

Before she knew it, Abbie had gripped Lucy's hair with both hands and yanked her forward. Abbie swung her own head forward and head-butted Lucy right above the eye.

Stunned, Lucy tried to recover, tried to move her hand to reach back for her gun, but Abbie had locked her in a fierce bear hug and held on tight. Lucy tried to struggle but it was becoming harder and harder, with each passing second, to do so. Maybe she had underestimated Abbie's strength. More likely, it was the narcotic, whatever Abbie had injected into her bloodstream.

"Sweet dreams, you stupid bitch," Abbie whispered, gripping Lucy tighter still. Lucy's defenses wavered to nothing. Her body went limp. She had underestimated Abbie. And now she was at her mercy.

CHAPTER 96

SABINE CHECKED THE clock in the guard's station outside the infirmary door. It was now 1:40 a.m. It had been twenty minutes. What was taking so long?

She couldn't turn on the security camera. Whatever was caught on camera was recorded in a database. If she activated the camera, even for an instant, Lucy would be recorded stringing Abbie up. They would be cooked, Sabine included.

Sabine grabbed her cell phone and punched up Lucy's private cell number. She and Lucy had agreed that any communication would take place by cell phone. They couldn't use the hand radios; other guards would hear them.

Sabine waited impatiently for one, two, three rings.

On the fourth ring, she heard a voice, breathless. *"Allô?"*

"Is everything okay?" Sabine asked in French.

"Yes, but there's blood," the voice answered in French. The voice was breathless, barely above a whisper.

"Blood? There's *blood?* What did you do, Lucy? You weren't supposed to *beat* her first!"

"Help me clean it up," the whispery voice replied.

"Help you—?" Sabine looked at her watch and sighed. The clock was ticking on their little mission. Ten minutes, tops, and they had to get out of there.

She cussed and left the guard station and buzzed herself through the infirmary door. She shouldn't have left this to Lucy. She should have done it herself.

She approached the window to the secured room and saw the empty bed where Abbie had once lain. As she got closer she saw a woman in a guard's uniform, with dark hair and, of course, a large gauze bandage on her face, bent over, scrubbing the floor with a towel. When Sabine rushed through the door she saw a body lying prone on the floor in Abbie's prison garb.

"What a mess," Sabine complained.

She started to ask Lucy why Abbie was still lying on the floor as opposed to hanging from the ceiling by a strap. But other questions invaded her mind all at once, in the space of one beat of her pulse.

Why did Lucy's uniform seem a bit large on her? And why had her hair grown a few inches? And why did Abbie's prison outfit suddenly look so small on her?

Questions that came a few moments too late, as Abbie, dressed in the guard's uniform and the gauze bandage, popped up from the floor and pointed a gun at her.

Lucy's uniform. Lucy's bandage.

Lucy's gun.

"Hands on your head," Abbie said in French. "I killed Lucy and I'll kill you if I have to."

"Please don't," Sabine replied in French, the situation now fully clear to her. Abbie Elliot surely had nothing to lose. She would kill Sabine in a heartbeat if need be. Why not? She was already serving a life sentence for murder. What more could they do to her?

"Turn around," Abbie ordered her. "If you want to live."

Her hands on her head, Sabine turned around. "Don't kill me," she repeated, as she felt the stab of a needle in the side of her neck. She jumped and removed the needle. Too late. The contents of the syringe had been injected.

Abbie trained the gun on Sabine. "That drug won't kill you," she said, "but *I* will if you make one move."

Sabine glanced over at Lucy, lying motionless on the floor. But she did seem to be breathing. Maybe Abbie wasn't going to kill them, after all.

"I want to thank you, Sabine," Abbie said. "You arranged everything perfectly to kill me tonight. You waited until you were near a shift change. You picked the dead of night, when all the prisoners are locked down, and when there is the smallest number of prison staff on duty. You kept things to just you and Lucy. You cleared out the infirmary, and I'd be willing to bet there isn't another guard on this entire wing, is there?"

Sabine began to swoon from whatever Abbie had injected into her.

"No, of course there isn't," Abbie continued. "You couldn't run the risk of another guard stopping by unannounced. This whole side of the prison is probably empty right now. Am I right?"

Sabine felt her legs giving out. She fell to her knees, catching herself with her hands. She was on all fours, like an animal.

"Why do you...thank me?" she asked.

Sabine's vision became spotty. She was losing consciousness.

Abbie approached her, got down on a knee so she could whisper in Sabine's ear. Ordinarily that might be a risky move, but Sabine was on the verge of collapsing.

"Because in creating the perfect conditions for me to be murdered," said Abbie, "you've also created the perfect conditions for me to escape."

CHAPTER 97

I LOOKED AT MY watch: 1:47 a.m. Thirteen minutes before the shift change. And who knew if the replacement guard might come a little early? I might have just a handful of minutes.

I looked back at my handiwork in the secured room. My mind was racing. The rush of adrenaline was clouding my thoughts. Had I done this right? Thought of everything? I knew, in my semipanicked state, that it was possible I'd made a mistake.

But there was no turning back now.

I closed the door to the secured room behind me. I ran through the main area to the infirmary's exit door. Before, there was no camera on me, so I didn't need to worry about appearances.

But now I did.

I took a breath to calm myself before I opened the door into G wing. I hoped like hell that I was right and that Sabine had cleared out this wing.

I opened the door with shaky hands. I looked down the corridor at the guard booth by the door leading downstairs to the parking garage. Empty. I looked the other way, at the guard booth near solitary. Also empty.

What I expected, but you never knew.

Very soon, the prison staff getting ready to leave would be coming down this very corridor in G wing to take the stairs down to the parking garage.

I went to the guard booth where Sabine and Lucy had conveniently turned off the security monitors. I turned them back on. I looked at the grainy, black-and-white image on the screen that monitored the secured room. It looked okay. It looked as I wanted it to look.

I found a set of keys, presumably Lucy's, and her key card. Her shift would be ending soon. She'd already visited her locker and picked up her keys. Her plan had been to kill me and then waltz downstairs and drive out of the garage.

I walked to the door leading to the underground parking garage, past the empty guard booth next to it—G-3, I think they called this booth. Some of the prison staff who would be passing by here soon, when their shift ended, might find the empty guard booth alarming. The regulations were clear, of course, that any possible exit out of this prison, including access to the parking garage, required a guard booth. But our prison was notoriously understaffed, it was the middle of the night, when every prisoner was locked down, and what bleary-eyed staffer leaving work at 2:00 a.m. feels like making waves?

That was my hope, at least.

I swiped Lucy's key card and the door handle released. My heart did a small leap.

I heard voices at the far end of the corridor, two or three women with the frivolous lilt to their voices that came with being happy to be leaving work—and leaving a tad early, at that. They were coming my way, to this same staircase.

I took the stairs down quickly. I could taste it now—freedom. When I got to the bottom of the staircase, there was a gray door and another slot for the key card. I swiped it and the door handle released.

The smell of gasoline greeted me in the underground parking garage. The surface area was large, but it was the overnight shift, and there were only about forty or fifty vehicles down here. Most of them were clustered in the front rows of the parking garage, nearest the door. A few were spread out along the back, separated by several rows from the cluster.

Shit.

The voices behind me would be coming down here soon, so I had to move fast. I had to find Lucy's car. Once those women got down here, I'd have a hard time explaining who I was, or why I didn't know which car was mine.

I weighed Lucy's car keys in my hand. Why the hell couldn't she have one of those key-fob remotes that made her car beep?

Playing the odds, but not necessarily using logic, I picked the cluster of vehicles closest to the door. I jogged down the first line of cars, looking for Lucy's car. I had no idea what kind of car she drove. That information would have been too risky for Giorgio to convey to me, even in code, over the telephone.

But I did know her license-plate number, which Giorgio had discovered simply by parking his car outside the prison two nights ago and waiting for Lucy to drive out.

As I jogged along, scanning the license plates in the third row, the parking garage door opened and the voices of those staffers echoed through the garage. I crouched down so they wouldn't see me. I peeked through a couple of cars at them.

Three women. All guards, cracking a joke as they walked toward me. Now what?

Move. I couldn't let them see me. If they did, it was game over.

I stayed in my crouch, moving quickly on the balls of my feet to the far end of the row. The women, without breaking stride and still chatting, sliced through the middle of the parked cars in the front cluster, the stride of their heavy boots echoing on the concrete. I was crouched behind a car on the end, ready to move to stay out of their line of sight.

They all stopped in the fourth row. Carpoolers?

No. Each of them got in a separate car, all within a few spots of each other.

Oh. Oh, sure. They worked the same shift. They arrived at approximately the same time. That made sense. One shift full of cars parks as close as possible to the door. Then the next shift comes in and parks farther back. Then the next shift comes and takes the better spots up close, which were vacated by the two previous shifts. The cycle would repeat itself.

The clump of cars here up front were the cars parked by the eight-to-two shift, which was just ending.

But Lucy worked a double shift today. She started at 2:00 p.m. She wouldn't be parked with this shift. She'd be parked with the two-to-eight shift.

I looked to my left, to the cars in the back cluster. About ten cars. Fewer than a dozen people had worked double shifts. One of those cars belonged to Lucy.

I heard two things simultaneously: the parking garage door opening again, as other prison staffers snuck out a few minutes early; and the squeal of tires as more cars came into the lot down a curved ramp in the far corner—the overnight shift arriving for duty, entering the prison from the side opposite the exit.

They were coming at me from both directions now.

I considered my options, which included literally sliding under a car and hiding. But it was only going to get worse. I looked at my watch: 1:54 a.m. The remainder of this shift was going to be coming down the stairs any minute. And a number of other employees were going to be arriving starting now, and parking in the available spaces in the back, by Lucy's car.

I was running out of time.

CHAPTER 98

I REMOVED LUCY'S cell phone from my pocket. Then I stood up from my crouch as though I didn't have a care in the world and started talking into the cell phone and walking toward the back of the lot. The three women who had come into the garage after me were in their cars now. If they wondered where I had come from, they didn't say anything. They just started their cars.

Some more prison employees were spilling into the lot, just getting off, but I was ahead of them. I hoped that if any of them were even remotely inclined to speak with me, they would be less likely to do so if I were chatting on my cell phone.

As I approached the sprinkling of cars in the back, my pace slowed, and I scanned the cars' license plates.

Avec Amour, 243, *Avec Amour.*

There. I saw it. It was a blue compact. Apparently, it was a Clio. I didn't know cars, and I'd never heard of a Clio. But I was sure this was Lucy's car.

License plate AA-243-AA.

I got into the car. Turned it on. Some dance music on the stereo was cranked way up and startled the piss out of me. The car clock said 1:56 a.m.

The car was a stick shift. It had been ages since I'd driven stick, but I'd have to make do. It wasn't like I had a choice.

I drove toward the exit of the underground garage. I managed to fall in line behind one of the other guards, one who was driving a beige Toyota sedan. Good, because the three cars in front of me were going to show me the way out. Not so good, because they weren't on my timetable. They were in a get-the-hell-out-of-work hurry. I was in a run-for-your-life hurry.

I followed the other three cars up the outgoing ramp. Idling on an incline is about the hardest thing to do when driving a stick shift, and I was out of practice. The car rocked back and forth as I balanced between the gas and the clutch, but I didn't have the rhythm down and the engine died. I cursed under my breath and started the car up again, trying very hard not to panic, and this time I used the emergency brake when idling.

The guard in the first car reached out her window and swiped her card through a slot. The wooden arm lifted. So did the garage door. The first car drove out and the wooden arm lowered again. Everyone moved up one spot. I let out the emergency brake, hit the gas too hard, lurched forward, and almost hit the car in front of me before slamming on the brake pedal and killing the engine.

"Dammit!" I hissed. Try again. Got the car running again and didn't look ahead or in my rearview mirror. It didn't do any good to wonder if anyone was eyeballing me. Instead I looked at the clock: 1:58 a.m.

By the time the third car got out and it was my turn, it was 1:59 a.m.

I slid Lucy's key card through the slot, the wooden arm lifted, the steel door rose, and I drove up and out onto the main road leading to the exit.

So far, so good.

But now it was 2:00 a.m. And I was still inside the prison walls.

CHAPTER 99

LUISA WALKED DOWN G wing toward the infirmary. She passed by the guard station at the door leading down to the underground parking garage, G-3. Empty. That was odd, but not entirely unheard-of at this time of night, when all prisoners were locked down. Budgets were tight. This time of night, the prison often wasn't staffed at full capacity.

Luisa could see from a distance that the guard booth at the infirmary, G-2—her assigned position—was empty as well. When she reached the booth, she found the check sheet—the form the departing guard had to fill out, verifying her head count and containing an inventory of all equipment—was resting on a clipboard, not filled out.

Sabine, she thought. Fucking Sabine.

Sabine, the head guard, would have anyone else written up for this. But Sabine seemed to think that the rules didn't apply to her. She was probably gallivanting around somewhere and would expect Luisa not to complain about the check sheet. In fact, she'd probably expect Luisa to do the inventory herself.

Luisa raised her hand radio and spoke into it. "This is Luisa at G station two for Sabine," she said in French. "Luisa at G station two for Sabine. Over."

She waited a minute and got nothing back.

She looked around the booth. The inmate sheet said they had an overnight guest tonight—Abbie Elliot, one of the president's assassins. If someone was staying overnight, that meant the secured room.

She looked at the security monitor. Sure enough, in bed 1, the bed closest to the camera, a motionless figure with dark hair was lying on her left side. The black-and-white picture was somewhat grainy, and the lighting was dim. The lights didn't turn all the way off in the secured room, because the camera couldn't see in the dark, but they dimmed enough to allow the inmates to sleep at night while still allowing the camera to monitor them. So Luisa couldn't quite make out the facial features of the sleeping figure, but she didn't think twice about it.

Filling out the form that Sabine should have completed her own damned self, Luisa checked the box for the inmate head count—easy in this case, just one person. Then she went to the equipment inventory. The four rifles were locked and loaded. The tear gas and batons, check. Mobile first-aid kits, check. Handcuffs, check. Glocks—

Wait.

There was a Glock missing from the stash. The guards weren't typically armed, for obvious security reasons—an inmate who subdued a guard with a gun would become very dangerous very quickly. Why did Sabine need a handgun right now?

"Luisa at G station two for Sabine," she said into her radio. "Luisa at G station two for Sabine. Over."

As she waited for a response, Luisa peered closely at the four screens corresponding to the infirmary cameras. The pharmacy was empty. The main room, empty. The secured room, just the one sleeping prisoner.

In terms of protocol, the next step was clear. Having found a serious equipment breach—it didn't get much more serious than a missing gun—and having been unable to immediately clarify the situation to her satisfaction, Luisa was supposed to call this in to administration as a "code 3 alert." Every guard on duty would be alerted that there was a gun unaccounted for.

But this would mean ratting out Sabine, of all people. Snitching on the head guard. The one who set the schedules and assignments, who allocated vacation time. The last place you wanted to be in this prison was on Sabine's bad side.

And there wasn't a single inmate in this entire prison who wasn't locked up in her cell, or, in Abbie Elliot's case, in the secured infirmary room.

Luisa thought a moment, then raised the radio to her mouth.

CHAPTER 100

I FOLLOWED THE three cars ahead of me at a normal speed toward the mammoth outside gate and the guard tower, which was elevated ten feet above the ground. Following the routine I'd observed over the last several months, when I would gaze out the window of the infirmary, the guard in the first car swiped her key card and waved to the guard in the tower. The gate opened and then closed behind the car after it had driven through.

The second car rolled up. The guard in the second car swiped and waved and the gates opened. But the guard in the tower was feeling chatty and there was an exchange of small talk.

"C'mon, dammit." The car clock clicked over to 2:03 a.m. In my rearview mirror I saw four, now five cars lining up behind me. I hoped the guard would see them, too, and show the rest of us a little courtesy, for God's sake.

At 2:04 a.m., the second car exited and the third car, the one just in front of me, pulled up. I rolled down my window. The third car's driver swiped and waved. The gate parted and the car drove out. There. That's more like it.

I rolled the car forward to the spot for the key card. I'd already lowered my window, so I put out the key card and swiped. I waved up at the guard tower with my left hand and looked up and to the left at the guard. I momentarily caught her eyes. The lighting was good, as it should be on the perimeter of the prison. I wasn't sure how clearly she saw me. I didn't recognize her, which was probably good; she'd probably never seen the face of Abbie Elliot before.

But she presumably had seen the face of Lucy the guard before.

The tower guard held her stare on me. She seemed to crane her neck a bit.

An objective observer might say that she stared at me for one or two seconds. It felt to me like one or two hours. I wasn't sure what she was seeing.

I did know that she was looking at someone in a prison-guard uniform driving Lucy's car, with Lucy's key card, with Lucy's hair color, and with Lucy's gauze bandage across half her face. And the person driving was doing so at a shift change, and the guard's records would clearly show that Lucy had just gone off the clock. Every ounce of logic transmitting signals to her brain told her that I should be Lucy the guard.

What she *wasn't* seeing were the two things that primarily distinguished me from Lucy: one was our weight differential, which was largely obscured because I was seated in a car. And the second was our faces. As much as I hated to admit it, I did bear some resemblance to Lucy, but our facial differences were still obvious. However, they were masked at the moment by the large gauze bandage, the distance of ten feet or so between the guard tower and me, and the guard's angle of view, which was downward and partially blocked by the roof of the car.

So yes, I had a lot going for me. But still she watched me.

And she had the right to order anyone, even prison staff, out of a vehicle at any time.

With my right hand, I felt Lucy's gun, tucked under my right leg.

My heartbeat did a little dance. A thought raced through my mind: what if she was friends with Lucy? What if she said something to

Lucy, some inside comment that I didn't understand? What if she asked me a—

I jumped as her voice crackled through the speaker near the key-card pad.

"*J'ai entendu ce que vous est arrivé aujourd'hui,*" she said. "*Êtes-vous bon?*"

I heard what happened to you today. Are you okay?

Not surprising that my attack on Lucy had been news throughout the prison.

"*Oui, c'est bon,*" I answered.

The car clock said it was 2:06 a.m.

Poor kid, the tower guard, Rhonda, thought. But what a soldier. She was attacked very early into her first shift today by that prisoner Abbie Elliot, but here Lucy was, working until the end of her double shift. The word was she'd had twenty, maybe thirty stitches on her face today.

"*Bonsoir,*" Rhonda said to Lucy. She pulled the toggle switch to open the main gate. Lucy drove through and the next car pulled up. Rhonda knew this next driver pretty well; she was one of the deputy administrators in—

"Addie, this is Luisa at G station two," said a voice in French through the tower guard's radio. "I have a code three alert."

CHAPTER 101

"LUISA, THIS IS Addie confirming a code three alert on a missing Glock handgun at G station two." The voice of the administrative commander—"Addie"—crackled through Luisa's radio.

"That's affirmative, Addie," Luisa responded in French.

"This was Sabine's post, Luisa?"

"Affirmative. I can't locate her."

"Are you secure at G station two?"

Luisa looked at the monitors. Nothing in the infirmary except the prisoner, sleeping peacefully. "Affirmative."

"All officers, this is Addie. All officers shall arm themselves immediately. And we'll issue a no further movement order pending a head-count confirmation."

Luisa frowned. This was turning into a big deal. In all likelihood, Sabine was fooling around somewhere with the Glock and had killed her radio. Maybe hazing one of the new prisoners or something. Oh, was she going to be pissed at Luisa.

Well, screw her. She gave the rest of the guards a bad name.

Luisa removed a Glock from the stash and stood near her station. Guarding the infirmary wasn't exactly a trying job. She had all of one inmate, who was locked inside a room. But the order was to arm, so she did.

She listened to the radio as each station called out its confirmation that all prisoners were accounted for. When they got to G wing, she called out, "Affirmative, one prisoner."

Then a thought occurred to her. It *was* Sabine, after all. One of the more sadistic guards. And the word was she was none too friendly toward Abbie Elliot. Maybe—maybe she'd decided to have some fun with Abbie tonight. Maybe a game of Russian roulette or something.

Kind of hard to believe, but there *was* a gun missing. Maybe Sabine was careless enough to leave it in the infirmary, knowing that Abbie was locked into that secured room.

Careless would be an understatement. It would be reckless as hell. But stranger things had happened around here. Luisa buzzed open the infirmary door and walked in.

She walked from bed to bed, scanning the place for the missing Glock. Her eyes passed over the clock on the wall.

It was 2:11 a.m.

When the roll call was completed a few moments later, Addie announced over the radio that all prisoners were present and accounted for. The no further movement order—requiring that all inmates basically freeze in their tracks until further notice—was moot. There wasn't a single prisoner out of her cell at twelve minutes past two in the morning: "All secure at zero two twelve hours," Addie said. "But let's find that weapon, officers."

Luisa looked under pillows and sheets in the main room. She kicked towels on the floor. She sighed. It was probably nothing. The odds of that Glock being in this room were slim to none.

"Rhonda at perimeter one, this is Addie. What is your status on Sabine?"

"Addie, this is Rhonda at perimeter one. Sabine has not passed through the gate."

Luisa approached the secured room but stopped short of the door. If she was considering every possibility, she had to consider the possibility that Abbie Elliot had the weapon, and she was waiting for an opportunity to use it in an ambush.

She wouldn't give her that opportunity.

She pushed the intercom button outside the room.

"Elliot, wake up," she said. "Stand away from the bed and raise your hands."

The body lying in bed 1 didn't stir. Luisa watched her chest expand and contract with the rhythms of sleep.

"Elliot!" she cried.

No movement.

Getting a little hot herself now, Luisa walked to the door. It was bulletproof; she'd be safe as long as she stayed on this side.

She raised a fist, prepared to pound on the glass. When she reached the door, she almost jumped out of her skin. She bounced backward, then righted herself, moved a few steps to the left so she could see more clearly what it was she thought she saw in her peripheral vision, in the far front corner of the room.

Something she couldn't see from the security camera monitor.

Because it was directly *under* the security camera.

It was Sabine, unconscious, handcuffed by the hands and feet to a chair.

"This is—this is Luisa at G station two," she stammered into the radio, her nerves choking her throat. "This is a code one alert. That's code one. Request an immediate lockdown."

CHAPTER 102

I DROVE LIKE my life depended on it. Because it did.

The prison was set apart from the rest of Limoges, and only one fairly narrow and poorly paved road led out of JRF toward the town. I had no choice but to follow the pace set by the three vehicles in front of me until we reached the first intersection.

Once I was free of them, I picked up the pace, though I didn't want to be overly reckless and draw attention. It didn't take me long to reach the train station, the Gare de Limoges-Bénédictins, located just north of the town center, opposite the Champ de Juillet garden and its majestic fountain.

I parked as close to the station as I could, in a small lot nearby. It wasn't a parking space per se; in fact, the lot was full and I was blocking two cars in the corner. Sorry about that, but I had more urgent matters on my mind.

I ran past several parked cars. A red compact. A blue Mini Cooper. A white Audi sedan. Tucked in the rear window of the Audi was a little teddy bear. My heart did a flip. Linette, my dear friend, always slept with one, even in prison.

I'm doing this for you as much as for me, honey, I thought.

I sprinted toward the train station. I'd heard it was a source of architectural pride here in Limoges, but at night it looked like a scary, scowling monster. It was a massive Gothic concrete structure with a domed glass top, pillars framing each side of the building, square lights resembling eyes on top of the pillars, and a concrete arch, in the shape of a frown, over the entrance. Next to the station was the monster's "staff"—a tall bell tower that could have doubled as a lighthouse for ships at sea.

Pulling Lucy's gauze bandage off my face, I ran into the station, got my bearings, and found the window marked BILLETS. I was still wearing Lucy's ill-fitting uniform and perspiring badly. I must have been quite a sight.

"Quand le prochain train part-il?" I asked the man behind the counter.

When is the next train leaving?

"À où?" he asked. To where?

I looked behind the man to the clock on the wall. It was 2:15 a.m.

"À n'importe où."

To anywhere, I answered. The next train to anywhere.

CHAPTER 103

BY 2:20 A.M., BOULEZ was at his wits' end. He had very clearly told Sabine that he wanted a call to his private cell phone when the task had been completed. What part of that hadn't she understood?

He nursed his Scotch, his cell phone in his other hand. He sat in his love seat and pondered his future. It would be bright, after this. He'd had all sorts of aspirations of climbing the ladder at the Ministry of Justice and Liberty, but he'd never dreamed of the good fortune that would befall him when Abbie Elliot walked into his life.

But dammit, she'd been difficult. If only she'd confessed, she could have lived. This was, ultimately, her own doing.

He jumped as his phone rang. But not his cell. His landline. His home phone was ringing?

He picked up the phone in the bedroom. "Hello?" he answered cautiously in French. He looked at his reflection in the dresser mirror.

"Sir, this is Aimée, the AC on duty right now."

The administrative commander. Sure. Sabine must have forgotten to call. But no matter now. They'd found Abbie, obviously. Someone had turned on the security camera and found her swinging from the ceiling by a bed strap. And now they were dutifully calling the warden.

"Yes, Aimée."

"Sir, I have some bad news."

And Boulez would be sure to treat it as such. Shock, indignation, the works.

"It's Abbie Elliot, sir."

"I see," he said. "Tell me what's happened." How calm and commanding he sounded. A leader in control in a time of crisis. No doubt for this prisoner there would be inquiries tomorrow morning, and he'd accommodate the media by making himself available for them. He'd already picked out the suit he'd wear, a new orange Hermès tie—

As he listened to Aimée, his blood went cold.

He closed his eyes and felt a catch in his throat, tension immediately forming above his eyes.

"Tell me...you're joking," he said to his hand.

It was a moment before he realized that he'd dropped the phone.

CHAPTER 104

THE CLERK SLID A ticket, and Lucy's credit card, over the counter to me.

"C'est le seul train pendant des heures," the clerk said to me.

It's the only train for hours. Don't miss it, in other words.

I thanked him and took the ticket. The clock behind him read 2:16 a.m.

I turned and ran through the station. It was open and airy, with ornate carvings on the domed ceiling and stained glass windows that were probably gorgeous in the sunlight. But it wasn't daytime and I wasn't sightseeing. I was running for my life across a train terminal.

I made a turn in the largely empty station and picked up my pace. An amorous couple sitting on a bench looked up, startled, and watched as I ran, as if they were wondering where I was headed.

It wasn't much of a mystery. I was running for the staircase. Which meant I could only be heading for one of two things at this time of night.

One, an exit out of the station.

Or two, the overnight train from London to Toulouse, stopping here in Limoges for a connection at 2:24 a.m.

I took the stairs down and ran onto the platform, almost slamming into one of the yellow pillars. I hopped onto the first car I saw, which I was pretty sure was a first-class car because there was a large 1 on the side.

I hadn't purchased a first-class ticket.

I found a porter almost instantly and handed him my ticket. "*Bonsoir,*" I said to the man, a chubby fellow with a cherubic face and wiry hair.

It was now 2:18 a.m. Made it with six minutes to spare.

"*Bonsoir,*" the man sang. After looking at my ticket, he said, "*Ah, mademoiselle. Vous êtes dans la mauvaise voiture. La couchette est deux voitures en bas.*"

He was telling me I had jumped onto the wrong car on the train. The *couchette*—the sleeping car—was two cars down.

He gave me the once-over. I was quite the picture, a sweaty, frazzled, out-of-breath woman in an ill-fitting prison guard's outfit.

"*Ah, trés bien,*" I said. I pointed behind me, to make sure I knew the direction. I asked him if I could just walk through the train cars, rather than hop off and hop back on two cars down.

"*Oui, c'est bon,*" he answered.

I turned to walk through the first-class cabin toward the next car over.

"*Bon voyage,*" the porter said to me.

"*Merci.*" I was certainly hoping that my *voyage* would be *bon*.

CHAPTER 105

"WE'VE INITIATED PROTOCOL," said LaFave, the captain of the prison's elite Unité d'Intervention Tactique—the Tactical Response Unit—on the phone with Boulez as Boulez traveled back to the prison.

"The prison is locked down?" Boulez said. "The bloodhounds are out?"

"Yes, sir. But as I said, I don't think she's in the prison, and I don't think she's on foot."

"You think she drove Lucy's car right out."

"Affirmative, sir." It had taken everyone a few minutes, unfortunately, to sort through the confusion. When Luisa first discovered that bed 1 in the infirmary's secured area contained not the prisoner but a drugged prison guard—Lucy—the initial reaction was that Abbie Elliot was somewhere still within the walls of the prison, carrying a Glock handgun. Lockdown procedures had been put in place and a search initiated. It took a few minutes before they realized the second, crucial piece of information—that while Lucy was lying in bed 1 in a drug-induced slumber, her car had been driven out of the prison, through the main gate, at 2:06 a.m.

They had lost precious minutes. Luisa called for the lockdown at 2:12, and they didn't realize that the prisoner had breached the perimeter until a minute ago—at 2:20 a.m.

LaFave grudgingly smiled. Had to admire her brass. Abbie Elliot had driven right out of the damn prison.

He looked at his watch, which was synced up to the official prison clock. It was 2:21. "So she's had basically a fifteen-minute head start," he said.

"How far can she get in fifteen minutes?"

Obviously, that answer varied. In LaFave's experience, a desperate inmate will ride whatever has worked for her so far—in this case, Lucy's car. Basic human nature says to keep running, as fast as you can; distance is the most important goal. Get as far away as possible, as quickly as possible.

"Her options include the following, as I see it," LaFave said. "She could get rid of the car and try to hide out in the countryside. There's plenty of terrain around here. She could take the bus. She could take the train. Or she could just drive."

"Drive where?"

LaFave sighed. "Anywhere, sir. The airport wouldn't make sense, because she has no passport. But there are plenty of roads she could travel in all directions, sir, and then she could access our highways."

"Can we block the roads?"

"Block the roads?" LaFave shook his head, even though he was talking on the phone. "It isn't feasible. By the time we got up the manpower to do it, she'd have had an opportunity to go almost any-where. The perimeter we'd have to draw would be—it would just be unworkable."

Boulez let out a string of expletives. LaFave held the phone away from his ear.

"Sir," he said, "in the time we've been on the phone, we've flashed her photo everywhere. The police have it. The toll collectors have it. And the police are being dispatched right now to the bus and train stations. That's a good start. Understand, Elliot was hoping that her ruse would last a long time. She hoped that Luisa would never walk up to that secured room, that she'd be content to watch things on that monitor from the hallway. She figured Luisa wouldn't be able to see Sabine, who was directly under the camera, and she wouldn't realize that the person lying in bed 1 was Lucy. And Abbie put enough drugs in those women to keep them quiet for several hours."

"And why are you telling me this, LaFave?"

"I'm saying," he replied, "that Abbie probably thinks we don't know she's gone yet."

"Ah. Maybe so."

"She thinks she has a little breathing room, sir. She thinks she has the flexibility to make some decisions. Like getting rid of a car that, very soon, is going to be hot. I mean, she's pretty smart, right? She seems to be."

Another set of expletives came over the phone line. Boulez wasn't feeling complimentary toward Abbie Elliot at the moment.

Boulez sighed through the phone. "She's very smart," he conceded. "So what's this smart lady who thinks she has some time on her hands going to do, LaFave?"

LaFave nodded to himself. "My bet?" he said. "If there's a train any time soon, she takes it."

CHAPTER 106

THOUGH THEY CAME from different directions, the three police cars descended on the Gare de Limoges-Bénédictins, the train station, almost simultaneously, pulling up abruptly at varying angles in the area typically reserved for taxis. The six officers drew their weapons and fanned out, four of them heading inside the station and two staying outside.

The lead patrol officer, a man named Darrow, walked so briskly it was almost a jog, his gun down at his side, his other hand clutching his cell phone, which displayed a photograph of Abbie Elliot that the prison had just flashed over. Darrow watched as a handful of bleary-eyed passengers walked in his direction, toward the main exit. They were carrying overnight bags or pulling suitcases behind them.

They'd just arrived.

Right. The overnight train. These people had come from London, or Paris, and disembarked at Limoges.

"Come on," he shouted to his partner. They raced toward the train tracks. A few people were strolling in front of them but they quickly parted as they heard the urgent footsteps of the officers running.

"Darrow," his radio blared from his belt. It was one of the officers

323

who had stayed outside, calling out to him in French. "The car is parked right outside. AA-243-AA."

"She's on that train," Darrow mumbled as he reached the staircase. Just as he heard the train pulling away.

He took the stairs two at a time, hit the bottom, and, from the platform, watched the rear of the train as it rolled down the tracks.

CHAPTER 107

THE TRAIN HAD COME from London via Paris's Gare d'Austerlitz, traveling at a speed of 125 miles per hour, with scheduled stops at Limoges, Brive-la-Gaillarde, Cahors, and, ultimately, Toulouse, at 6:44 a.m. The stop at Limoges had taken place at 2:24 a.m.

The train rolled into the station at its next stop, Brive-la-Gaillarde, on schedule, sixty-four minutes later, at 3:28 a.m. The train passed under the bridge connecting the train terminal to the passenger platform. The platform was empty. A few minutes ago, there had been two people who were planning on getting on this train. Those people had been politely encouraged to leave.

The train stopped next to a platform covered by a pitched roof. The doors to the train opened with a hiss. Only three passengers disembarked. A black male, a white, gray-haired female, and a white male, who appeared to be in his twenties.

No big surprise that the number was small. Brive-la-Gaillarde was not full of tourist sites. The people disembarking were most likely residents. No, most people on this train were going all the way to the end, to Toulouse.

The police hadn't expected Abbie Elliot to disembark here. The smart money said she hoped to get to Toulouse, and from there to Barcelona, Spain. Getting out of the country would probably seem optimal to her, and besides, she spoke fluent Spanish.

But they couldn't count on that, obviously. They had to intercept her at the first stop after she got on at Limoges.

"Approach," said the operations commander from his perch, lying flat on top of the bridge under which the train had passed. Members of the RAID assault team, dressed in black, jumped down from their nearby posts and crept toward the train, holding their Beretta pistols out in front of them. Spotters at various points, using night-vision binoculars, monitored the inside of the train cars. No sign of Abbie Elliot in any of the passenger cars. No evidence that she had moved out of her sleeping car.

Using a stolen Visa card, Abbie Elliot had purchased a ticket in the *couchette* that was fourth from the end. A porter had confirmed that a woman matching Abbie's description, wearing a JRF guard's uniform, had embarked at Limoges-Bénédictins.

Three members of the assault team entered the *couchette* for which Abbie Elliot had purchased her ticket. Others entered the adjoining cars on either side, in the event the target tried to flee.

The commandant waited, drumming his fingers on the bridge. They had no eyes in the *couchette*. All he could do was wait for word.

It came surprisingly quickly.

"She's not in there," came a voice through his earpiece.

The commandant didn't hesitate. "Take the train," he said. "All forces, take the train."

In the blink of an eye, powerful lights splashed over the train, like something on a Hollywood movie set. A helicopter appeared from the south and hovered overhead. Twenty local police officers joined with the elite ten-man RAID unit as they invaded all cars of the train at once, armed with Berettas or HK MP5 submachine guns.

They checked every seat. They checked baggage compartments.

They checked bathrooms. They checked every sleeping car. They called out various status updates through their mikes and into the operation commander's earpiece.

When it was all done, twenty-three minutes had passed.

And Abbie Elliot was nowhere to be found.

CHAPTER 108

BOULEZ WAS ON his third Scotch of the night—or, more appropriately, of the early morning. It was 4:00 a.m. on the button.

He looked at the vanity wall in his office, which was now minus two framed photographs that he'd punched in anger over the last hour. His knuckles were bleeding. It was the least of his problems right now.

"She got on the train," said LaFave. "There doesn't seem to be any doubt about that."

"But then she got off." Boulez shook his head. The bitter golden liquid in his glass was numbing him, but it only halfway did the trick, like a Novocain shot that didn't fully take. His stomach was doing gymnastics.

"There's still hope, sir. The trains are closed to her. The bus station is covered. She's on foot, presumably—"

"She planned this well." Boulez waved a hand. "She had nothing but time to plot every step. She knew about the London train, and she made a big show of purchasing a ticket and probably even talking to that train porter. She wanted to make sure we thought she was on that train." He eased himself out of his chair. "Leave me, LaFave."

He looked over at his special-unit commander. "And don't stop until you find her."

When LaFave had left, Boulez opened his cell phone and found the number in his contacts list. It was a call he'd prayed he wouldn't have to make.

"This is Warden Antoine Boulez from L'Institution de Justice et Réforme pour les Femmes. I need to speak with Colonel Durand immediately. Yes, I am fully aware what time it is. What is the message? You want to know what you should tell him?"

So apparently Durand hadn't received word yet; he was sleeping, as any sane person would be at this hour. Boulez would have the privilege of delivering the news.

He said, "Tell the colonel that Abbie Elliot has escaped."

CHAPTER 109

I DROVE SLOWLY along the A85, following the MapQuest directions, gradually calming as I gained an increasing distance from Limoges.

I was far from safe. I was driving a stolen car that wasn't registered to me. If I was pulled over by the French police, I was toast.

But I'd stopped worrying about roadblocks. I was too far away. They'd have no particular reason to know that I was heading north.

The truth was, I had no idea what they knew, or how long they'd known it. For all I knew, the guard who replaced Sabine at 2:00 a.m. was still sitting at her station, thinking everything was hunky-dory.

If they'd become aware, then presumably they would have looked at the train station and figured I took the overnight train to Toulouse. I'd left plenty of bread crumbs, all the way up to that porter, who sent me two cars down to the *couchette*. It allowed me to walk through the train cars and disembark from a different car—where the porter couldn't see me get off—and then head for the exit by the back staircase.

Did it work? Did they chase me south while I drove north? Well, I was still on the run. So I guess it did.

I surely didn't condone the criminal pasts of my friend Linette and her fiancé, Giorgio. But if they were going to commit crimes, it sure was handy that they became car thieves.

The Audi sedan—the one parked by the train station, with the teddy bear in the back window—drove very nicely indeed. The stuffed animal for the signal had been Giorgio's idea, a touching salute to Linette.

I stretched my arms, releasing nervous energy. I'd done a good job of thinking this through, but the truth was, I was in way over my head. I had no idea what kind of resources they could employ to find me.

Thanks to Giorgio, I had two hundred euros, two changes of clothes, a box of granola bars, two liters of Vittel water, MapQuest directions to where I was going, and a sleeping bag. The money was awfully generous of Giorgio—more than I'd requested, and tough on him, I knew—but it really didn't amount to a whole lot. It would run out soon.

All these worries aside, I wouldn't be denied a small measure of euphoria, a buzz of electricity coursing through me. I had the window down and let the thick air lick my cheek and brush my hair. I was free. I didn't know for how long, but I was free.

I only knew one thing for sure: between the money running out and the relentless pursuit of me that was forthcoming, I only had a small window of time to figure out what I needed to figure out, and to prove it.

Make that two things I knew. After two and a half hours outside the prison walls, I knew with absolute certainty that I couldn't go back. I couldn't live in that soul-killing hellhole for another minute.

I was either going to solve this puzzle or I was going to die trying.

BOOK FOUR

SEPTEMBER 2011

CHAPTER 110

THE TOWN OF ONZAIN, France, is unknown even to some French natives; I recall getting a blank stare from Linette when I'd recommended it as a honeymoon destination. Onzain is in the Loire region, about two hours southwest of Paris, tucked between Blois and Amboise, just off the A10 on the way to Tours.

Jeffrey and I had come here in 1998, back when Richie was only two years old. We'd left him with Jeff's parents in Connecticut and spent a week in France. First in Paris, then in the Loire Valley, touring the glorious castles and the vineyards, marveling at the majestic countryside, and getting tipsy on unbelievable wine, including a Sancerre that became my favorite thereafter, mostly because it reminded me of that brief window of time when Jeffrey Elliot and I were insatiably in love.

The MapQuest directions got me as far as the exit for Blois, which is not to say that the directions stopped there, but rather that they stopped making sense at that point. No matter. Once I was through Blois I was navigating tiny roads clustered within a town—maybe that town was Blois, maybe not; it had been thirteen years, after all—and I just kept looking for the large rectangular signs that said

LE DOMAINE in their elaborate font until I made it through to a narrow, two-lane road that paralleled the Loire River.

It was dawn, that gorgeous interval when the countryside was awakening, when the air still had that slightly crisp feel, even with the extended summer this year. I drove in complete solitude the final twelve miles until I saw the open gates on the right.

Le Domaine was an old thirty-acre feudal estate, complete with an ivy-covered castle and neighboring mansion, which later became a hunting lodge before it settled into its current form, a series of rental cottages. Though the owners had succumbed to modernity and put in tennis courts and an Olympic-size pool, which I could have done without, its true appeal lay in the acres of manicured gardens, the tranquil pond, and the vast swath of untouched forest. It was, as I remembered it more than a dozen years ago, the most romantic place on earth.

The Audi's tires crunched over the gravel as I made my way through the entrance to the parking area. I tucked the Audi in the farthest corner of the lot, against a row of hedges. I got out and stretched my arms and legs and inhaled the clean air.

"Well, girl, you made it this far," I said.

I was dressed well. Giorgio had packed one of Linette's nicest outfits for me, presumably so I wouldn't look out of place driving an expensive foreign car as I made my way across central France. I was wearing a navy jacket, white blouse, and gray skirt. I pulled my hair out of the rubber band in which I had gathered it; most of it had already fallen loose, anyway, as my dirty locks were barely shoulder length.

Directly in front of me was the castle, which housed the reception area and restaurant. It was bordered with manicured shrubs, its walls covered in leaves that had turned gorgeous shades of auburn and yellow. I could see through the windows that preparations had already begun for room service and housekeeping for the cottages. To my right were the rows of cottages. The fifth from the end was where we stayed, a standard room with exposed wooden beams and flowered wallpaper and rustic furniture. It was where

Jeffrey and I spent the better part of three days. It was where we conceived Elena.

I shuddered and snapped into focus. I got into the backseat and changed into the running outfit Giorgio had given me. My wardrobe request had been twofold: first, something nice, so I could walk into pretty much anyplace looking like a relatively normal person; and, in addition, running clothes, which served a dual purpose—I could blend in anywhere, and if it ever became necessary, I could run like hell.

I strolled the gardens in my running clothes, passing a couple members of the waitstaff pushing carts along the stone path from one of the service cottages. My role was simple enough: a tourist staying here who had gone for a morning run and was cooling off with a stroll. I acted as though I were out of breath and smiled at them. They pleasantly said, *"Bonjour,"* and I pleasantly replied, *"Buenos dias."* I'd come to learn that my dark hair and slightly olive complexion, thanks to an Italian grandparent, allowed me to pass for a Spaniard or Italian, and if anyone were ever trying to place me later, it would be better if they didn't remember me as *that American.*

I walked along the stone paths. The sun had barely risen, so it was nearly pitch-black as I navigated the forest area. The paths wound almost all the way through the acres of forest. Almost. I discovered that there was a decent patch of woodland in the back where nobody seemed to tread.

I looked back to be sure I was alone. It was just me among an acre of quiet trees. The ground was blanketed by fallen leaves that crunched under my feet as I found a secluded spot behind a thick tree.

I took another deep breath and burst into tears. I dove into the leaves, rolled through them, dug my hands into dirt, tasted and smelled and felt freedom for the first time in more than a year. I cried out and laughed and moaned. I looked up through the trees at the morning sky and marveled at its majesty. I could stare up at the sky as long as I wished. I was free.

Finally, I rested my head against the tree trunk and felt my eyes swim beneath my eyelids. I'd been up all night and I wouldn't be any help to myself if I didn't catch a little sleep.

Just a little. And then I had some work to do.

Because they were coming for me. And I knew one man, in particular, who wouldn't rest until he found me.

CHAPTER 111

THE PLANE TOUCHED down at the Aéroport de Limoges-Belle-garde at a few minutes before seven in the morning. Colonel Bernard Durand—Square Jaw, to Abbie—took the stairs briskly and walked straight into the back of a waiting black car.

"Good morning, Colonel," said a man named Rouche, the highest-ranking DCRI official for the Limousin region, which included Limoges.

"I want an update," Durand answered in French.

"Yes, sir. The army is on the ground, fanning out with a hard-target search of every home within a five-mile radius. Her photo has been flashed to all known transportation options. And we've alerted the CNI," he said, referring to the Spanish intelligence agency, the Centro Nacional de Inteligencia. "They're searching every train, every bus, every car, every plane that crosses the border."

In addition to Spain, France shares borders with Belgium, Luxembourg, Germany, Switzerland, Italy, and Monaco. Rouche explained that each country's intelligence services had been notified and were prepared to search vehicles of all kinds at the border.

Spain had been considered the most likely option, given its relative proximity to Limoges and the fact that Abbie Elliot spoke its language fluently, but Durand didn't buy it. She'd used the overnight train as a head fake, to get the authorities moving south. More likely, he thought, she was moving in the opposite direction.

Or not moving at all. The Limousin region was almost entirely rural countryside, offering countless places to hide.

"She'll want things to die down first," Durand speculated. "She'll hunker down for a few days somewhere before she makes her move." He looked over at Rouche. "Now explain to me again how this happened."

Rouche went over it again. It was the third time Durand had heard it. He always liked to hear the explanation more than once; at least one additional fact would emerge with each recounting of the events.

"It was the overnight shift," said Rouche. "The prison staff is lighter, because the inmates are locked down."

"And yet she escaped."

"The first one in twenty-two years, sir."

Yes. Well, Durand had always found Abbie to be formidable, from the first time he interrogated her at DCRI headquarters to their last encounter, when she was the lone holdout, refusing to confess even with a generous promise of a twenty-year sentence, even after the other three women's spirits had been broken like twigs.

"I want to know everything Abbie did within the past week," he directed. "Everyone she talked to. Every visitor. Every phone call. Everything she read. Everything she did."

"Yes, sir. The warden, Boulez, is overseeing it personally as we speak."

The warden. He couldn't keep a prisoner imprisoned, which, the last Durand checked, was pretty much the beginning and end of a warden's job.

"I don't want Boulez overseeing his own dick," said Durand. "I want you handling this. Do you understand, Rouche?"

"Understood, sir."

Durand leaned back for the first time against the seat. "If she stayed close, the army will find her. But if she didn't, do you know what that means, Rouche?"

Rouche looked perplexed. He didn't want to admit he wasn't following.

"It means she had help," said Durand. "And that's how we find her."

CHAPTER 112

MY HEAD JERKED forward as I spun out of a dream that drifted away like smoke. My heart was pounding. I held perfectly still and listened until I was satisfied that I was hearing only the sounds of nature, not the urgent footfalls of a nationwide manhunt.

I didn't have a watch, so I didn't know what time it was. The sun, filtering its rays down through the tree branches and their few remaining leaves, was high. I figured it was somewhere around eleven in the morning.

I walked about thirty yards or so, back to the stone path. Now I had company. Couples milled aimlessly about, hand in hand, admiring the forest and enjoying their time away from the real world. A few of them looked me over briefly, but they were vacationing, not conducting critical analysis, and I had to assume they would soon forget me altogether.

I took the Audi and spent the afternoon in downtown Blois, first stopping at a café for a croissant and *café américain*. A simple bread twist and basic coffee, but the meal was like a symphony to my taste buds. I had a copy of *Le Monde* laid out on a table along with a notepad. I was facing a wall so I could keep my back to the other patrons. Nobody would expect to see the infamous fugitive sitting in this quaint little restaurant, but I didn't have to make anyone's job any easier.

There was a bar in this place, and therefore a television, and the news was all about me. If I turned around I probably would have seen an unflattering photograph of myself splashed across the screen.

The front page of *Le Monde* didn't cover me; news of my escape had presumably come well after the paper went to press. Anyway, I was concerned with the section devoted to arts and entertainment, where a half page was dedicated to none other than Damon Kodiak. I'd read about him in prison, his upcoming movie about Adolf Hitler. Apparently the opening-weekend box office in the States had exceeded all expectations. Damon was probably happy that Hollywood had turned its back on the project, leaving him to privately finance the movie; all the more money for him now. And this week he was off to Europe, hitting all the major cities. The premiere in Germany was expected to be controversial, to say the least, which would surely translate into millions in box-office receipts. How nice for Damon.

Enough of that jerk. I left the café and walked over to the train station to familiarize myself with it. I wondered briefly if the police would have it covered. They didn't. There was only a single uniformed officer, whom I avoided.

I found a *pharmacie* in town and got some hair products. I added some basic toiletries and accessories—soap, shampoo, some eyeliner, and lipstick. Then I grabbed a cheap Mickey Mouse watch, scissors, a hand mirror, a small flashlight, sunglasses, and more bottles of water. I went down the street to another store and bought a cheap costume wig that roughly matched my current hair color and a baseball cap bearing the emblem of some soccer team.

On my way back to Le Domaine, I wondered, just briefly, how things were going at JRF.

CHAPTER 113

COLONEL DURAND WALKED over to the guard, Lucy Denoyer, who was seated in a chair, rubbing her forehead. He squatted down so he could make eye contact with her. She had a rough look about her, not helped at all by the vicious scar across her left cheek.

"I don't believe you," he said to Lucy in French.

"I'm telling the truth." Her answer, also in French, was not convincing—especially given that her eyes were averted—though it could have been because of her nerves. Lucy, after all, was royally fucked at best. Her negligence—if it was just negligence—bordered on the criminally inept.

"You expect me to believe that you were simply checking on the prisoner in the secured room. You, having served a double shift, and having been brutally scarred earlier in the day by the very person lying in that room—you just wanted to check on her well-being before you headed home."

Lucy folded her arms. She wasn't going to move off that story.

Durand looked over a map of the prison. "You could have taken the stairs down to the parking garage from E Wing, where you were assigned," he said. "But you took a detour all the way to G Wing because you wanted to check to make sure Abbie was resting comfortably. *That's* your statement."

Lucy's head bobbed up and down.

"And this was acceptable to Sabine? The chief correctional officer let you waltz into the infirmary to pay a friendly visit to the woman who'd attacked you earlier today?"

"She said it was okay." Lucy shrugged. "Sabine's my boss."

"And while checking on Abbie's well-being, you decided to violate regulations and arm yourself with a loaded Glock."

"I didn't bring that gun in," Lucy snapped. "Abbie already had it."

"Abbie already had the gun?" Durand searched her eyes, though the guard avoided eye contact. "Abbie Elliot somehow got through a secured door in the infirmary, then through the secured booth outside the infirmary, stole a loaded Glock, snuck back into the secured room, and somehow locked herself back in, all without Sabine noticing."

Lucy's posture tightened; her shoulders closed in. Classic defensive reaction.

"And you're sure that Sabine told you it was perfectly fine to visit Abbie?"

"Sabine said it was okay. I already *told* you."

Durand rose to a standing position. Lucy's eyes peeked up at him.

"I wonder what Sabine will say about that," said Durand.

He walked out of the room. One of the first directives that Durand had issued to the local DCRI agents responding to the prison, upon learning of the escape at 4:00 a.m, was to sequester the guards involved in the escape. Most escapes from prison didn't happen without help. The guards were natural suspects. Keep them separated, he demanded, so they couldn't get their stories straight.

They'd been heavily drugged, anyway, and hadn't snapped back to the real world until sometime after five. By the time their eyes opened, Lucy and Sabine had long been isolated from each other.

He walked into the next room, H-12.

"Tell me again," he said to Sabine, who was seated in a chair in the center of the room. Upon superficial appraisal, Sabine seemed even less pleasant than Lucy. But he saw something behind those hard, bloodshot eyes, and that something was fear.

"I was off my station," Sabine said. "I already told you. It was—wrong, I know, but I'm the head guard, and sometimes I conduct surprise inspections of the others." Sabine kept her eyes focused on the floor. "Lucy must have gone in there while I was gone."

"You didn't see Lucy go in there?" When Sabine didn't respond immediately, Durand took her by the shoulders and gave her one abrupt shake. *"You didn't see Lucy go into the infirmary?"*

"No! I keep telling you, no!"

Durand nodded. One of them was lying. More likely, both of them. Each making up the story that painted herself in the best light.

"G Wing has guard stations at the infirmary, the underground parking garage, and solitary. Why was only one of those three stations staffed?"

"Solitary was empty," said Sabine. "A guard isn't required if—"

"Because *you* emptied it." Durand grabbed a file off the nearby table. "Earlier that evening, you transferred three inmates out of Le Mitard."

Sabine tucked her chin into her chest. Her breathing was becoming more rapid.

"You cleared out G Wing, Officer. You cleared it out so that you were the only guard stationed there. You cleared a path for Abbie Elliot to escape." He threw the file down on the desk. "What did Abbie promise you?"

Sabine's head snapped up. "You think—I helped her *escape?*"

Durand watched her carefully as she continued to protest. Her reaction had been visceral, natural—convincing, he thought. She had lied about plenty so far, but she wasn't lying about this.

He walked out of the room into the hallway, where the local DCRI guy, Rouche, huddled with him.

"The guards were working together, no doubt," said Durand, looking back at the rooms. "But I don't think they were helping Abbie escape."

Rouche nodded. "You think it was just Lucy wanting some payback for Abbie attacking her earlier in the day? Sabine turns a blind eye and lets it happen?"

Durand made a face. "But with a loaded *Glock?* That violates twenty different regulations, and it's just plain stupid. She had a canister of OC spray and a baton and plenty of other things she could have used. Every guard knows that a firearm is the last resort, because it can be taken off you."

Rouche shrugged his shoulders. "Then what? If not a conspiracy to break Abbie out, if not an old-fashioned assault—then what?"

Durand sighed and shook his head absently. "They were trying to kill her," he surmised. He thought some more and nodded firmly. "They were trying to kill her and she used that to her advantage and escaped."

"Wow. Maybe so." Rouche brought a hand to his chin. "But even if you're right—even if they wanted to kill her—does that get us any closer to finding Abbie Elliot?"

Durand thought about that. "It might," he said. "If we can figure out why."

CHAPTER 114

BOULEZ STARED AT himself in the bedroom mirror. He hardly recognized the man staring back. He was beyond tired, of course, having lost a night's sleep. And he was essentially still in a state of shock, still unable to fathom what had transpired. He was like someone who had taken several punches in such rapid succession that he hadn't yet realized he should fall down.

But he was ready to fall now. The final blow had come a half hour ago, a call from the man himself, the Minister of Justice and Liberty. Boulez had been relieved of his duties. Not demoted. Not suspended. Not placed on administrative leave. Fired. Gone. *Au revoir.*

He fingered his cuff links out of his shirt and pulled at his tie. His career was in ashes now. And that might be the least of his concerns. The DCRI was all over Lucy and Sabine, interrogating them separately and probing for inconsistencies. What would they say? Would they put this on Boulez? It would make sense. He could deny things all he wanted, but it might be two against one. If each guard, separately, broke down and confessed to trying to murder Abbie Elliot, and if each of them said the directive came from the top, Boulez's denials wouldn't be convincing.

Boulez froze as he felt something change in the bedroom. Something intangible, an adjustment to the temperature or something—

He whipped around and saw the man. He hadn't heard him. How had he—

"I won't say anything," Boulez said to the man. "I can keep a—"

Boulez didn't finish his sentence. He didn't take another breath. The bullet between his eyes saw to that. The impact sent him back against the chest of drawers. The last thing he saw was a small insect crawling across the ceiling. The last thing he felt was the release of his bowels. The last thing he thought was: I can't believe she beat me, I can't believe Abbie Elliot won.

CHAPTER 115

I DROVE BACK FROM downtown Blois to Le Domaine as dusk settled over Onzain. I parked my car in the same distant corner of
the lot and, in the backseat, changed from my nice clothes to the
running outfit. I carried a bag of items from the pharmacy and the
sleeping bag and made my way back to the forest, the portion that
was off the beaten path, where I planned to hide and, I hoped, sleep
in obscurity.

I found a good spot and positioned the sleeping bag just as I
wanted it. Then I walked about ten yards away and sat behind a thick
tree trunk. I needed the flashlight to read the directions on the kit.
It had been more than a decade since I'd dyed my hair, and that was
in a beauty salon, not following the instructions on a box. But how
hard could it be?

When would I leave this little hideout? I had to admit that I felt pretty
safe here. It was tempting, though illogical, to stay here for days.

But I had to get moving. I had a small window of opportunity and
once it closed, it would stay closed.

"Oh, Abbie," I whispered to myself. "You better know what you're
doing."

CHAPTER 116

"OBVIOUSLY, I HAVE no intention of revealing any communications with my client." Jules Laurent, Abbie Elliot's defense attorney, raised his chin defiantly.

Durand remembered him from the trial. A good lawyer, he thought. Not some polished shyster but a sincere advocate. He had protested when DCRI agents stormed his law office in Paris this morning, but he hadn't been given a choice in the matter. He had arrived at the prison just before dusk, under a DCRI escort.

"You are aware, Mr. Laurent, that client confidentiality will not shield you if you aided and abetted an escape."

"I didn't do anything of the kind," Jules said. "Abbie never said anything to me about breaking out of prison."

"She never said anything about prison?"

Jules said, "She never said anything about *breaking out of* prison."

Durand blinked. The lawyer was making a careful distinction.

"She thought they were trying to kill her in here," Durand said, then waited for a reaction.

Surprise registered in the lawyer's eyes, in the parting of his lips. Not *you-must-be-kidding* surprise but *how-did-you-know* surprise. But

Jules seemed to be calculating what he could reveal to Durand, and so far he'd come up with nothing.

Jules raised a finger and then went to his briefcase. "This I can give you, because it's not confidential information," he said. "These are papers I just filed with the court yesterday."

Jules handed Durand a series of documents. Durand wasn't a lawyer but he got the point easily enough: Abbie Elliot's lawyer was asking the court to subpoena a number of documents, some located within France and some abroad.

Durand read them over once, twice, three times. They included specific arguments showing how the production of these documents would assist Abbie Elliot in proving that she did not murder the president of France and his bodyguard.

Durand burst out of the door and found Rouche conferring with some other DCRI officials down the corridor in H wing. He motioned Rouche over.

"Who was the guy at the U.S. Embassy during the trial?" Durand asked. "The pain in the ass who kept complaining that we were violating Abbie Elliot's civil rights?"

"Oh, right, right." Rouche searched his memory. "Ingle . . . Inger—"

"Ingersoll," said Durand. "Daniel Ingersoll."

"That's it, sir."

"Find him," said Durand. "Get him on the phone right away."

CHAPTER 117

DAWN. ONZAIN WAS just another tranquil Loire Valley village. The car drove slowly on the road that tracked the Loire River. It missed the turnoff for Le Domaine the first time, then doubled back and slowly drove into the entrance, over the gravel, which made more noise than was desirable.

The sun was just emerging over the horizon. The trip had taken longer than expected. Darkness would have been preferable, but there was nothing that could be done about that now.

He surveyed the surroundings. Highly doubtful that Abbie was in one of the cottages. That would require a passport and probably a credit card. Presumably, she had neither of those. But that conclusion was qualified by the cold fact that underestimating Abbie Elliot had been a hazardous practice indeed.

Still, logic dictated that the cottages were a last option. Especially because there was a pretty obvious alternative—the large tract of forest covering one end of the grounds. There would be any number of places to stow away in there.

He sighed. The forest was sizable. This could take a while. And with each passing moment the damn sun peeked higher over the horizon and lit up more of the countryside. For obvious reasons, he preferred to find Abbie asleep.

He reflexively patted his belt, reassuring himself that his gun was still there. Then he started walking. He found a stone path that wound around a pond and disappeared into the trees. A nature walk, or something like that. He took the steps lightly, on the balls of his feet, holding a Maglite flashlight but not turning it on. He didn't want to signal his arrival any more than necessary.

He stopped, turned on the flashlight, and swept it quickly over a patch of trees. Nothing. He turned it back off. Kept walking.

The path began to curve, tapering away from a large swath of forest. He stopped and tried to get his bearings. The path covered a lot of ground, but not all of it. Part of the natural forest was preserved.

There were a couple of acres of forest to his left, where no hotel resident was invited or expected to tread.

If it were me, he thought to himself, that's where I'd hide.

He drew his gun, crouched down, and listened. Then he left the path and walked into the thick trees. He moved slowly, reluctant to bring his body weight down on the crunchy leaves. He used the flashlight sparingly, just enough to wave light over an area to see if anything warranted a second look before clicking it back off. He repeated the procedure many times—gentle steps forward, wave the flashlight, click off.

His hand jumped as the circle of yellow light hit something. He took a breath. Paused. Flashed the light again over the same area.

It was mostly hidden behind a tree trunk. But he could make out a small portion of it.

Hair. A woman's hair. A sleeping bag.

Abbie.

He shuffled forward, keeping the flashlight trained on the sleeping bag, not her head. The light on her head might awaken her, and he didn't know how she might react. But the sleeping bag didn't have eyes. It allowed him to monitor her movements without alerting her. Or so he hoped.

He got within ten yards. Abbie hadn't stirred. Eight yards. Five yards. Close enough now so that it didn't really matter if she re-acted—he'd be on top of her.

He moved right, to get a better angle, to see the rest of what was obscured by the tree. He shined the light again. The entire sleeping bag. She was asleep.

He crouched down, moved toward her.

But something about the hair—it wasn't—

A wig. It was a wig, lying atop a gym bag, stuffed inside the sleeping bag. A nice diversion, he thought, as his instincts kicked in and told him to move, but it was too late.

"Don't move," came a voice from behind him. "I have a gun and I'll use it."

He froze in place, like an action-figure doll, his legs spread apart, his arms out and poised for movement. Well played, Abbie, he thought.

"Turn your head, and only your head, around toward me."

He turned and squinted as the beam of a flashlight blinded him.

"Fancy meeting you here, Christien," Abbie said.

CHAPTER 118

IF THERE WAS one thing that I learned to do well during my fun-filled stay at JRF, it was to sleep very, very lightly.

Christien was good, though. He'd figured out my misdirection with the sleeping bag before he'd even touched it. Another second, tops, and he would have spun around, and who knows what might have happened?

I trained the gun and the flashlight on him from a distance of about ten yards. I took one step toward him.

"Drop the gun," I said.

"You said not to move." The cool baritone, the thick British accent.

"That's very humorous, Christien." I threw down the flashlight. I could make him out well enough and I wanted two hands on my Glock. My hands and forearms were trembling and my heart was pumping at full throttle. "Drop the gun."

"Think a moment, love." He looked back at me again. "If I drop this gun from five feet, you have decent odds it goes off. Do you want a firearm discharging? Do you want to draw that kind of attention?"

I tried to steady the gun. "Okay, Christien, point made. I want you to slowly—"

In one fell swoop, Christien's right leg swept forward and he did a one-eighty, spinning around into a crouch, training his firearm on me. In the time it took me to get a handful of words out of my mouth, he had made a move and turned the tables on me.

For one beat of my pulse, I thought I was a dead woman.

His gun aimed squarely at me, he slowly rose.

"Now be a sport, love, and do put down that bloody gun."

My pulse was pounding so violently my whole body shook. It was James Bond versus a terrified amateur.

"How...the hell...did you find me?" I asked through gritted teeth.

He grunted. "How many times did you go on about this vacation spot to Winnie and me? All you knew of France was Paris and this place. I played the odds." He moved the gun ever so slightly, like a nod of the head. "Now put the gun down, Abbie, before I grow impatient."

"I'll die first," I said, and I meant it.

He paused a beat, as if this very outcome were on the table. "I don't want that."

"No?" I asked. "You just stopped by to wish me well?"

He looked over the sight of the gun at me. "In a manner of speaking, yes."

"With a gun."

"I knew *you* had one," he said. "I couldn't predict how you might react."

My eyes were weak from lack of sleep. And sunlight was now streaking through the trees, playing tricks on my eyes. It was hard to focus. This wasn't a fair fight.

"Who did it, Christien?" I spat. "Which one of you? Or was it all of you?"

He didn't answer for a long moment. I wasn't doing myself any favors here. But my frustration and anger were beginning to overtake my terror.

Christien moved a step forward. "You have no idea what you're doing, Abbie."

"I'm figuring out who killed the president," I said. "And framed us."

Christien took another step in my direction. Three more strides and our guns would be touching, barrel to barrel.

"You're not going to shoot me," he said.

"Sure about that?"

Another step toward me. "Yes, I am."

"Careful, Christien. I'm a girl with nothing to lose." My finger braced against the trigger. The gun felt heavy in my hands, in more ways than one. I'd never held a firearm in my life before yesterday. I'd never fired one. I'd never killed a *spider,* much less a human being.

But there was a first time for everything. One step closer and I wouldn't have a choice. I'd either shoot him or lose my weapon.

"I didn't come here to kill you," Christien said.

"Then why?"

He watched me a moment. "Put the gun down and find out," he said.

CHAPTER 119

"NO DEAL, CHRISTIEN." I braced myself. "Take another step and I pull the trigger."

Christien blinked. Then his expression eased.

"Right, then," he said. "I'm going to reach into my back pocket." His right hand was still raised with the gun. He showed me the palm of his other hand before it disappeared behind him. If he had some trick in store, I was probably at his mercy.

Because the truth was, if he wanted to kill me, I'd already be dead. I may have tricked him initially with my diversion, the sleeping bag, but he'd managed to even things up in no time, and he seemed pretty comfortable with a handgun. It was still aimed at my face, and his hand hadn't budged an inch.

His left hand reappeared, holding a thick envelope. "This is for you," he said.

I stepped back, keeping my gun aimed at him, just as his was aimed at me. "Drop it on the ground," I said.

"Fair enough." He tossed it lightly into a pile of leaves.

"What is it?"

"A ticket," he said. "A flight departing this afternoon from Bordeaux-Mérignac to Brasília. There's also a passport, a credit card, and five hundred euros. You're an American named Allison Larson. Though I'm sorry, I didn't realize you'd become a blonde. It suits you, by the way."

"I'm flying to Brazil?"

He nodded. "Extradition is tricky from there. Assuming they ever found you. We might have to move you to Argentina or Venezuela eventually. But Brazil is best for a start. Someone will meet you there and make sure you sail through customs. I still have some friends around the globe."

Brazil. Freedom, he was saying. I didn't know anything about extradition from Brazil to France. I surely couldn't take Christien's word for it. Could I?

"By nightfall tomorrow," Christien said, "you'll be sipping caipirinhas at Praia de Pipa."

"Why?" I asked. "Why are you doing this?"

"Becau—" Christien's voice choked off. It was a simple question, but he was struggling with it. My eyes had adjusted enough for me to get a pretty good bead on his face, and I could see his eyes filling.

"I don't want anyone else to die," he said.

His emotion ignited something in me. I felt rage and frustration rise like a fist inside my chest.

"Who did this?" I asked again. "And why? *Tell me,* Christien! Tell me why this all had to happen!"

Christien backpedaled effortlessly, keeping the gun on me as he retreated.

"I've figured out most of it," I said.

"Even if you think you have," he answered, "you'll never be able to prove it."

"Then tell me everything or I swear to God, Christien, I'll shoot you."

Christien paused, then lowered his gun. "No, you won't," he replied. "You're not a killer, Abbie."

"Damn you," I hissed, the tears falling now, every ounce of my being filled with poisonous rage. "Damn all of you!"

"Go to Brazil and give yourself a chance," he said. "Or stay in France and die."

"Christien. *Christien!*" I screamed, but it was to no avail.

Just like that, he had fled into the shadows.

CHAPTER 120

I FOUND THE A10 easily enough and started following the signs to Tours and Bordeaux. I was hedging my bets here. I hadn't made a decision yet on what I would do, but it was clear that my brilliant plan to hide out in Onzain hadn't been so brilliant, after all. If Christien could figure it out, then so could my old friend Square Jaw—Colonel Durand—who no doubt was leading the search for me. So I had to move.

My mind was racing, trying to connect as many dots as I could, trying to figure out what exactly had happened during those two days in Monte Carlo. And, more immediately, trying to unravel Christien's motives. Was he being straight with me? Was there a trap awaiting me at the Bordeaux airport? Anything, at this point, was possible.

Brazil. I'd never been there. I'd heard it was an up-and-comer, but, frankly, any place where I tasted freedom would be paradise. It really wasn't a question of evaluating the choice of destinations. It was just a simple question of priorities.

Should I escape and buy myself some semblance of a life?

Or stay here and risk my life for some long-shot hope that I could figure this all out and get my friends out of prison?

I put my foot down hard on the Audi's accelerator. I had almost four hours in the car before I'd reach the airport.

CHAPTER 121

JEFFREY ELLIOT AND Simon Schofield approached the gates of the U.S. Embassy in Paris a few minutes shy of 10:00 a.m. They'd come from different routes. Jeffrey had flown a charter jet, courtesy of the French government, from Washington, D.C., to Paris overnight. Simon had simply taken one of his own private jets and traveled from Switzerland, arriving an hour ago.

They showed their passports to the U.S. Marines at the gates. Then they stopped in the front entry station, apart from the main building. "Please turn your cell phones on and off, and then check them here," said one of the guards. Each of the men complied, leaving the phones in a black basket and getting a receipt for them, which they would show when they returned. Standard routine at the U.S. Embassy, and Jeffrey and Simon had been here before.

They passed through a metal detector and walked with an escort into the building and up to the office of the Justice Department attaché, Daniel Ingersoll. They waited outside the door with a marine for ten minutes before they entered.

Ingersoll was wearing a crisp white shirt and a dark purple tie. He was talking into a headset while taking notes. He motioned for the two men to have a seat.

When he was off the phone, he removed the headset and looked at the two men. "Thanks for coming, gentlemen."

"You said it was important," said Simon.

"It is, yes." Ingersoll folded his hands and took a moment. "I consider it my duty to watch out for Americans who come to this country. I can't be their lawyer, but I can certainly be their advocate in other ways. I tried to perform that role for your wives. I don't know how well I did, but I tried."

"And?" Jeffrey rolled his hand, as though he were eager for the punch line.

"I think I owe you two the same courtesy," said Ingersoll. "I've just been made aware that the day before Ms. Elliot escaped from prison, her lawyer—you remember Jules Laurent?—had filed some documents with the court."

Ingersoll slid two copies of the documents across his desk, one each for Jeffrey and Simon.

"I thought you should see them right away," he told them.

Jeffrey and Simon read the documents thoroughly, stopping on certain items, scratching their heads, rubbing their eyes. They looked at each other in disbelief. They looked back at Ingersoll, as if he had any further information.

"When I find out more," said Ingersoll, "I'll be sure to call."

Each man nodded, still stunned. They trudged out in silence with the marine escort through the embassy and out into the open air. They handed the receipts to the marines at the entry station and got their cell phones back.

They got into a cab and drove to a bar about a mile west of the U.S. Embassy, still on the right bank of the Seine and within sight of the Eiffel Tower. The air was crisp and the sun was high; it was really a beautiful day, but the weather was lost on the two Americans at the moment.

Colton Gordon was already in the bar, nursing a glass of Belvedere.

"*Sawubona*, gents," he said, using an old Zulu greeting from his native South Africa.

"I'll have what he's drinking," Jeffrey said to the waitress. "Make it a double."

CHAPTER 122

MORE THAN FOUR hours after I'd left my hideout in Onzain, I made it to the airport. I almost missed the turnoff, a mistake that would have taken me into the town of Mérignac instead of to the airport itself. The route to the airport circled around the town of Bordeaux. I followed the signs for guest parking and pulled into the lot. It was an easy walk through the rental-car lots to the terminal. There was a row of manicured grapevines leading to the entrance. But there was not, as far as I could see, a row of manicured law enforcement officials waiting to take me into custody.

Then again, every minute, at this point, was another adventure.

My passport said that my name was Allison Larson, that I lived in a town in Illinois called Downers Grove, that I was forty-one, and that I had arrived in France six days ago. Christien had written a note that outlined my story: I was a recently divorced mother of two (that part was soon to be true); I had stayed at the Hôtel Burdigala on the Rue Georges Bonnac in Bordeaux; I went on a wine tour; and I visited three friends here, whose names and addresses and bios Christien had provided. Now I was headed to Brasília to meet some women I'd known since high school—at Downers Grove North, in case I was grilled—whose names, ages, and bios were also provided.

Oh, and now I'd have to explain that I dyed my hair blond in Bordeaux just for the fun of it, which is why I looked different from my brunette passport photo.

I stood at the door to the terminal and paused. I let a couple with a small child pass me, watching them stroll in with the carefree whimsy of people on holiday, about to embark on an adventure.

Christien had gone to a lot of trouble to make sure I was able to make it through customs with a good cover story, if I were asked. He'd given me a convincing passport and a credit card and cash. Why would he do all that, if he weren't trying to help me?

"Okay, Christien," I said to myself. "I guess I'm going to have to trust you."

I took a breath and entered the terminal.

Five minutes later, a man standing near the door of the terminal entrance broke from an embrace with his female companion. He opened his cell phone and dialed the number.

"She just arrived," he said.

CHAPTER 123

I MADE IT THROUGH security at Bordeaux-Mérignac and sat at the gate for my departing flight, which was scheduled to take off at 1:50 p.m. Around me, a few female American students were talking about a boy one of them had met here in Bordeaux. I enjoyed a brief moment of peace, of hope, as I pondered something that once seemed impossible: a new life.

All told, my journey would take me more than twenty-four hours. One day. And then I would be Allison Larson, American expatriate, or someone else Christien invented for me. If, that is, I could trust him.

I closed my eyes as the flight attendant's voice came over the loudspeaker, first in French, then English. We were now boarding. Starting with first-class passengers and elite members of the airline's loyalty program.

Now boarding for a new life. A life with fresh air and blue skies and the sweet intoxication of freedom.

I hadn't won, exactly. I hadn't solved the puzzle or corrected the injustice. I was close, I thought, but I remembered what Christien had said to me in Onzain: even if I were right, I couldn't prove anything.

He might be right. I didn't know for sure. But if I was taken back into custody, I'd *never* know for sure.

Get away, I told myself. Escape.

Then maybe you can come up with the answer. Surely you'll think of something, Abbie. But get away first.

The overhead loudspeaker called for the back rows of coach class, including the row I was in, to board.

I took a breath, got up, and got in line.

CHAPTER 124

CHRISTIEN WALKED ALONG the Left Bank of the Seine, squinting into the sun and feeling the light wind through the open collar of his shirt. He passed a small playground, where a woman was helping her toddler down the slide with some effort. He thought of his own children, and what they'd been through. He thought of his wife, and what she went through.

He checked his watch. It was twenty past one. Abbie's flight would be boarding now. "Off you go, then," he said.

He felt the vibration of his phone in his pants pocket.

He fished out the phone. The number was blocked, which meant it was his contact at Bordeaux-Mérignac. Christien had asked him to call when Abbie got on board.

He took a look around him and then answered his cell.

"She left," said his contact over the phone.

Christien sighed. "Right, then."

"No, mate, I mean—she left. She was at the bleedin' gate as they were boarding and she just turned around and hightailed it out of the airport."

Christien took a second to contain his reaction. He rolled his neck and clenched and unclenched his jaw.

He'd given her a chance. And he'd given her a warning. She'd made her decision understanding the consequences.

"You made your bed, love," he mumbled to himself. He watched the children on the playground for another moment before he moved on.

CHAPTER 125

I MADE IT TO Paris a little after seven in the evening. The sun was low in the west but hadn't yet set. For all practical purposes, as I maneuvered through the streets, it was dusk, a hazy darkness.

It might have been the biggest mistake of my life, not getting on that plane. But in the end, it came down to three words: Serena, Bryah, and Winnie. I was their only chance, and even if I couldn't bring Winnie back, I could clear her name along with ours. Sure, I could tell myself that I could try to figure everything out from the comfort of a South American beach, but the truth was the best place was right here in France. Where a nationwide manhunt for me was currently under way.

I didn't really know where I was going. I knew I wanted to be on the Left Bank and close to the Seine. When Jeffrey and I had been in Paris years ago, we stayed at some hotel on the Rue Dauphine. Even if the hotel was still there, and I could remember its name, I'd never stay there now, having learned my lesson in Onzain. The French government could probably go back that far in their records and figure—as Christien did—that I might return to a familiar haunt.

I kept driving and turned, somewhat randomly, onto Rue de

l'Ancienne Comédie, a narrow street on which I found a hotel bearing the emblem HÔTEL COMÉDIE. It looked fine to me. I found a public parking garage about three blocks away for the Audi.

I walked back. On a lamppost, pasted on top of several other makeshift advertisements for rock bands or movies, was a square poster with a picture of me on it. There was one on the window of a restaurant I passed, too. A newsstand displayed a copy of today's *Le Monde*, which also had a prominent photo of me above the fold.

I felt incredibly conspicuous. I pulled down the hat I was wearing and lowered my chin—the kind of thing someone not wanting to be seen would do. Was I better off pretending I didn't have a care in the world? I had no idea. I was in a city of millions, but I felt as though I were wearing a sandwich board that said FUGITIVE.

There was the hint of a chill in the night air and the city was buzzing with diners at the outdoor cafés. I stopped at a boutique on the Rue de Buci that was open late and bought a black cocktail dress, heels, a purse, panty hose, and simple jewelry. Down the street, I grabbed a baguette and a bottle of water. At both the boutique and the café, I kept up the theme I began in Onzain, playing a Spaniard. The same reasoning applied now: I wanted someone's first memory of me to be that I was Spanish, not American. The saleswoman at the boutique was under the impression that I couldn't speak a word of French, much less English, though pointing and handing over cash were internationally recognized modes of communication.

I stuffed all my purchases into my gym bag. By the time I made it back to the Hôtel Comédie, I had acquired a fresh coat of perspiration for my troubles. In a span of three city blocks, I had seen my face staring back at me on posters and newspapers no less than eight times.

I walked into the hotel, trying not to look like number one on France's Most Wanted list. A pimply teenage boy was sitting behind the desk. He took one look at me and said, "Hello," meaning he had sized me up as American.

Instead of saying hello back, I said, *"Buenas tardes. ¿Habla usted español?"*

"Ah...*sí.*" He answered tentatively.

"You prefer...English?" I asked. "Ees okay. I speak...leetle English."

I was proud of myself, using broken English, just as a Spaniard would if she didn't know the language well.

"You would like a room?" the boy asked.

"*Sí.* Yes."

"Passport?" he said, sticking with the relevant noun and avoiding verbs where possible. Communication with a Foreigner 101.

"*¿Quieres mi pasaporte?*" I fished in my bag, still patting myself on the back for my cleverness with the Spanish thing.

Until, that is, I handed Pimple Boy my passport.

Which identified me as Allison Larson, American.

Shit. Just what I'd feared. Tired + strung out = stupid mistakes.

"*Êtes-vous une Américaine?*" he asked me, introducing a third language into our conversation. Maybe I should respond in Russian.

"Yes, I'm American," I said, throwing in an embarrassed laugh. "I'm learning Spanish and trying to practice it as much as I can."

Good thing for me that Pimple Boy wasn't the cerebral type. He spent approximately one second thinking about what I'd said before he realized that he couldn't care less. He seemed far more interested in the movie he was watching on his iPhone or whatever it was. I requested a high floor and he gave me a room on the sixth. I paid in cash. He processed my passport and had me fill out a form and handed me a key for room 606.

God, I thought as I took the elevator up, exhaling relief. That was close. Not a bad recovery on my part, but what a stupid slipup. A Spaniard with a U.S. passport. Nice one, Abbie.

Room 606 was decent. Red wallpaper with pictures of hot-air balloons. A window overlooking the street. Thick blue carpet, a queen-size bed, a small but clean bathroom with a detachable spray nozzle in the shower.

I walked out of the room and strolled up and down the hall. There was a staircase on one end that led all the way to the ground floor, or maybe a basement. The other end of the hallway was a dead end.

I went back into my room, stripped off my clothes, and took the hottest shower I'd ever taken in my life. I moaned with relief as I scrubbed off the sweat and grime and let hot water rush over my face and in my eyes and down my neck.

Stupid, stupid, the Spanish thing. And no matter how well I may have recovered, I'd done the one thing, above all, that I hadn't wanted to do.

I'd made myself memorable to the clerk.

I wasn't thinking clearly. My brain was getting foggy. I needed to sleep, to really sleep tonight.

Colonel Durand's eyes lifted from the documents Abbie Elliot's lawyer had filed in court. He'd been studying them relentlessly, sure that they held the clue to where she would be hiding.

But he looked up when his lieutenant, a woman named Verose, burst through his office door. "The Hôtel Comédie," she said to Durand. "She checked in an hour ago."

Durand shot out of his chair with an adrenaline boost. "Make sure every exit is blocked until we get there," he said.

"Already done, sir."

Durand came around the desk and broke into a jog. "Let's go," he said.

CHAPTER 126

AT TWENTY-THREE MINUTES after 9:00 p.m., a man wearing a business suit walked into the hotel and looked around the small reception and parlor area. He nodded to a man and a woman seated on a couch, posing as a couple; they were undercover officers of the Paris police force. They all made eye contact but nobody spoke.

The man said something to the pimple-faced teenager behind the counter, who at this point was fully aware of what was transpiring. It was not twenty minutes ago that a French police officer had stopped in to see whether an American named Allison Larson had checked into the hotel. Since then, officers had waited at the two exits—the front door and the rear staircase—while they waited for undercover agents, and the DCRI, to respond.

The man pushed the button for the elevator in the lobby. When it opened, it was empty. The man reached in and hit the kill switch, turning it off.

The man said something into his collar. Then he went through a door at the rear of the lobby, which led to the back staircase running throughout the hotel. Another undercover officer nodded in recognition. The man took the stairs down to the basement and pushed open the outside door. Coming down the ramp from the street level to meet him was a team of ten agents of the French RAID squad, dressed in black combat gear and carrying Beretta pistols.

He held the door for them and they streamed in. They took the staircase, moving in a standard formation upward until they reached the sixth floor.

They quickly moved down the hallway and surrounded the door that was the third on the right, room 606. One of the officers slipped a key card into the door. It made the familiar whiny, automated sound of a latch opening and they burst into the room.

It was empty.

The overhead light was off, but the bathroom light was on. A wet towel hung from a bar in the bathroom and a glass had been used by the sink. The fruity smells of shampoo and soap filled the room. She hadn't left anything behind—not clothes or a bag, nothing. Not two hours after checking in, she was gone, and it sure looked like she wasn't coming back.

I jumped at the burst of new light appearing through the window. I counted the number of windows from the end to make doubly sure that, yes, it was indeed my hotel room I was seeing. Someone had turned on the overhead light in room 606. The police, I assumed, or Durand's people with French intelligence.

It could have been the hotel clerk who made me, after I botched that whole encounter. But I didn't think so. Pimple Boy didn't strike me as the discerning type.

It was Christien. Christien had given me up.

He'd handed me a chance to escape and somehow knew that I hadn't taken it. Now all bets were off. If he ever had been on my side, he sure wasn't any longer. "Go to Brazil and give yourself a chance," he'd said. "Or stay in France and die."

I lowered my binoculars and dropped them in my gym bag. So much for Allison Larson. And now Durand knew I was in Paris. This area was going to be crawling with law enforcement any minute.

Time to move.

CHAPTER 127

DURAND STOOD WITH his forehead against the window, looking out onto the street from room 606. His lieutenant, Verose, walked up to him.

"She must have gone down the rear staircase before we talked to the clerk," she said. "Which means she must have taken a quick shower and left within an hour of checking in. Lucky her."

Durand peered down at the street below, where a throng of young people was heading toward the party scene on the Rue de Buci.

"I'm not sure I'd call it lucky," he said. "I think she suspected her alias wouldn't hold up. She wanted a shower, probably a change of clothes, but she didn't want to stick around." He looked at Verose. "Tell me again about the tip."

Verose wasn't surprised. Durand always did this, always asked for the story to be repeated over and over again, trying to find new nuggets of information. "A man handed an envelope to a police captain leaving work on the Quai des Orfèvres. The captain says the man was so smooth, he didn't catch a glimpse of him before he was gone. The note inside the envelope said that Abbie Elliot was traveling with an American passport under the name of Allison Larson and was heading to Paris."

Durand put his palms flat against the window. It wasn't adding up. "And what is the status of her cell mate's fiancé?" he asked. "The car thief?"

"Giorgio Ambrezzi? We still haven't found him, sir," she said. "Neither of his employers has heard from him and he hasn't returned to his apartment. It stands to reason that he stole a car for her and left it for her at the Limoges train station, but we don't know that for certain. And even if he did help her, that doesn't mean he knows where she is."

"Or what she's planning." Durand moaned. Abbie Elliot was giving him indigestion. "And the plane ticket?" he asked.

"Sir, it was purchased yesterday in Paris. There is a bona fide Visa card issued in the name of Allison Larson. And as far as we can tell, there was a real Allison Larson who lived in the United States, outside Chicago, until her death last month."

"Hmph. And this Giorgio person—the car thief? Is he capable of this type of fraud?"

"It's not in his background, sir. But it's certainly possible. Why, are you thinking it might be someone else?"

Durand thought about that. "Maybe," he said. "So Allison Larson had a boarding pass for a flight out of France and was on her way to Brazil," he said. "She'd gotten out. She was gone. She'd won. But instead, she changes her mind and drives back to Paris. She's coming right back to us, Verose. Why?"

Verose shrugged. "Maybe Brazil is an unknown to her. She might not make it through customs, for all she knows. And Paris? If you're going to hide, a city of more than two million people isn't a bad place."

"Is that what she's doing? Hiding?" Durand shook his head. He thought for a second and made a decision. "You still have that friend at *Le Monde*, Verose?"

"Yes, sir."

"Good." He nodded to himself. "I want a story leaked tonight. We believe that she's made it across the Spanish border."

Verose understood. The DCRI routinely used the press for its own purposes. "You want her to feel comfortable here in Paris," she ventured.

"I want her guard down, yes," Durand said. "Tomorrow morning, I want her to read in the papers that we think she's in Barcelona."

CHAPTER 128

I WALKED ALONG the Seine, trying to enjoy the brisk air and the subdued energy of a Paris evening. I crossed the bridge at the Place de la Concorde, just at the west end of the Jardin des Tuileries, the beautiful garden that runs between the Place de la Concorde and the Louvre, at the garden's eastern end. When I was an ordinary citizen, this had been my favorite part of Paris for a daytime stroll. But it wasn't daytime, I wasn't out for a stroll, and I was no ordinary citizen.

I turned onto the Avenue des Champs-Élysées and walked west, toward the Arc de Triomphe. No, I was no ordinary citizen. I was a fugitive, the most wanted person in all Europe. At any point as I walked, people could catch a glimpse of my face and wonder. They could mention it to a police officer. They could make a phone call.

I was doing my best not to look like someone who'd just escaped from prison. I was no longer wearing a baseball cap pulled low over my face. My ratty gym bag was gone. Now I was an upscale shopper on the Champs-Élysées, a woman dressed in a new cocktail dress and heels, carrying shopping bags from a high-end boutique. But I still had the same face, a face that had been splashed across French television for months on end, and, if anyone needed a reminder, was now displayed on lampposts and store windows all around this city. Sooner or later, somebody would recognize me if I stayed in Paris.

After a fifteen-minute walk, I stopped at the Cinema Lamarcke, located not quite halfway between the Arc de Triomphe and the Place de la Concorde, where the Champs-Élysées intersects the Rue de Marignan and the Rue Marbeuf.

I took a deep breath. A dark movie theater wasn't a bad place to get lost.

The Lamarcke was showing four movies on six screens. I was a bit behind on pop culture of late, so I didn't recognize the titles or most of the actors. I picked the movie that had the latest showing, a 2005 film called *La Trahison*. It was scheduled to begin at 10:45.

The Lamarcke was an entire complex: it included a brasserie, whose patrons were still enjoying their meals; a women's boutique; a store that sold children's clothing; a travel store; and a small café, which was closed. You had to take an escalator down to the movie theaters.

Downstairs, there were two theaters to the left and four to the right. One of the theaters on the left was the gigantic theater they called the Lamar. It was named after the man who founded this theater, Lamar Lamarcke, a French thespian of the late 1800s.

I handed my movie ticket to the clerk and walked down the hallway to the two theaters on the left. I poked my head into the Lamar, though it wasn't showing my movie. I walked up the ramp and looked around. On the screen, Cameron Diaz was kicking someone in the face and screaming. The theater was enormous—probably seven or eight hundred seats, including a giant balcony.

I then walked down to the neighboring theater, which was showing my movie. It had the same setup, but the balcony was smaller and there were fewer and narrower rows on the main floor. It was dwarfed by its neighbor, the Lamar.

I freshened up in the women's bathroom. It had sleek, modern fixtures of stainless steel, a clean marble floor, and five stalls. When I walked back out into the hallway, I almost ran into a janitor, who was pushing an oversize garbage can with assorted cleaning products hanging from it.

"*Bonsoir,*" he sang. He was a chipper elderly man.

"*Bonsoir,*" I answered, but he was already past me. He reached the end of the hallway and opened a door, flipped on a light, and pushed the garbage can inside. From what I could tell, it was a pretty spacious room. I saw a ladder propped up against the wall, a snow shovel—did it ever snow in Paris?—and a whole rack of cleaning supplies on the wall.

I sat on a bench and put my head against the soft wall. I was dreadfully tired. I'd already made a big blunder at the hotel and nearly been caught. And who knew what other mistakes I had made or would make?

The janitor whistled a carefree song as he walked past me again, his duties for the evening presumably completed, his supplies stored away, and a time card ready to be punched. A simple life. How desperately I envied him.

A sprinkling of moviegoers filtered into the smaller theater for the 10:45 showing. Probably fifty people, tops, doing the late-night movie thing. I envied them, too. Frivolous entertainment hadn't been a priority for me for well over a year now.

I stayed outside the theater on that bench until I could hear the sounds of the movie beginning, the melodramatic opening music.

When I was alone, I walked over to the janitor's closet and opened it up.

CHAPTER 129

THE JANITOR'S CLOSET wasn't all that spacious and it wasn't remotely comfortable, but it was a place to hide for the time being. I couldn't be sure when, or if, someone would open this closet. So I parked myself behind the garbage can and lay completely flat. I threw some large, thick drop cloths over me and tried to calculate what someone opening the door would see.

Presumably, no one would be expecting a person lying on the floor camouflaged by drop cloths and obscured by a garbage can. But I didn't know what to think. I didn't have a better idea. That janitor sure looked like he was done for the night, so I had to play the odds as best I could.

I'd slept on worse floors, of course. I'd slept in cell 413, after all, where rodents regularly trolled and where the odor of fungus and decay was overpowering. I'd take the intense smell of cleaning chemicals any day over that prison.

My mind started playing tricks on me as I drifted in and out of sleep. I lost track of time and didn't even hear the movie end. Sleep deprivation was a powerful thing.

My watch said it was almost three-thirty in the morning. Surely the last movie had long ago ended and the Lamarcke was in hibernation for the night.

I tentatively pushed open the door into darkness and listened. I could not hear the faintest sound. The Lamarcke was definitely closed.

I walked over to the movie theater that had been showing the 10:45 movie, the smaller one next to the Lamar. The door opened. If it had been locked, I don't know what I would have done.

I walked in and took the stairs up to the balcony. I found a cozy space in the back and nestled in. No jammies for me. I still had my cocktail dress and heels. I would use my purse for a pillow.

Durand would be searching every hotel in Paris tonight for Allison Larson, or anyone who fit my description and who managed to get around the passport requirement. He would probably be searching parking garages, expecting me to be sleeping in my car. He would probably have officers out on the streets and in the nightclubs and the train stations.

But I was pretty sure he wouldn't be looking for me in the Cinema Lamarcke.

Still, Durand was close now. He knew I was in Paris and he knew he had missed me by no more than an hour or so at the hotel. I had rushed through a shower, changed, and run out of there down the back staircase. If I'd so much as caught a catnap—which I had seriously contemplated doing—I'd be in French custody right now.

I shuddered at the thought. No way, I told myself again. No way was I going back to prison.

I stretched my back. My shoulders ached from tension. The truth was, I didn't know what Durand knew, or how close he was.

I ran my hand over my purse for comfort. Inside it was a wad of my remaining cash and a bit of makeup.

And, of course, the Glock I took off Lucy at the prison. I had no intention of shooting another human being. No matter what happened, I wasn't a killer and I wasn't going to let them turn me into one.

But I did keep a single bullet in the chamber. It was reserved for one possible outcome—the outcome, if I were honest with myself, that was the most likely end to all this. And it was the worst outcome of all.

The bullet was reserved for the possibility that Durand would catch me before I could prove my innocence.

And in that event, the bullet would be for me.

CHAPTER 130

COLONEL DURAND'S BLACK sedan pulled in through the gates of the Palais de Justice at seven in the morning. He was with his top aide, Verose. He would spend the day in Paris; indeed, he would spend every day in Paris until he found Abbie Elliot.

"They found his body last night, after he wouldn't answer his front door or his phone," Verose told him. "He was in his bedroom. A single bullet between his eyes. Not from close range, sir."

Not from close range. No chance of a suicide. Which meant that the warden, Boulez, had been murdered.

Had Abbie killed the warden? Things were getting stranger by the day.

"Tell me about today," Durand said.

"We'll have more than two hundred agents and officers on the streets," said Verose. "All of them in plain clothes. We have flashed a directive to every hotel, asking them to be on the lookout for her passport. Every transportation hub is covered. She won't leave Paris, sir."

Durand nodded to a guard as he entered the building. "You're assuming she *wants* to leave Paris," he said.

* * *

Another car was parked just down the street from the Palais de Justice. Christien Brookes sat at the wheel, watching Durand and his associate enter the Palais. On the seat beside him was today's edition of *Le Monde*. The headline—ABBIE À ESPAGNE?—stared back at him. The front-page story described how French authorities believed that Abbie Elliot either was headed to Spain or had already made it across the border to Barcelona.

He smirked at the headline. A nice plant by Durand, no doubt. A smart move, too. Durand obviously missed Abbie last night. But he was probably close. And why not make her feel safe while he inched ever closer?

Speaking of which—how *did* Durand miss Abbie last night? Christien didn't know. He'd done all he could do, slipping that note to the French police and tipping them off about the name Allison Larson. Somehow, she had avoided capture. Maybe she hadn't stayed in a hotel, and thus hadn't used her passport.

Or maybe Abbie wasn't even *in* Paris. Christien didn't know for certain. He lacked the resources to keep tabs on her. Sure, he had a friend waiting for her at Bordeaux-Mérignac, a former colleague at SIS who now lived in nearby Lyon and did Christien a favor. But he didn't have anyone following her afterward. He didn't know where she went after she scurried out of the airport.

Still, he liked Paris as the most likely option. He was pretty sure she was here.

And he was pretty sure he knew why.

He removed the .45 from under his seat and fitted the suppressor on it. He wouldn't need it for a while yet, but it never hurt to check the fitting.

"Why didn't you just get on that bloody plane?" he whispered.

CHAPTER 131

SIX P.M. THE limousine pulled up and two men, Simon Schofield and Colton Gordon, stepped out. Crowds of spectators flanked each side of the entrance. Flashbulbs went off, but only a few. Though they were men of wealth and power and immaculate in their tuxedos, Simon and Colton were relative unknowns under these circumstances.

They walked along the red carpet into the entrance. They were stopped by a man holding a list on a clipboard. They gave their names. They passed an area where others had stopped to have their photographs taken against a backdrop of black and red. But nobody was itching to take photos of Colton or Simon. They weren't famous and they weren't much to look at. They had money. That was their ticket tonight. That was always their ticket.

They took the escalator downstairs, where a healthy crowd had already gathered. Hors d'oeuvres were passed by waiters in white jackets. The themed appetizers were elaborate—*matjeshering*-and-apple canapés, made with salted herring; onion tarts; *kartoffel kloesse*, plump potato dumplings; *brunede kartofler*, delectable sugar-browned potatoes—and the Champagne and liquor flowed freely.

Colton and Simon looked around in amusement. This wasn't really their scene. They usually hobnobbed with traders and speculators and financiers. But they belonged here—they'd earned a spot here tonight—and they might as well enjoy it.

Colton took a bite of an onion tart and washed it down with a swallow of Champagne. "So she's in Barcelona," he said.

"If you believe *Le Monde*. And the authorities." Simon shrugged. "Never know with Abbie, do you? I have to admit, I underestimated her."

Colton watched Simon a moment. He wasn't used to hearing Simon concede anything. "You think we should be worried, *brah*? Our *gats* are hanging out in the wind, are they?"

Simon looked about, ensuring that nobody was listening to this conversation. They weren't. Most of them were tipsy, if not drunk, and had less weighty issues on their minds. "I think all the bases are covered, Colt. Don't go getting excited."

Colton didn't appreciate the admonishment. He patted his jacket, the inside pocket that held his firearm. "No need to get excited when I have my lady with me."

"Great, Colt." Simon rolled his eyes. "If we'd left things up to you, you'd have walked over to our wives at that hotel pool and gunned them down. You almost ruined everything by going to Monte Carlo as it was."

"Did I? Maybe if you'd told me you had yourself a *fokken* plan, I wouldn't have. But you kept all that to yourself, *brah*." Colt guzzled his Champagne and pointed the glass at Simon. "Besides, by yourself, what did you have? A key card? A bit of Serena's hair and blood? You didn't have any plan for carrying it out." He shook his head. "You were just a jealous husband who wanted to pay back his wife. I'd wager that, left to your own devices, you couldn't have pulled it off, when it came down to it."

Simon had to acknowledge the point. All those months after discovering Serena's affair, as Simon stewed and plotted revenge, he'd always wondered exactly how he'd do it, or if he even could. When Serena had mentioned her planned ladies' weekend in Monte Carlo, Simon thought he had an opportunity. He figured the trip was a ruse to cover Serena's scheme to spend the weekend with her lover. He played the doting husband, insisting on personally traveling to Monte Carlo weeks in advance to scout out the perfect hotel—which allowed him the chance, when the manager of the Hôtel Métropole stepped out of his office, for Simon to slip the master key card—one that opened every hotel room—off the manager's key ring. Getting DNA evidence from Serena over the following weeks was easy: a plucked eyebrow from the bathroom sink; a fingerprint on a wineglass; a spot of blood on a cutting board when Serena nicked her finger while slicing a tomato.

He had planned it well. But he *hadn't* planned on Colton making his own trip to Monte Carlo to keep a jealous eye on Bryah. He hadn't counted on Colton summoning the other husbands down, either—including Simon, who, unbeknownst to Colton, was already *in* Monte Carlo.

And he hadn't planned for anything that came afterward.

From the front of the reception area, they heard the clank and squeak of a microphone as someone removed it from its stand and spoke into it.

"Everyone," said the man in French-accented English. "If I could have everyone's attention, *s'il vous plaît.*"

After a moment the roomful of guests had settled down and turned toward the front.

"Thank you, all. Thank you for joining us tonight," the man said. "I'd like to welcome each and every one of you to the Cinema Lamarcke."

CHAPTER 132

"NOTHING, SIR. NO REPORTS," said Verose. She looks tired, Durand thought. They were all tired.

Durand, through his headset, had received many of the updates himself as he paced the spacious office he was given in the Palais de Justice throughout the day. Nothing at the airports. Nothing at the bus stations. Zero at the train stations. No positive identifications from the tollbooths.

"She's lying low," Verose said to him.

"Maybe." Durand wasn't convinced. "But when has Abbie Elliot ever lain low?"

Outside the Cinema Lamarcke, another limousine stopped at the curb. The photographers lining the red carpet crept forward and started snapping their pictures before the door had even opened, before the supermodel—the occupant's date—had first stepped out of the car. Television reporters from the French media and correspondents from American network television stations teased their hair and cleared their throats as they prepared for short interviews on the red carpet.

One of them, an anorexic reporter wearing too much hair spray, posed before the camera and flashed her best smile. "This is Tabby Hudson from *Entertainment Tonight*," she said. "We are live at Paris's historic Cinema Lamarcke on the Champs-Élysées for the French premiere of the controversial box-office sensation *Der Führer*. And the star, Damon Kodiak, has just arrived!"

CHAPTER 133

DAMON KODIAK STOOD on the stage inside the Lamar, the complex's gigantic theater, microphone in hand. The supporting cast of *Der Führer,* having just been introduced, lined the stage behind him. Damon had made a few remarks and now choked up. He paused for dramatic effect, looking over the eight hundred people in attendance. "If we don't challenge ourselves," he said softly, "then we are not artists. And more important than that—more important than anything else, my friends—we are not artists if we don't challenge our *audience.* Ladies and gentlemen, I give you *Der Führer.*"

The crowd erupted in applause. The cast walked off the stage and took their seats. Damon was last, soaking in the adoration before bowing once and walking down the steps.

The lights dimmed until it was pitch-black in the theater. The audience settled into a hush of quiet anticipation.

But, unlike the rest of the cast, Damon Kodiak did not take a seat in the front row of the theater. He did not take a seat at all.

Instead, in the darkness, he pivoted and turned toward a corner of the theater where a member of the Lamarcke staff stood like a sentry. As Damon neared him, the man pushed on the wall—a door, actually.

Damon disappeared through it.

Moments later, the movie began with grainy, black-and-white footage of Adolf Hitler addressing a crowd from a balcony. This movie was Damon's crowning achievement. But he wouldn't be watching.

The audience, brimming with anticipation, hadn't noticed Damon's covert exit. Why would they? Their eyes were on the screen, not the corner of the theater. They were eager for the start of this controversial movie.

Except, of course, for two members of the audience, seated in the fourth row on the aisle, who were much more concerned with Damon himself than with his movie.

"Did he just slip out?" Colton whispered to Simon.

CHAPTER 134

DAMON KODIAK CLOSED the door behind him and looked up to the projectionist's booth in the empty theater connected to the Lamar. He waved and smiled to Sam, who had been with the Lamarcke ever since Damon's first movie premiere here, eleven years ago. *Der Führer* was Damon's seventh premiere in this theater and they knew his secret well. And kept it, all these years.

Damon found a seat in the tenth row, square in the middle. The room went black, the curtain parted, and the movie began. Damon's heart fluttered as he watched the two boxing gloves, one bearing the American flag and the other the hammer and sickle of the Soviet Union. They smashed together in an explosion and the scene cut to Rocky Balboa on the verge of knocking out Clubber Lang in their rematch, one of the final scenes of *Rocky III*.

And then there was the opening scene of *Rocky IV.* It had been Damon's acting debut, twenty-six years back, a lifetime ago, when it was all about the art, all about the dream. Damon was a skinny college dropout who wrote poetry and went to the movies every night of the week that he wasn't working one of his two jobs, delivering flowers and painting elementary school classrooms in the local school district.

He'd been nothing more than an extra in *Rocky IV*, a nonspeaking part, one of the security guards at the press conference held to publicize a match between the Russian fighter, Drago, and the American ex-champ, Apollo Creed. He remembered his one day on the set, shaking hands with Sly Stallone and feeling his knees weaken and praying his voice wouldn't crack when he said, "Great to meet you."

He settled into his seat. This was Damon's secret. It had started back with his first starring role, four years after *Rocky IV*, when he knew that his whole career could go bust after one major movie if it flopped. He was so nervous he couldn't stay in his seat at the premiere. Now he had a ritual, which had become a superstition—ducking out of his premieres and prearranging a screening of his acting debut. But now it wasn't about nerves or fear of failure so much as it was a refresher, a reminder of how much this all meant to him. It kept him grounded in a—wait—what—

What was that noise—

At once, something cold pressed into his neck from the right. A hand gripped his left shoulder. From behind him, he felt the body heat, and then he heard a voice he remembered from not so long ago.

"I don't have much time, Damon," said Abbie. "So you better start talking."

CHAPTER 135

AFTER THE INITIAL shock wore off, and I'd made it clear that yes, it was me, and yes, I had a gun, and yes, I was more than willing to use it, Damon grew perfectly still, his hands gripping the armrests of his seat and his eyes trained forward. "How did you know?" he asked.

"How did I know... you'd come here? You told me, you idiot," I said. "You told me all about your little secret when you attend your movie premieres."

Damon let out a brief moan. He obviously didn't remember telling me.

"You have five minutes to tell me what happened or I pull this trigger," I said. "Keep in mind, Damon, that I'm already serving a life sentence for murder. I kill you, I don't kill you, same sentence either way."

Damon didn't move, but his breathing was becoming labored. It probably had something to do with the gun against his neck, and the fact that I was pressing it harder still to make my point.

"Tell me how this started," I said. "And make it fast."

"How this started? I don't *know* how this started—"

"Now, you listen to me," I said through gritted teeth, fear and anger choking my throat. "You and I both know you lied on the witness stand. You ruined my life. So if you think I won't happily *end* yours—"

"Okay, okay, just—don't shoot." I was now gripping his hair tightly with one hand and drilling the gun into his ear with the other. "Okay, I'll tell you," he said.

Colonel Durand checked his watch as he paced his office. He had reports coming in from more than a dozen agents throughout Paris, who were themselves receiving reports from other agents in the city. He'd been giving instructions and monitoring events through his headset all day long. He'd probably walked five miles within this office.

Now it was dusk. With darkness falling over Paris, the focus would shift, because Abbie's behavior would change. She would be looking for a place to sleep. If she picked a hotel, the odds were good they would catch her. If she didn't, she'd be looking for something like an isolated park or a warm train station.

But all that, he realized, was assuming that Abbie simply chose Paris as a place to hide. If she had a particular goal in mind, then all generalizations about fugitive behavior went out the window.

He jumped as his aide, Verose, burst through his office door. "Sir, you have to see this," she said. "Someone has a television on in the conference room."

There was a flat-screen television on the wall of his office. Verose worked the remote until she found the channel she wanted.

On France 24, a correspondent was just signing off on a report from the Cinema Lamarcke on the Champs-Élysées.

Durand blinked twice, staring at the television in disbelief. Was it that easy?

He ran out of his office without a word.

CHAPTER 136

"LOOK, WHAT HAPPENED between us on that boat—it was real, okay?" Damon said to me with some effort, given the gun that was now shoved into his ear. "I wasn't part of any plan. But when I left you—when I got off the yacht—I was walking down the dock and I saw it. I saw the whole thing happen." He sighed nervously, as if reliving something horrifying. "I saw them . . . shoot Devo and Luc in their car."

I tried to steady my nerves. I had kept my hands busy, either gripping Damon's hair or steadying the gun against his ear, to stop them from trembling. My heart was hammering so violently that I had trouble hearing Damon. I didn't think this moment was ever really going to come. Now that it was, I wasn't sure how to handle it.

"I . . . threw myself down on the dock," Damon continued. "It was just instinct to duck down. I probably made a lot of noise. Anyway, they heard me. I . . . I didn't know what to do. I was still processing everything and suddenly they were on the dock, pointing guns at me, and I was on my knees begging them not to kill me. I'd never been so scared in my entire life."

I knew something about fear. I was terrified right now, and I was the one holding the gun. Sweat was dripping into my eyes and my pulse was working so feverishly I was beginning to wonder if this was what it felt like to have a heart attack.

"You have to believe me, Abbie, I was just trying to get out of there alive. I told them who I was and that I'd give them anything—I'd give them money, I'd put them in a movie, anything at all—if they'd spare my life."

"And destroy four other women's lives." The bitter edge to my words made my voice unrecognizable to me.

"I wasn't trying to destroy anything," he said. "I was trying to survive. I knew if I didn't go along with them, they'd kill me."

"Who's 'they,' Damon?" I asked. "Who did this?"

As the other guests watched a young Adolf Hitler struggling to peddle his paintings on the streets of Vienna, Simon Schofield and Colton Gordon huddled and considered their options. "This is our chance," Colton whispered. "We might not get another one."

It was the only reason they'd come to the party tonight, to get a word with Damon before the movie premiere, to make sure that Damon was on the same page with them, to give him a few not-so-friendly reminders. But the star of the show had been mobbed from the moment he stepped out of his limousine. Getting a second alone with Damon Kodiak at this event was harder than getting an audience with the pope.

But now they had a chance. Damon had slipped out of the theater. Maybe he was off to the bathroom, or to the alley for a smoke. Maybe an interview with the press. But if he left through that door, odds were he'd return the same way. They could follow through that door and wait for the chance for their little chat.

Simon looked over at Colton, whose face was illuminated by the light coming off the movie screen. This was becoming a pattern: Colton preferring action over deliberation, always leading with his chin, while Simon played the voice of reason, viewing the bigger picture and plotting out the consequences. Lord knows, Colt had almost blown everything in Monte Carlo when he called the other husbands to join him—but Simon made sure to fly them down on one of his jets, where he could manipulate the passenger manifest and keep their arrival clandestine.

Then again, they'd worked together well as a team. Simon might never have acted without Colton, who was so fierce with rage after watching the wives at the nightclub, and then that orgy on the yacht.

"It's now or never, *brah,* hey?"

Simon felt his pulse surge, just as it had that night.

"All right, Colt," he said. "Let's do it."

CHAPTER 137

"WHO WAS IT?" I repeated, grinding the barrel of the Glock into Damon's ear. "Who killed them?"

It sounded like Damon was beginning to cry. I suddenly realized that I'd been doing the same, that my face was wet with both perspiration and tears.

"No," Damon said, his head dropping. "I can't."

"I already know most of it," I said. "I know about Simon."

It took me way too long to figure it out. But once I started suspecting our husbands, things began to tumble like dominos in my mind. Such as when we first showed up at the Hôtel Métropole, and the receptionist looking up our reservation said, "Simon Schofield"—Simon, not Serena. *Simon* had made the reservation and put it under his name. I didn't know exactly how he did it. But at some time, in some way, somehow, Simon had gotten hold of a key card to our suite.

And Simon, with a net worth approaching a billion dollars, would have been the one who got to the warden, Boulez, too, bribing him to get me to confess and make the case against me airtight. And for all that money, he also managed to get Serena a plum spot in cell block A—Simon's way of apologizing in some small way to his wife for framing her for murder.

"Simon bankrolled your movie, didn't he?" I asked. "This film that Hollywood wouldn't finance. Hush money for you. Right, Damon? That was the deal? You keep quiet about what you know and screw us at trial, and *Der Führer* gets made?"

Damon didn't answer. However Simon had arranged for the money, he'd managed to do it without leaving a trail. Joe Morro at *The New York Times* couldn't find any record of it, and he'd looked pretty hard.

"I'm done playing games." I stood up, putting my full weight behind the gun shoved into Damon's ear. My rage was overtaking everything else now. I hadn't come here to kill Damon Kodiak. I'd come here to get answers. It didn't do me any good to kill him. He was my evidence. He was my only chance. *It didn't do any good to kill him.* But he'd helped them, at the very least, and destroyed me at my trial, and if I wasn't going to make it out of this theater tonight, why should *he*?

Damon, practically lying in a fetal position, started shouting out. "It was the British one and the South African!" he cried. "The South Af—Colt? Colton?—Colton wanted to kill me but the Brit said no. Winnie's husband. He said no, killing me would make this an international scandal because I was a movie star. Two guys dead in a car in Monte Carlo was one thing, but killing a world-famous movie star would bring a huge spotlight on things."

"Killing 'two guys'?" I asked. "One of them was the pres—"

"They didn't know he was President Devereux, Abbie!" Damon insisted, speaking quickly, as if his life depended on it. "Any more than you or I did. You think they would have done any of this if they'd known they were killing the president of France?"

I paused. I was woozy from the adrenaline spikes and sleep deprivation and pure, unadulterated bitterness. But it made sense. They had followed us to Monte Carlo and found us sleeping with other men, but they didn't know who "Devo" was any more than I did.

Right. They thought they were killing two ordinary people. They didn't realize they were creating an international incident.

"The Brit—the British one, he was so calm and cool—he snuck back on the yacht. When he came back, the murder weapon was gone—"

"He left it in my purse."

"—and he had the camcorder. The one that recorded the sex video." Damon was panting as the information poured out in spurts. "The Brit made me touch it. He made me hold it. He made me hold it so my—so my fingerprints were on it. He said to me, 'If we go down, so do you,' or something like that. That was their insurance. If I turned them in, I'd be turning *myself* in, too. It wouldn't matter if I was guilty or innocent. Even if I could keep myself out of prison, if I was associated with this in any way, my career would be finished. Finished!

"And the next day," he went on, vomiting information now, once again pleading for his life, as he did on that dock, "after we all realized that the guy they killed was President Devereux, they got worried that I might change my mind. They were freaking out. So was I. The president of France? This thing had suddenly become so huge! So they offered me the money for the movie. They made me dependent on them. They made us partners. And yes, that part was Simon. It was Simon and Colton's money."

"And what…" I said, my throat catching. "What about my husband, Jeffrey?"

Damon shook his head furiously. "Never met him or saw him. I don't know, Abbie. I swear. I have no idea."

It was all hurtling toward me at once. Much of this I'd already suspected, in the quiet, deliberative hours I'd spent with nothing to do in JRF. But now my pulse was racing so fiercely I could hardly hold still. I was a twitch of the finger away from murdering the number one film star in the world right now.

And I was still light-years away from proving any of this.

Or maybe not.

CHAPTER 138

"PLEASE DON'T KILL ME," Damon pleaded. "Try to see it from my persp—"

"Shut up."

While Damon lay on his side, like a small child, beaten and fearful, I did a two-step maneuver and climbed over the seat so that I was next to him. He didn't move in the process. He watched me with wide eyes as I gripped his shirt.

"You're going to do one more thing for me," I said, "and if you do it right, I promise you I won't kill you."

"What...What—"

"You're going to repeat what you just told me," I said, "to a thousand of your closest friends next door. Get up, movie star."

The man standing sentry by the door through which Damon Kodiak had exited crossed his arms and shook his head. "I'm sorry, gentlemen," he said in English with a heavy accent. "Nobody passes through."

"We saw him go through, lad," Colton said. "We need a word with him just now."

The man shook his head. He was younger and stronger than both of them.

Colton gave Simon a fiery look. Simon had seen that expression before. Colton was about to reach for his gun.

Simon shook his head. He reached for something else—money. A thousand euros, to be exact.

The man looked at the cash offered. His expression softened.

"Two thousand," he countered.

As I pushed Damon forward, I felt my legs gain strength. Could this actually work? I never gave myself much of a chance at succeeding. Now, for the first time, I thought I might pull this off. I felt my head clear, my heartbeat decelerate.

Damon wasn't having a good evening. He was blubbering like a baby, his head hanging low, his posture slumped and defeated, as I gripped the back of his tuxedo jacket and pressed my gun between his shoulder blades.

We reached the end of the aisle, at the front of the theater, when I heard the *thump* of a door opening.

"No," I said.

Colton and Simon, in tuxedos, likewise jumped at the sight of me. Colton reached into his jacket. I didn't have to think very hard about what he was reaching for.

"I'll shoot him!" I warned, bracing myself.

But as soon as the words came out, I realized how empty they were. Killing Damon Kodiak would be perfectly fine with Colton and Simon. He was my last hope to prove my innocence and their guilt. He was their last outstanding liability. I'd be doing them the biggest favor in the world.

Colton raised a gun and aimed it at us.

During the standoff between Abbie and Colton, and with a fight scene from *Rocky IV* playing in the theater, nobody heard or saw the man take the stairs down from the balcony and walk onto the soft carpet of the aisle. Back in the day, this kind of silent movement had been part of Christien's SIS training, and he'd been sure to wear soft-soled shoes tonight. He dropped to a crouch, his feet in a wide stance. Christien raised his weapon, the suppressor attached, and started moving.

CHAPTER 139

THE MOVIE SCREEN in front of us abruptly went blank and the overhead lights came on. Whoever was running the projector had realized that nobody was watching *Rocky IV* at this point. And he was probably calling the police right now.

"Don't come any closer!" I called out to Colton.

"*Ag*, you're a wild *stukkie*, I'll give ya that," said Colton as he inched toward me with his gun raised.

I still had my gun pressed into Damon's back. But it made no sense. Colton would shoot both of us, and claim that Damon got caught in the cross fire. Surely I, the fugitive holding a hostage, would take the blame for everything.

My whole body was in an uncontrollable quiver. I felt helpless. I had a gun but could I... could I really use it? I could do a lot of things to protect myself—I *had* done a lot of things—but shoot someone?

I could see the wild, fiery look in Colton's eyes as he advanced on me. He flanked to his left for a better angle.

Do something, Abbie.

"I'll shoot," I said again, thinking it would buy me a few seconds. That's what Colton wanted, more than anything. He wanted Damon to die by *my* hand, not his. Then he could shoot me and tell a really good story.

"I'll do it, Colton. I'll kill him." I moved the gun to Damon's forehead. Damon was on the verge of collapsing.

A menacing grin played on Colton's face. He was now maybe ten feet from me. He had us in his sights. I watched him pause a moment. One last chance for me to do his dirty work for him and kill Damon Kodiak.

His eyes gained focus. He steeled himself.

Then he froze for a beat, his face going blank. The gun fell from his hands a moment before his legs gave out and he collapsed to the floor. A pool of blood quickly expanded near his forehead.

I looked to the right. Christien. Christien was standing at the top of the same aisle that Damon and I had traveled, holding a gun with a long piece on the end. I assumed it was a suppressor. I certainly hadn't heard him fire the bullet.

Simon stood against the wall just below the movie screen, stunned. He looked at Christien and then at me.

"Christien!" he said. He cleared his throat, as though he were trying to recover. "Christien, thank God—"

"Simon, tell me something." Christien aimed the gun at him. "Who told the warden that my Winnie was an acceptable loss?"

"Not me," he said, raising his hands in surrender. "That was all Boulez."

"Yes, well, I've already dealt with Boulez."

"Christien, I swear—"

Those were the last words that Simon Schofield ever spoke. A dark circle appeared between his eyes and his limp body crumpled to the ground.

Christien lowered his weapon to his side and looked at me. He was wearing the same expression I'd seen in Onzain, one of despair and regret. A single tear trickled down his face as he approached me.

Damon broke free of me and started to run toward the other theater. I couldn't have stopped him if I wanted to. And I didn't want to.

I pointed my gun at Christien, who stood before me, helpless, his own weapon at his side. For all I knew, he wanted me to shoot.

"Christien," I said. "Was Jeffrey part of this?"

Christien's shoulders relaxed. He seemed to be past the deception. It was over, and he knew it. "I can give whatever answer you'd like," he said.

I thought I knew what he meant. "The truth," I said. "Once and for all, Christien, I want the *truth*."

CHAPTER 140

WE HAD PRECIOUS few seconds. The police or theater security would be here any moment now.

"You were the one who snuck into our hotel suite and got the DNA evidence," I guessed. "Simon had the key card somehow but you pulled it off. An easy task for a former SIS agent, right?"

Christien grimaced. "Not so easy, it turned out. I only got to the first bedroom—yours and Win's—before I heard someone in the hallway. I settled for what I could get and got out of there. Simon had been kind enough to bring some trace evidence of Serena with him on the trip, so that gave us three out of four wives."

That explained the lack of Bryah's DNA at the crime scene.

"Who killed Devo and Luc?" I asked.

Christien paused only a beat before he released a heavy sigh. At this point, he probably figured, there was no point in withholding anything. Quite the opposite, in fact—it seemed as though he wanted this off his chest.

"Colt shot the bodyguard," he said. "But I wanted Winnie's man for myself."

"Keep going, Christien. And hurry."

"Simon stood lookout at the harbor, watching for any cars entering."

I closed my eyes and lowered the gun. "And Jeffrey watched the dock," I said. It was a guess. I hoped beyond all reason that I was wrong.

"Jeff was the one who spotted the movie star coming off the yacht."

It felt like a needle through my heart. I'd suspected it, but it was different hearing it confirmed as fact. My husband, the father of my children, had been complicit in murdering two people and framing me. He'd watched as I was sent to prison for the rest of my life.

From the top of the theater, the entrance for regular customers, we both heard the sound of urgent footsteps. The cavalry was coming.

Christien quickly turned back to me. "You don't owe me anything, love, but for Winnie?"

I choked up at the mention of her name. So did Christien.

"My sister will take Nat and Dory," he said, referring to his children. "But do make sure they're okay. And tell them—"

Christien's voice cut out. He took a deep breath. His eyes were shimmering with tears. "Tell them Pappy tried to do the right thing in the end."

The door at the rear of the theater burst open. Colonel Bernard Durand came through, followed by a number of his agents, all with their guns drawn. Durand called out to us to drop our weapons as DCRI agents flooded the theater.

Through a heavy throat, I said, "You have my word, Christien."

I dropped my weapon and held my hands up high, so that there would be no misunderstanding. Durand didn't need extra incentive to shoot me.

I made eye contact with the colonel, who reached the end of the other aisle and then began to move toward me. Other agents, coming down the aisle nearer me, rushed past me. It was only then that I realized that Christien was gone. He'd fled through the fire door. And they were chasing him.

I made sure to show Square Jaw my palms. Even this creep wouldn't shoot somebody in full surrender mode.

But as he approached me, Durand's expression softened. Around him, agents were checking on Colton and Simon, but Durand was simply walking up to me. He even dropped his weapon to his side.

As we stood nearly face-to-face, I lowered my hands and held them out, readying them for handcuffs. Durand looked at my hands as if amused by my gesture.

And I wouldn't swear to this, but I even thought I saw the trace of a smile cross his face.

CHAPTER 141

OUTSIDE THIS TINY movie theater, it was bedlam. The guests watching *Der Führer* had been oblivious to what had happened. The only gunshots, after all, had come from Christien's suppressor, and the soundproofing was obviously good in the Lamarcke.

But once DCRI had shown up, everything turned upside down. The police were engaged in full-scale crowd control, corralling the guests and paparazzi on hand. These reporters were accustomed to covering celebrity divorces and judging red-carpet fashion shows; they hardly knew what to say to me as I navigated through them, with Colonel Durand lightly holding my arm at the bicep.

We walked into fresh air, where more photographers were snapping our photos and the Champs-Élysées was swarming with onlookers. Someone opened the rear door of a long black sedan and Durand helped me into the car.

Durand sat across from me in the spacious rear compartment and heaved a heavy sigh.

"You know the truth," I said to him.

He nodded.

I cocked my head. "How?"

Durand came forward, his elbows on his knees. "I wish I could take credit for solving this...puzzle. But the truth, Miss Abbie, is otherwise. It was the papers you filed with the court just before you escaped."

At my direction, my lawyer, Jules, had issued requests to subpoena a number of documents, including the cell phone records of our husbands on the days surrounding the president's murder. We requested the passenger manifests for all Simon's jets, hoping to find evidence of travel to or from Monte Carlo. We also requested all documents connected with the financing of Damon Kodiak's new movie, *Der Führer.* We had asked for the surveillance videos from the Hôtel Métropole for every day from the time that Simon had made our reservation until the president's murder.

And finally, we had requested the phone records of my favorite warden, Antoine Boulez, for the entire time I was housed at JRF.

And we explained our theory that the husbands had been complicit in the murders and a frame-up. Simon had the key card, which he used to gather DNA evidence. They bribed Damon to go along with their story by financing an otherwise unfinanceable movie. And in further covering up those crimes, they bribed Boulez to pressure me to confess, as the others had done.

"You gave me reason for suspicion," Durand said. "So I...pursued the matter more...vigorously."

He produced from his pocket a small voice recorder. "Colton, Simon, and your husband," he said to me before hitting PLAY.

The sound wasn't perfect, and had some accompanying static. I leaned forward and listened with a combination of dread and morbid curiosity.

"You've got to relax, Jeffrey." Simon's voice. "This court filing will be embarrassing, yes. But ultimately she can't prove anything."

"You don't know Abbie like I do."

Jeffrey's voice. I felt a catch in my throat.

"No, but I do know the evidence," said Simon. "Or lack thereof. The manifests were taken care of long ago, you'll recall. There is absolutely no evidence of any of us traveling in or out of Monte Carlo. None. Zero. And the phone records?"

"*Ag, brah,* that just proves we talked to each other." Colton joining in. "And I don't think we used them much at all once we were together."

"We didn't," said Simon. "For this very reason. Christien was adamant, remember, Jeff? He said cell calls could be triangu—triangulated, I think was the word. So we didn't use them. You're panicking, Jeff. You're just not remembering."

"Okay, fine," Jeffrey answered, sounding very much panicked, as Simon had pointed out. "And your phone calls to Boulez, Simon? Could those be traced back to you?"

"They could," Simon replied, "if I were a complete idiot. But lucky for us, Jeff, I'm not. The calls I've made to Boulez will not trace back to me. And neither will the cash—if they ever even discover the cash, which they won't. Boulez had strict instructions to keep the money out of a bank account. I promised him I'd make up for the lost interest earnings with an extra million on the back end, once his job was completed."

I did a slow burn. "Once his job was completed" meant my confession or my death.

"And the Hôtel Métropole?" Simon went on. "She's reaching. She can't prove I got hold of a key card. And it seems our good friend Christien, wherever he may be, lived up to his billing when he snuck into the suite. If there was any evidence of him being there, they'd have found it by now."

"We still have the actor," Jeffrey said. "How do we control for that?"

"Jeffrey, Jeffrey." Simon sounded as though he were laughing. "If the actor comes forward now, he admits to perjury on the witness stand. And you'll recall, if you can make your brain work a little harder, that we have that camcorder with his fingerprints on it."

"Right. Okay. But there's still the money for the movie."

"Yes, you're correct, Jeffrey. It's possible that Kodiak will be forced to disclose that information. But even if he does, what does it prove?

We set up the financing so that Colton and I had equity in the deal. For this very reason, Jeff. So if it ever came to light, we would simply look like people making an investment."

"And I don't know if you've noticed, *brah,* but this movie is setting records," Colton added. "We're in for tens of millions of dollars of return."

"Right, Colt. So Jeff, in the end, what does that money prove? It proves that Colton and I are shrewd investors. And I'll tell you, Jeff, that I will have no trouble admitting to that under oath."

The men's laughter cut off in mid-burst. Durand killed the recorder and sat back in his seat. "When I saw your papers, I spoke with your colleague at the embassy, Mr. Ingersoll. We…collaborated on a plan."

I was still shell-shocked by all this, but I nodded.

"He invited the Americans…your husband and Simon, to the embassy. He showed them your court papers to…elicit?…elicit a reaction. And while they met, we planted recording devices in their cell phones, which they left with the marine guards at the station outside."

The car began to move into traffic on a boulevard that was filling up with police cars and ambulances and media trucks and people who were just plain curious. I put my head back against the cushion and closed my eyes.

"You know what's pathetic?" I said. "All that time during the investigation and trial, while I was trying to figure out who framed us, I considered everyone in the world a suspect. I even considered you, Colonel. But I never once considered our husbands."

The colonel clucked his tongue again. "This is not…pathetic. It is because you are a good person. You would not suspect those closest to you."

I sighed. I never thought I'd see the day that Colonel Durand called me a good person.

"Miss Abbie," said Durand, "I am so very sorry."

CHAPTER 142

THE PRESIDING JUDGE looked stately but slightly uncomfortable in his red robe. He and the other judges listened attentively as the prosecutor, Maryse Ballamont, completed her formal recitation to the court.

"I will ask the accused to please rise," said the presiding judge. As before, his French was translated through our headphones into English.

Serena, Bryah, and I had been seated with our lawyers at the table outside the cage where defendants normally sat. Technically, they could have placed us inside the cage, as they had previously. But it would have been a pure formality, and a tacky gesture under the circumstances.

The presiding judge nodded to each of us respectfully. "There is a principle deeply embedded in our republic's consciousness that it is far better for the guilty to go free than to convict even a single innocent person. There is nothing more offensive, no greater harm that a government can inflict against an individual, than to imprison her wrongly. Ms. Gordon, Ms. Schofield, Ms. Elliot: the French Republic owes you an apology."

I closed my eyes and inhaled deeply and let those words wash over me. Words I thought I would never hear.

"On motion of the prosecution and with the consent of the defense, the court finds unanimously that the newly discovered evidence has demonstrated beyond any doubt that the accused are not guilty of the crimes as charged in the transfer judgment. The accused are to be released from custody at once. This court is adjourned."

The courtroom erupted in applause. Serena, Bryah, and I held hands and then broke down into tight embraces and then, finally, inevitably, into violent and joyful sobs. So much passed between us in those moments. We had each fallen so far and so hard, our lives turned entirely inside out, only to unexpectedly come out the other end in one piece.

In one piece, but not unscathed. Each of our children had, in a very real sense, lost their mothers, only to regain them at the expense of their fathers. Katie Mei, for over a year, had only a father, and now in an instant her mother was back and Simon was dead. Bryah's boy suffered the same result.

And my Richie and Elena—teenagers, both of them, since Elena had her birthday last month: I tried to tell myself that it was different for them, because they didn't live with Jeffrey, they'd been at boarding school, they were more emancipated than Bryah's and Serena's young kids. But it was a reach, I knew. They were old enough to understand that their father had been part of a horrific crime and had done what still, after all this time, seemed utterly unthinkable—he had framed me for it. They had believed in my innocence, and even if they hadn't, no doubt they would have stood by me anyway. But now it was different. They knew their father was guilty, and at least part of the crime he'd committed was against me—and, in that sense, against them as well.

And I couldn't leave myself out of the list of casualties, either. I was alive and I was free and I was reunited with my children. But I didn't kid myself. Something like this changes you. It breaks you into pieces and puts you back together, but the sum total is different. I felt like a car that had been in a violent collision—you can get it to run again, but it's never quite the same.

It would be a long time, I knew, before the bitterness left me. A longer time still before I could trust anyone again. I didn't want the book deals offered to me. I didn't want to sit down with *60 Minutes* or *People* magazine for an exclusive interview. I only wanted the one thing I couldn't have—my life, before all this happened.

Richie and Elena came through the barrier and laid themselves gently against me. I cupped their heads and fought back more tears. We'd been together three days now, since the French flew them to Paris and put all of us together in a hotel in the Latin Quarter. That, I thought, had been decent of Durand. Technically, I was still a convicted felon, so the compromise was that they made me stay under police guard while we ordered room service and watched pay-per-view movies on DCRI's tab.

Over Richie's and Elena's heads I saw Giorgio Ambrezzi and Dan Ingersoll in the gallery. I felt a squeeze of my heart when I thought of Linette, the love of Giorgio's life, dead not because of anything she did but because of me. I couldn't have done this without Giorgio. I never could have escaped from prison. Colonel Durand seemed to understand this on some level, judging from comments he'd made to me, but there was no direct proof of Giorgio's complicity and, in any event, Durand clearly lacked the appetite to pursue the matter. All's well that ends well, or something like that.

Dan Ingersoll had been more than a government official doing his job. He'd been my friend. He'd gone to bat for me as much as he could and, according to Durand, it had been Dan's idea to bring Jeff and Simon to the embassy so Durand could plant recording devices in their cell phones.

He was pretty cute, too. He'd mentioned to me more than once over the last three days that his time in Paris would be ending soon, that he'd be back at the Justice Department in D.C. by next summer.

I smiled at him, he smiled back at me, and I realized that these tiny little encounters and interactions and things, just *things* in life, were what I missed most.

Now that the court had adjourned, the cameras were flashing feverishly. I found it rather invasive, but at least the coverage of me had flip-flopped from negative to positive. And after everything I'd been through, having a few cameras in my face was like a walk in the park.

"It's going to be like this for a little while," I told Richie and Elena, as we began to navigate our way through the reporters and paparazzi.

"You deserve it, Mom," Elena said. "They spent a year tearing you down as some bad person. Let them build you up for a while now that you're a hero."

I stopped and looked at Elena. Those weren't words my eleven-year-old would have spoken, before I was arrested. But they were the words of the thirteen-year-old standing before me.

I had missed those crucial fifteen months, terrifying and confusing and exhilarating times that Elena had endured without her mother. I would make up for it as best I could now. If they wanted to stay in boarding school in Connecticut, that's where I was going to move. If they wanted to return to Georgetown, so be it.

"Hero?" I laughed. "I'm no hero, kiddo. I'm just a survivor."

Richie planted a kiss on my cheek. "You're *our* hero, Mom," he said.

It wouldn't be the last time today that I smiled through tears.

CHAPTER 143

THE WALK THROUGH the basement of the Palais de Justice brought back a flood of emotions and memories so violent, so overwhelming, that I had to remind myself to breathe. I also had to remind myself of my newfound status. *You're free, Abbie, it wasn't a dream.* I would always equate France with my captivity, with my utter degradation, with a period of time when everything was stolen from me.

I will dream about this dungeon, about JRF, about my interrogation at DCRI—all of this—for the rest of my life. No matter how fiercely I scrub my teeth, I will always taste it. No matter how tightly I shut my eyes, I will always see it. No matter how low the temperature on the air-conditioning, I will always feel the rabid heat of cell 413.

The escort guard stopped at the cell. *"Voulez-vous aller à l'intérieur?"* he asked me.

I shook my head no. I would stay on this side of the cage.

Jeffrey was sitting on a bench that was fixed to the wall, hunched over, his elbows on his knees. His hair was greasy, his face unshaven, his white shirt stained with sweat at the armpits.

The last act that Colonel Bernard Durand performed before he resigned his post was arresting Jeffrey at the hotel where he was staying, near the U.S. Embassy. I'm told that Jeffrey took it bravely, that he handled himself well.

"We're leaving today," I said.

He nodded. "The kids didn't come with you?"

"You couldn't possibly expect them to."

Jeffrey rubbed his hands together. He had to appreciate how terribly he'd betrayed his family. "This might sound pathetic, Abbie, but none of this was my idea. I went along with it. I did. But I didn't come up with the idea, and I didn't plan it or execute it. I went along for the ride. There's a difference."

"You're right," I said. "It does sound pathetic."

He didn't answer. He was totally and completely broken.

"You got your lawyer?" I asked.

He nodded. "He thinks we might be able to fight it. There's not—not a lot of direct proof."

That was probably true. Simon and Colton were dead, and Christien was still on the run. Simon and Colton had admitted to plenty on the tape that Durand had recorded, but Jeffrey hadn't admitted to a thing. Clearly he knew about their involvement, but knowing they did something and being a part of it were two different things.

Damon Kodiak was under arrest for perjury. Thus far, at least as far as I knew, he wasn't talking. But even if they could get him to talk, he'd already told me that he had no knowledge of Jeff's involvement.

Ironic, I thought. Jeffrey's incompetence and cowardice might ultimately be his saving grace.

"You're going to deny you were part of the lookout at the harbor?" I asked.

He shrugged his shoulders. "What do *you* think I should do?"

"Hey, my name's Abbie, not Dear Abby."

For just a moment, Jeffrey's face brightened. It was an old line of mine, back when we were dating, when we were madly in love and life was full of doors that were open, not closed.

"I still love you," he said. For the first time, he turned and looked at me. "I never stopped. I know what I did. The affair. But I didn't do that because I didn't love you. I did it because I was afraid you'd stop loving me."

I turned away. "I'm not going to do this, Jeffrey. You made a decision and you betrayed me. And then you made another decision and you betrayed me and your children. You stole their *mother* away! Don't expect me to ever forgive you for that."

A long silence hung between us. Maybe this is why I came here, to say these words to him, just one long-overdue scolding before I went back to America and rebooted my life. Or maybe there was a small part of me that simply wanted to see him behind bars.

"I know what you did," he said. "The phone call from the new French president? My lawyer told me. That was...thank you, Abbie."

I shrugged. "He asked me if there was anything he could do for me."

"And you asked him to show me mercy," he said. "I don't deserve that."

"No, you don't."

But he was still the father of my children. And if there was a possibility that the fracture between Jeffrey and the kids could ever heal, I had to try to make that happen. I was so tired of seeing things torn down and destroyed. I wanted to see things grow.

I moved quickly back through the claustrophobic hallway and chose the stairs over the elevator. I ran up and out of the Palais de Justice and kept running until I was crossing the bridge over the gorgeous Seine.

I wanted things to be better. And the first step was going home.

Acknowledgments

Many thanks to Daniel Morro of the Department of Homeland Security, currently assigned to the U.S. Embassy in Paris, for advice, insight, and observations on Paris and the French criminal justice system. He and his wife, Kathleen Morro, were incredibly gracious answering our questions and helping us explore the wonderful city of Paris.

Thank you to assistant U.S. attorney Laura Ingersoll, who served as the Department of Justice's attaché to the U.S. Embassy in Paris, for spending many hours explaining the substantive and technical details of a French criminal trial. Arnaud Baleste, *capitaine de police* for the Brigade Criminelle in Paris, was very generous with his technical and practical observations about murder investigations in France. When necessary, this novel took some creative license on certain details, which should be attributed to the authors alone.

Thank you to the following for allowing a tour of the Dwight Correctional Center near Dwight, Illinois: David Eldridge, former chief of staff to the director of the Illinois Department of Corrections; Sharyn Elman, the department's chief public information officer; and Sheryl Thompson, the warden at Dwight. Thank you for all the questions you answered and the insight you provided. Although a women's prison in Illinois differs substantially from the fictional prison depicted in this novel, and none of the horrors depicted herein bear any relation to Dwight, the information provided was tremendously helpful.

THE NEW NOVEL IN THE NO. 1 BESTSELLING
PRIVATE SERIES, AVAILABLE NOW

Private: No. 1 Suspect

James Patterson
& Maxine Paetro

Jack Morgan is accused of a horrific murder – and not even his own world-class investigators can prove he didn't do it.

Since former US Marine Jack Morgan started Private, it has become the world's most effective investigation firm – sought out by the famous and the powerful to discreetly handle their most intimate problems. Private's investigators are the smartest, the fastest, and the most technologically advanced in the world – and they always uncover the truth.

When his former lover is found murdered in Jack's bed, he is instantly the number one suspect. While Jack is under police investigation and fighting to clear his name, the mob strong-arms him into recovering $30 million in stolen pharmaceuticals for them. And the beautiful owner of a chain of luxury hotels persuades him to quietly investigate a string of murders at her high-class establishments.

With Jack and his team stretched to breaking point, one of his most trusted colleagues threatens to leave Private, and Jack realises he is facing his biggest challenge yet.

Century · London

Turn the page for a sneak preview of

CHAPTER 1

THE CAR WAS waiting for me at LAX. Aldo was out at the curb, holding a sign reading, "Welcome Home Mr. Morgan."

I shook Aldo's hand, threw my bags into the trunk, and slid onto the cushy leather seat in the back. I'd done six cities in three days, the return leg from Stockholm turning into a twenty-five-hour journey through airline hell to home.

I was wiped out. And that was an understatement.

"Your packet, Jack," Aldo said, handing a folder over the divider. The cover was marked "Private," the name of my private investigation firm. Our main office was in LA, and we had branches in six countries with clients all over the map who demanded and paid well for services not available through public means.

I had worried lately that we were growing too big too fast,

that if big was the enemy of good, *great* didn't stand a chance. And most of all, I wanted Private to be great.

I tucked the folder from Accounting into my briefcase and as the car surfed into the fast lane, I took out my BlackBerry. Unread messages ran into triple digits, so I chose selectively as I thumbed through the list.

The first e-mail was from Viviana, the stunner who'd sat next to me from London to New York. She sold 3-D teleconferencing equipment, not exactly must-have technology, but it was definitely interesting.

There was a text from Paolo, my security chief in Rome, saying, "Our deadbeat client is now just dead. Details to follow." I mentally kissed a two-hundred-thousand-euro fee good-bye and moved to texts from the home team.

Justine Smith, my confidante and number two at Private, wrote, "We've got some catching up to do, bud. I've left the porch light on." I smiled, thinking that as much as I wanted to see her, I wanted to shower and hit the rack even more.

I sent Justine a reply, then opened a text from Rick Del Rio. "Noccia wants to see you pronto, that prick."

The text was like a gut punch.

Carmine Noccia was the scion of the major Mob family by that name, capo of the Las Vegas branch, and my accidental buddy because of a deal I'd had to make with him six months before. If I never saw Carmine Noccia again, it would be way too soon.

I typed a four-letter reply, sent it to Del Rio, and put my phone back into my pocket as the car turned into my driveway. I collected my bags and watched Aldo back out, making sure he didn't get T-boned on Pacific Coast Highway.

I swiped my electronic key fob across the reader and went through the gate, pressed my finger to the biometric pad, and entered my home sweet home.

For a half second, I thought I smelled roses, but I chalked it up to the delight of standing again in my own house.

I started stripping in the living room and by the time I'd reached the bathroom, I was down to my boxers, which I kicked off outside the shower stall.

I stood under water as hot as I could stand it, then went into my bedroom and hit the wall switch that turned on the lights on either side of the bed.

For a long moment, I stood frozen in the doorway. I couldn't understand what I saw—because it made no sense. How could Colleen be in my bed? Her sweater was soaked with blood.

What the hell was this?

A tasteless prank?

I shouted her name, and then I was on my knees beside the bed, my hand pressing the side of her neck. Her skin was as warm as life—but she had no pulse.

Colleen was wearing a knee-length skirt and a blue cardigan, clothes I'd seen her wear before. Her rose-scented hair was fanned out around her shoulders and her violet-blue eyes were closed. I gripped her shoulders and gently shook her, but her head just lolled.

Oh, Jesus. No.

Colleen was dead.

How in God's name had this happened?

CHAPTER 2

I'D SEEN COUNTLESS dead while serving in Afghanistan. I've worked murders as part of my job for years, and I've even witnessed the deaths of friends.

None of that protected me from the horror of seeing Colleen's bloody and lifeless form. Her blood spattered the bedspread, soaking through. Her sweater was so bloody I couldn't see her wounds. Had she been stabbed? Shot? I couldn't tell.

The covers were pulled tight and I saw no sign of a struggle. Everything in the room was exactly as I had left it four days ago—everything but Colleen's dead body, right here.

I thought about Colleen's attempted suicide after we'd broken up six months ago—the scars were visible: silver lines on her wrists. But this was no suicide.

There was no weapon on or near the bed.

It looked as if Colleen had come into my bedroom, put her head on the pillow, and then been killed while she slept.

And that made no sense.

Just then, my lagging survival instinct kicked in. Whoever had killed Colleen could still be in the house. I went for the window seat where I kept my gun.

My hands shook as I lifted the hinged top of the window seat and grabbed the metal gun box. It was light. Empty.

I opened the closet doors, looked under the bed, saw no one, no shells, no nothing. I stepped into jeans, pulled on a T-shirt, then walked from window to window to door, checking locks, staring up at skylights looking for broken panes.

And I backtracked through my mind.

I was certain the front door had been locked when I came home. And now I was sure that every other entry point was secure.

That could only mean that someone had entered my house with an electronic gate key and biometric access—someone who knew me. Colleen had been my assistant and my lover for a year before we'd broken up. I hadn't deleted her codes.

Colleen wasn't the only one with access to my house, but maybe I wouldn't have to guess who had killed her.

My house was watched by the best surveillance system ever made. There were cameras posted on all sides, over the doorways, sweeping the highway, and taking in 180 degrees of beachfront beyond my deck.

I opened the cabinet doors on the entertainment unit in the living room and flipped the switch turning on the six video monitors stacked in two columns of three. All six screens lit up—and all six screens were blank. I stabbed the buttons on the remote control again and again before I realized the hard drive was gone. Only a detached cord remained.

I grabbed the phone by the sofa and called Justine's direct line at the office. It was almost seven. Would she still be there?

She answered on the first ring.

"Jack, you hungry after all?"

"Justine. Something bad has happened."

My voice cracked as I forced myself to say it.

"It's Colleen. She's dead. Some *bastard* killed her."

JAMES PATTERSON

**To find out more about James Patterson
and his bestselling books, go to
www.jamespatterson.co.uk**

Also by James Patterson

ALEX CROSS NOVELS

Along Came a Spider • Kiss the Girls • Jack and Jill •
Cat and Mouse • Pop Goes the Weasel • Roses are Red •
Violets are Blue • Four Blind Mice • The Big Bad Wolf •
London Bridges • Mary, Mary • Cross • Double Cross •
Cross Country • Alex Cross's Trial (*with Richard DiLallo*) •
I, Alex Cross • Cross Fire • Kill Alex Cross

THE WOMEN'S MURDER CLUB SERIES

1st to Die • 2nd Chance (*with Andrew Gross*) • 3rd Degree
(*with Andrew Gross*) • 4th of July (*with Maxine Paetro*) •
The 5th Horseman (*with Maxine Paetro*) • The 6th Target
(*with Maxine Paetro*) • 7th Heaven (*with Maxine Paetro*) •
8th Confession (*with Maxine Paetro*) • 9th Judgement
(*with Maxine Paetro*) • 10th Anniversary (*with Maxine Paetro*) •
11th Hour (*with Maxine Paetro*)

DETECTIVE MICHAEL BENNETT SERIES

Step on a Crack (*with Michael Ledwidge*) • Run for Your Life
(*with Michael Ledwidge*) • Worst Case (*with Michael Ledwidge*) •
Tick Tock (*with Michael Ledwidge*) • I, Michael Bennett
(*with Michael Ledwidge, to be published June 2012*)

PRIVATE NOVELS

Private (*with Maxine Paetro*) •
Private London (*with Mark Pearson*) •
Private Games (*with Mark Sullivan*) •
Private: No. 1 Suspect (*with Maxine Paetro*)

NON-FICTION

Torn Apart (*with Hal and Cory Friedman*) •
The Murder of King Tut (*with Martin Dugard*)

ROMANCE

Sundays at Tiffany's (*with Gabrielle Charbonnet*) •
The Christmas Wedding (*with Richard DiLallo*)

FAMILY OF PAGE-TURNERS

MAXIMUM RIDE SERIES

The Angel Experiment • School's Out Forever •
Saving the World and Other Extreme Sports •
The Final Warning • Max • Fang • Angel •
Nevermore (*to be published August 2012*)

DANIEL X SERIES

The Dangerous Days of Daniel X (*with Michael Ledwidge*) •
Daniel X: Watch the Skies (*with Ned Rust*) •
Daniel X: Demons and Druids (*with Adam Sadler*) •
Daniel X: Game Over (*with Ned Rust*)

WITCH & WIZARD SERIES

Witch & Wizard (*with Gabrielle Charbonnet*) •
Witch & Wizard: The Gift (*with Ned Rust*) •
Witch & Wizard: The Fire (*with Jill Dembowski*)

MIDDLE SCHOOL SERIES

Middle School: The Worst Years of My Life
(*with Chris Tebbetts and Laura Park*) •
Middle School: Get Me Out of Here!
(*with Chris Tebbetts and Laura Park*)

ILLUSTRATED NOVELS

Daniel X: Alien Hunter Graphic Novel (*with Leopoldo Gout*) •
Maximum Ride: Manga Vol. 1 (*with NaRae Lee*) •
Maximum Ride: Manga Vol. 2 (*with NaRae Lee*) •
Maximum Ride: Manga Vol. 3 (*with NaRae Lee*) •
Maximum Ride: Manga Vol. 4 (*with NaRae Lee*) •
Maximum Ride: Manga Vol. 5 (*with NaRae Lee*) •

For more information about James Patterson's novels, visit
www.jamespatterson.co.uk

Or become a fan on Facebook

I'm proud to support the National Literacy Trust, an independent charity that changes lives through literacy.

Did you know that millions of people in the UK struggle to read and write? This means children are less likely to succeed at school and less likely to develop into confident and happy teenagers. Literacy difficulties will limit their opportunities throughout adult life.

The National Literacy Trust passionately believes that everyone has a right to the reading, writing, speaking and listening skills they need to fulfil their own and, ultimately, the nation's potential.

My own son didn't use to enjoy reading, which was why I started writing children's books – reading for pleasure is an essential way to encourage children to pick up a book. The National Literacy Trust is dedicated to delivering exciting initiatives to encourage people to read and to help raise literacy levels. To find out more about the great work that they do, visit their website at www.literacytrust.org.uk.

James Patterson